CURRENTS
IN
FICTION

CURRENTS IN FICTION

CURRENTS IN NONFICTION

CURRENTS IN POETRY

CURRENTS IN DRAMA

CURRENTS IN FICTION

VIRGINIA ALWIN

Professor of English and Education
Northern Arizona University
Flagstaff, Arizona

Glencoe
McGraw-Hill

New York, New York
Columbus, Ohio
Woodland Hills, California
Peoria, Illinois

Vocabulary studies are reprinted from *A Book of Stories,* by Brother H. Raphael, F.S.C. © The Macmillan Company 1960.

ACKNOWLEDGMENTS

For permission to use material in this book, grateful acknowledgment is made to the following:

Astor-Honor, Inc.: For Chapters 9 and 11 from *Things Fall Apart* by Chinua Achebe. Copyright © 1958 by Chinua Achebe.

The Atlantic Monthly: For "A Ride on the Short Dog," by James Still. Copyright, 1951, by The Atlantic Monthly Company.

Mr. Joseph N. Bell: For "I'm Coming In," by Joseph N. Bell.

Brandt & Brandt: For "The Most Dangerous Game," by Richard Connell. Copyright, 1924, by Richard Connell. Copyright renewed, 1952, by Louise Fox Connell. For "The Milk Pitcher," by Howard Brubaker. Copyright, 1929, by Howard Brubaker. Both reprinted by permission of Brandt & Brandt.

Collins-Knowlton-Wing, Inc.: For "Gold-Mounted Guns," by F. R. Buckley. Reprinted by permission of Collins-Knowlton-Wing, Inc. Copyright 1922, 1949 by F. R. Buckley.

Mrs. George Curry: For "Miss Hinch," by Henry Sydnor Harrison.

Curtis Brown, Ltd.: For "Unreasonable Doubt," by Stanley Ellin. Reprinted by permission of the author. © 1958 by Stanley Ellin.

Doubleday & Company, Inc.: For "The Ransom of Red Chief," by O. Henry. Copyright 1907 by Doubleday & Company, Inc. Reprinted by permission of the publisher.

Farrar, Straus & Cudahy, Inc. and Brandt & Brandt: For "Charles," by Shirley Jackson, from *The Lottery* by Shirley Jackson, Copyright © 1948, 1949 by Shirley Jackson.

Henry Gregor Felsen: For "Necktie Party," by Henry Gregor Felsen.

Houghton Mifflin Company: For "Bargain" from *The Big It,* by A. B. Guthrie, Jr. Reprinted by permission of the publisher, Houghton Mifflin Company.

Cover design by David Zerba, Nason Design Associates, Inc.

Send all inquiries to:
Glencoe/McGraw-Hill
21600 Oxnard Street, Suite 500
Woodland Hills, CA 91367
ISBN 0-02-194010-X
18 19 20 21 22 23 24 25   05 04 03 02 01 00

ACKNOWLEDGMENTS (*continued*)

Harold Matson Company, Inc.: For "The Biscuit Eater," by James Street. Copyright 1929 by The Curtis Publishing Company. Copyright renewed 1966 by Mrs. Lucy Nash. For "All Summer in a Day," by Ray Bradbury. Copyright 1958 by Ray Bradbury.

John Murray (Publishers) Ltd., the Trustees of the Estate of Sir Arthur Conan Doyle, and Mary Yost Associates: For "The Red-Headed League" by Sir Arthur Conan Doyle.

The New Yorker: For "The Test," by Angelica Gibbs. Reprinted by permission. Copyright © 1940 The New Yorker Magazine, Inc.

Harold Ober Associates, Inc.: For "The Frill," by Pearl S. Buck. Copyright © 1933 by Pearl S. Buck. Renewed. For "Death of Red Peril," by Walter D. Edmonds. Copyright © 1928 by Walter D. Edmonds. Renewed.

William Saroyan: For "An Ornery Kind of Kid," by William Saroyan, from *The Assyrian and Other Stores* (where it appeared under the title "The Pheasant Hunter"), published by Harcourt, Brace and Company, Inc.

Irving Shepard: For "To Build a Fire," by Jack London. Permission granted by Irving Shepard, copyright owner.

The Viking Press, Inc. and The Bodley Head Ltd.: For "The Open Window," by H. H. Munro, from *The Short Stories of Saki* by H.H. Munro. Reprinted by permission of The Viking Press, Inc. All rights reserved.

Contents

We are surprised by the unexpected in

There are ornery kids in

Some people don't play fair in

*Angry young people are goaded
into action in*

CURRENTS
IN
Fiction

Reading the Short Story

Reading is a way you can experience many adventures that might never happen to you in real life. The twenty-two short stories in this book will involve you in many different incidents. You will be amused, thrilled, held in suspense, made to wonder, and perhaps even horrified. In some stories the author will carefully and subtly prepare you for the outcome; in other stories a sudden turn of events will surprise you.

In each of the stories you will meet interesting and unusual characters. You will become involved with them during a significant or crucial moment in their lives. This moment might be the time during which they reveal their true character for the first time. It may be a moment of revelation during which they learn some important lesson about life and people. Or it may be that point in time in which they face a "life and death" crisis on their own. Unlike real people, these characters will hold nothing back from you. You will see deeply into their hearts, and you will learn how their minds work. You will discover their darkest secrets and know their deepest fears. You will come to know them better than you know some of your closest friends. Some of these characters you might like and admire, others you may hate and despise. But no matter what feelings they arouse in you, you will be interested in learning about their fate.

In addition to introducing you to interesting and exciting people, these stories will take you to places you may never have visited before. You will be transported to New York, Paris, London, China, a jungle island, Haiti, and the distant planet Venus. Even time will hold no boundaries for you: you will be involved in stories that take place in the past and future as well as in the present. Your passport to these exciting adventures will be provided by your imagination and the writers' craft.

Mr. Nuttel is told
an eerie story about . . .

The Open Window

H. H. MUNRO (SAKI)

"**M**Y aunt will be down presently, Mr. Nuttel," said a very self-possessed young lady of fifteen; "in the meantime you must try and put up with me."

Framton Nuttel endeavoured to say the correct something which should duly flatter the niece of the moment without unduly discounting the aunt that was to come. Privately he doubted more than ever whether these formal visits on a succession of total strangers would do much towards helping the nerve cure which he was supposed to be undergoing.

"I know how it will be," his sister had said when he was preparing to migrate to this rural retreat; "you will bury yourself down there and not speak to a living soul, and your nerves will be worse than ever from moping. I shall just give you letters of introduction to all the people I know there. Some of them, as far as I can remember, were quite nice."

Framton wondered whether Mrs. Sappleton, the lady to whom he was presenting one of the letters of introduction, came into the nice division.

"Do you know many of the people round here?" asked the niece, when she judged that they had had sufficient silent communion.

"Hardly a soul," said Framton. "My sister was staying here, at the rectory, you know, some four years ago, and she gave me letters of introduction to some of the people here."

He made the last statement in a tone of distinct regret.

"Then you know practically nothing about my aunt?" pursued the self-possessed young lady.

"Only her name and address," admitted the caller. He was wondering whether Mrs. Sappleton was in the married or widowed state.

An undefinable something about the room seemed to suggest masculine habitation.

"Her great tragedy happened just three years ago," said the child; "that would be since your sister's time."

"Her tragedy?" asked Framton; somehow in this restful country spot tragedies seemed out of place.

"You may wonder why we keep that window wide open on an October afternoon," said the niece, indicating a large French window that opened on to a lawn.

"It is quite warm for the time of the year," said Framton; "but has that window got anything to do with the tragedy?"

"Out through that window, three years ago to a day, her husband and her two young brothers went off for their day's shooting. They never came back. In crossing the moor to their favourite snipe-shooting ground they were all three engulfed in a treacherous piece of bog. It had been that dreadful wet summer, you know, and places that were safe in other years gave way suddenly without warning. Their bodies were never recovered. That was the dreadful part of it." Here the child's voice lost its self-possessed note and became falteringly human. "Poor aunt always thinks that they will come back some day, they and the little brown spaniel that was lost with them, and walk in at that window just as they used to do. That is why the window is kept open every evening till it is quite dusk. Poor dear aunt, she has often told me how they went out, her husband with his white waterproof coat over his arm, and Ronnie, her youngest brother, singing, 'Bertie, why do you bound?' as he always did to tease her, because she said it got on her nerves. Do you know, sometimes on still, quiet evenings like this, I almost get a creepy feeling that they will all walk in through that window—"

She broke off with a little shudder. It was a relief to Framton when the aunt bustled into the room with a whirl of apologies for being late in making her appearance.

"I hope Vera has been amusing you?" she said.

"She has been very interesting," said Framton.

"I hope you don't mind the open window," said Mrs. Sappleton briskly; "my husband and brothers will be home directly from shooting, and they always come in this way. They've been out for snipe in the marshes today, so they'll make a fine mess over my poor carpets. So like you men-folk, isn't it?"

She rattled on cheerfully about the shooting and the scarcity of birds, and the prospects for duck in the winter. To Framton it was all purely horrible. He made a desperate but only partially successful effort to turn the talk on to a less ghastly topic; he was conscious that his hostess was giving him only a fragment of her attention, and her eyes were constantly straying past him to the open window and the lawn beyond. It was certainly an unfortunate coincidence that he should have paid his visit on this tragic anniversary.

"The doctors agree in ordering me complete rest, an absence of mental excitement, and avoidance of anything in the nature of violent physical exercise," announced Framton, who laboured under the tolerably widespread delusion that total strangers and chance acquaintances are hungry for the least detail of one's ailments and infirmities, their cause and cure. "On the matter of diet they are not so much in agreement," he continued.

"No?" said Mrs. Sappleton, in a voice which only replaced a yawn at the last moment. Then she suddenly brightened into alert attention —but not to what Framton was saying.

"Here they are at last!" she cried. "Just in time for tea, and don't they look as if they were muddy up to the eyes!"

Framton shivered slightly and turned towards the niece with a look intended to convey sympathetic comprehension. The child was staring out through the open window with dazed horror in her eyes. In a chill shock of nameless fear Framton swung round in his seat and looked in the same direction.

In the deepening twilight three figures were walking across the lawn towards the window; they all carried guns under their arms, and one of them was additionally burdened with a white coat hung over his shoulders. A tired brown spaniel kept close at their heels. Noiselessly they neared the house, and then a hoarse young voice chanted out of the dusk: "I said, Bertie, why do you bound?"

Framton grabbed wildly at his stick and hat; the hall-door, the gravel-drive, and the front gate were dimly noted stages in his headlong retreat. A cyclist coming along the road had to run into the hedge to avoid imminent collision.

"Here we are, my dear," said the bearer of the white mackintosh, coming in through the window; "fairly muddy, but most of it's dry. Who was that who bolted out as we came up?"

"A most extraordinary man, a Mr. Nuttel," said Mrs. Sappleton;

"could only talk about his illnesses, and dashed off without a word of good-bye or apology when you arrived. One would think he had seen a ghost."

"I expect it was the spaniel," said the niece calmly; "he told me he had a horror of dogs. He was once hunted into a cemetery somewhere on the banks of the Ganges by a pack of pariah dogs, and had to spend the night in a newly dug grave with the creatures snarling and grinning and foaming just above him. Enough to make any one lose their nerve."

Romance at short notice was her specialty.

Questions for discussion

1. What kind of girl is fifteen-year-old Vera? What does the author mean when he says that her speciality is "romance at short notice"? Is this a common characteristic of girls of her age?
2. Why did Vera ask Mr. Nuttel the question: "Then you know practically nothing about my aunt?"
3. At what point did you catch on to what Vera was doing? Why does she do this sort of thing? Did it amuse you to watch her at work on Mr. Nuttel? Did you feel sorry for Mr. Nuttel?
4. Why does the author choose to make Vera's victim a person who is suffering from a bad case of nerves?
5. What was Mr. Nuttel's reaction when Mrs. Sappleton mentioned the open window and the men who would be coming through it? What do you suppose Vera was thinking and feeling at that moment?
6. What do you think was Vera's reaction to Mr. Nuttel's headlong flight from the ghastly scene?
7. What was your reaction during the story? At the end of the story? How, for instance, did you feel when Mrs. Sappleton said: "One would think he (Mr. Nuttel) had seen a ghost"?
8. Would you say that this is a story in which something happens to a character or in which a character makes something happen?
9. When you looked at the title "The Open Window," did you see a picture in your mind? Did you wonder why the window was open? What part it would play in the story?

"The Open Window" names an object which plays a most important part in the story. This is true of the titles of several stories in this book. Sometimes a title is the name of a character in the story or a description of that character. Sometimes it states a character's problem or a situation in which he finds himself. And sometimes a title states the story's theme; that is, it summarizes what the author is trying to tell you about people and life.

It is likely that authors take considerable time and care in choosing the titles of their stories so that they will contribute to the effects the stories will have on you. If you would take a little time to wonder about the title of each story in this book before you read the story itself, you will probably enjoy the reading experience more. You will find yourself coming to that spot in the story which reveals why the story has this particular title and you will experience the pleasure of recognition.

Vocabulary growth

WORD BUILDING. One reason there are 600,000 words in English is that we build one word upon another. For example, we start with *television*, and make *televise* by changing the ending. Or we start with *nautical*, drop off the ending, add a new prefix, and come up with *astronaut* or *cosmonaut*.

Words formed in this way are built upon *base words* or *roots*. They are made by adding *prefixes* before the base and *suffixes* after the root.

1. The following nouns appear in the story. They are made by adding a suffix to the verb. Sometimes there is a minor spelling change at the end of the verb. Find the verb and suffix for each.

collision	statement	delusion
succession	ailment	acquaintance
introduction	coincidence	attention
communion	avoidance	agreement

2. We also make adjectives out of nouns and verbs by adding suffixes, sometimes also changing the spelling. The following adjectives appear in the story. Find the base word, noun or verb, and the suffix for each.

restful	desperate
treacherous	tragic
creepy	muddy
horrible	sympathetic
nameless	successful

For composition

1. How did Framton Nuttel feel about his experience? How would he

tell about it to his sister? Imagine that you are Framton, writing a letter to her. "Dear Alice" you might begin—"You can't imagine what happened to your dear Mrs. Sappleton just a year after you left here."

2. How would Vera tell the story? Imagine that you are Vera writing in her diary. Recount the experience as she might write it.

Mr. Willoughby overhears
a fantastic story and has an . . .

Unreasonable Doubt

STANLEY ELLIN

MR. Willoughby found a seat in the club car and gingerly settled into it. So far, he reflected with overwhelming gratitude, the vacation was a complete success. Not a hint of the headaches he had lived with the past year. Not a suggestion of the iron band drawing tight around the skull, the gimlet boring into it, the hammers tapping away at it.

"Tension," the doctor had said. "Physically you're sound as a nut, but you sit over your desk all day worrying over one problem after another until your mind is as tight as a mainspring. Then you take the problems home and worry them to death there. Don't get much sleep, do you?"

Mr. Willoughby admitted that he did not.

"I thought so," said the doctor. "Well, there's only one answer. A vacation. And I do mean a real vacation where you get away from it all. Seal your mind up. Don't let anything get into it but idle talk. Don't think about any problems at all. Don't even try a crossword puzzle. Just close your eyes and listen to the world go round. That'll do it," he assured him.

And it *had* done it, as Mr. Willoughby realized even after only one day of the treatment. And there were weeks of blissful relaxation ahead. Of course, it wasn't always easy to push aside every problem that came to mind. For example, there was a newspaper on the smoking-table next to his chair right now, its headline partly revealing the words NEW CRISIS IN—Mr. Willoughby hastily averted his head and thrust the paper into the rack beneath the table. A small triumph, but a pleasant one.

He was watching the rise and fall of the landscape outside the window, dreamily counting mile posts as they flashed by, when he first became aware of the voice at his elbow. The corner of his chair

was backed up near that of his neighbor, a stout, white-haired man
who was deep in talk with a companion. The stout man's voice was
not loud, but it was penetrating. The voice, one might say, of a trained
actor whose every whisper can be distinctly heard by the gallery. Even
if one did not choose to be an eavesdropper it was impossible not to
follow every word spoken. Mr. Willoughby, however, deliberately
chose to eavesdrop. The talk was largely an erudite discourse on legal
matters; the stout man was apparently a lawyer of vast experience and
uncanny recollective powers; and, all in all, the combination had the
effect on Mr. Willoughby of chamber music being played softly by
skilled hands.

Then suddenly his ears pricked like a terrier's. "The most interesting case I ever worked on?" the stout man was saying in answer to
his companion's query. "Well, sir, there's one I regard not only as the
most interesting I ever handled, but which would have staggered any
lawyer in history, right up to Solomon himself. It was the strangest,
most fantastic, damndest thing that ever came my way. And the way
it wound up—the real surprise after it was supposedly over and done
with—is enough to knock a man out of his chair when he thinks of it.
But let me tell it to you just as it took place."

Mr. Willoughby slid down in his chair, pressed his heels into the
floor, and surreptitiously closed the gap between his chair and his
neighbor's. With his legs extended, his eyes closed, and his arms folded
peaceably on his chest he was a fair representation of a man sound
asleep. Actually, he had never been more wide-awake in his life.

Naturally [the stout man said], I won't use the right names of
any of these people, even though all this took place a long time ago.
That's understandable when you realize it involves a murder. A cold-
blooded murder for profit, beautifully planned, flawlessly executed,
and aimed at making a travesty of everything written in the law books.

The victim—let's call him Hosea Snow—was the richest man in
our town. An old-fashioned sort of man—I remember him wearing
a black derby and a stiff collar on the hottest days in summer—he
owned the bank, the mill, and a couple of other local interests. There
wasn't any secret among folks as to how much he was worth. On the
day of his death it came to about two million dollars. Considering
how low taxes were in those days, and how much a dollar could buy,
you can see why he was held in such high esteem.

His only family consisted of two nephews, his brother's sons, Ben
and Orville. They represented the poor side of the family, you might

say. When their father and mother died all that was left to them was a rundown old house which they lived in together.

Ben and Orville were nice-looking boys in their middle twenties about that time. Smooth-faced, regular features, much of a size and shape, they could have been a lot more popular than they were, but they deliberately kept apart from people. It wasn't that they were unfriendly—any time they passed you on the street they'd smile and give you the time of day—but they were sufficient unto themselves. Nowadays you hear a lot of talk about sibling rivalries and fraternal complexes, but it would never fit those two boys.

They worked in their uncle's bank, but their hearts were never in it. Even though they knew that when Hosea died his money would be divided between them it didn't seem to cheer the boys any. Fact is, Hosea was one of those dried-out, leathery specimens who are likely to go on forever. Looking forward to an inheritance from somebody like that can be a trying experience, and there's no question that the boys had been looking forward to that inheritance from the time they first knew what a dollar was worth.

But what they seemed to be concerned with, meanwhile, was something altogether different from banking and money—something Hosea himself could never understand or sympathize with, as he told me on more than one occasion. They wanted to be song writers, and, for all I know, they had some talent for it. Whenever there was any affair in town that called for entertainment, Ben and Orville would show up with some songs they had written all by themselves. Nobody ever knew which of them did the words and which did the music, and that in itself was one of the small mysteries about them that used to amuse the town. You can pretty well judge the size and disposition of the place if something like that was a conversation piece.

But the situation was all shaken up the day Hosea Snow was found dead in his big house, a bullet hole right square in the middle of his forehead. The first I heard of it was when a phone call got me out of bed early in the morning. It was the County Prosecutor telling me that Ben Snow had murdered his uncle during the night, had just been arrested, and was asking me to come to the jail right quick.

I ran over to the jail half dressed, and was pulled up short by the sight of Ben locked in a cell, reading a newspaper, and seemingly indifferent to the fact that he was on his way to a trapdoor with a rope around his neck.

"Ben," I said, "you didn't do it, did you?"

"They tell me I did," he said in a matter-of-fact voice.

I don't know which bewildered me more—what he said or the unconcerned way he said it.

"What do you mean?" I asked him. "And you'd better have a good story to tell me, boy, because you're in serious trouble."

"Well," he said, "in the middle of the night the police and the County Prosecutor walked in on Orville and me, because Uncle Hosea was killed, and after some talking they said I did it. When I got tired of them nagging me about it I said, all right, I did do it."

"You mean," I said, "they've got evidence against you?"

He smiled. "That'll come out in court," he said. "All you've got to do is call Orville as my witness at the trial, and you won't have any trouble. I'm not going to testify for myself, so they can't cross-examine me. But don't you worry any. Orville'll take care of everything."

I felt a terrible suspicion creeping into my mind, but I didn't let myself consider it. "Ben," I said, "have you and Orville been reading law books?"

"We've been looking into them," he admitted. "They're mighty interesting"—and that was all I could get out of him. I got even less from Orville when I went over to the bank and tried to talk to him about his testimony.

Considering that, you can imagine my state of mind when we finally came to trial. The case was the biggest sensation the town had ever known, the courthouse was packed, and here I was in the middle of things with no idea of what I could do for Ben, and Ben himself totally indifferent. I felt sick every time I got a look at the prosecutor's smug and smiling face. Not that I could blame him for looking like the cat that ate the canary. The crime was a brutal one, he and the police had solved it in jig time, and here he was with an airtight case.

In his opening address to the jury he threw the works at them. The motive was obvious: Ben Snow stood to inherit a million dollars from his uncle's death. The method was right there on the clerk's desk where everyone could see it: an old pistol that Ben Snow's father had left among his effects years before, and which was found—one bullet freshly discharged from it—right in the kitchen where Ben and Orville were drinking coffee when the police broke in on them. And the confession signed by Ben before witnesses settled things beyond the shadow of a doubt.

The only thing I could do in the face of this was to put blind faith in Ben and do what he wanted me to. I had Orville Snow called as my first witness—and my only witness, too, as far as I could see—and then, without any idea of what he was going to say, I put him on the stand. He took the oath, sat down, straightened the crease in his trousers, and looked at me with the calm unconcern his brother had shown throughout the whole terrible business.

You see, I knew so little about the affair that it was hard to think of even a good opening question for him. Finally, I took the bull by the horns and said, "Would you please tell the jury where you were the night of the crime?"

"Glad to," said Orville. "I was in Uncle Hosea's house with a gun in my hand. If the police had only gotten to me before they started pestering Ben about this, I could have told them so right off. Fact is, I was the one who killed uncle."

Talk about sensations in court! And in the middle of the uproar I saw Ben eagerly signaling me over to him. "Now, whatever you do," he whispered to me, "don't you ask that this trial be stopped. It's got to go to the jury, do you understand?"

I understood, all right. I had had my suspicions all along, but for the sake of my own conscience I just didn't want to heed them. Now I knew for sure, and for all I hated Ben and Orville right then I had to admire them just a little bit. And it was that little bit of admiration which led me to play it Ben's way. With the prosecutor waiting hang-dog for me to ask that the trial be stopped I went back to Orville on the witness stand and had him go ahead with his story as if nothing spectacular had happened.

He told it like a master. He started way back when the desire for his uncle's money had seeped into his veins like a drug, and went along in detail right up to the killing itself. He had the jury hypno-tized, and just to make sure the job was complete I wound up my closing speech by reminding them that all they needed in finding a man innocent was a reasonable doubt of his guilt.

"That is the law of this state," I told them. "Reasonable doubt. It is exactly what you are feeling now in the light of Orville Snow's confession that he alone committed the crime his brother was charged with!"

The police grabbed Orville right after the verdict of "Not Guilty" was brought in. I saw him that evening in the small cell Ben had been kept in, and I already knew what he was going to tell me.

"Ben's my witness," he said. "Just keep me off the witness stand and let him do the talking."

I said to him, "One of you two killed your uncle, Orville. Don't you think that as your lawyer I ought to know which of you it was?"

"No, I don't," said Orville, pleasantly enough.

"You're putting a lot of faith in your brother," I told him. "Ben's free and clear now. If he doesn't want to testify for you the way you did for him, he gets two million dollars and you get the gallows. Doesn't that worry you any?"

"No," said Orville. "If it worried us any we wouldn't have done it in the first place."

"All right," I said, "if that's the way you want it. But tell me one thing, Orville, just for curiosity's sake. How did you decide which one of you should kill Hosea?"

"We cut cards," said Orville, and that was the end of it, as far as he was concerned.

If Ben's trial had stirred up the town, Orville's had people coming in from all over the county. It was the prosecutor's turn to look sick now when he faced that crowd. He knew in his bones what was coming, and he couldn't do a blessed thing about it. More than that, he was honestly outraged at what looked to be an obscene mockery of the law. Ben and Orville Snow had found a loophole in justice, so to speak, and were on their way to sneaking through it. A jury couldn't convict a man if it had a reasonable doubt of his guilt; a man couldn't be retried for a crime when a jury had acquitted him of it; it wasn't even possible to indict the two boys together for conspiracy to commit murder, because that was a lesser charge in the murder indictment and covered by it. It was enough to make any prosecutor wild with frustration.

But this one held himself in check until Ben had finished telling his story to the jury. Ben told that story every bit as well as Orville had told his at the previous trial. He made it so graphic you could almost see him there in the room with his uncle, the gun flashing out death, the old man crumpling to the floor. The jurymen sat there spellbound, and the prosecutor chewed his nails to the quick while he watched them. Then when he faced Ben on the stand he really cut loose.

"Isn't all this a monstrous lie?" he shouted. "How can you be innocent of this crime one day, and guilty of it the next?"

Ben raised his eyebrows. "I never told anybody I was innocent," he said indignantly. "I've been saying right along I was guilty."

There was no denying that. There was nothing in the record to dispute it. And I never felt so sure of myself, and so unhappy, as when I summed up the case for the jury. It took me just one minute, the quickest summing-up in my record.

"If I were sitting among you good people in that jury box," I said, "I know just what I'd be thinking. A heinous crime has been committed, and one of two men in this very courtroom has committed it. But I can take my oath that I don't know which of them it was, any more than you do, and like it or not I'd know I had to bring in a verdict of 'Not Guilty.' "

That was all they needed, too. They brought in their verdict even quicker than the jury had in Ben's case. And I had the dubious pleasure of seeing two young men, one of them guilty of murder, smilingly walk out of that room. As I said, I hated them, but I felt a sort of infuriated admiration for them too. They had gambled everything in their loyalty to each other, and the loyalty had stood the test of fire . . .

The stout man was silent. From his direction came the sound of a match striking, and then an eddy of expensive cigar smoke drifted under Mr. Willoughby's nostrils. It was the pungent scent of the present dissolving the fascinating web of the past.

"Yes, sir," the stout man said, and there was a depth of nostalgia in his voice, "you'd have to go a long way to find a case to match that."

"You mean," said his companion, "that they actually got away with it? That they found a way of committing the perfect murder?"

The stout man snorted. "Perfect murder, bosh! That's where the final, fantastic surprise comes in. They *didn't* get away with it!"

"They didn't?"

"Of course not. You see, when they—good heavens, isn't this our station?" the stout man suddenly cried, and the next instant he went flying past Mr. Willoughby's outstretched feet, briefcase in hand, overcoat flapping over his arm, companion in tow.

Mr. Willoughby sat there dazed for a moment, his eyes wide-open, his mouth dry, his heart hammering. Then he leaped to his feet—but it was too late: the men had disappeared from the car. He took a few frantic steps in the direction they had gone, realized it was pointless, then ran to a window of the car overlooking the station.

The stout man stood on the platform almost below him, buttoning his coat, and saying something to his companion. Mr. Willoughby made a mighty effort to raise the window, but failed to budge it. Then he rapped on the pane with his knuckles, and the stout man looked up at him.

"H-o-w?" Mr. Willoughby mouthed through the closed window, and saw with horror that the stout man did not understand him at all. Inspiration seized him. He made a pistol of his hand, aimed the extended forefinger at the stout man, and let his thumb fall like a hammer on a cartridge. "Bang!" he yelled. "Bang, bang! H-o-w?"

The stout man looked at him in astonishment, glanced at his companion, and then putting his own forefinger to his temple, made a slow circling motion. That was how Mr. Willoughby last saw him as the train slowly, and then with increasing speed, pulled away.

It was when he moved away from the window that Mr. Willoughby became aware of two things. One was that every face in the car was turned toward him with rapt interest. The other was that an iron band was drawing tight around his skull, a gimlet was boring into it, tiny hammers were tapping at it.

It was, he knew with utter despair, going to be a perfectly terrible vacation.

Questions for discussion

1. Is this a typical "Whodunit" story? What is it that creates the suspense in the story—who did it, or whether they would get away with it? Did you think that they would get away with it?

2. At what point in the story did your interest suddenly pick up? What, specifically, was it that interested you?

3. At the point where the lawyer begins his story, how do you feel? With whom were you identifying yourself at that moment, with the person telling the story or with the person overhearing it? Have you any idea why? Did the same thing happen to you when you were reading "The Open Window"?

4. How did the lawyer feel at various times during the trial? Why? How did he feel towards his two clients? Why?

5. Do you object to how the story ends? Would it have been a better story if you knew how the "story within the story" came out? Does

this sometimes happen in real life—that we are left without knowing how an event turned out or what finally happened to a person? Has it ever happened to you? Have you ever read any other story which intentionally leaves you without knowing what happened at the end?

6. Why did the author title this story "Unreasonable Doubt" rather than "Reasonable Doubt"? That is, what was the doubt, who had it, and in what way was it unreasonable?

7. Notice how the author ties together the introduction and the conclusion of the story. What does the first paragraph of the story accomplish? Why does the author begin the story this way? Why doesn't he just tell the story of "the remarkable case of the Snow boys"?

This might be called "a story within a story." This method was also used in "The Open Window." Did you notice that in both stories the person who hears this "story within the story" is of uncertain emotional health. He has a bad case of nerves. Why does the author choose to use this kind of person to play the listener's role?

Vocabulary growth

CONTEXT. The context of a word is the sentence or passage in which it appears—the other words with which it is used. Sometimes the context gives the reader clues to a new and unfamiliar word. Sometimes the clues are obvious; at other times the reader has to dig them out. The effort is worth while because the reader not only gets more meaning out of the passage but adds a bit of information about a new word to his vocabulary. Each time he meets the word in later contexts, he acquires more meanings for it.

In the story, you met these sentences: "Even if one did not choose to be an *eavesdropper*, it was impossible not to follow every word spoken. Mr. Willoughby, however, deliberately chose to *eavesdrop*." Just what does it mean to *eavesdrop*. What did Mr. Willoughby do? 1) He "followed every word spoken" by the stout man. 2) "Then suddenly his ears pricked up like a terrier's." 3) "Mr. Willoughby slid down on his chair, pressed his heels into the floor and surreptitiously closed the gap between his chair and his neighbor's . . . he was a fair representation of a man sound asleep. Actually, he had never been more wide awake in his life."

Now, we can put the clues together. Eavesdropping involves listening secretly to a conversation one is not supposed to hear. Originally, the word was applied to those who stood under the eaves of a house to hear conversation going on inside.

Context clues will not usually give you a complete meaning for a new word, but they will give you enough meaning to aid your reading. From the context, figure out the meaning of the italicized words in each of the following sentences from the story.

a. "Not a suggestion of the iron band drawing tight around the skull, the *gimlet* boring into it." (page 9).

b. "Mr. Willoughby hastily *averted* his head and thrust the paper into the rack beneath the table." (Reread the whole paragraph, page 9).

c. "It was enough to make any prosecutor wild with *frustration*." (Reread the whole paragraph, page 14).

For composition

What happened? You are the stout man. You are explaining to your friend what happened to the brothers. Did they have a fight over the spoils? Did one of the brothers inform on the other? Were both of them arrested finally? Tell the rest of the story that Mr. Willoughby wanted so much to hear.

A clever detective pursues
a clever fugitive in . . .

Miss Hinch

HENRY SYDNOR HARRISON

In going from a given point on 126th Street to a subway station at 125th, it is not usual to begin by circling the block to 127th Street, especially in sleet, darkness, and deadly cold. When two people pursue such a course at the same time, moving unobtrusively on opposite sides of the street, in the nature of things the coincidence is likely to attract the attention of one or the other of them.

In the bright light of the entrance to the tube they came almost face to face, and the clergyman took a good look at her. Certainly she was a decent-looking old body, if any woman was: white-haired, wrinkled, spectacled, and stooped. A poor but thoroughly respectable domestic servant of the better class she looked, in her old black hat, neat veil, and grey shawl; and her brief glance at the reverend gentleman was precisely what it should have been from her to him—deference itself. Nevertheless, he, going more slowly down the draughty steps, continued to study her from behind with a singular intentness.

An express was just thundering in, which the clergyman, handicapped as he was by his clubfoot and stout cane, was barely in time to catch. He entered the same car with the woman and chanced to take a seat directly across from her. It must have been then after twelve o'clock, and the wildness of the weather was discouraging to travel. The car was almost deserted. Even in this underground retreat the bitter breath of the night blew and bit, and the old woman shivered under her shawl. At last, her teeth chattering, she got up in an apologetic sort of way, and moved toward the better protected rear of the car, feeling the empty seats as she went, plainly in search of hot pipes. The clergyman's eyes followed her candidly, and watched her sink down, presently, into a seat on his own side of the car. A young couple sat between them now; he could no longer see the

19

woman, beyond occasional glimpses of her black knees and her faded bonnet, fastened on with a long steel hatpin.

Nothing could have seemed more natural or more trivial than this change of seats on the part of a thin-blooded and half-frozen passenger. But it happened to be at a time of mutual doubt and misgivings, of alert suspicions and hair-trigger watchfulness, when men looked askance into every strange face and the smallest incidents were likely to take on a hysterical importance. Through days of fruitless searching for a fugitive outlaw of extraordinary gifts, the nerves of the city had been slowly strained to the breaking-point. All jumped, now, when anybody cried "Boo!" and the hue and cry went up falsely twenty times a day.

The clergyman pondered; mechanically he turned up his coat collar and fell to stamping his icy feet. He was an Episcopal clergyman, by his garb—rather short, very full-bodied, not to say fat, bearded and somewhat puffy-faced, with heavy cheeks cut by deep creases. Well-lined against the cold though he was, however, he, too, began to suffer visibly, and presently was forced to retreat in his turn, seeking out a new place where the heating apparatus gave a better account of itself. He found one, two seats beyond the old serving-woman, limped into it, and soon relapsed into his own thoughts.

The young couple, now half a dozen seats away, were thoroughly absorbed in each other's society. The fifth traveler, a withered old gentleman sitting next the middle door across the aisle, napped fitfully upon his cane. The woman in the hat and shawl sat in a sad kind of silence; and the train hurled itself roaringly through the tube. After a time, she glanced timidly at the meditating clergyman, and her look fell swiftly from his face to the discarded "ten o'clock extra" lying by his side. She removed her dim gaze and let it travel casually about the car; but before long it returned, pointedly, to the newspaper. Then, with some hesitation, she bent forward and said, above the noises of the train:

"Excuse me, Father, but would you let me look at your paper a minute, sir?"

The clergyman came out of his reverie instantly, and looked up with a quick smile.

"Certainly. Keep it if you like: I am quite through with it. But," he added, in a pleasant deep voice, "I am an Episcopal minister, not a priest."

"Oh, sir—I beg your pardon! I thought—"

He dismissed the apology with a nod and a good-natured hand.

The woman opened the paper with decent cotton-gloved fingers. The garish headlines told the story at a glance: "Earth Opened and Swallowed Miss Hinch—Headquarters Virtually Abandons Case— Even Jessie Dark," so the bold capitals ran on—"Seems Stumped." Below the spread was a luridly written but flimsy narrative "By Jessie Dark," which at once confirmed the odd implication of the caption. "Jessie Dark," it appeared, was one of those most extraordinary of the products of yellow journalism, a woman "crime expert," now in action. More than this, she was a "crime expert" to be taken seriously it seemed—no mere office-desk sleuth, but an actual performer with, unexpectedly enough, a somewhat formidable list of notches on her gun. So much, at least, was to be gathered from her paper's display of "Jessie Dark's Triumphs":

March 2, 1901. Caught Julia Victorian, alias Gregory, the brains of the "Heally Ring" kidnapers.

October 7–29, 1903. Found Mrs. Trotwood and secured the letter that convicted her of the murder of her lover, Ellis E. Swan.

December 17, 1903. Ran down Charles Bartsch in a Newark laundry and trapped a confession from him.

July 4, 1904. Caught Mary Calloran and recovered the Stratford jewels.

And so on—nine "triumphs" in all; and nearly every one of them, as the least observant reader could hardly fail to notice, involved the capture of a woman.

Nevertheless, it could not be pretended that the "snappy" paragraphs in this evening's extra seemed to foreshadow a new or tenth triumph for Jessie Dark at an early date; and the old serving-woman in the car presently laid down the sheet with a look of marked depression.

The clergyman looked at her again. Her expression was so speaking that it seemed to be almost an invitation; besides, public interest in the great case made conversation between total strangers the rule wherever two or three were gathered together.

"You were reading about this strange mystery, perhaps."

The woman with a sharp intake of breath answered, "Yes, sir. Oh, sir, it seems as if I couldn't think of anything else."

"Ah?" he said, without surprise. "It certainly appears to be a remarkable affair."

Remarkable, indeed, the affair seemed. In a tiny little room within ten steps of Broadway at half-past nine o'clock on a fine evening, Miss Hinch had killed John Catherwood with the light sword she used in her famous representation of the Father of His Country. Catherwood, it was known, had come to tell her of his coming marriage, and ten thousand amateur detectives, fired by unusual rewards, had required no further motive of a creature already notorious for fierce jealousy. So far the tragedy was commonplace enough, and even vulgar. What had redeemed it to romance from this point on was the extraordinary faculty of the woman, which had made her celebrated while she was still in her teens. Coarse, violent, utterly unmoral she might be, but she happened also to be the most astonishing impersonator of her time. Her brilliant "act" consisted of a series of character changes, many of them done in full view of the audience with the assistance only of a small table of properties half concealed under a net. Some of these transformations were so amazing as to be beyond belief, even after one had sat and watched them. Not her appearance only, but voice, speech, manner, carriage, all shifted incredibly to fit the new part; so that the woman appeared to have no permanent form or fashion of her own, but to be only so much plastic human material out of which her cunning could mold at will man, woman, or child, great lady of the Louisan Court or Tammany statesman with the modernest of East Side modernisms upon his lips.

With this strange skill, hitherto used only to enthrall large audiences and wring extortionate contracts from managers, the woman known as Miss Hinch—she appeared to be without a first name—was now fighting for her life somewhere against the police of the world. Without artifice, she was a tall, thin-chested young woman with strongly marked features and considerable beauty of a bold sort. What she would look like at the present moment nobody could venture a guess. Having stabbed John Catherwood in her dressing-room at the Amphitheater, she had put on her hat and coat, dropped two wigs and her make-up kit into a handbag, and walked out into Broadway. Within ten minutes the dead body of Catherwood was found and the chase had begun. At the stage door, as she passed out, Miss Hinch had met an acquaintance, a young comedian named Dargis, and exchanged a word of greeting with him. That had been ten days ago. After Dargis, no one had seen her. The earth, indeed, seemed to have opened and swallowed her. Yet her natural features were almost as well known as the President's, and the newspapers of a continent were daily reprinting them in a thousand variations.

"A very remarkable case," repeated the clergyman, rather absently; and his neighbor, the old woman, respectfully agreed that it was. Then, as the train slowed up for the stop at 86th Street, she added with sudden bitterness:

"Oh, they'll never catch her, sir—never! She's too smart for 'em all, Miss Hinch is."

Attracted by her tone, the stout divine inquired if she was particularly interested in the case.

"Yes, sir—I got reason to be. Jack Catherwood's mother and me was at school together, and great friends all our life long. Oh, sir," she went on, as if in answer to his look of faint surprise, "Jack was a fine gentleman, with manners and looks and all beyond his people. But he never grew away from his old mother—no, sir, never! And I don't believe ever a Sunday passed that he didn't go up and set the afternoon away with her, talking and laughing just like he was a little boy again. Maybe he done things he hadn't ought, as high-spirited lads will, but oh, sir, he was a good boy in his heart—a good boy. And it does seem too hard for him to die like that—and that hussy free to go her way, ruinin' and killin'—"

"My good woman," said the clergyman presently, "compose yourself. No matter how diabolical this woman's skill is, her sin will assuredly find her out."

The woman dutifully lowered her handkerchief and tried to compose herself, as bidden.

"But, oh, she's that clever—diabolical, just as ye say, sir. Through poor Jack we of course heard much gossip about her, and they do say that her best tricks was not done on the stage at all. They say, sir, that, sittin' around a table with her friends, she could begin and twist her face so strange and terrible that they would beg her stop, and jump up and run from the table—frightened out of their lives, sir, grown-up people, by the terrible faces she could make. And let her only step behind her screen for a minute—for she kept her secrets well, Miss Hinch did—and she'd come walking out to you, and you could go right up to her in the full light and take her hand, and still you couldn't make yourself believe it was her."

"Yes," said the clergyman, "I have heard that she is remarkably clever—though, as a stranger in this part of the world—I never saw her act. I must say, it is all very interesting and strange."

He turned his head and stared through the rear of the car at the dark flying walls. At the same moment the woman turned her head and stared full at the clergyman. When the train halted again, at Grand Central Station, he turned back to her.

"I'm a visitor in the city, from Denver, Colorado," he said pleasantly, "and knew little or nothing about the case until an evening or two ago, when I attended a meeting of gentlemen here. The men's club of St. Matthias' Church—perhaps you know the place? Upon my word, they talked of nothing else. I confess they got me quite interested in their gossip. So tonight I bought this paper to see what this extraordinary woman detective it employs had to say about it. We don't have such things in the West, you know. But I must say I was disappointed after all the talk about her."

"Yes, sir, indeed, and no wonder, for she's told Mrs. Catherwood herself that she never made such a failure as this so far. It seemed like she could always catch women, up to this. It seemed like she knew in her own mind just what a woman would do, where she'd try to hide and all, and so she could find them time and time when the men detectives didn't know where to look. But, oh, sir, she's never had to hunt for such a woman as Miss Hinch before!"

"No! I suppose not," said the clergyman. "Her story here in the paper certainly seems to me very poor."

"Story, sir! Bless my soul!" suddenly exploded the old gentleman across the aisle, to the surprise of both. "You don't suppose the clever little woman is going to show her hand in those stories, with Miss Hinch in the city and reading every line of them! In the city, sir— such is my positive belief!"

The approach to his station, it seemed, had roused him from his nap just in time to overhear the episcopate criticism. Now he answered the looks of the old woman and the clergyman with an elderly cackle.

"Excuse my intrusion, I'm sure! But I can't sit silent and hear anybody run down Jessie Dark—Miss Mathewson in private life, as perhaps you don't know. No, sir! Why, there's a man at my boarding-place—astonishing young fellow named Hardy, Tom Hardy—who's known her for years! As to those stories, sir, I can assure you that she puts in there exactly the opposite of what she really thinks!"

"You don't tell me!" said the clergyman encouragingly.

"Yes, sir! Oh, she plays the game—yes, yes! She has her private ideas, her clues, her schemes. The woman doesn't live who is clever enough to hoodwink Jessie Dark. I look for developments any day —any day, sir!"

A new voice joined in. The young couple down the car, their attention caught by the old man's pervasive tones, had been frankly listening; and it was illustrative of the public mind at the moment that, as they now rose for the station and drew nearer, the young man felt perfectly free to offer his contribution.

"Dramatic situation, isn't it, when you stop to think. Those two clever women pitted against each other in a life-and-death struggle, fighting it out silently in the underground somewhere—keen professional pride on one side and the fear of the electric chair on the other. Good heavens, there's—"

"Oh, yes! Oh, yes!" exclaimed the old gentleman rather testily. "But my dear sir, it's not professional pride that makes Jessie Dark so resolute to win. It's sex jealousy, if you follow me—no offense, madam! Yes, sir! Women never have the slightest respect for each other, either! I tell you, Jessie Dark'd be ashamed to be beaten by another woman. Read her stories between the lines, sir—as I do. Invincible determination—no weakening—no mercy! You catch my point, sir?"

"It sounds reasonable," answered the Colorado clergyman, with his courteous smile. "All women, we are told, are natural rivals at heart—"

"Oh, I'm for Jessie Dark every time!" the young fellow broke in eagerly—"especially since the police have practically laid down. But—"

"Why, she's told my young friend Hardy," the old gentleman rode him down, "that she'll find Hinch if it takes her lifetime! Knows a thing or two about actresses, she says. Says the world isn't big enough for the creature to hide from her. Well! What do you think of that?"

"Tell what we were just talking about, George," said the young wife, looking at her husband with admiring eyes.

"But, oh, sir!" began the old woman timidly, "Jack Catherwood's been dead ten days now, and—and—"

"Ten days, madam! And what is that, pray?" exploded the old gentleman, rising triumphantly. "A lifetime, if necessary! Oh, never fear! Mrs. Victorian was considered pretty clever, eh? Wasn't she? Remember what Jessie Dark did for her? Nan Parmalee, too—though the police did their best to steal her credit. She'll do just as much for Miss Hinch—you may take it from me!"

"But how's she going to make the capture, gentlemen?" cried the young fellow, getting his chance at last. "That's the point my wife and I've been discussing. Assuming that she succeeds in spotting this woman-devil, what will she do? Now—"

"Do! Yell for the police!" burst from the old gentleman at the door.

"And have Miss Hinch shoot her—and then herself, too? Wouldn't she have to—"

"Grand Central!" cried the guard for the second time; and the young fellow broke off reluctantly to find his bride towing him strongly toward the door.

"Hope she nabs her soon, anyway," he called back to the clergyman over his shoulder. "The thing's getting on my nerves. One of these kindergarten reward-chasers followed my wife for five blocks the other day, just because she's got a pointed chin, and I don't know what might have happened if I hadn't come along and—"

Doors rolled shut behind him, and the train flung itself on its way. Within the car a lengthy silence ensued. The clergyman stared thoughtfully at the floor, and the old woman fell back upon her borrowed paper. She appeared to be re-reading the observations of Jessie Dark with considerable care. Presently she lowered the paper and began a quiet search for something under the folds of her shawl; and at length, her hands emerging empty, she broke the silence in a lifted voice.

"Oh, sir—have you a pencil you could lend me, please? I'd like to mark something in the piece to send to Mrs. Catherwood. It's what she says here about the disguises, sir."

The kindly divine felt in his pockets, and after some hunting produced a pencil—a white one with blue lead. She thanked him gratefully.

"How is Mrs. Catherwood bearing all this strain and anxiety?" he asked suddenly. "Have you seen her today?"

"Oh, yes, sir! I've been spending the evening with her since nine o'clock, and am just back from there now. Oh, she's very much broke up, sir."

She looked at him uncertainly. He stared straight in front of him, saying nothing, though conceivably he knew, in common with the rest of the reading world, that Jack Catherwood's mother lived, not on 126th Street, but on East Houston Street. Possibly he might have wondered if his silence had not been an error of judgment. Perhaps that misstatement had not been a slip, but something clever?

The woman went on with a certain eagerness: "Oh, sir, I only hope and pray those gentlemen may be right, but it does look to Mrs. Catherwood, and me too, that if Jessie Dark was going to catch her at all, she'd have done it before now. Look at those big bold blue eyes she had, sir, with the lashes an inch long, they say, and that terrible long chin of hers. They do say she can change the color of her eyes, not forever of course, but put a few of her drops into them and make them look entirely different for a time. But that chin, ye'd say—"

She broke off; for the clergyman, without preliminaries of any sort, had picked up his heavy stick and suddenly risen.

"Here we are at Fourteenth Street," he said, nodding pleasantly. "I must change here. Good night. Success to Jessie Dark, I say!"

He was watching the woman's faded face and he saw just that look of respectful surprise break into it that he had expected.

"Fourteenth Street! I'd no notion at all we'd come so far. It's where I get out, too, sir, the express not stopping at my station."

"Ah?" said the clergyman, smiling a little.

He led the way, limping and leaning on his stick. They emerged upon the chill and cheerless platform, not exactly together, yet still with some reference to their acquaintanceship on the car. But the clergyman, after stumping along a few steps, all at once realized that he was walking alone, and turned. The woman had halted. Over the intervening space their eyes met.

"Come," said the man gently. "Come, let us walk about a little to keep warm."

"Oh, sir—it's too kind of you, sir," said the woman, coming forward.

From other cars two or three blue-nosed people had got off to make the change; one or two more came straggling in from the street; but scattered over the bleak concrete expanse, they detracted little from the isolation that seemed to surround the woman and the clergyman. Step for step, the odd pair made their way to the extreme northern end of the platform.

"By the way," said the clergyman, halting abruptly, "may I see that paper again for a moment?"

"Oh, yes, sir—of course," said the woman, producing it from beneath her shawl. "I thought you had finished with it, and I—"

He said that he wanted only to glance at it for a moment; but he fell to looking through it page by page, with considerable care. The woman glanced at him several times. At last she said hesitatingly:

"I thought, sir, I'd ask the ticket-chopper could he say how long before the next train. I'm very late as it is, sir, and I still must stop to get something to eat before I go to bed."

"An excellent idea," said the clergyman.

He explained that he, too, was already behind time, and was spending the night with cousins in Jersey, to boot. Side by side, they retraced their steps down the platform, questioned the chopper with scant results, and then, as by tacit consent, started back again. However, before they had gone far, the woman stopped short and, with a white face, leaned against a pillar.

"Oh, sir, I'm afraid I'll just have to stop and get a bite somewhere before I go on. You'll think me foolish, sir, but I missed my supper entirely tonight, and there is quite a faint feeling coming over me."

The clergyman looked at her with apparent concern. "Do you know, my friend, you seem to anticipate all my own wants. Your mentioning something to eat just now reminded me that I myself was all but famishing." He glanced at his watch, appearing to deliberate. "Yes—it will not take long. Come, we'll find a modest eating-house together."

"Oh, sir," she stammered, "but—you wouldn't want to eat with a poor old woman like me, sir."

"And why not? Are we not all equal in the sight of God?"

They ascended the stairs together, like any prosperous parson and his poor parishioner, and coming out into Fourteenth Street, started west. On the first block they came to a restaurant, a brilliantly lighted, tiled and polished place of a quick-lunch variety.

But the woman timidly preferred not to stop here, saying that the glare of such places was very bad for her old eyes. The divine accepted the objection as valid, without an argument. Two blocks farther on they found on a corner a quieter resort, an unpretentious little haven which yet boasted a "Ladies' Entrance" down the side street.

They entered by the front door, and sat down at a table, facing each other. The woman read the menu through, and finally, after some embarrassed uncertainty, ordered poached eggs on toast. The clergyman ordered the same. The simple meal was soon despatched. Just as they were finishing it, the woman said apologetically:

"If you'll excuse me, sir—could I see the bill of fare a minute? I think I'd best take a little pot of tea to warm me up, if they do not charge too high."

"I haven't the bill of fare," said the clergyman.

They looked diligently for the cardboard strip, but it was nowhere to be seen. The waiter drew near.

"Yes, sir! I left it there on the table when I took the order."

"I'm sure I can't imagine what's become of it," repeated the clergyman, rather insistently.

He looked hard at the woman, and found that she was looking hard at him. Both pairs of eyes fell instantly.

The waiter brought another bill of fare; the woman ordered tea; the waiter came back with it. The clergyman paid for both orders with a bill that looked hard-earned.

The tea proved to be very hot; it could not be drunk down at a gulp. The clergyman, watching the woman sidewise as she sipped, seemed to grow more restless. His fingers drummed the tablecloth: he could hardly sit still. All at once he said: "What is that calling in the street? It sounds like newsboys."

The woman put her old head on one side and listened. "Yes, sir. There seems to be an extra out."

"Upon my word," he said after a pause. "I believe I'll go get one. Good gracious! Crime is a very interesting thing, to be sure!"

He rose slowly, took down his shovel-hat from the hanger near him, grasped his heavy stick, limped to the door. Leaving it open behind him, much to the annoyance of the proprietor in the cashier's cage, he stood a moment in the little vestibule, looking up and down the street. Then he took a few slow steps eastward, beckoning with his hand as he went, and so passed out of sight of the woman at the table.

The eating-place was on the corner, and outside the clergyman paused for half a breath. North, east, south, and west he looked, and nowhere he found what his flying glance sought. He turned the corner into the darker cross-street, and began to walk, at first slowly, continually looking about him. Presently his pace quickened, quickened, so that he no longer even stayed to use his stout cane. In another moment he was all but running, his clubfoot pounding the icy sidewalk heavily as he went. A newsboy thrust an extra under his very nose, but he did not even see it.

Far down the street, nearly two blocks away, a tall figure in a blue coat stood and stamped in the freezing sleet; and the hurrying divine sped straight toward him. But he did not get very near. For, as he passed the side entrance at the extreme rear of the restaurant, a departing guest dashed out so recklessly as to run full into him, stopping him dead.

Without looking at her, he knew who it was. In fact, he did not look at her at all, but turned his head hurriedly north and south, sweeping the dark street with a swift eye. But the old woman, having drawn back with a sharp exclamation as they collided, rushed breathlessly into apologies:

"Oh, sir—excuse me! A newsboy popped his head into the side door just after you went out, and I ran to get you the paper. But he got away too quick for me, sir, and so I—"

"Exactly," said the clergyman in his quiet deep voice. "That must have been the very boy I myself was after."

On the other side, two men had just turned into the street, well muffled against the night, talking cheerfully as they trudged along. Now the clergyman looked full at the woman, and she saw that there was a smile on his face.

"As he seems to have eluded us both, suppose we return to the subway?"

"Yes, sir; it's full time I—"

"The sidewalk is so slippery," he went on gently, "perhaps you had better take my arm."

Behind the pair in the dingy restaurant, the waiter came forward to shut the door, and lingered to discuss with the proprietor the sudden departure of his two patrons. However, the score had been paid with a liberal tip for service, so there was no especial complaint to make. After listening to some unfavorable comments on the ways of the clergy, the waiter returned to his table to set it in order.

On the floor in the carpeted aisle between tables lay a white piece of cardboard, which his familiar eye recognized as part of one of his own bills of fare, face downward. He stooped and picked it up. On the back of it was some scribbling, made with a blue lead pencil.

The handwriting was very loose and irregular, as if the writer had had his eyes elsewhere while he wrote, and it was with some difficulty that the waiter deciphered this message:

"Miss Hinch 14th St. subway Get police quick."

The waiter carried this curious document to the proprietor, who read it over a number of times. He was a dull man, and had a dull man's suspiciousness of a practical joke. However, after a good deal of irresolute discussion, he put on his overcoat and went out for a policeman. He turned west, and halfway up the block met an elderly bluecoat trudging east. The policeman looked at the scribbling, and dismissed it profanely as a wag's foolishness of the sort that was bothering the life out of him a dozen times a day. He walked along with the proprietor, and as they drew near to the latter's place of business both became aware of footsteps thudding nearer up the cross-street from the south. As they looked up, two young policemen, accompanied by a man in a uniform like a street-car conductor's, swept around the corner and dashed straight into the restaurant.

The first policeman and the proprietor ran in after them, and found them staring about rather vacantly. One of the arms of the law demanded if any suspicious characters had been seen about the place, and the dull proprietor said no. The officers, looking rather flat, explained their errand. It seemed that a few moments before, the third man, who was a ticket-chopper at the subway station, had found a mysterious message lying on the floor by his box. Whence it had come, how long it had lain there, he had not the slightest idea. However, there it was. The policeman exhibited a crumpled scrap torn from a newspaper, on which was scrawled in blue pencil:

"Miss Hinch Miller's Restaurant Get police quick."

The first policeman, who was both the oldest and the fattest of the three, produced the message on the bill of fare, so utterly at odds with this. The dull proprietor, now bethinking himself, mentioned the clergyman and the old woman who had taken poached eggs and tea together, called for a second bill of fare, and departed so unexpectedly by different doors. The ticket-chopper recalled that he had seen the same pair at his station; they had come up, he remembered, and questioned him about trains. The three policemen were momentarily puzzled by this testimony. But it was soon plain to them if either the woman or the clergyman really had any information about Miss Hinch—a highly improbable supposition in itself—they would never have stopped with peppering the neighborhood with silly little contradictory messages.

"They're a pair of old fools tryin' to have sport with the police, and I'd like to run them in for it," growled the fattest of the officers; and his was the general verdict.

The little conference broke up. The dull proprietor returned to his cage, the waiter to his table; the subway man departed for his chopping box; the three policemen passed out into the bitter night. They walked together, grumbling, and their feet, perhaps by some subconscious impulse, turned toward the subway. And in the next block a man came running up to them.

"Officer, look what I found on the sidewalk a minute ago. Read that scribble!"

"Police! Miss Hinch 14th St subw"

The hand trailed off on the *w* as though the writer had been suddenly interrupted. The fat policeman blasphemed and threatened arrests. But the second policeman, who was dark and wiry, raised his head from the bill of fare and said suddenly: "Tim, I believe there's something in this."

"There'd ought to be ten days on the Island in it for thim," growled fat Tim.

"Suppose, now," said the other policeman, staring intently at nothing, "the old woman was Miss Hinch, herself, f'r instance, and the parson was shadowing her while pretendin' he never suspicioned her, and Miss Hinch not darin' to cut and run for it till she was sure she had a clean getaway. Well, now, Tim, what better could he do—"

"That's right!" exclaimed the third policeman. " 'Specially when ye think that Hinch carries a gun, an'll use it, too! Why not have a look in at the subway station?"

The proposal carried the day. The three officers started for the

subway, the citizen following. They walked at a good pace and
without more talk; and both their speed and their silence had a
psychological reaction. As the minds of the policemen turned inward
upon the odd behavior of the pair in Miller's Restaurant, the con-
viction that, after all, something important might be afoot grew and
strengthened within each one of them. Unconsciously their pace
quickened. It was the wiry policeman who first broke into a run, but
the two others had been for twenty paces on the verge of it.

However, these consultations had taken time. The stout clergyman and the poor old woman had five minutes' start on the officers
of the law, and that, as it happened, was all that the occasion required. On Fourteenth Street, as they made their way arm in arm
to the station, they were seen and remembered by a number of
belated pedestrians. It was observed by more than one that the
woman lagged as if she were tired, while the club-footed divine,
supporting her on his arm, steadily kept her up to his own brisk gait.

So walking, the pair descended the subway steps, came out upon
the bare platform again, and presently stood once more at the extreme uptown end of it, just where they had waited half an hour
before. Near by a careless porter had overturned a bucket of water,
and a splotch of thin ice ran out and over the edge of the concrete.
Two young men who were taking lively turns up and down distinctly heard the clergyman warn the woman to look out for this ice.
Far away to the north was to be heard the faint roar of the approaching train.

The woman stood nearer the track, and the clergyman stood in
front of her. In the vague light their looks met, and each was struck
by the pallor of the other's face. In addition, the woman was breathing hard, and her hands and feet betrayed some nervousness. It was
difficult now to ignore the fact that for an hour they had been cling-
ing desperately to each other, at all costs; but the clergyman made
a creditable effort to do so. He talked ramblingly, in a voice sounding
only a little unnatural, for the most part of the deplorable weather
and his train to Jersey, for which he was now so late. And all the
time both of them were incessantly turning their heads toward the
station entrances, as if expecting some arrival.

As he talked, the clergyman kept his hands unobtrusively busy.
From the bottom edge of his black sack-cloth he drew a pin, and
stuck it deep into the ball of the middle finger. He took out a hand-

kerchief to dust the hard sleet from his hat; and under his overcoat he pressed the handkerchief against his bleeding finger. While
making these small arrangements, he held the woman's eyes with
his own, talking on; and, still holding them, he suddenly broke off
his random talk and peered at her cheek with concern.

"My good woman, you've scratched your cheek somehow! Why,
bless me, it's bleeding quite badly."

"Never mind—never mind," said the woman and swept her eyes
hurriedly toward the entrance.

"But good gracious, I must mind! The blood will fall on your
shawl. If you will permit me—ah!"

Too quick for her, he leaned forward, and, through the thin veil,
swept her cheek hard with the handkerchief; removing it, he held
it up so that she might see the blood for herself. But she did not
glance at the handkerchief; and neither did he. His gaze was riveted
upon her cheek, which looked smooth and clear where he had
smudged the clever wrinkles away.

Down the steps and upon the platform pounded the feet of three
flying policemen. But it was evident now that the train would thunder in just ahead of them. The clergyman, standing close in front
of the woman, took a firmer grip on his heavy stick, and a look of
stern triumph came into his face.

"You're not so terribly clever, after all!"

The woman had sprung back from him with an irrepressible exclamation, and in that instant she was aware of the police.

However, her foot slipped upon the treacherous ice—or it may
have tripped on the stout cane, when the clergyman suddenly shifted
its position. And in the next breath the train came roaring past.

By one of those curious chances which sometimes refute all experience, the body of the woman was not mangled or mutilated in
the least. There was a deep blue bruise on the left temple, and apparently that was all; even the ancient hat remained on her head,
skewered fast by the long pin. It was the clergyman who found the
body huddled at the side of the dark track where the train had
flung it—he who covered the still face and superintended the removal
to the platform. Two eyewitnesses of the tragedy pointed out the
ice on which the unfortunate woman had slipped, and described
their horror as they saw her companion spring forward just too late
to save her.

Not wishing to bring on a delirium of excitement among the bystanders, two policemen drew the clergyman quietly aside and showed him the mysterious messages. Much affected by the shocking end of his sleuthery as he was, he readily admitted having written them. He briefly recounted how the woman's strange movements on 126th Street had arrested his attention and how, watching her closely on the car, he had finally detected that she wore a wig. Unfortunately, however, her suspicions had been aroused by his interest in her, and thereafter a long battle of wits had ensued between them—he trying to summon the police without her knowledge, she dogging him close to prevent that, and at the same time watching her chance to give him the slip. He rehearsed how, in the restaurant, when he had invented an excuse to leave her for an instant, she had made a bolt and narrowly missed getting away; and finally how, having brought her back to the subway and seeing the police at last near, he had decided to risk exposing her make-up with this unexpectedly shocking result.

"And now," he concluded in a shaken voice, "I am naturally most anxious to know whether I am right—or have made some terrible mistake. Will you look at her, officer, and tell me if it is indeed—she?"

But the fat policeman shook his head over the well-known ability of Miss Hinch to look like everybody but herself.

"It'll take God Almighty to tell ye that, sir, saving your presence. I'll leave it f'r headquarters," he continued, as if that were the same thing. "But, if it is her, she's gone to her reward, sir."

"God pity her!" said the clergyman.

"Amen! Give me your name, sir. They'll likely want you in the morning."

The clergyman gave it: Rev. Theodore Shaler, of Denver; city address, a number on East 11th Street. Having thus discharged his duty in the affair, he started sadly to go away; but, passing by the silent figure stretched on a bench under the ticket-seller's overcoat, he bared his head and stopped for one last look at it.

The parson's gentleness and efficiency had already won favorable comments from the bystanders, and of the first quality he now gave a final proof. The dead woman's balled-up handkerchief, which somebody had recovered from the track and laid upon her breast, had slipped to the floor; and the clergyman, observing it, stooped silently to restore it again. This last small service chanced to bring his head close to the head of the dead woman; and, as he straightened up again, her projecting hatpin struck his cheek and ripped a straight line down it. This in itself would have been a trifle, since scratches soon heal. But it happened that the point of the hatpin caught the lining of the clergyman's perfect beard and ripped it clean from him; so that, as he rose with a suddenly shrill cry, he turned upon the astonished onlookers the bare, smooth chin of a woman, curiously long and pointed.

There were not many such chins in the world, and the urchins in the street would have recognized this one. Amid a sudden uproar which ill became the presence of the dead, the police closed in on Miss Hinch and handcuffed her with violence, fearing suicide, if not some new witchery; and at the station-house an unemotional matron divested the famous impersonator of the last and best of her disguises.

This much the police did. But it was everywhere understood that it was Jessie Dark who had really made the capture, and the papers next morning printed pictures of the unconquerable little woman and of the hatpin with which she had reached back from another world to bring her greatest adversary to justice.

Questions for discussion

1. This is a detective story but it is not a "Whodunit." Perhaps we could call it a "Whichoneisit." The story's effectiveness depends in great part on its ability to keep you mystified until the very end. Was there any point before the very end of the story at which you were quite sure that you knew which one was Miss Hinch?
2. It might be interesting now to go back and look for the clues which could have given you the answer. Did you pick up the clue of the hat pin? The pointed chin? The white pencil with the blue lead? At the same time look for those things by which the author probably intended to throw you off the track.
3. Every story is built around a conflict between two opposing forces. Here the two forces are two people. This kind of conflict is probably the most exciting to read about. Why is this true? In what ways were Jessie Dark and Miss Hinch what might be called well-matched opponents?
4. Conflicts are of many kinds and of many degrees of intensity. This one is unusually intense. What are some of the factors which make it so?

During the subway ride the young man describes the conflict between these two unusual women. How does he put it?

5. The old man on the subway quotes Jessie Dark's determination to catch the fugitive. What had Jessie Dark said? Why is this statement more significant to you now that you have finished the story than it was when you first read it?

6. In what way do the various aspects of the setting contribute to the story?

7. The next story in this book, "The Most Dangerous Game," is also one of "hot pursuit." This time watch for clues at every step.

Vocabulary growth

WORDS ARE INTERESTING. On page 20 you read, "Nothing could have seemed more natural or more *trivial* than this change of seats . . ." What does *trivial* mean? The word is made up of two Latin words, *tri*, "three," and *via*, "roads." The Romans long ago put these words together to form *triviatis*, meaning "of the crossroads." Since the crossroads in those days were the places where the same things happened over and over again, *triviatis* came to mean "commonplace." For us today *trivial* means "unimportant, trifling, or petty."

WORD FORMATION. On page 22 you read, "Some of these transformations were so amazing as to be beyond belief." *Transformation* is built on the base word *form*, meaning "shape or structure." The prefix *trans-* means "to change thoroughly"; the suffix *-ion* shows that the word is a noun. Thus a transformation is a thorough change in shape or structure.

The base word *form* appears in many English words. Using the following word parts, how many words can you build upon *form*?

Prefixes	Suffixes
de-	-or (-er)
in-	-ation
con-	-ance
trans-	-ive
per-	

CONTEXT. On page 22 you will find the sentence, "Coarse, violent, utterly unmoral, she happened to be the most astonishing *impersonator* of her time." From the context of the whole paragraph, work out the meaning of *impersonator*.

On page 33 appears this sentence: "As he talked the clergyman kept his hands *unobtrusively* busy." From the context of the paragraph, work out the meaning of *unobtrusively*.

For composition

1. You are a writer on Miss Dark's paper. Before the final night on which she died, she told you how she knew who Miss Hinch was. Write a human interest story, telling of her guess and of her plans to unmask and capture the guilty woman.
2. You are one of the young men waiting in the cold on the platform of the subway. Tell what you saw and heard, beginning with the arrival of the two women on the platform.

Rainsford and the general
were certainly playing . . .

The Most Dangerous Game

RICHARD CONNELL

"OFF there to the right—somewhere—is a large island," said
Whitney. "It's rather a mystery—"

"What island is it?" Rainsford asked.

"The old charts call it 'Ship-Trap Island,' " Whitney replied. "A
suggestive name, isn't it? Sailors have a curious dread of the place.
I don't know why. Some superstition—"

"Can't see it," remarked Rainsford, trying to peer through the
dank tropical night that was palpable as it pressed its thick, warm
blackness in upon the yacht.

"You've good eyes," said Whitney, with a laugh, "and I've seen
you pick off a moose moving in the brown fall bush at four hundred
yards, but even you can't see four miles or so through a moonless
Caribbean night."

"Not four yards," admitted Rainsford. "Ugh! It's like moist black
velvet."

"It will be light enough where we're going," promised Whitney.
"We should make it in a few days. I hope the jaguar guns have
come. We'll have good hunting up the Amazon. Great sport,
hunting."

"The best sport in the world," agreed Rainsford.

"For the hunter," amended Whitney. "Not for the jaguar."

"Don't talk rot, Whitney," said Rainsford. "You're a big-game
hunter, not a philosopher. Who cares how a jaguar feels?"

"Perhaps the jaguar does," observed Whitney.

"Bah! They've no understanding."

"Even so, I rather think they understand one thing—fear. The
fear of pain and the fear of death."

"Nonsense," laughed Rainsford. "This hot weather is making you

soft, Whitney. Be a realist. The world is made up of two classes—
the hunters and the hunted. Luckily, you and I are hunters. Do you
think we've passed that island yet?"

"I can't tell in the dark. I hope so."

"Why?" asked Rainsford.

"The place has a reputation—a bad one."

"Cannibals?" suggested Rainsford.

"Hardly. Even cannibals wouldn't live in such a God-forsaken
place. But it's got into sailor lore, somehow. Didn't you notice that
the crew's nerves seemed a bit jumpy today?"

"They were a bit strange, now that you mention it. Even Captain
Nielsen—"

"Yes, even that tough-minded old Swede, who'd go up to the
devil himself and ask him for a light. Those fishy blue eyes held a
look I never saw there before. All I could get out of him was: 'This
place has an evil name among seafaring men, sir.' Then he said to
me, very gravely: 'Don't you feel anything?'—as if the air about us
was actually poisonous. Now, you mustn't laugh when I tell you this
—I did feel something like a sudden chill.

"There was no breeze. The sea was as flat as a plate-glass window. We were drawing near the island then. What I felt was a—
a mental chill; a sort of sudden dread."

"Pure imagination," said Rainsford. "One superstitious sailor can
taint the whole ship's company with his fear."

"Maybe. But sometimes I think sailors have an extra sense that
tells them when they are in danger. Sometimes I think evil is a
tangible thing—with wave lengths, just as sound and light have. An
evil place can, so to speak, broadcast vibrations of evil. Anyhow,
I'm glad we're getting out of this zone. Well, I think I'll turn in now,
Rainsford."

"I'm not sleepy," said Rainsford. "I'm going to smoke another
pipe up on the afterdeck."

"Good night, then, Rainsford. See you at breakfast."

"Right. Good night, Whitney."

There was no sound in the night as Rainsford sat there, but the
muffled throb of the engine that drove the yacht swiftly through the
darkness, and the swish and ripple of the wash of the propeller.

Rainsford, reclining in a steamer chair, indolently puffed on his
favorite briar. The sensuous drowsiness of the night was on him.

"It's so dark," he thought, "that I could sleep without closing my eyes; the night would be my eyelids—"

An abrupt sound startled him. Off to the right he heard it, and his ears, expert in such matters, could not be mistaken. Again he heard the sound, and again. Somewhere, off in the blackness, someone had fired a gun three times.

Rainsford sprang up and moved quickly to the rail, mystified. He strained his eyes in the direction from which the reports had come, but it was like trying to see through a blanket. He leaped upon the rail and balanced himself there, to get greater elevation; his pipe, striking a rope, was knocked from his mouth. He lunged for it; a short, hoarse cry came from his lips as he realized he had reached too far and had lost his balance. The cry was pinched off short as the blood-warm waters of the Caribbean Sea closed over his head.

He struggled up to the surface and tried to cry out, but the wash from the speeding yacht slapped him in the face and the salt water in his open mouth made him gag and strangle. Desperately he struck out with strong strokes after the receding lights of the yacht, but he stopped before he had swum fifty feet. A certain cool-headedness had come to him; it was not the first time he had been in a tight place. There was a chance that his cries could be heard by someone aboard the yacht, but that chance was slender, and grew more slender as the yacht raced on. He wrestled himself out of his clothes, and shouted with all his power. The lights of the yacht became faint and ever-vanishing fireflies; then they were blotted out entirely by the night.

Rainsford remembered the shots. They had come from the right, and doggedly he swam in that direction, swimming with slow, deliberate strokes, conserving his strength. For a seemingly endless time he fought the sea. He began to count his strokes; he could do possibly a hundred more and then—

Rainsford heard a sound. It came out of the darkness, a high screaming sound, the sound of an animal in an extremity of anguish and terror.

He did not recognize the animal that made the sound—he did not try to; with fresh vitality he swam toward the sound. He heard it again; then it was cut short by another noise, crisp, staccato.

"Pistol shot," muttered Rainsford, swimming on.

Ten minutes of determined effort brought another sound to his ears—the most welcome he had ever heard—the muttering and growling of the sea breaking on a rocky shore. He was almost on the rocks before he saw them; on a night less calm he would have been shattered against them. With his remaining strength he dragged himself from the swirling waters. Jagged crags appeared to jut into the opaqueness; he forced himself upward, hand over hand. Gasping, his hands raw, he reached a flat place at the top. Dense jungle came down to the very edge of the cliffs. What perils that tangle of trees and underbrush might hold for him did not concern Rainsford just then. All he knew was that he was safe from his enemy, the sea, and that utter weariness was on him. He flung himself down at the jungle edge and tumbled headlong into the deepest sleep of his life.

When he opened his eyes he knew from the position of the sun that it was late in the afternoon. Sleep had given him new vigor; a sharp hunger was picking at him. He looked about him, almost cheerfully.

"Where there are pistol shots, there are men. Where there are men, there is food," he thought. But what kind of men, he wondered, in so forbidding a place? An unbroken front of snarled and jagged jungle fringed the shore.

He saw no sign of a trail through the closely knit web of weeds and trees; it was easier to go along the shore, and Rainsford floundered along by the water. Not far from where he had landed, he stopped.

Some wounded thing, by the evidence a large animal, had thrashed about in the underbrush; the jungle weeds were crushed down and the moss was lacerated; one patch of weeds was stained crimson. A small, glittering object not far away caught Rainsford's eye and he picked it up. It was an empty cartridge.

"A twenty-two," he remarked. "That's odd. It must have been a fairly large animal too. The hunter had his nerve with him to tackle it with such a light gun. It's clear that the brute put up a good fight. I suppose the first three shots I heard were when the hunter flushed his quarry and wounded it. The last shot was when he trailed it here and finished it."

He examined the ground closely and found what he had hoped to find—the print of hunting-boots. They pointed along the cliff in the direction he had been going. Eagerly he hurried along, now slipping on a rotten log or a loose stone, but making headway; night was beginning to settle down on the island.

Bleak darkness was blacking out the sea and jungle when Rainsford sighted the lights. He came upon them as he turned a crook in the coast line, and his first thought was that he had come upon a village, for there were many lights. But as he forged along he saw to his great astonishment that all the lights were in one enormous building—a lofty structure with pointed towers plunging upward into the gloom. His eyes made out the shadowy outlines of a palatial château; it was set on a high bluff, and on three sides of it cliffs dived down to where the sea licked greedy lips in the shadows.

"Mirage," thought Rainsford. But it was no mirage, he found, when he opened the tall spiked iron gate. The stone steps were real enough; the massive door with a leering gargoyle for a knocker was real enough; yet about it all hung an air of unreality.

He lifted the knocker, and it creaked up stiffly, as if it had never before been used. He let it fall, and it startled him with its booming loudness. He thought he heard steps within; the door remained closed. Again Rainsford lifted the heavy knocker, and let it fall. The door opened then, opened as suddenly as if it were on a spring, and Rainsford stood blinking in the river of glaring gold light that poured out. The first thing Rainsford's eyes discerned was the largest man Rainsford had ever seen—a gigantic creature, solidly made and black-bearded to the waist. In his hand the man held a long-barrelled revolver, and he was pointing it straight at Rainsford's heart.

Out of the snarl of beard two small eyes regarded Rainsford.

"Don't be alarmed," said Rainsford, with a smile which he hoped was disarming. "I'm no robber. I fell off a yacht. My name is Sanger Rainsford of New York City."

The menacing look in the eyes did not change. The revolver pointed as rigidly as if the giant were a statue. He gave no sign that he understood Rainsford's words, or that he had even heard them. He was dressed in uniform, a black uniform trimmed with gray astrakhan.

"I'm Sanger Rainsford of New York," Rainsford began again. "I fell off a yacht. I am hungry."

The man's only answer was to raise with his thumb the hammer of his revolver. Then Rainsford saw the man's free hand go to his forehead in a military salute, and he saw him click his heels together and stand at attention. Another man was coming down the broad marble steps, an erect, slender man in evening clothes. He advanced and held out his hand.

In a cultivated voice marked by a slight accent that gave it added precision and deliberateness, he said: "It is a very great pleasure and honor to welcome Mr. Sanger Rainsford, the celebrated hunter, to my home." Automatically Rainsford shook the man's hand.

"I've read your book about hunting snow leopards in Tibet, you see," explained the man. "I am General Zaroff."

Rainsford's first impression was that the man was singularly handsome; his second was that there was an original, almost bizarre quality about the general's face. He was a tall man past middle age, for his hair was a vivid white; but his thick eyebrows and pointed military mustache were as black as the night from which Rainsford had come. His eyes, too, were black and very bright. He had high cheekbones, a sharp-cut nose, a spare, dark face, the face of a man used to giving orders, the face of an aristocrat. Turning to the giant in uniform, the general made a sign. The giant put away his pistol, saluted, withdrew.

"Ivan is an incredibly strong fellow," remarked the general, "but he has the misfortune to be deaf and dumb. A simple fellow, but, I'm afraid, like all his race, a bit of a savage."

"Is he Russian?"

"He is a Cossack," said the general, and his smile showed red lips and pointed teeth. "So am I."

"Come," he said, "we shouldn't be chatting here. We can talk later. Now you want clothes, food, rest. You shall have them. This is a most restful spot."

Ivan had reappeared, and the general spoke to him with lips that moved but gave forth no sound.

"Follow Ivan, if you please, Mr. Rainsford," said the general. "I was about to have my dinner when you came. I'll wait for you. You'll find that my clothes will fit you, I think."

It was to a huge, beam-ceilinged bedroom with a canopied bed big enough for six men that Rainsford followed the silent giant. Ivan laid out an evening suit, and Rainsford, as he put it on, noticed that it came from a London tailor who ordinarily cut and sewed for none below the rank of duke.

The dining room to which Ivan conducted him was in many ways remarkable. There was a medieval magnificence about it; it suggested a baronial hall of feudal times with its oaken panels, its high ceiling, its vast refectory table where twoscore men could sit down to eat. About the hall were the mounted heads of many animals—lions, tigers, elephants, moose, bears; larger or more perfect specimens Rainsford had never seen. At the great table the general was sitting alone.

"You'll have a cocktail, Mr. Rainsford," he suggested. The cocktail was surpassingly good; and, Rainsford noted, the table appointments were of the finest—the linen, the crystal, the silver, the china.

They were eating *borsch*, the rich, red soup with whipped cream so dear to Russian palates. Half apologetically General Zaroff said: "We do our best to preserve the amenities of civilization here. Please forgive any lapses. We are well off the beaten track, you know. Do you think the champagne has suffered from its long ocean trip?"

"Not in the least," declared Rainsford. He was finding the general a most thoughtful and affable host, a true cosmopolite. But there was one trait of the general's that made Rainsford uncomfortable. Whenever he looked up he found the general studying him, appraising him narrowly.

"Perhaps," said General Zaroff, "you were surprised that I recognized your name. You see, I read all books on hunting published in English, French, and Russian. I have but one passion in my life, Mr. Rainsford, and it is the hunt."

"You have some wonderful heads here," said Rainsford as he ate a particularly well-cooked filet mignon. "That Cape buffalo is the largest I ever saw."

"Oh, that fellow. Yes, he was a monster."

"Did he charge you?"

"Hurled me against a tree," said the general. "Fractured my skull. But I got the brute."

"I've always thought," said Rainsford, "that the Cape buffalo is the most dangerous of all big game."

For a moment the general did not reply; he was smiling his curious red-lipped smile. Then he said slowly: "No. You are wrong, sir. The Cape buffalo is not the most dangerous big game." He sipped his wine. "Here in my preserve on this island," he said in the same slow tone, "I hunt more dangerous game."

Rainsford expressed his surprise. "Is there big game on this island?"

The general nodded. "The biggest."

"Really?"

"Oh, it isn't here naturally, of course. I have to stock the island."

"What have you imported, General?" Rainsford asked. "Tigers?"

The general smiled. "No," he said. "Hunting tigers ceased to interest me some years ago. I exhausted their possibilities, you see. No thrill left in tigers, no real danger. I live for danger, Mr. Rainsford."

The general took from his pocket a gold cigarette case and offered his guest a long black cigarette with a silver tip; it was perfumed and gave off a smell like incense.

"We will have some capital hunting, you and I," said the general. "I shall be most glad to have your society."

"But what game—" began Rainsford.

"I'll tell you," said the general. "You will be amused, I know. I think I may say, in all modesty, that I have done a rare thing. I have invented a new sensation. May I pour you another glass of port, Mr. Rainsford?"

"Thank you, General."

The general filled both glasses, and said: "God makes some men poets. Some He makes kings, some beggars. Me He made a hunter. My hand was made for the trigger, my father said. He was a very rich man with a quarter of a million acres in the Crimea, and he was an ardent sportsman. When I was only five years old he gave me a little gun, specially made in Moscow for me, to shoot sparrows with. When I shot some of his prize turkeys with it, he did not punish me; he complimented me on my marksmanship. I killed my first bear in the Caucasus when I was ten. My whole life had been one prolonged hunt. I went into the army—it was expected of noblemen's sons—and for a time commanded a division of Cossack cavalry, but my real interest was always the hunt. I have hunted every kind of game in every land. It would be impossible for me to tell you how many animals I have killed."

The general puffed at his cigarette.

"After the debacle in Russia I left the country, for it was imprudent for an officer of the Czar to stay there. Many noble Russians lost everything. I, luckily, had invested heavily in American securities, so I shall never have to open a tearoom in Monte Carlo or drive a taxi in Paris. Naturally, I continued to hunt—grizzlies in your Rockies, crocodiles in the Ganges, rhinoceroses in East Africa. It was in Africa that the Cape buffalo hit me and laid me up for six months. As soon as I recovered I started for the Amazon to hunt jaguars, for I had heard they were unusually cunning. They weren't." The Cossack sighed. "They were no match at all for a hunter with his wits about him, and a high-powered rifle. I was bitterly disappointed. I was lying in my tent with a splitting headache one night when a terrible thought pushed its way into my mind. Hunting was beginning to bore me! And hunting, remember, had been my life. I have heard that in America businessmen often go to pieces when they give up the business that has been their life."

"Yes, that's so," said Rainsford.

The general smiled. "I had no wish to go to pieces," he said. "I must do something. Now, mine is an analytical mind, Mr. Rainsford. Doubtless that is why I enjoy the problems of the chase."

"No doubt, General Zaroff."

"So," continued the general, "I asked myself why the hunt no longer fascinated me. You are much younger than I am, Mr. Rainsford, and have not hunted as much, but you perhaps can guess the answer."

"What was it?"

"Simply this: hunting had ceased to be what you call 'a sporting proposition.' It had become too easy. I always got my quarry. Always. There is no greater bore than perfection."

The general lit a fresh cigarette.

"No animal had a chance with me any more. That is no boast; it is a mathematical certainty. The animal had nothing but his legs and his instinct. Instinct is no match for reason. When I thought of this it was a tragic moment for me, I can tell you."

Rainsford leaned across the table, absorbed in what his host was saying.

"It came to me as an inspiration what I must do," the general went on.

"And that was?"

The general smiled the quiet smile of one who has faced an obstacle and surmounted it with success. "I had to invent a new animal to hunt," he said.

"A new animal? You're joking."

"Not at all," said the general. "I never joke about hunting. I needed a new animal. I found one. So I bought this island, built this house, and here I do my hunting. The island is perfect for my purposes—there are jungles with a maze of trails in them, hills, swamps—"

"But the animal, General Zaroff?"

"Oh," said the general, "it supplies me with the most exciting hunting in the world. No other hunting compares with it for an instant. Every day I hunt, and I never grow bored now, for I have a quarry with which I can match my wits."

Rainsford's bewilderment showed in his face.

"I wanted the ideal animal to hunt," explained the general. "So I said: 'What are the attributes of an ideal quarry?' And the answer was, of course: 'It must have courage, cunning, and, above all, it must be able to reason.'"

"But no animal can reason," objected Rainsford.

"My dear fellow," said the general, "there is one that can."

"But you can't mean—" gasped Rainsford.

"And why not?"

"I can't believe you are serious, General Zaroff. This is a grisly joke."

"Why should I not be serious? I am speaking of hunting."

"Hunting? Good God, General Zaroff, what you speak of is murder."

The general laughed with entire good nature. He regarded Rainsford quizzically. "I refuse to believe that so modern and civilized a young man as you harbors romantic ideas about the value of human life. Surely your experiences in the war—"

"Did not make me condone cold-blooded murder," finished Rainsford stiffly.

Laughter shook the general. "How extraordinarily droll you are!" he said. "One does not expect nowadays to find a young man of the educated class, even in America, with such a naïve and, if I may say so, mid-Victorian point of view. It's like finding a snuffbox in a limousine. Ah, well, doubtless you had Puritan ancestors. So many Americans appear to have had. I'll wager you'll forget your notions when you go hunting with me. You've a genuine thrill in store for you, Mr. Rainsford."

"Thank you, I'm a hunter, not a murderer."

"Dear me," said the general, quite unruffled, "again that unpleasant word. But I think I can show you that your scruples are quite unfounded."

"Yes?"

"Life is for the strong, to be lived by the strong, and, if needs be, taken by the strong. The weak of the world were put here to give the strong pleasure. I am strong. Why should I not use my gift? If I wish to hunt, why should I not? I hunt the scum of the earth—sailors from tramp ships—lascars, blacks, Chinese, whites, mongrels—a thoroughbred horse or hound is worth more than a score of them."

"But they are men," said Rainsford hotly.

"Precisely," said the general. "That is why I use them. It gives me pleasure. They can reason, after a fashion. So they are dangerous."

"But where do you get them?"

The general's eyelid fluttered down in a wink. "This island is called Ship-Trap," he answered. "Sometimes an angry god of the high seas sends them to me. Sometimes, when Providence is not so kind, I help Providence a bit. Come to the window with me."

Rainsford went to the window and looked out toward the sea.

"Watch! Out there!" exclaimed the general, pointing into the night. Rainsford's eyes saw only blackness, and then, as the general pressed a button, far out to sea Rainsford saw the flash of lights.

The general chuckled. "They indicate a channel," he said, "where there's none: giant rocks with razor edges crouch like a sea monster with wide-open jaws. They can crush a ship as easily as I crush this nut." He dropped a walnut on the hardwood floor and brought his heel grinding down on it. "Oh, yes," he said, casually, as if in answer to a question, "I have electricity. We try to be civilized here."

"Civilized? And you shoot down men?"

A trace of anger was in the general's black eyes, but it was there for but a second, and he said, in his most pleasant manner: "Dear me, what a righteous young man you are! I assure you I do not do the thing you suggest. That would be barbarous. I treat these visitors with every consideration. They get plenty of good food and exercise. They get into splendid physical condition. You shall see for yourself tomorrow."

"What do you mean?"

"We'll visit my training school," smiled the general. "It's in the cellar. I have about a dozen pupils down there now. They're from the Spanish bark, 'San Lucar,' that had the bad luck to go on the rocks out there. A very inferior lot, I regret to say. Poor specimens and more accustomed to the deck than to the jungle."

He raised his hand, and Ivan, who served as waiter, brought thick Turkish coffee. Rainsford, with an effort, held his tongue in check.

"It's a game, you see," pursued the general blandly. "I suggest to one of them that we go hunting. I give him a supply of food and an excellent hunting knife. I give him three hours' start. I am to follow, armed only with a pistol of the smallest caliber and range. If my quarry eludes me for three whole days, he wins the game. If I find him," the general smiled, "he loses."

"Suppose he refuses to be hunted?"

"Oh," said the general, "I give him his option, of course. He need not play that game if he doesn't wish to. If he does not wish to hunt I turn him over to Ivan. Ivan once had the honor of serving as official knouter to the Great White Czar, and he has his own ideas of sport. Invariably, Mr. Rainsford, invariably they choose the hunt."

"And if they win?"

The smile on the general's face widened. "To date I have not lost," he said.

Then he added, hastily: "I don't wish you to think me a braggart, Mr. Rainsford. Many of them afford only the most elementary sort of problem. Occasionally I strike a tartar. One almost did win. I eventually had to use the dogs."

"The dogs?"

"This way, please. I'll show you."

The general steered Rainsford to a window. The lights from the window sent a flickering illumination that made grotesque patterns on the courtyard below, and Rainsford could see moving about there a dozen or so huge black shapes; as they turned toward him, their eyes glittered greenly.

"A rather good lot, I think," observed the general. "They are let out at seven every night. If anyone should try to get into my house —or out of it—something extremely regrettable would occur to him." He hummed a snatch of song from the Folies Bergère.

"And now," said the general, "I want to show you my new collection of heads. Will you come with me to the library?"

"I hope," said Rainsford, "that you will excuse me tonight, General Zaroff. I'm really not feeling at all well."

"Ah, indeed?" the general inquired solicitously. "Well, I suppose that's only natural, after your long swim. You need a good, restful night's sleep. Tomorrow you'll feel like a new man, I'll wager. Then we'll hunt, eh? I've one rather promising prospect—"

Rainsford was hurrying from the room.

"Sorry you can't go with me tonight," called the general. "I expect rather fair sport—a big, strong black. He looks resourceful—Well, good night, Mr. Rainsford; I hope you have a good night's rest."

The bed was good and the pajamas of the softest silk, and he was tired in every fiber of his being, but nevertheless Rainsford could not quiet his brain with the opiate of sleep. He lay, eyes wide open. Once he thought he heard stealthy steps in the corridor outside his room. He sought to throw open the door; it would not open. He went to the window and looked out. His room was high up in one of the towers. The lights of the château were out now, and it was dark and silent, but there was a fragment of sallow moon, and by its wan light he could see, dimly, the courtyard; there, weaving, in and out in the pattern of shadow, were black, noiseless forms; the hounds heard him at the window and looked up, expectantly, with their green eyes. Rainsford went back to the bed and lay down. By many methods he tried to put himself to sleep. He had achieved a doze when, just as morning began to come, he heard, far off in the jungle, the faint report of a pistol.

General Zaroff did not appear until luncheon. He was dressed faultlessly in the tweeds of a country squire. He was solicitous about the state of Rainsford's health.

"As for me," sighed the general, "I do not feel so well. I am worried, Mr. Rainsford. Last night I detected traces of my old complaint."

To Rainsford's questioning glance the general said: "Ennui. Boredom."

Then, taking a second helping of crêpe suzette, the general explained: "The hunting was not good last night. The fellow lost his head. He made a straight trail that offered no problems at all. That's the trouble with these sailors; they have dull brains to begin with, and they do not know how to get about in the woods. They do excessively stupid and obvious things. It's most annoying. Will you have another glass of Chablis, Mr. Rainsford?"

"General," said Rainsford firmly, "I wish to leave this island at once."

The general raised his thickets of eyebrows; he seemed hurt. "But, my dear fellow," the general protested, "you've only just come. You've had no hunting—"

"I wish to go today," said Rainsford. He saw the dead black eyes of the general on him, studying him. General Zaroff's face suddenly brightened.

He filled Rainsford's glass with venerable Chablis from a dusty bottle.

"Tonight," said the general, "we will hunt—you and I."

Rainsford shook his head. "No, General," he said. "I will not hunt."

The general shrugged his shoulders and nibbled delicately at a hothouse grape. "As you wish, my friend," he said. "The choice rests entirely with you. But may I not venture to suggest that you will find my idea of sport more diverting than Ivan's?"

He nodded toward the corner where the giant stood, scowling, his thick arms crossed on his hogshead of chest.

"You don't mean—" cried Rainsford.

"My dear fellow," said the general, "have I not told you I always mean what I say about hunting? This is really an inspiration. I drink to a foeman worthy of my steel—at last."

The general raised his glass, but Rainsford sat staring at him.

"You'll find this game worth playing," the general said enthusiastically. "Your brain against mine. Your woodcraft against mine. Your strength and stamina against mine. Outdoor chess. And the stake is not without value, eh?"

"And if I win—" began Rainsford huskily.

"I'll cheerfully admit myself defeated if I do not find you by midnight of the third day," said General Zaroff. "My sloop will place you on the mainland near a town."

The general read what Rainsford was thinking.

"Oh, you can trust me," said the Cossack. "I will give you my word as a gentleman and a sportsman. Of course, you, in turn, must agree to say nothing of your visit here."

"I'll agree to nothing of the kind," said Rainsford.

"Oh," said the general, "in that case— but why discuss that now? Three days hence we can discuss it over a bottle of Veuve Cliquot, unless—"

The general sipped his wine.

Then a businesslike air animated him. "Ivan," he said to Rainsford, "will supply you with hunting clothes, food, a knife. I suggest you wear moccasins; they leave a poorer trail. I should suggest too that you avoid the big swamp in the southeast corner of the island. We call it Death Swamp. There's quicksand there. One foolish fellow tried it. The deplorable part of it was that Lazarus followed him. You can imagine my feelings, Mr. Rainsford. I loved Lazarus; he was the finest hound in my pack. Well, I must beg you to excuse me now. I always take a siesta after lunch. You'll hardly have time for a nap, I fear. You'll want to start, no doubt. I shall not follow till dusk. Hunting at night is so much more exciting than by day, don't you think? Au revoir, Mr. Rainsford, au revoir."

General Zaroff, with a deep, courtly bow, strolled from the room.

From another door came Ivan. Under one arm he carried khaki hunting clothes, a haversack of food, a leather sheath containing a long-bladed hunting knife; his right hand rested on a cocked revolver thrust in the crimson sash around his waist. . . .

Rainsford had fought his way through the bush for two hours.

"I must keep my nerve. I must keep my nerve," he said through tight teeth.

He had not been entirely clear-headed when the château gates snapped shut behind him. His whole idea at first was to put distance between himself and General Zaroff, and, to this end, he had plunged along, spurred on by the sharp rowels of something very like panic. Now he had got a grip on himself, had stopped, and was taking stock of himself and the situation.

He saw that straight flight was futile; inevitably it would bring him face to face with the sea. He was in a picture with a frame of water, and his operations, clearly, must take place within that frame.

"I'll give him a trail to follow," muttered Rainsford, and he struck off from the rude path he had been following into the trackless wilderness. He executed a series of intricate loops; he doubled on his trail again and again, recalling all the lore of the fox hunt, and all the dodges of the fox. Night found him leg-weary, with hands and face lashed by the branches, on a thickly wooded ridge. He knew it would be insane to blunder on through the dark, even if he had the strength. His need for rest was imperative and he thought: "I have played the fox, now I must play the cat of the fable." A big tree with a thick trunk and outspread branches was near by, and, taking care to leave not the slightest mark, he climbed up into the crotch, and stretching out on one of the broad limbs, after a fashion, rested. Rest brought him new confidence and almost a feeling of security. Even so zealous a hunter as General Zaroff could not trace him there, he told himself; only the devil himself could follow that complicated trail through the jungle after dark. But, perhaps, the general was a devil—

An apprehensive night crawled slowly by like a wounded snake, and sleep did not visit Rainsford, although the silence of a dead world was on the jungle. Toward morning when a dingy gray was varnishing the sky, the cry of some startled bird focused Rainsford's attention in that direction. Something was coming through the bush, coming slowly, carefully, coming by the same winding way Rainsford had come. He flattened himself down on the limb, and through a screen of leaves almost as thick as tapestry, he watched. The thing that was approaching was a man.

It was General Zaroff. He made his way along with his eyes fixed in utmost concentration on the ground before him. He paused almost beneath the tree, dropped to his knees, and studied the ground before him. Rainsford's impulse was to hurl himself down like a panther, but he saw that the general's right hand held something small and metallic—an automatic pistol.

The hunter shook his head several times as if he were puzzled. Then he straightened up and took from his case one of his black cigarettes; its pungent incenselike smoke floated up to Rainsford's nostrils.

Rainsford held his breath. The general's eyes had left the ground and were traveling inch by inch up the tree. Rainsford froze there, every muscle tensed for a spring. But the sharp eyes of the hunter stopped before they reached the limb where Rainsford lay; a smile spread over his brown face. Very deliberately he blew a smoke ring into the air; then he turned his back on the tree and walked carelessly away, back along the trail he had come. The swirls of the underbrush against his hunting boots grew fainter and fainter.

The pent-up air burst hotly from Rainsford's lungs. His first thought made him feel sick and numb. The general could follow a trail through the woods at night; he could follow an extremely difficult trail; he must have uncanny powers; only by the merest chance had the Cossack failed to see his quarry.

Rainsford's second thought was even more terrible. It sent a shudder of cold horror through his whole being. Why had the general smiled? Why had he turned back?

Rainsford did not want to believe what his reason told him was true, but the truth was as evident as the sun that had by now pushed through the morning mists. The general was playing with him. The general was saving him for another day's sport! The Cossack was the cat; he was the mouse. Then it was that Rainsford knew the full meaning of terror.

"I will not lose my nerve. I will not."

He slid down from the tree, and struck off again into the woods. His face was set and he forced the machinery of his mind to function. Three hundred yards from his hiding place he stopped where a huge dead tree leaned precariously on a smaller living one. Throwing off his sack of food, Rainsford took his knife from its sheath and began to work with all his energy.

The job was finished at last, and he threw himself down behind a fallen log a hundred feet away. He did not have to wait long. The cat was coming again to play with the mouse.

Following the trail with the sureness of a bloodhound came General Zaroff. Nothing escaped those searching black eyes, no crushed blade of grass, no bent twig, no mark, no matter how faint, in the moss. So intent was the Cossack on his stalking that he was upon the thing Rainsford had made before he saw it. His foot touched the protruding bough that was the trigger. Even as he touched it, the general sensed his danger and leaped back with the agility of an ape. But he was not quite quick enough; the dead tree, delicately adjusted to rest on the cut living one, crashed down and struck the general a glancing blow on the shoulder as it fell; but for his alertness, he must have been smashed beneath it. He staggered, but he did not fall; nor did he drop his revolver. He stood there rubbing his injured shoulder, and Rainsford, with fear again gripping his heart, heard the general's mocking laugh ring through the jungle.

"Rainsford," called the general, "if you are within sound of my voice, as I suppose you are, let me congratulate you. Not many men know how to make a Malay man-catcher. Luckily, for me, I too have hunted in Malacca. You are proving interesting, Mr. Rainsford. I am going now to have my wound dressed; it's only a slight one. But I shall be back. I shall be back."

When the general, nursing his bruised shoulder, had gone, Rainsford took up his flight again. It was flight now, a desperate, hopeless flight, that carried him on for some hours. Dusk came, then darkness, and still he pressed on. The ground grew softer under his moccasins; the vegetation grew ranker, denser; insects bit him savagely. Then, as he stepped forward, his foot sank into the ooze. He tried to wrench it back, but the muck sucked viciously at his foot as if it were a giant leech. With a violent effort, he tore his foot loose. He knew where he was now. Death Swamp and its quicksand.

His hands were tight closed as if his nerve were something tangible that someone in the darkness was trying to tear from his grip. The softness of the earth had given him an idea. He stepped back from the quicksand a dozen feet or so and, like some huge prehistoric beaver, he began to dig.

Rainsford had dug himself in in France when a second's delay meant death. That had been a placid pastime compared to his digging now. The pit grew deeper; when it was above his shoulders, he climbed out and from some hard saplings cut stakes and sharpened them to a fine point. These stakes he planted in the bottom of the pit with the points sticking up. With flying fingers he wove a rough carpet of weeds and branches and with it he covered the mouth of the pit. Then, wet with sweat and aching with tiredness, he crouched behind the stump of a lightning-charred tree.

He knew his pursuer was coming; he heard the padding sound of feet on the soft earth, and the night breeze brought him the perfume of the general's cigarette. It seemed to Rainsford that the general was coming with unusual swiftness; he was not feeling his way along, foot by foot. Rainsford, crouching there, could not see the general, nor could he see the pit. He lived a year in a minute. Then he felt an impulse to cry aloud with joy, for he heard the sharp crackle of the breaking branches as the cover of the pit gave way; he heard the sharp scream of pain as the pointed stakes found their mark. He leaped up from his place of concealment. Then he cowered back. Three feet from the pit a man was standing, with an electric torch in his hand.

"You've done well, Rainsford," the voice of the general called.

"Your Burmese tiger pit has claimed one of my best dogs. Again you score. I think, Mr. Rainsford, I'll see what you can do against my whole pack. I'm going home for a rest now. Thank you for a most amusing evening."

At daybreak Rainsford, lying near the swamp, was awakened by a sound that made him know that he had new things to learn about fear. It was a distant sound, faint and wavering, but he knew it. It was the baying of a pack of hounds.

Rainsford knew he could do one of two things. He could stay where he was and wait. That was suicide. He could flee. That was postponing the inevitable. For a moment he stood there, thinking. An idea that held a wild chance came to him, and, tightening his belt, he headed away from the swamp. The baying of the hounds drew nearer, then still nearer, nearer, ever nearer. On a ridge Rainsford climbed a tree. Down a watercourse, not a quarter of a mile away, he could see the bush moving. Straining his eyes, he saw the lean figure of General Zaroff; just ahead of him Rainsford made out another figure whose wide shoulders surged through the tall jungle weeds; it was the giant Ivan, and he seemed pulled forward by some unseen force; Rainsford knew that Ivan must be holding the pack in leash.

They would be on him any minute now. His mind worked frantically. He thought of a native trick he had learned in Uganda. He slid down the tree. He caught hold of a springy young sapling and to it he fastened his hunting knife, with the blade pointing down the trail; with a bit of wild grapevine he tied back the sapling. Then he ran for his life. The hounds raised their voices as they hit the fresh scent. Rainsford knew now how an animal at bay feels.

He had to stop to get his breath. The baying of the hounds stopped abruptly, and Rainsford's heart stopped too. They must have reached the knife.

He shinned excitedly up a tree and looked back. His pursuers had stopped. But the hope that was in Rainsford's brain when he climbed died, for he saw in the shallow valley that General Zaroff was still on his feet. But Ivan was not. The knife, driven by the recoil of the springing tree, had not wholly failed.

Rainsford had hardly tumbled to the ground when the pack resumed the chase.

"Nerve, nerve, nerve!" he panted, as he dashed along. A blue

gap showed between the trees dead ahead. Ever nearer drew the
hounds. Rainsford forced himself on toward that gap. He reached it.
It was the shore of the sea. Across a cove he could see the gloomy
gray stone of the château. Twenty feet below him the sea rumbled
and hissed. Rainsford hesitated. He heard the hounds. Then he
leaped far out into the sea. . . .

When the general and his pack reached the place by the sea, the
Cossack stopped. For some minutes he stood regarding the blue-
green expanse of water. He shrugged his shoulders. Then he sat down,
took a drink of brandy from a silver flask, lit a perfumed cigarette,
and hummed a bit from *Madame Butterfly*.

General Zaroff had an exceedingly good dinner in his great pan-
eled dining hall that evening. With it he had a bottle of Pol Roger
and a half bottle of Chambertin. Two slight annoyances kept him
from perfect enjoyment. One was the thought that it would be difficult to replace Ivan; the other was that his quarry had escaped him;
of course, the American hadn't played the game—so thought the
general as he tasted his after-dinner liqueur. In his library he read,
to soothe himself, from the works of Marcus Aurelius. At ten he went
up to his bedroom. He was deliciously tired, he said to himself, as
he locked himself in. There was a little moonlight, so, before turning
on his light, he went to the window and looked down at the courtyard. To the great hounds he called: "Better luck another time!"
Then he switched on the light.

A man, who had been hiding in the curtains of the bed, was
standing there.

"Rainsford!" screamed the general. "How in God's name did
you get here?"

"Swam," said Rainsford. "I found it quicker than walking through
the jungle."

The general sucked in his breath and smiled. "I congratulate
you," he said. "You have won the game."

Rainsford did not smile. "I am still a beast at bay," he said, in a
low, hoarse voice. "Get ready, General Zaroff."

The general made one of his deepest bows. "I see," he said.
"Splendid! One of us is to furnish a repast for the hounds. The other
will sleep in this very excellent bed. On guard, Rainsford." . . .

He had never slept in a better bed, Rainsford decided.

Questions for discussion

1. Perhaps you were aware as you read this story that it actually took several pages of reading before the story of the pursuit of the "hunted" by the "hunter" itself began to develop. The author used those opening paragraphs to establish the setting and to create the proper atmosphere for the story. You'll remember that the author of "Miss Hinch" did the same thing. This is good technique for a story of mystery and suspense. Can you see why? You see first a strange place, then a strange person, and finally the strange game played by that strange person in the strange place.

   Sometimes the setting plays a very important part in a story, so important that what happened could not have happened just like that in any other place or time. When this is true, the author usually makes it a point to show you that place and time very clearly at the beginning of the story. He knows that if you can visualize the place and feel the atmosphere, you will understand what takes place and why, and appreciate it all the more.

   Although atmosphere is perhaps most important in this story and in "Miss Hinch," it plays a significant part in several of the other stories in this book too. Watch for it.

2. Go back and read the first few pages again. How do they prepare you for what happens later? Look for references to "evil," "dread," "terror," and to "hunting." What is said and what happens at the beginning of the story that gains real significance later on in the story?

3. Probably the most significant line in this story is this: "The world is made up of two classes—the hunters and the hunted." Many people who have read this story have remembered this line for years afterward. What does it mean to you? What is your reaction to this idea?

4. At what point did you begin to realize what the game was? At what point did you begin to suspect who the next "hunted" would be?

5. Notice how the author reveals the general's character and his intentions through his own words. The general makes a series of statements about himself. The first is: "I have but one passion in life, and it is the hunt." From this you realize how deadly serious this game is to him. What are the other statements he makes? What do you learn from each one?

6. What do you think of the general's philosophy: "Life is for the strong"?

7. Were you surprised by the ending of this story? Did you expect a different ending? Why? What does this ending tell you about the author's own personal beliefs?

Vocabulary growth

WORD ORIGINS. The word *lore* came to England when that country was invaded more than a thousand years ago by Germanic peoples called Angles and Saxons. To them it meant "learning" or "something taught." What do you think *lore* means in this sentence, "But it's got into sailor *lore* somehow."?

In ancient Roman times, some people were so afraid of the gods that they would scarcely step outside the house without a prayer or sacrifice. They could not believe that anything in the physical world happened just from natural causes. To those who held this extreme fear of the gods, the Romans applied the word *superstitio*. They made it up from two words, *super*: above, and *stare*: to stand. A superstitious person was one who thought that fearsome gods were constantly standing above him, waiting to do him some harm or mischief.

CONTEXT. " 'Can't see it,' remarked Rainsford, trying to peer through the dank tropical night that was *palpable* as it pressed its thick, warm blackness in upon the yacht."

Which words in this sentence give you a clue to the meaning of *palpable*? What do you think it means? Check your guess with the dictionary.

For composition

One doesn't need to go to some faraway jungle island to find someone who is playing a dangerous game. Most countries, communities, or groups of people have someone in their midst who, because of his nature or character, is playing a dangerous game which is likely to prove disastrous for himself or for someone else. Look around you for a person who is playing a dangerous game. (Perhaps it is driving a car.) Write a character sketch of him in which you include what he does, what it is that compels him to play this game, and what you predict the outcome will be.

The dangers were great but the cadet
in Navy plane 323 called in to say . . .

I'm Coming In

JOSEPH N. BELL

W HEN the first light went out at 6:45, the Texas sun had just
poked its nose over the horizon and the hundreds of Navy training
planes nestling on the ramp looked like gray ghosts in the dim morning light. Mounting the steps to the squadron control tower a few
minutes earlier, I had noticed, far off to the north in the dew-infested
haze, a lowering bank of black clouds. I remember feeling relieved
that I wasn't flying that day, but had instead drawn the assignment
as tower duty officer. Later, I would have been happy to trade places
with almost anyone in the squadron.

In the glass-encased tower atop the hangar, all the disconnected
threads of the complex operations of a wartime naval-air-training
squadron were gathered and loosely held—until an emergency arose
and the thread tautened and hauled in or played out as the emergency called for. Here, we were in direct radio contact with hundreds
of practicing pilots, some fearful, some cocky, some cautious and
some simply doing a job as best they knew how. This day one would
survive an experience that dozens of others would never forget.

Perhaps as I looked over the early-morning weather report, I was
thinking of my own cadet days and how little I knew about the
airplanes I flew then. A "norther"—one of those vicious Texas storms
which sweep in so often with little warning and batter an area with
driving rain, howling wind and biting cold—was due later in the day.
Flying conditions were expected to be very bad by afternoon; but
now the sun was climbing in the sky, a few fleecy clouds were scut-
tling by, and the EVERYTHING OUT sign was underscored on the flight
schedule board.

Only a few minutes after the field had been cleared of planes
headed out to practice formation flying or landings at remote prac-

tice fields, a revised weather report came in. The norther was moving much faster than had been expected; it would now hit in midmorning. A look outside to the north confirmed the emergency. The bank of black clouds which had looked so far away in the predawn light now loomed ominously in the near distance, bearing down on us with the malevolence that only a pilot can see in approaching bad weather.

I was reaching for the phone to ask permission to recall our planes when it jingled of its own accord. The commanding officer was on the other end. "Call 'em back," he told me succinctly.

I passed the word to the tower radio operator and he began to repeat into his transmitter: "Attention all Twelve Baker planes. Return to base immediately."

The planes came piling back to the field for about fifteen minutes; then the ranks of the landing aircraft began to thin.

The clouds were almost on us, thick, black and low-flying. The planes coming in now were obviously all piloted by cadets, judging by the long, slow, cautious approaches they were making. The enlisted man at my side was checking the numbers of the landing aircraft against a schedule sheet.

"How many still out?" I asked him.

He ran down the list. "About fifteen."

I picked up the radio transmitter and intoned: "All Twelve Baker planes not now on the ground: do not attempt to return to the main base. We are weathered in here. Put down at the nearest practice field and call in your position. All Twelve Baker planes still in the air, acknowledge."

We peered anxiously into the gloom. Two planes were in their approach. Three more were circling the field, flying well under the 500-foot traffic-circle altitude because the overcast was now solid just a few hundred feet above the ground. The five around the field landed without mishap; then an uneasy quiet descended. Actually, the place was noisy; taxiing planes, groups of shouting pilots gathered on the ramp or in the hangar, mechanics testing engines, all contributed to the din. But the sound we were listening for, the noisy, angry growl of an aircraft engine in low pitch preparing for a landing, was absent.

I asked for another check and was told there were nine planes unaccounted for. I repeated my radio message several times, and then we waited.

At last we began to hear from them. Three cadets and an instructor—a whole practice formation—had landed on one of our outlying fields and were safe. That left five. Two cadets called in; they were down together on another practice field. Three still unaccounted for: two cadets and an officer instructor. I began calling them individually by name and number, and the instructor answered promptly.

"I'm above the overcast," he said, "on my way in. The overcast isn't very thick—maybe a few hundred feet. I'll make it back home O.K."

Then, as we were to learn later, he shoved his earphones toward the top of his head to rest his ears—and there they remained until he landed. He never heard the drama that followed.

Two aviation cadets: fate unknown. Our cadets were in basic training. They'd survived about 100 flying hours in primary trainers and were flying heavy planes for the first time. None had yet received training in instrument flying, but we were fast approaching instrument conditions. We continued to call the missing cadets. It seemed like an eternity, but it couldn't have been more than five minutes later when one of them answered. He had landed in a plowed field and washed out his landing gear. But he wasn't badly hurt—just a few scratches. I told him to stand by his plane until we picked him up. That left one.

Another slice of eternity, then—happily—we heard from him too. When his voice came in distinctly on the tower radio, there was an audible catching of breath behind me. For the first time, I realized that a dozen or more of the older instructors—returned from their flights—had climbed to the tower to watch and listen. Their thoughts, like mine, were not contained by the glass walls of the tower; they had taken wing and joined with that one lonely kid who was somewhere in the mist over strange territory in a strange airplane.

His voice was almost plaintive as he said, "Twelve Baker tower, this is Three-two-three. Can you hear me? Over."

Three-two-three. Today I have no idea of that boy's name, but the number I'll never forget. It was implanted indelibly on my memory in the few minutes that followed. I reached for the transmitter to answer him when another hand slipped in ahead of mine. The commanding officer had been in the group of observers.

He picked up the transmitter and said: "We read you loud and clear, Three-two-three. Where are you?"

A pause. Then, apologetically, "I don't know. I'm above the overcast and I can't see the ground."

The occupants of the tower looked at one another wordlessly.

"Give us your last known position, Three-two-three," said the skipper.

"I was practicing landings at Field Twenty-one. I took off, found myself in fog and just kept climbing, I guess. I broke through in a minute or so, but then there were nothing but clouds under me. That was about ten minutes ago. I've been trying to find a hole in them ever since."

"Make a tight circle right where you are," the skipper told him, "and wait for instructions."

He fidgeted with the transmitter and looked at the rest of us pensively. No word had been spoken when the executive officer burst into the tower.

"I think I hear a plane somewhere over the field," he told us.

We threw open several windows and listened intently. Very faintly we heard the unmistakable sound of an aircraft engine.

"Three-two-three," said the skipper, his voice tinged with excitement, "put your engine in full low pitch and gun it. We think we can hear you near the field."

The silence was almost painful; then we heard the louder throb of a laboring engine, repeated.

"O.K., Three-two-three, we've located you. Continue to circle. How much gas do you have?"

Another pause, then, "I figure about fifteen or twenty minutes, sir."

The C.O.'s thumb released the microphone cut-on and he chewed his lip speculatively. More to himself than to us, he said, "That isn't time enough to send somebody out to look for him. Couldn't do much anyway. Kinda tough to teach a boy instrument flying in five minutes from another plane—if we could find him."

He clicked the transmitter on and off several times; then said into it, rather slowly and very distinctly, "Son, this is the squadron commander. I want you to listen very carefully and think about this before you give me an answer. The overcast here is about three hundred feet off the ground. We understand that it's about five to eight hundred feet thick right now. There's no chance of finding a hole in it. This stuff is all over South Texas, and it isn't going to get any better. To fly through it, you'd have to use your instruments. You haven't much room underneath, so your letdown would have to be slow and easy, and you've never had any instrument flying. I can try to tell you what to do, but letting down through this soup would be a tough job for an experienced pilot with instrument training. I recommend that you climb to two thousand feet, trim up your plane, set it on a heading of east and bail out. Now you think it over for a minute. And keep in that tight circle."

There was scarcely any hesitation. "I'll try to bring it down, sir," the cadet voice said tightly.

The skipper pulled a handkerchief from his pocket, mopped his face, loosened his tie and sat down before the transmitter.

Behind me, almost inaudibly, I heard a voice say, "That boy's my student."

The skipper looked up and asked the instructor who had spoken, "Is he a good pilot?"

The instructor half shrugged and spread his palms out and down. "Average, maybe a little above. He's a big kid, kinda quiet, tries hard —too hard, sometimes. He was studying to be an engineer," he added irrelevantly; "knows the engine inside out. He can think too. I wish he could fly as well as he can tell you what makes the thing work."

The way he said it, it sounded almost like a prayer.

The skipper had listened intently, but now he turned back to the transmitter. I remember thinking, *God, help him to say the right thing.* I knew how lonely it could feel up there with nothing but clouds below, and the vital question of how far under those clouds the ground lay gnawing at you incessantly, magnifying the lost feeling that your last bond with earthly things had been forever severed. It was the loneliest feeling in the world, yet a feeling, too, of oneness with something much bigger and more important and awe-inspiring than those things which lay somewhere under the clouds.

I felt a tremendous bond with that boy in the airplane, whose voice quavered a little now as he said, "What do I do first, sir?"

"What does your altimeter say?"

"It reads fifteen hundred feet. The clouds look like they're about five hundred feet below me."

The skipper's voice was incisive now. "Turn to a heading of three hundred and sixty degrees and climb another five hundred feet. Then fly straight and level at an air speed of one hundred knots. When you get squared away there, throttle back, holding the same air speed, until you're letting down about two hundred feet a minute. You can check your rate of descent on an instrument just above your right knee. Memorize the attitude of the plane, the instruments, everything—because that's the way you'll want it to be when you're in the soup. Practice it a few times where you can see what you're doing, and ask questions. O.K.?"

"I got it, sir. I'll try it."

The noise of the motor seemed to be growing fainter out the window.

"Make a hundred-and-eighty-degree turn," said the skipper. "How's it going?"

The voice was faltering a little more now. "I guess I know what to do. I just hope I can do it. Let me practice a few more times."

Five minutes ticked interminably by. The officers in the tower shifted from one foot to the other. The C.O. perspired. And 323 practiced and asked questions.

Finally the skipper said into the transmitter, "All right, son; we'll have to get on with it. Want to change your mind about the parachute? They never fail."

The cadet voice became incisive, "No, sir. I'm ready now."

"O.K. Climb up well above the overcast and get your instruments and your rate of letdown set. Then just keep all those things constant when you hit the soup. Remember, your stick controls your air speed. If it starts to build up, ease back on the stick. But try to keep your air speed right at a hundred knots. Don't make any violent corrections or get panicky when you don't have a reference point. Don't look around you and don't trust your senses. Just keep your eyes on the instruments and keep them steady where you want them. Ready?"

"Yes, sir."

The skipper swallowed something, made a false start, cleared his throat and started again. "Here we go. We can hear the plane clearly now. Hold your present heading and trim up your plane for the letdown. Tell me when you've started letting down, but don't try to talk to me after you hit the overcast. Just concentrate on your instruments then."

"I'm coming down," said the familiar cadet voice, now strangely calm. "My instruments all seem to be O.K. I'll be in the overcast in about thirty seconds. Stay with me, sir."

If the instruments were right and he held his rate of descent constant, he should break through in three to four minutes in a very gentle glide. The skipper kept talking, cajoling, explaining, encouraging. The silence from the other end was ominous. The skipper covered the transmitter and made a sweeping gesture with his free hand.

"Keep a lookout in every direction. If you spot him break through, holler—quick."

Then back to the transmitter. Time hung suspended in an 800-foot bank of clouds. I had the feeling that every man there, in his own way, was asking God to direct this boy. I know that's what I was doing. I was immersed in the thought that if a supreme Mind governs all of us, that Mind was present with the cadet in 323, telling him what to do right now. So powerful was this thought that only a repeated, concerted, happy shout penetrated my consciousness, "There he is! He's broken through!"

In the haze in the middle distance was a plane.

"We can see you!" the skipper shouted into the transmitter; then, abashed, he modulated his tone to a businesslike pitch. "Take a heading of two hundred seventy and come on in. You're headed into the wind and down the right runway. The field is clear. Acknowledge."

He put the transmitter down, grinning with crazy relief. But, strangely, there was no answer. The plane, clearly visible now, was approaching the end of the runway. He came in, nose cocked high, and touched down perfectly. I could see a hand wave from the cockpit as the plane reached the middle of the runway. The professional perfection of the landing and the almost casual wave of the hand suddenly chilled me and set my insides to churning. As the plane turned to taxi in, we could see for the first time the number on its side.

The skipper clutched the schedule sheet with a look of overwhelming horror. I didn't have to look at the schedule. The plane that had just landed was the missing instructor's. Outside, there was no sound.

"So help me," cried the skipper, "I've crashed him out in the middle of nowhere!"

He stood, looking down at the taxiing plane as if by sheer desire he could change the number on its side. The silence in the tower was intense.

Then the Exec said quietly, "Let's get some officers out to Field

Twenty-one. We can keep under the stuff, and maybe we can find him."

The Exec threw an arm over the skipper's shoulder and we started to file from the room, when suddenly, wonderfully, that same plaintive voice came with shattering clarity over the squadron radio.

"Say, sir," it said, "you landed me at the wrong field. I broke through all right, like you said, and I saw a runway and I got down O.K. But once I got down, I saw I had the wrong place. This looks like one of our practice fields. What should I do now?"

The skipper's eyes were at once sad and grateful. He handed the transmitter to me without a word and walked wearily out of the room. There was an audible letting out of breath behind me.

I picked up the transmitter. "Just stay where you are, Three-two-three!" I said. "For Pete's sake, just stay where you are!"

Questions for discussion

1. Observe that this story is told from the first person point of view. The person telling the story is one of the witnesses to what is happening to the boy in plane 323. Why does the author choose to have the tower-duty officer tell the story? Why not the cadet in 323? What sentence in the story gives the answer to this question?
2. As you read the story did you feel as though you were in plane 323? Or did you feel that you were in the flight tower? Who was feeling more suspense, the cadet above the storm or those down on the ground?
3. Read the first paragraph once again. Observe how much the author accomplishes in this short paragraph of only four sentences. What exactly does he tell you? Do you remember your feelings at this point during the first reading of the story?
4. In this first paragraph there is one sentence which summarizes the entire story. What is the sentence? From it you knew what the outcome would be. Did your knowing lessen the suspense for you? Why or why not?
5. Did you observe how the author used the "countdown" method to create suspense? That is, the planes were accounted for one by one until finally "that left one" and all attention centered on "that one lonely kid in 323." Where else have you seen such a method used?
6. There are several lines which might have given you a clue to what would happen. What are they?
7. How do you think the cadet in 323 felt? From what do you get

your evidence? How did the people in the tower feel? How do you know this?

8. Why did the tower-duty officer say the last sentence in the first paragraph?

9. In what way are the endings of "Miss Hinch," "The Most Dangerous Game," and this story alike? Do you think that this likeness in structure is just a coincidence, or is there a reason for it?

Vocabulary growth

HOMOGRAPHS. Two words, spelled alike, but having quite different meanings are called *homographs*. In the first paragraph of the story you read about "a *lowering* bank of clouds." This phrase does not mean that the clouds were coming lower to the ground. The word is not pronounced *lō′er·ing*. The *ow* is pronounced like the *ow* in *cow*. The word means "dark, as if about to rain or snow.''

CONTEXT. Sometimes a writer gives you a clue to the meaning of an unfamiliar word by restating it in other words. The restatement is sometimes set off by commas, sometimes by dashes. Turn to page 61 and find the clue that tells you what *norther* means in Texas.

WORDS ARE INTERESTING. The word *omen* means "a sign of something good or evil that is about to happen." Scholars do not know how this word came about. They believe that the *o-* may have come from a word meaning "to hear" and that the *-men* means just what it says. Thus *omen* may originally have meant something for men to hear—and to pay attention to. The word *ominous*, which appears in the story, comes from *omen*. But *ominous* has only the meaning of "something bad, threatening." An *omen* may be good or bad; anything described as *ominous* is all bad.

For composition

You are the student pilot whose number is Three-two-three. What happened to you? How did you feel? Why did you decide not to abandon the plane and take to your parachute? Tell the story of being lost in the fog and of landing by instruments on an unfamiliar field. How did you feel when you found that it was the wrong field?

In the cold of the Far North a man's
survival depends on his ability . . .

To Build a Fire

JACK LONDON

MAY had broken cold and gray, exceedingly cold and gray, when
the man turned aside from the main Yukon trail and climbed the
high earth bank, where a dim and little-traveled trail led eastward
through the spruce timberland. It was a steep bank, and he paused
for breath at the top, excusing the act to himself by looking at his
watch. It was nine o'clock. There was no sun nor hint of sun,
though there was not a cloud in the sky. It was a clear day, and yet
there seemed an intangible pall over the face of things, a subtle gloom
that made the day dark, and that was due to the absence of sun.
This fact did not worry the man. He was used to the lack of sun. It
had been days since he had seen the sun, and he knew that a few
more days must pass before that cheerful orb, due south, would just
peep above the skyline and dip immediately from view.

The man flung a look back along the way he had come. The
Yukon trail lay a mile wide and hidden under three feet of ice. On
top of this ice were as many feet of snow. It was all pure white,
rolling in gentle undulations where the ice jams of the freeze-up had
formed. North and south, as far as his eye could see, it was unbroken
white, save for a dark hairline that curved and twisted from around
the spruce-covered island to the south, and that curved and twisted
away into the north, where it disappeared behind another spruce-
covered island. This dark hairline was the trail—the main trail—that
led south five hundred miles to the Chilcoot Pass, Dyea, and salt
water, and that led north seventy miles to Dawson, and still on to
the north a thousand miles to Nulato, and finally to St. Michael on
Bering Sea, a thousand. miles and half a thousand more.

But all this—the mysterious, far-reaching hairline trail, the absence of sun from the sky, the tremendous cold, and the strangeness

70

and weirdness of it all—made no impression on the man. It was not because he was long used to it. He was a newcomer in the land, a cheechako,[1] and this was his first winter. The trouble with him was that he was without imagination. He was quick and alert in the things of life, but only in the things, and not in the significances. Fifty degrees below zero meant eighty-odd degrees of frost. Such fact impressed him as being cold and uncomfortable, and that was all. It did not lead him to meditate upon his frailty as a creature of temperature, and upon man's frailty in general, able only to live within certain narrow limits of heat and cold, and from there on it did not lead him to the conjectural field of immortality and man's place in the universe. Fifty degrees below zero stood for a bite of frost that hurt and that must be guarded against by the use of mittens, ear flaps, warm moccasins, and thick socks. Fifty degrees below zero was to him just precisely fifty degrees below zero. That there should be anything more to it than that was a thought that never entered his head.

As he turned to go on he spat speculatively. There was a sharp, explosive crackle that startled him. He spat again. And again, in the air, before it could fall to the snow, the spittle crackled. He knew that at fifty below spittle crackled on the snow, but this spittle had crackled in the air. Undoubtedly it was colder than fifty below—how much colder he did not know. But the temperature did not matter. He was bound for the old claim on the left fork of Henderson Creek, where the boys were already. They had come over across the divide from the Indian Creek country, while he had come the roundabout way to take a look at the possibilities of getting out logs in the spring from the islands in the Yukon. He would be in to camp by six o'clock —a bit after dark, it was true, but the boys would be there, a fire would be going, and a hot supper would be ready. As for lunch, he pressed his hand against the protruding bundle under his jacket. It was also under his shirt, wrapped up in a handkerchief and lying against the naked skin. It was the only way to keep the biscuits from freezing. He smiled agreeably to himself as he thought of those biscuits, each cut open and sopped in bacon grease, and each enclosing a generous slice of fried bacon.

He plunged in among the big spruce trees. The trail was faint. A foot of snow had fallen since the last sled had passed over, and

[1] **Cheechako:** term for a tenderfoot, used in cold regions

he was glad he was without a sled, traveling light. In fact, he carried nothing but the lunch wrapped in the handkerchief. He was surprised, however, at the cold. It certainly was cold, he concluded, as he rubbed his numb nose and cheekbones with his mittened hand. He was a warm-whiskered man, but the hair on his face did not protect the high cheek-bones and the eager nose that thrust itself aggressively into the frosty air.

At the man's heels trotted a dog, a big native husky, the proper wolf dog, gray-coated and without any visible or temperamental difference from its brother, the wild wolf. The animal was depressed by the tremendous cold. It knew that it was no time for traveling. Its instinct told it a truer tale than was told to the man by the man's judgment. In reality it was not merely colder than fifty below zero; it was colder than sixty below, than seventy below. It was seventy-five below zero. Since the freezing point is thirty-two above zero, it meant that one hundred and seven degrees of frost obtained. The dog did not know anything about thermometers. Possibly in its brain there was no sharp consciousness of a condition of very cold such as was in the man's brain. But the brute had its instinct. It experienced a vague but menacing apprehension that subdued it and made it slink along at the man's heels, and that made it question eagerly every unwonted movement of the man, as if expecting him to go into camp or to seek shelter somewhere and build a fire. The dog had learned fire, and it wanted fire, or else to burrow under the snow and cuddle its warmth away from the air.

The frozen moisture of its breathing had settled on its fur in a fine powder of frost, and especially were its jowls, muzzle, and eyelashes whitened by its crystaled breath. The man's red beard and mustache were likewise frosted, but more solidly, the deposit taking the form of ice and increasing with every warm, moist breath he exhaled. Also, the man was chewing tobacco, and the muzzle of ice held his lips so rigidly that he was unable to clear his chin when he expelled the juice. The result was that a crystal beard of the color and solidity of amber was increasing its length on his chin. If he fell down it would shatter itself, like glass, into brittle fragments. But he did not mind the appendage. It was the penalty all tobacco chewers paid in that country, and he had been out before in two cold snaps. They had not been so cold as this, he knew, but by the spirit thermometer at Sixty Mile he knew they had been registered at fifty below and at fifty-five.

He held on through the level stretch of woods for several miles, crossed a wide flat, and dropped down a bank to the frozen bed of a small stream. This was Henderson Creek, and he knew he was ten miles from the forks. He looked at his watch. It was ten o'clock. He was making four miles an hour, and he calculated that he would arrive at the forks at half-past twelve. He decided to celebrate that event by eating his lunch there.

The dog dropped in again at his heels, with a tail drooping discouragement, as the man swung along the creek bed. The furrow of the old sled trail was plainly visible, but a dozen inches of snow covered the marks of the last runners. In a month no man had come up or down that silent creek. The man held steadily on. He was not much given to thinking, and just then particularly he had nothing to think about save that he would eat lunch at the forks and that at six o'clock he would be in camp with the boys. There was nobody to talk to; and, had there been, speech would have been impossible because of the ice muzzle on his mouth. So he continued monotonously to chew tobacco and to increase the length of his amber beard.

Once in a while the thought reiterated itself that it was very cold and that he had never experienced such cold. As he walked along he rubbed his cheekbones and nose with the back of his mittened hand. He did this automatically, now and again changing hands. But rub as he would, the instant he stopped his checkbones went numb, and the following instant the end of his nose went numb. He was sure to frost his cheeks; he knew that, and experienced a pang of regret that he had not devised a nose strap of the sort Bud wore in cold snaps. Such a strap passed across the cheeks, as well, and saved them. But it didn't matter much, after all. What were frosted cheeks? A bit painful, that was all; they were never serious.

Empty as the man's mind was of thought, he was keenly observant, and he noticed the changes in the creek, the curves and bends and timber jams, and always he sharply noted where he placed his feet. Once, coming around a bend, he shied abruptly, like a startled horse, curved away from the place where he had been walking, and retreated several paces back along the trail. The creek, he knew, was frozen clear to the bottom—no creek could contain water in that arctic winter—but he knew also that there were springs that bubbled out from the hillsides and ran along under the snow and on top of the ice of the creek. He knew that the coldest snaps never froze these springs, and he knew likewise their danger. They were traps. They hid pools of water under the snow that might be three inches deep, or three feet. Sometimes a skin of ice half an inch thick covered them, and in turn was covered by the snow. Sometimes there were alternate layers of water and ice skin, so that when one broke through he kept on breaking through for a while, sometimes wetting himself to the waist.

That was why he had shied in such panic. He had felt the give under his feet and heard the crackle of a snow-hidden ice skin. And to get his feet wet in such a temperature meant trouble and danger. At the very least it meant delay, for he would be forced to stop and build a fire, and under its protection to bare his feet while he dried his socks and moccasins. He stood and studied the creek bed and its banks, and decided that the flow of water came from the right. He reflected a while, rubbing his nose and cheeks, then skirted to the left, stepping gingerly and testing the footing for each step. Once clear of the danger, he took a fresh chew of tobacco and swung along at his four-mile gait.

In the course of the next two hours he came upon several similar traps. Usually the snow above the hidden pools had a sunken, candied appearance that advertised the danger. Once again, however, he had a close call; and once, suspecting danger, he compelled the dog to go on in front. The dog did not want to go. It hung back until the man shoved forward, and then it went quickly across the white, unbroken surface. Suddenly it broke through, floundered to one side, and got away to firmer footing. It had wet its forefeet and legs, and almost immediately the water that clung to it turned to ice. It made quick efforts to lick the ice off its legs, then dropped down in the snow and began to bite out the ice that had formed between the toes. This was a matter of instinct. To permit the ice to remain would mean sore feet. It did not know this. It merely obeyed the mysterious prompting that arose from the deep crypts of its being. But the man knew, having achieved a judgment on the subject, and he removed the mitten from his right hand and helped tear out the ice-particles. He did not expose his fingers more than a minute, and was astonished at the swift numbness that smote them. It certainly was cold. He pulled on the mitten hastily, and beat the hand savagely across his chest.

At twelve o'clock the day was at its brightest. Yet the sun was too far south on its winter journey to clear the horizon. The bulge of the earth intervened between it and Henderson Creek, where the man walked under a clear sky at noon and cast no shadow. At half-past twelve, to the minute, he arrived at the forks of the creek. He was pleased at the speed he had made. If he kept it up, he would certainly be with the boys by six. He unbuttoned his jacket and shirt and drew forth his lunch. The action consumed no more than a quarter of a minute, yet in that brief moment the numbness laid hold of the exposed fingers. He did not put the mitten on, but, instead, struck the fingers a dozen sharp smashes against his leg. Then he sat down on a snow-covered log to eat. The sting that followed upon the striking of his fingers against his leg ceased so quickly that he was startled. He had had no chance to take a bite of biscuit. He struck the fingers repeatedly and returned them to the mitten, baring the other hand for the purpose of eating. He tried to take a mouthful, but the ice muzzle prevented. He had forgotten to build a fire and thaw out. He chuckled at his foolishness, and as he chuckled he noted the numbness creeping into the exposed fingers. Also he noted that the stinging which had first come to his toes when he sat down was already passing away. He wondered whether the toes were warm or numb. He moved them inside the moccasins and decided that they were numb.

He pulled the mitten on hurriedly and stood up. He was a bit frightened. He stamped up and down until the stinging returned into the feet. It certainly was cold, was his thought. That man from Sulphur Creek had spoken the truth when telling how cold it sometimes got in the country. And he had laughed at him at the time! That showed one must not be too sure of things. There was no mistake about it, it *was* cold. He strode up and down, stamping his feet and threshing his arms, until reassured by the returning warmth. Then he got out matches and proceeded to make a fire. From the undergrowth, where high water of the previous spring had lodged a supply of seasoned twigs, he got his firewood. Working carefully from a small beginning, he soon had a roaring fire, over which he thawed the ice from his face and in the protection of which he ate his biscuits. For the moment the cold of space was outwitted. The dog took satisfaction in the fire, stretching out close enough for warmth and far enough away to escape being singed.

When the man had finished, he filled his pipe and took his comfortable time over a smoke. Then he pulled on his mittens, settled the ear flaps of his cap firmly about his ears, and took the creek trail up the left fork. The dog was disappointed and yearned back toward the fire. This man did not know cold. Possibly all the generations of his ancestry had been ignorant of cold, of real cold, of cold one hundred and seven degrees below the freezing point. But the dog knew; all its ancestry knew, and it had inherited the knowledge. And it knew that it was not good to walk abroad in such fearful cold. It was the time to lie snug in a hole in the snow and wait for a curtain of cloud to be drawn across the face of outer space whence this cold came. On the other hand, there was no keen intimacy between the dog and the man. The one was the toil-slave of the other, and the only caresses it had ever received were the caresses of the whiplash and of harsh and menacing throat sounds that threatened the whiplash. So the dog made no effort to communicate its apprehension to the man. It was not concerned in the welfare of the man; it was for its own sake that it yearned back toward the fire. But the man whistled, and spoke to it with the sound of whiplashes, and the dog swung in at the man's heels and followed after.

The man took a chew of tobacco and proceeded to start a new amber beard. Also, his moist breath quickly powdered with white his mustache, eyebrows, and lashes. There did not seem to be so many springs on the left fork of the Henderson, and for half an hour the man saw no signs of any. And then it happened. At a place where there were no signs, where the soft, unbroken snow seemed to advertise solidity beneath, the man broke through. It was not deep. He wet himself halfway to the knees before he floundered out to the firm crust.

He was angry, and cursed his luck aloud. He had hoped to get into camp with the boys at six o'clock, and this would delay him an hour, for he would have to build a fire and dry out his footgear. This was imperative at that low temperature—he knew that much; and he turned aside to the bank, which he climbed. On top, tangled in the underbrush about the trunks of several small spruce trees, was a high-water deposit of dry firewood—sticks and twigs, principally, but also larger portions of seasoned branches and fine, dry, last year's grasses. He threw down several large pieces on top of the snow. This served for a foundation and prevented the young flame from drowning itself in the snow it otherwise would melt. The flame he got by touching a match to a small shred of birch bark that he took from his pocket. This burned even more readily than paper. Placing it on the foundation, he fed the young flame with wisps of dry grass and with the tiniest dry twigs.

He worked slowly and carefully, keenly aware of his danger. Gradually, as the flame grew stronger, he increased the size of the twigs with which he fed it. He squatted in the snow, pulling the twigs out from their entanglement in the brush and feeding directly to the flame. He knew there must be no failure. When it is seventy-five below zero a man must not fail in his first attempt to build a fire —that is, if his feet are wet. If his feet are dry, and he fails, he can run along the trail for half a mile and restore his circulation. But the circulation of wet and freezing feet cannot be restored by running when it is seventy-five below. No matter how fast he runs, the wet feet will freeze the harder.

All this the man knew. The old-timer on Sulphur Creek had told him about it the previous fall, and now he was appreciating the advice. Already all sensation had gone out of his feet. To build the fire, he had been forced to remove his mittens, and the fingers had quickly gone numb. His pace of four miles an hour had kept his heart pumping blood to the surface of his body and to all the extremities. But the instant he stopped, the action of the pump eased down. The cold of space smote the unprotected tip of the planet, and he, being on that unprotected tip, received the full force of the blow. The blood of his body recoiled before it. The blood was alive, like the dog, and like the dog it wanted to hide away and cover itself up from the fearful cold. So long as he walked four miles an hour, he pumped that blood, willy-nilly, to the surface; but now it ebbed away and sank down into the recesses of his body. The extremities were the first to feel its absence. His wet feet froze the faster, and his exposed fingers numbed the faster, though they had not yet begun to freeze. Nose and cheeks were already freezing, while the skin of all his body chilled as it lost its blood.

But he was safe. Toes and nose and cheeks would be only touched by the frost, for the fire was beginning to burn with strength. He was feeding it with twigs the size of his finger. In another minute he would be able to feed it with branches the size of his wrist, and then he could remove his wet footgear, and, while it dried, he could keep his naked feet warm by the fire, rubbing them at first, of course, with snow. The fire was a success. He was safe. He remembered the advice of the old-timer on Sulphur Creek, and smiled. The old-timer had been very serious in laying down the law that no man must travel alone in the Klondike after fifty below. Well, here he was; he had had the accident; he was alone; and he had saved himself. Those old-timers were rather womanish, some of them, he thought. All a man had to do was to keep his head, and he was all right. Any man who was a man could travel alone. But it was surprising, the rapidity with which his cheeks and nose were freezing. And he had not thought his fingers could go lifeless in so short a time. Lifeless they were, for he could scarcely make them move together to grip a twig, and they seemed remote from his body and from him. When he touched a twig, he had to look and see whether or not he had hold of it. The wires were pretty well down between him and his finger-ends.

All of which counted for little. There was the fire, snapping and crackling and promising life with every dancing flame. He started to untie his moccasins. They were coated with ice; the thick German socks were like sheaths of iron halfway to the knees; and the moccasin strings were like rods of steel all twisted and knotted as by some conflagration. For a moment he tugged with his numb fingers, then, realizing the folly of it, he drew his sheath knife.

But before he could cut the strings it happened. It was his own fault, or, rather, his mistake. He should not have built the fire under the spruce tree. He should have built it in the open. But it had been easier to pull the twigs from the bush and drop them directly on the fire. Now the tree under which he had done this carried a weight of snow on its boughs. No wind had blown for weeks, and each bough was fully freighted. Each time he had pulled a twig he had communicated a slight agitation to the tree—an imperceptible agitation, so far as he was concerned, but an agitation sufficient to bring about the disaster. High up in the tree one bough capsized its load of snow. This fell on the boughs beneath, capsizing them. This process continued, spreading out and involving the whole tree. It grew like an avalanche, and it descended without warning upon the man and the fire, and the fire was blotted out! Where it had burned was a mantle of fresh and disordered snow.

The man was shocked. It was as though he had just heard his own sentence of death. For a moment he sat and stared at the spot where the fire had been. Then he grew very calm. Perhaps the old-timer on Sulphur Creek was right. If he had only had a trailmate he would have been in no danger now. The trailmate could have built the fire. Well, it was up to him to build the fire over again, and this second time there must be no failure. Even if he succeeded, he would most likely lose some toes. His feet must be badly frozen by now, and there would be some time before the second fire was ready.

Such were his thoughts, but he did not sit and think them. He was busy all the time they were passing through his mind. He made a new foundation for a fire, this time in the open, where no treacherous tree could blot it out. Next he gathered dry grasses and tiny twigs from the high-water flotsam. He could not bring his fingers together to pull them out, but he was able to gather them by the handful. In this way he got many rotten twigs and bits of green moss that were undesirable, but it was the best he could do. He worked methodically, even collecting an armful of the larger branches to be used later when the fire gathered strength. And all the while the dog sat and watched him, a certain yearning wistfulness in its eyes, for it looked upon him as the fire provider, and the fire was slow in coming.

When all was ready, the man reached in his pocket for a second piece of birch bark. He knew the bark was there, and, though he could not feel it with his fingers, he could hear its crisp rustling as he fumbled for it. Try as he would, he could not clutch hold of it. And all the time, in his consciousness, was the knowledge that each instant his feet were freezing. This thought tended to put him in a panic, but he fought against it and kept calm. He pulled on his mittens with his teeth, and threshed his arms back and forth, beating his hands with all his might against his sides. He did this sitting down, and he stood up to do it; and all the while the dog sat in the snow, its wolf brush of a tail curled around warmly over its forefeet, its sharp wolf ears pricked forward intently as it watched the man. And the man, as he beat and threshed with his arms and hands, felt a great surge of envy as he regarded the creature that was warm and secure in its natural covering.

After a time he was aware of the first far-away signals of sensation in his beaten fingers. The faint tingling grew stronger till it evolved into a stinging ache that was excruciating, but which the man hailed with satisfaction. He stripped the mitten from his right hand and fetched forth the birch bark. The exposed fingers were quickly going numb again. Next he brought out his bunch of sulphur matches. But the tremendous cold had already driven the life out of his fingers. In his effort to separate one match from the others, the whole bunch fell in the snow. He tried to pick it out of the snow, but failed. The dead fingers could neither touch nor clutch. He was very careful. He drove the thought of his freezing feet, and nose, and cheeks, out of his mind, devoting his whole soul to the matches. He watched, using the sense of vision in place of that of touch, and when he saw his fingers on each side of the bunch, he closed them—that is, he willed to close them, but the wires were down, and the fingers did not obey. He pulled the mitten on the right hand, and beat it fiercely against his knee. Then, with both mittened hands, he scooped the bunch of matches, along with much snow, into his lap. Yet he was no better off.

After some manipulation he managed to get the bunch between the heels of his mittened hands. In this fashion he carried it to his mouth. The ice crackled and snapped when by a violent effort he opened his mouth. He drew the lower jaw in, curled the upper lip out of the way, and scraped the bunch with his upper teeth in order to separate a match. He succeeded in getting one, which he dropped on his lap. He was no better off. He could not pick it up. Then he devised a way. He picked it up in his teeth and scratched it on his leg. Twenty times he scratched before he succeeded in lighting it. As it flamed he held it with his teeth to the birch bark. But the burning brimstone went up his nostrils and into his lungs, causing him to cough spasmodically. The match fell into the snow and went out.

The old-timer on Sulphur Creek was right, he thought in the moment of controlled despair that ensued: after fifty below, a man should travel with a partner. He beat his hands, but failed in exciting any sensation. Suddenly he bared both hands, removing the mittens with his teeth. He caught the whole bunch between the heels of his hands. His arm muscles, not being frozen, enabled him to press the hand heels tightly against the matches. Then he scratched the bunch along his leg. It flared into flame, seventy sulphur matches at once! There was no wind to blow them out. He kept his head to one side to escape the strangling fumes, and held the blazing bunch to the birch bark. As he so held it, he became aware of sensation in his hand.

His flesh was burning. He could smell it. Deep down below the surface he could feel it. The sensation developed into pain that grew acute. And still he endured it, holding the flame of the matches clumsily to the bark that would not light readily because his own burning hands were in the way, absorbing most of the flame.

At last, when he could endure no more he jerked his hands apart. The blazing matches fell sizzling into the snow, but the birch bark was alight. He began laying dry grasses and the tiniest twigs on the flame. He could not pick and choose, for he had to lift the fuel between the heels of his hands. Small pieces of rotten wood and green moss clung to the twigs, and he bit them off as well as he could with his teeth. He cherished the flame carefully and awkwardly. It meant life, and it must not perish. The withdrawal of blood from the surface of his body now made him begin to shiver, and he grew more awkward. A large piece of green moss fell squarely on the little fire. He tried to poke it out with his fingers, but his shivering frame made him poke too far, and he disrupted the nucleus of the little fire, the burning grasses and tiny twigs separating and scattering. He tried to poke them together again, but, in spite of the tenseness of the effort, his shivering got away with him, and the twigs were hopelessly scattered. Each twig gushed a puff of smoke and went out. The fire provider had failed. As he looked apathetically about him, his eyes chanced on the dog, sitting across the ruins of the fire from him, in the snow, making restless, hunching movements, slightly lifting one forefoot and then the other, shifting its weight back and forth on them with wistful eagerness.

The sight of the dog put a wild idea into his head. He remembered the tale of the man, caught in a blizzard, who killed a steer and crawled inside the carcass, and so was saved. He would kill the dog and bury his hands in the warm body until the numbness went out of them. Then he could build another fire. He spoke to the dog, calling it to him; but in his voice was a strange note of fear that frightened the animal, who had never known the man to speak in such a way before. Something was the matter, and its suspicious nature sensed danger—it knew not what danger, but somewhere, somehow, in its brain arose an apprehension of the man. It flattened its ears down at the sound of the man's voice, and its restless, hunching movements and the liftings and shiftings of its forefeet became more pronounced; but it would not come to the man. He got on his hands and knees and crawled toward the dog. This unusual posture again excited suspicion, and the animal sidled mincingly away.

The man sat up in the snow for a moment and struggled for calmness. Then he pulled on his mittens, by means of his teeth, and got upon his feet. He glanced down at first in order to assure himself that he was really standing up, for the absence of sensation in his feet left him unrelated to the earth. His erect position in itself started to drive the webs of suspicion from the dog's mind; and when he spoke peremptorily with the sound of whiplashes in his voice, the dog rendered its customary allegiance and came to him. As it came within reaching distance, the man lost his control. His arms flashed out to the dog, and he experienced genuine surprise when he discovered that his hands could not clutch, that there was neither bend nor feeling in the fingers. He had forgotten for the moment that they were frozen and that they were freezing more and more. All this happened quickly, and before the animal could get away, he encircled its body with his arms. He sat down in the snow, and in this fashion held the dog, while it snarled and whined and struggled.

But it was all he could do, hold its body encircled in his arms and sit there. He realized that he could not kill the dog. There was no way to do it. With his helpless hands he could neither draw nor hold his sheath knife nor throttle the animal. He released it, and it plunged wildly away, with tail between its legs, and still snarling. It halted forty feet away and surveyed him curiously, with ears sharply pricked forward. The man looked down at his hands in order to locate them, and found them hanging on the ends of his arms. It struck him as curious that one should have to use his eyes in order to find out where his hands were. He began threshing his arms back and forth, beating the mittened hands against his sides. He did this for five minutes, violently, and his heart pumped enough blood up to the surface to put a stop to his shivering. But no sensation was aroused in the hands. He had an impression that they hung like weights on the ends of his arms, but when he tried to run the impression down, he could not find it.

A certain fear of death, dull and oppressive, came to him. This fear quickly became poignant as he realized that it was no longer a mere matter of freezing his fingers and toes, or of losing his hands and feet, but that it was a matter of life and death with the chances against him. This threw him into a panic, and he turned and ran up the creek-bed along the old, dim trail. The dog joined in behind and kept up with him. He ran blindly, without intention, in fear such as he had never known in his life. Slowly, as he ploughed and floundered through the snow, he began to see things again,—the banks of the creek, the old timber-jams, the leafless aspens, and the sky. The running made him feel better. He did not shiver. Maybe, if he ran on, his feet would thaw out; and, anyway, if he ran far enough, he would reach camp and the boys. Without doubt he would lose some fingers and toes and some of his face; but the boys would take care of him, and save the rest of him when he got there. And at the same time there was another thought in his mind that said he would never get to the camp and the boys; that it was too many miles away, that the freezing had too great a start on him, and that he would soon be stiff and dead. This thought he kept in the background and refused to consider. Sometimes it pushed itself forward and demanded to be heard, but he thrust it back and strove to think of other things.

It struck him as curious that he could run at all on feet so frozen that he could not feel them when they struck the earth and took the weight of his body. He seemed to himself to skim along above the surface, and to have no connection with the earth. Somewhere he had once seen a winged Mercury, and he wondered if Mercury felt as he felt when skimming over the earth.

His theory of running until he reached camp and the boys had one flaw in it: he lacked the endurance. Several times he stumbled, and finally he tottered, crumpled up, and fell. When he tried to rise, he failed. He must sit and rest, he decided, and next time he would merely walk and keep on going. As he sat and regained his breath, he noted that he was feeling quite warm and comfortable. He was not shivering, and it even seemed that a warm glow had come to his chest and trunk. And yet, when he touched his nose or cheeks, there was no sensation. Running would not thaw them out. Nor would it thaw out his hands and feet. Then the thought came to him that the frozen portions of his body must be extending. He tried to keep this thought down, to forget it, to think of something else; he was aware of the panicky feeling that it caused, and he was afraid of the panic. But the thought asserted itself, and persisted, until it produced a vision of his body totally frozen. This was too much, and he made another wild run along the trail. Once he slowed down to a walk, but the thought of the freezing extending itself made him run again.

And all the time the dog ran with him, at his heels. When he fell down a second time, it curled its tail over its forefeet and sat in front of him, facing him, curiously eager and intent. The warmth and security of the animal angered him, and he cursed it till it flattened down its ears appeasingly. This time the shivering came more quickly upon the man. He was losing in his battle with the frost. It was creeping into his body from all sides. The thought of it drove him on, but he ran no more than a hundred feet, when he staggered and pitched headlong. It was his last panic. When he recovered his breath and control, he sat up and entertained in his mind the conception of meeting death with dignity. However, the conception did not come to him in such terms. His idea of it was that he had been making a fool of himself, running around like a chicken with its head cut off—such was the simile that occurred to him. Well, he was bound to freeze, anyway, and he might as well take it decently. With this new-found peace of mind came the first glimmerings of drowsiness. A good idea, he thought, to sleep off to death. It was like taking an anesthetic. Freezing was not so bad as people thought. There were lots worse ways to die.

He pictured the boys finding his body next day. Suddenly he found himself with them, coming along the trail and looking for himself. And, still with them, he came around a turn in the trail and found himself lying in the snow. He did not belong with himself any more, for even then he was out of himself, standing with the boys and looking at himself in the snow. It certainly was cold, was his thought. When he got back to the States, he could tell the folks what real cold was. He drifted on from this to a vision of the old-timer on Sulphur Creek. He could see him quite clearly, warm and comfortable, and smoking a pipe.

"You were right, old hoss; you were right," the man mumbled to the old-timer of Sulphur Creek.

Then the man drowsed off into what seemed to him the most comfortable and satisfying sleep he had ever known. The dog sat facing him and waiting. The brief day drew to a close in a long, slow twilight. There were no signs of a fire to be made, and, besides, never in the dog's experience had it known a man to sit like that in the snow and make no fire. As the twilight drew on, its eager yearning for the fire mastered it, and with a great lifting and shifting of forefeet, it whined softly, then flattened its ears down in anticipation of being chidden by the man. But the man remained silent. Later the dog whined loudly. And still later it crept close to the man and caught the scent of death. This made the animal bristle and back away. A little longer it delayed, howling under the stars that leaped and danced and shone brightly in the cold sky. Then it turned and trotted up the trail in the direction of the camp it knew, where were the other food-providers and fire-providers.

Questions for discussion

1. In this story, the conflict is not between man and man, as it is in "Miss Hinch" and "The Most Dangerous Game," but between man and the elements. In "I'm Coming In," the aspect of the elements with which the Navy cadet was contending was a storm; in "To Build a Fire" it was the tremendous cold. Isn't it true that one of these, the storm or the cold, was so presented that it could actually be considered as a character in the story rather than as a part of the setting? Which one was it?

2. Did you observe that in this story the man is never named? The author simply presents him as "the man." Have you any idea why he does this?

3. What was your reaction to the man? Did you visualize him? Did you think of him as having a personality? Did you sympathize with him? Can you explain the reason for your reaction to him?

4. Notice the difference in the point of view from which these two stories were written. In "I'm Coming In," the story is told by someone who is on the scene. In "To Build a Fire," it is told by someone off the scene, standing to one side, observing, and reporting what he sees. These two different approaches are likely to have different effects on you, the reader. For instance, did you identify yourself with any character in either of the stories? During which story did you feel more suspense? Why? About which of the two characters did you feel more concern, the Navy cadet or the man who tried to build a fire?

5. What sensations did you feel as you read this story? That is, what did you see? What did you feel? What did you hear?

6. Would this have been a better story if it had ended differently?

7. At what point did you begin to suspect that something was going to happen to him? At what point did you begin to wonder whether he would make it or not?

8. Because of the title you know from the very beginning that the man

is going to have to build a fire. The suspense is created by what you don't know. What did you wonder about while you were reading the first few paragraphs?

9. The author of this story was making some significant comment about man and his relation with the elements. What was it? What might one say about this matter if one combined the observation suggested in this story with that made in "I'm Coming In"?

Vocabulary growth

WORD ORIGIN. W*eird* is a strange sort of word. To the average person it even seems to be oddly spelled. It is from an old Scotch word meaning "fate." It is also related to an Anglo-Saxon word meaning "what is to come." It is used today to refer to ghosts, evil spirits or mysterious supernatural things. If you think about it, you can see the connection between the modern usage and the old meaning of the word.

CONTEXT. 1. In the first paragraph we read, "It was a clear day, and yet there seemed an *intangible pall* over the face of things." From the context of the paragraph, work out a meaning for *intangible pall*.

2. In the third paragraph we read, "He was quick and alert in the things of life, but only in the things, and not in their *significances*." From the context of the whole paragraph work out a meaning for *significances* that fits the quoted sentence.

For composition

1. Was the man in this story the victim of bad luck? Or was his luck the result of the mistakes he made? What were those mistakes? Descide why the man came to his fate. Write your opinion and support it by facts from the story.

2. What do you think about the dog? Was he wise to leave when he did? Should he have stayed with the man? Was he being disloyal in leaving? Write your opinion of the dog's behavior and support it by facts from the story.

The Red-Headed League

SIR ARTHUR CONAN DOYLE

I had called upon my friend, Mr. Sherlock Holmes, one day in the autumn of last year, and found him in deep conversation with a very stout, florid-faced, elderly gentleman, with fiery red hair. With an apology for my intrusion, I was about to withdraw, when Holmes pulled me abruptly into the room, and closed the door behind me.

"You could not possibly have come at a better time, my dear Watson," he said cordially.

"I was afraid that you were engaged."

"So I am. Very much so."

"Then I can wait in the next room."

"Not at all. This gentleman, Mr. Wilson, has been my partner and helper in many of my most successful cases, and I have no doubt that he will be of the utmost use to me in yours also."

The stout gentleman half rose from his chair, and gave a bob of greeting, with a quick little questioning glance from his small, fat-encircled eyes.

"Try the settee," said Holmes, relapsing into his arm-chair, and putting his finger-tips together, as was his custom when in judicial moods. "I know, my dear Watson, that you share my love of all that is bizarre and outside the conventions and humdrum routine of everyday life. You have shown your relish for it by the enthusiasm which has prompted you to chronicle, and, if you will excuse my saying so, somewhat to embellish so many of my own little adventures."

"Your cases have indeed been of the greatest interest to me," I observed.

"You will remember that I remarked the other day, just before we went into the very simple problem presented by Miss Mary

Sutherland, that for strange effects and extraordinary combinations we must go to life itself, which is always far more daring than any effort of the imagination."

"A proposition which I took the liberty of doubting."

"You did, Doctor, but none the less you must come round to my view, for otherwise I shall keep piling fact upon fact on you, until your reason breaks down under them and acknowledges me to be right. Now, Mr. Jabez Wilson here has been good enough to call upon me this morning, and to begin a narrative which promises to be one of the most singular which I have listened to for some time. You have heard me remark that the strangest and most unique things are very often connected not with the larger but with the smaller crimes, and occasionally, indeed, where there is room for doubt whether any positive crime has been committed. As far as I have heard, it is impossible for me to say whether the present case is an instance of crime or not, but the course of events is certainly among the most singular that I have ever listened to. Perhaps, Mr. Wilson, you would have the great kindness to recommence your narrative. I ask you not merely because my friend Dr. Watson has not heard the opening part, but also because the peculiar nature of the story makes me anxious to have every possible detail from your lips. As a rule, when I have heard some slight indication of the course of events I am able to guide myself by the thousands of other similar cases which occur to my memory. In the present instance I am forced to admit that the facts are, to the best of my belief, unique."

The portly client puffed out his chest with an appearance of some little pride, and pulled a dirty and wrinkled newspaper from the inside pocket of his greatcoat. As he glanced down the advertisement column, with his head thrust forward, and the paper flattened out upon his knee, I took a good look at the man, and endeavoured after the fashion of my companion to read the indications which might be presented by his dress or appearance.

I did not gain very much, however, by my inspection. Our visitor bore every mark of being an average commonplace British tradesman, obese, pompous, and slow. He wore rather baggy grey shepherds' check trousers, a not over-clean black frock-coat, unbuttoned in the front, and a drab waistcoat with a heavy brassy Albert chain, and a square pierced bit of metal dangling down as an ornament. A frayed top-hat, and a faded brown overcoat with a wrinkled velvet collar lay upon a chair beside him. Altogether, look as I would, there was nothing remarkable about the man save his blazing red head, and the expression of extreme chagrin and discontent upon his features.

Sherlock Holmes's quick eye took in my occupation and he shook his head with a smile as he noticed my questioning glances. "Beyond the obvious facts that he has at some time done manual labour, that he takes snuff, that he is a Freemason, that he has been in China, and that he has done a considerable amount of writing lately, I can deduce nothing else."

Mr. Jabez Wilson started up in his chair, with his forefinger upon the paper, but his eyes upon my companion.

"How, in the name of good fortune, did you know all that, Mr. Holmes?" he asked. "How did you know, for example, that I did manual labor? It's as true as gospel, and I began as a ship's carpenter."

"Your hands, my dear sir. Your right hand is quite a size larger than your left. You have worked with it, and the muscles are more developed."

"Well, the snuff, then, and the Freemasonry?"

"I won't insult your intelligence by telling you how I read that, especially as, rather against the strict rules of your order, you use an arc-and-compass breastpin."

"Oh, of course, I forgot that. But the writing?"

"What else can be indicated by that right cuff so very shiny for five inches, and the left one with the smooth patch near the elbow where you rest it upon the desk?"

"Well, but China?"

"The fish which you have tattooed immediately above your right wrist could only have been done in China. I have made a small study of tattoo marks, and have even contributed to the literature of the subject. That trick of staining the fishes' scales of a delicate pink is quite peculiar to China. When, in addition, I see a Chinese coin hanging from your watch-chain, the matter becomes even more simple."

Mr. Jabez Wilson laughed heavily. "Well, I never!" said he. "I thought at first you had done something clever, but I see that there was nothing in it after all."

"I begin to think, Watson," said Holmes, "that I make a mistake in explaining. 'Omne ignotum pro magnifico,' [1] you know, and

---

[1] *Omne ignotum pro magnifico:* Every unknown thing is taken for something magnificent. (Latin)

my poor little reputation, such as it is, will suffer shipwreck if I am so candid. Can you not find the advertisement, Mr. Wilson?"

"Yes, I have got it now," he answered, with his thick, red finger planted half-way down the column. "Here it is. This is what began it all. You just read it for yourself, sir."

I took the paper from him and read as follows:—

"To THE RED-HEADED LEAGUE.—On account of the bequest of the late Ezekiah Hopkins, of Lebanon, Penn., U.S.A., there is now another vacancy open which entitles a member of the League to a salary of four pounds a week for purely nominal services. All red-headed men who are sound in body and mind, and above the age of twenty-one years, are eligible. Apply in person on Monday, at eleven o'clock, to Duncan Ross, at the offices of the League, 7, Pope's Court, Fleet Street."

"What on earth does this mean?" I ejaculated, after I had twice read over the extraordinary announcement.

Holmes chuckled, and wriggled in his chair, as was his habit when in high spirits. "It is a little off the beaten track, isn't it?" said he. "And now, Mr. Wilson, off you go at scratch, and tell us all about yourself, your household, and the effect which this advertisement had upon your fortunes. You will first make a note, Doctor, of the paper and the date."

"It is *The Morning Chronicle*, of April 27, 1890. Just two months ago."

"Very good. Now, Mr. Wilson?"

"Well, it is just as I have been telling you, Mr. Sherlock Holmes," said Jabez Wilson, mopping his forehead, "I have a small pawnbroker's business at Coburg Square, near the City. It's not a very large affair, and of late years it has not done more than just give me a living. I used to be able to keep two assistants, but now I only keep one; and I would have a job to pay him, but that he is willing to come for half wages, so as to learn the business."

"What is the name of this obliging youth?" asked Sherlock Holmes.

"His name is Vincent Spaulding, and he's not such a youth either. It's hard to say his age. I should not wish a smarter assistant, Mr. Holmes; and I know very well that he could better himself, and earn twice what I am able to give him. But after all, if he is satisfied, why should I put ideas in his head?"

"Why, indeed? You seem most fortunate in having an employee who comes under the full market price. It is not a common experience among employers in this age. I don't know that your assistant is not as remarkable as your advertisement."

"Oh, he has his faults, too," said Mr. Wilson. "Never was such a fellow for photography. Snapping away with a camera when he ought to be improving his mind, and then diving down into the cellar like a rabbit into its hole to develop his pictures. That is his main fault; but on the whole, he's a good worker. There's no vice in him."

"He is still with you, I presume?"

"Yes, sir. He and a girl of fourteen, who does a bit of simple cooking, and keeps the place clean—that's all I have in the house, for I am a widower, and never had any family. We live very quietly, sir, the three of us; and we keep a roof over our heads, and pay our debts, if we do nothing more.

"The first thing that put us out was that advertisement. Spaulding, he came down into the office just this day eight weeks with this very paper in his hand, and he says:

" 'I wish to the Lord, Mr. Wilson, that I was a red-headed man.'

" 'Why that?' I asks.

" 'Why,' says he, 'here's another vacancy on the League of the Red-Headed Men. It's worth quite a fortune to any man who gets it, and I understand that there are more vacancies than there are men, so that the trustees are at their wits' end what to do with the money. If my hair would only change colour, here's a nice little crib all ready for me to step into.'

" 'Why, what is it, then?' I asked. You see, Mr. Holmes, I am a very stay-at-home man, and, as my business came to me instead of my having to go to it, I was often weeks on end without putting my foot over the doormat. In that way I didn't know much of what was going on outside, and I was always glad of a bit of news.

" 'Have you never heard of the League of the Red-Headed Men?' he asked, with his eyes open.

" 'Never.'

" 'Why, I wonder at that, for you are eligible yourself for one of the vacancies.'

" 'And what are they worth?' I asked.

" 'Oh, merely a couple of hundred a year, but the work is slight, and it need not interfere much with one's other occupations.'

"Well, you can easily think that that made me prick up my ears, for the business has not been over good for some years, and an extra couple of hundred would have been very handy.

" 'Tell me all about it,' said I.

" 'Well,' said he, showing me the advertisement, 'you can see for yourself that the League has a vacancy, and there is the address where you should apply for particulars. As far as I can make out, the League was founded by an American millionaire, Ezekiah Hopkins, who was very peculiar in his ways. He was himself red-headed, and he had a great sympathy for all red-headed men; so, when he died, it was found that he had left his enormous fortune in the hands of trustees, with instructions to apply the interest to the providing of easy berths to men whose hair is of that colour. From all I hear it is splendid pay, and very little to do.'

" 'But,' said I, 'there would be millions of red-headed men who would apply.'

" 'Not so many as you might think,' he answered. 'You see, it is really confined to Londoners, and to grown men. This American had started from London when he was young, and he wanted to do the old town a good turn. Then, again, I have heard it is no use your applying if your hair is light red, or dark red, or anything but real, bright, blazing, fiery red. Now, if you cared to apply, Mr. Wilson, you would just walk in; but perhaps it would hardly be worth your while to put yourself out of the way for the sake of a few hundred pounds.'

"Now, it is a fact, gentlemen, as you may see for yourselves, that my hair is of a very full and rich tint, so that it seemed to me that, if there was to be any competition in the matter, I stood as good a chance as any man that I had ever met. Vincent Spaulding seemed to know so much about it that I thought he might prove useful, so I just ordered him to put up the shutters for the day, and to come right away with me. He was very willing to have a holiday, so we shut the business up, and started off for the address that was given us in the advertisement.

"I never hope to see such a sight as that again, Mr. Holmes. From north, south, east, and west every man who had a shade of red in his hair had tramped into the City to answer the advertisement. Fleet Street was choked with red-headed folk, and Pope's Court looked like a coster's orange barrow. I should not have thought there were so many in the whole country as were brought together by that single advertisement. Every shade of colour they were—straw, lemon, orange, brick, Irish-setter, liver, clay; but, as Spaulding said, there were not many who had the real vivid flame-coloured tint. When I saw how many were waiting, I would have given it up in despair; but Spaulding would not hear of it. How he did it I could not imagine, but he pushed and pulled and butted until he got me through the crowd, and right up to the steps which led to the office. There was a double stream upon the stair, some going up in hope, and some coming back dejected; but we wedged in as well as we could, and soon found ourselves in the office."

"Your experience has been a most entertaining one," remarked Holmes, as his client paused and refreshed his memory with a huge pinch of snuff. "Pray continue your very interesting statement."

"There was nothing in the office but a couple of wooden chairs and a deal table, behind which sat a small man, with a head that was even redder than mine. He said a few words to each candidate as he came up, and then he always managed to find some fault in them which would disqualify them. Getting a vacancy did not seem to be such a very easy matter after all. However, when our turn came, the little man was more favourable to me than to any of the others, and he closed the door as we entered, so that he might have a private word with us.

" 'This is Mr. Jabez Wilson,' said my assistant, 'and he is willing to fill a vacancy in the League.'

" 'And he is admirably suited for it,' the other answered. 'He has every requirement. I cannot recall when I have seen anything so fine,' He took a step backwards, cocked his head on one side, and gazed at my hair until I felt quite bashful. Then suddenly he plunged forwards, wrung my hand, and congratulated me warmly on my success.

" 'It would be injustice to hesitate,' said he. 'You will, however, I am sure, excuse me for taking an obvious precaution.' With that he seized my hair in both his hands, and tugged until I yelled with pain. 'There is water in your eyes,' said he, as he released me. 'I perceive that all is as it should be. But we have to be careful, for we have twice been deceived by wigs and once by paint. I could tell you tales of cobbler's wax which would disgust you with human nature.' He stepped over to the window, and shouted through it at the top of his voice that the vacancy was filled. A groan of disappointment came up from below, and the folk all trooped away in different directions, until there was not a red head to be seen except my own and that of the manager.

" 'My name,' said he, 'is Mr. Duncan Ross, and I am myself one of the pensioners upon the fund left by our noble benefactor. Are you a married man, Mr. Wilson? Have you a family?'

"I answered that I had not.

"His face fell immediately.

" 'Dear me!' he said gravely, 'that is very serious indeed! I am sorry to hear you say that. The fund was, of course, for the propagation and spread of the red-heads as well as for their maintenance. It is exceedingly unfortunate that you should be a bachelor.'

"My face lengthened at this, Mr. Holmes, for I thought that I was not to have the vacancy after all; but after thinking it over for a few minutes, he said that it would be all right.

" 'In the case of another,' said he, 'the objection might be fatal, but we must stretch a point in favour of a man with such a head of hair as yours. When shall you be able to enter upon your new duties?'

" 'Well, it is a little awkward, for I have a business already,' said I.

" 'Oh, never mind about that, Mr. Wilson!' said Vincent Spaulding. 'I shall be able to look after that for you.'

" 'What would be the hours?' I asked.

" 'Ten to two.'

"Now, a pawnbroker's business is mostly done of an evening, Mr. Holmes, especially Thursday and Friday evening, which is just before pay-day; so it would suit me very well to earn a little in the mornings. Besides, I knew that my assistant was a good man, and that he would see to anything that turned up.

" 'That would suit me very well,' said I. 'And the pay?'

" 'Is four pounds a week.'

" 'And the work?'

" 'Is purely nominal.'

" 'What do you call purely nominal?'

" 'Well, you have to be in the office, or at least in the building, the whole time. If you leave, you forfeit your whole position for ever. The will is very clear upon that point. You don't comply with the conditions if you budge from the office during that time.'

" 'It is only four hours a day, and I should not think of leaving,' said I.

" 'No excuse will avail,' said Mr. Duncan Ross, 'neither sickness, nor business, nor anything else. There you must stay, or you lose your billet.'

" 'And the work?'

" 'Is to copy out the *Encyclopedia Britannica*. There is the first volume of it in that press. You must find your own ink, pens, and blotting-paper, but we provide this table and chair. Will you be ready tomorrow?'

" 'Certainly,' I answered.

" 'Then, good-bye, Mr. Jabez Wilson, and let me congratulate you once more on the important position which you have been fortunate enough to gain.' He bowed me out of the room, and I went home with my assistant, hardly knowing what to say or do, I was so pleased at my own good fortune.

"Well, I thought over the matter all day, and by evening I was in low spirits again; for I had quite persuaded myself that the whole affair must be some great hoax or fraud, though what its object might be I could not imagine. It seemed altogether past belief that anyone could make such a will, or that they would pay such a sum for doing anything so simple as copying out the *Encyclopedia Britannica*. Vincent Spaulding did what he could to cheer me up, but by bedtime I had reasoned myself out of the whole thing. However, in the morning I determined to have a look at it anyhow, so I bought a penny bottle of ink, and with a quill pen, and seven sheets of foolscap paper, I started off for Pope's Court.

"Well, to my surprise and delight everything was as right as possible. The table was set out ready for me, and Mr. Duncan Ross was there to see that I got fairly to work. He started me off upon the letter A, and then he left me; but he would drop in from time to time to see that all was right with me. At two o'clock he bade me good day, complimented me upon the amount that I had written, and locked the door of the office after me.

"This went on day after day, Mr. Holmes, and on Saturday the manager came in and planked down four golden sovereigns for my week's work. It was the same next week, and the same the week after. Every morning I was there at ten, and every afternoon I left at two. By degrees Mr. Duncan Ross took to coming in only once of a morning, and then, after a time, he did not come in at all. Still, of course, I never dared to leave the room for an instant, for I was not sure when he might come, and the billet was such a good one, and suited me so well, that I would not risk the loss of it.

"Eight weeks passed away like this, and I had written about Abbots, and Archery, and Armour, and Architecture, and Attica, and hoped with diligence that I might get on to the B's before very long. It cost me something in foolscap, and I had pretty nearly filled a shelf with my writings. And then suddenly the whole business came to an end."

"To an end?"

"Yes, sir. And no later than this morning. I went to my work as usual at ten o'clock, but the door was shut and locked, with a little square of cardboard hammered on to the middle of the panel with a tack. Here it is, and you can read for yourself."

He held up a piece of white cardboard, about the size of a sheet of note-paper. It read in this fashion:

THE RED-HEADED LEAGUE IS DISSOLVED
Oct. 9, 1890

Sherlock Holmes and I surveyed this curt announcement and the rueful face behind it, until the comical side of the affair so completely over-topped every other consideration that we both burst out into a roar of laughter.

"I cannot see that there is anything very funny," cried our client, flushing up to the roots of his flaming head. "If you can do nothing better than laugh at me, I can go elsewhere."

"No, no," cried Holmes, shoving him back into the chair from which he had half risen. "I really wouldn't miss your case for the world. It is most refreshingly unusual. But there is, if you will excuse my saying so, something just a little funny about it. Pray what steps did you take when you found the card upon the door?"

"I was staggered, sir. I did not know what to do. Then I called at the offices round, but none of them seemed to know anything about it. Finally, I went to the landlord, who is an accountant living on the ground floor, and I asked him if he could tell me what had become of the Red-Headed League. He said that he had never heard of any such body. Then I asked him who Mr. Duncan Ross was. He answered that the name was new to him.

" 'Well,' said I, 'the gentleman at No. 4.'

" 'What, the red-headed man?'

" 'Yes.'

" 'Oh,' said he, 'his name was William Morris. He was a solicitor, and was using my room as a temporary convenience until his new premises were ready. He moved out yesterday.'

" 'Where could I find him?'

" 'Oh, at his new offices. He did tell me the address. Yes, 17 King Edward Street, near St. Paul's.'

"I started off, Mr. Holmes, but when I got to that address it was a manufactory of artificial knee-caps, and no one in it had ever heard of either Mr. William Morris or Mr. Duncan Ross."

"And what did you do then?" asked Holmes.

"I went home to Saxe-Coburg Square, and I took the advice of my assistant. But he could not help me in any way. He could only say that if I waited I should hear by post. But that was not quite good enough, Mr. Holmes. I did not wish to lose such a place without a struggle, so, as I had heard that you were good enough to give advice to poor folk who were in need of it, I came right away to you."

"And you did very wisely," said Holmes. "Your case is an exceedingly remarkable one, and I shall be happy to look into it. From what you have told me I think that it is possible that graver issues hang from it than might at first sight appear."

"Grave enough!" said Mr. Jabez Wilson. "Why, I have lost four pounds a week."

"As far as you are personally concerned," remarked Holmes, "I do not see that you have any grievance against this extraordinary league. On the contrary, you are, as I understand, richer by some thirty pounds, to say nothing of the minute knowledge which you have gained on every subject which comes under the letter A. You have lost nothing by them."

"No, sir. But I want to find out about them, and who they are, and what their object was in playing this prank—if it was a prank—upon me. It was a pretty expensive joke for them, for it cost them two-and-thirty pounds."

"We shall endeavour to clear up these points for you. And, first, one or two questions, Mr. Wilson. This assistant of yours

who first called your attention to the advertisement—how long
has he been with you?"

"About a month then."

"How did he come?"

"In answer to an advertisement."

"Was he the only applicant?"

"No, I had a dozen."

"Why did you pick him?"

"Because he was handy, and would come cheap."

"At half wages, in fact."

"Yes."

"What is he like, this Vincent Spaulding?"

"Small, stout-built, very quick in his ways, no hair on his face,
though he's not short of thirty. Has a white splash of acid upon his
forehead."

Holmes sat up in his chair in considerable excitement.

"I thought as much," said he. "Have you ever observed that his
ears are pierced for ear-rings?"

"Yes, sir. He told me that a gipsy had done it for him when
he was a lad."

"Hum!" said Holmes, sinking back in deep thought. "He is
still with you?"

"Oh, yes, sir; I have only just left him."

"And has your business been attended to in your absence?"

"Nothing to complain of, sir. There's never very much to do
of a morning."

"That will do, Mr. Wilson. I shall be happy to give you an
opinion upon the subject in the course of a day or two. Today is
Saturday, and I hope that by Monday we may come to a conclusion."

"Well, Watson," said Holmes, when our visitor had left us,
"what do you make of it all?"

"I make nothing of it," I answered, frankly. "It is a most
mysterious business."

"As a rule," said Holmes, "the more bizarre a thing is the less
mysterious it proves to be. It is your commonplace, featureless
crimes which are really puzzling, just as a commonplace face is the
most difficult to identify. But I must be prompt over this matter."

"What are you going to do, then?" I asked.

"To smoke," he answered. "It is quite a three-pipe problem,
and I beg that you won't speak to me for fifty minutes." He curled

himself up in his chair, with his thin knees drawn up to his hawk-like nose, and there he sat with his eyes closed and his black clay pipe thrusting out like the bill of some strange bird. I had come to the conclusion that he had dropped asleep, and indeed was nodding myself, when he suddenly sprang out of his chair with the gesture of a man who had made up his mind, and put his pipe down upon the mantelpiece.

"Sarasate plays at the St. James's Hall this afternoon," he remarked. "What do you think, Watson? Could your patients spare you for a few hours?"

"I have nothing to do today. My practice is never very absorbing."

"Then put on your hat, and come. I am going through the City first, and we can have some lunch on the way. I observe that there is a good deal of German music on the program, which is rather more to my taste than Italian or French. It is introspective, and I want to introspect. Come along!"

We travelled by the Underground as far as Aldersgate; and a short walk took us to Saxe-Coburg Square, the scene of the singular story which we had listened to in the morning. It was a pokey, little, shabby-genteel place, where four lines of dingy two-storied brick houses looked out into a small railed-in enclosure, where a lawn of weedy grass and a few clumps of faded laurel bushes made a hard fight against a smoke-laden and uncongenial atmosphere. Three gilt balls and a brown board with JABEZ WILSON in white letters, upon a corner house, announced the place where our red-headed client carried on his business. Sherlock Holmes stopped in front of it with his head on one side and looked it all over, with his eyes shining brightly between puckered lids. Then he walked slowly up the street and then down again to the corner, still looking keenly at the houses. Finally he returned to the pawnbroker's, and, having thumped vigorously upon the pavement with his stick two or three times, he went up to the door and knocked. It was instantly opened by a bright-looking, clean-shaven young fellow, who asked him to step in.

"Thank you," said Holmes, "I only wished to ask you how you would go from here to the Strand."

"Third right, fourth left," answered the assistant promptly, closing the door.

"Smart fellow, that," observed Holmes as we walked away. "He is, in my judgment, the fourth smartest man in London, and for daring I am not sure that he has not a claim to be third. I have known something of him before."

"Evidently," said I, "Mr. Wilson's assistant counts for a good deal in this mystery of the Red-Headed League. I am sure that you inquired your way merely in order that you might see him."

"Not him."

"What then?"

"The knees of his trousers."

"And what did you see?"

"What I expected to see."

"Why did you beat the pavement?"

"My dear Doctor, this is a time for observation, not for talk. We are spies in an enemy's country. We know something of Saxe-Coburg Square. Let us now explore the paths which lie behind it."

The road in which we found ourselves as we turned round the corner from the retired Saxe-Coburg Square presented as great a contrast to it as the front of a picture does to the back. It was one of the main arteries which convey the traffic of the City to the north and west. The roadway was blocked with the immense stream of commerce flowing in a double tide inwards and outwards, while the footpaths were black with the hurrying swarm of pedestrians. It was difficult to realize as we looked at the line of fine shops and stately business premises that they really abutted on the other side upon the faded and stagnant square which we had just quitted.

"Let me see," said Holmes, standing at the corner, and glancing along the line, "I should like just to remember the order of the houses here. It is a hobby of mine to have an exact knowledge of London. There is Mortimer's the tobacconist, the little newspaper shop, the Coburg branch of the City and Suburban Bank, the Vegetarian Restaurant, and McFarlane's carriage-building depot. That carries us right on to the other block. And now, Doctor, we've done our work, so it's time we had some play. A sandwich, and a cup of coffee, and then off to violin land, where all is sweetness, and delicacy, and harmony, and there are no red-headed clients to vex us with their conundrums."

My friend was an enthusiastic musician, being himself not only a very capable performer, but a composer of no ordinary merit. All the afternoon he sat in the stalls wrapped in the most perfect happiness, gently waving his long thin fingers in time to the music, while his gently smiling face and his languid, dreamy eyes were as unlike those of Holmes the sleuth-hound, Holmes the relentless, keen-witted, ready-handed criminal agent, as it was possible to conceive. In his singular character the dual nature alternately asserted itself, and his extreme exactness and astuteness represented, as I have often thought, the reaction against the poetic and contemplative mood which occasionally predominated in him. The swing of his nature took him from extreme languor to devouring energy; and, as I knew well, he was never so truly formidable as when, for days on end, he had been lounging in his arm-chair amid his improvisations and his black-letter editions. Then it was that the lust of the chase would suddenly come upon him, and that his brilliant reasoning power would rise to the level of intuition, until those who were unacquainted with his methods would look askance at him as on a man whose knowledge was not that of other mortals. When I saw him that afternoon so enwrapped in the music at St. James's Hall I felt that an evil time might be coming upon those whom he had set himself to hunt down.

"You want to go home, no doubt, Doctor," he remarked, as we emerged.

"Yes, it would be as well."

"And I have some business to do which will take some hours. This business at Coburg Square is serious."

"Why serious?"

"A considerable crime is in contemplation. I have every reason to believe that we shall be in time to stop it. But today being Saturday rather complicates matters. I shall want your help tonight."

"At what time?"

"Ten will be early enough."

"I shall be at Baker Street at ten."

"Very well. And, I say, Doctor! there may be some little danger, so kindly put your army revolver in your pocket." He waved his hand, turned on his heel, and disappeared in an instant among the crowd.

I trust that I am not more dense than my neighbours, but I was always oppressed with a sense of my own stupidity in my dealings with Sherlock Holmes. Here I had heard what he had heard, I had seen what he had seen, and yet from his words it was evident that he saw clearly not only what had happened, but what was about to happen, while to me the whole business was still confused and grotesque. As I drove home to my house in Kensington

I thought over it all, from the extraordinary story of the red-headed copier of the *Encyclopedia* down to the visit to Saxe-Coburg Square, and the ominous words with which he had parted from me. What was this nocturnal expedition, and why should I go armed? Where were we going, and what were we to do? I had the hint from Holmes that this smooth-faced pawnbroker's assistant was a formidable man—a man who might play a deep game. I tried to puzzle it out, but gave it up in despair, and set the matter aside until night should bring an explanation.

It was a quarter past nine when I started from home and made my way across the Park, and so through Oxford Street to Baker Street. Two hansoms were standing at the door, and, as I entered the passage, I heard the sound of voices from above. On entering his room, I found Holmes in animated conversation with two men, one of whom I recognized as Peter Jones, the official police agent; while the other was a long, thin, sad-faced man, with a very shiny hat and oppressively respectable frock coat.

"Ha! our party is complete," said Holmes, buttoning up his pea-jacket, and taking his heavy hunting-crop from the rack. "Watson, I think you know Mr. Jones, of Scotland Yard? Let me introduce you to Mr. Merryweather, who is to be our companion in tonight's adventure."

"We're hunting in couples again, Doctor, you see," said Jones in his consequential way. "Our friend here is a wonderful man for starting a chase. All he wants is an old dog to help him to do the running down."

"I hope a wild goose may not prove to be the end of our chase," observed Mr. Merryweather gloomily.

"You may place considerable confidence in Mr. Holmes, sir," said the police agent loftily. "He has his own little methods, which are, if he won't mind my saying so, just a little too theoretical and fantastic, but he has the makings of a detective in him. It is not too much to say that once or twice, as in that business of the Sholto murder and the Agra treasure, he has been more nearly correct than the official force."

"Oh, if you say so, Mr. Jones, it is all right!" said the stranger, with deference. "Still, I confess that I miss my rubber. It is the first Staturday night for seven-and-twenty years that I have not had my rubber."

"I think you will find," said Sherlock Holmes, "that you will play for a higher stake tonight than you have ever done yet, and that the play will be more exciting. For you, Mr. Merryweather, the stake will be some thirty thousand pounds; and for you, Jones, it will be the man upon whom you wish to lay your hands."

"John Clay, the murderer, thief, smasher, and forger. He's a young man, Mr. Merryweather, but he is at the head of his profession, and I would rather have my bracelets on him than on any criminal in London. He's a remarkable man, is young John Clay. His grandfather was a royal duke, and he himself has been to Eton and Oxford. His brain is as cunning as his fingers, and though we meet signs of him at every turn, we never know where to find the man himself. He'll crack a crib in Scotland one week, and be raising money to build an orphanage in Cornwall the next. I've been on his track for years, and have never set eyes on him yet."

"I hope that I may have the pleasure of introducing you tonight. I've had one or two little turns also with Mr. John Clay, and I agree with you that he is at the head of his profession. It is past ten, however, and quite time that we started. If you two will take the first hansom, Watson and I will follow in the second."

Sherlock Holmes was not very communicative during the long drive, and lay back in the cab humming the tunes which he had heard in the afternoon. We rattled through an endless labyrinth of gas-lit streets until we emerged into Farringdon Street.

"We are close there now," my friend remarked. "This fellow Merryweather is a bank director and personally interested in the matter. I thought it as well to have Jones with us also. He is not a bad fellow, though an absolute imbecile in his profession. He has one positive virtue. He is as brave as a bulldog, and as tenacious as a lobster if he gets his claws upon anyone. Here we are, and they are waiting for us."

We had reached the same crowded thoroughfare in which we had found ourselves in the morning. Our cabs were dismissed, and, following the guidance of Mr. Merryweather, we passed down a narrow passage, and through a side door, which he opened for us. Within there was a small corridor, which ended in a very massive iron gate. This also was opened, and led down a flight of winding stone steps, which terminated at another formidable gate. Mr. Merryweather stopped to light a lantern, and then conducted us down a dark, earth-smelling passage, and so, after opening a third door, into a huge vault or cellar, which was piled all round with crates and massive boxes.

"You are not very vulnerable from above," Holmes remarked, as he held up the lantern and gazed about him.

"Nor from below," said Mr. Merryweather, striking his stick upon the flags which lined the floor. "Why, dear me, it sounds quite hollow!" he remarked, looking up in surprise.

"I must really ask you to be a little more quiet," said Holmes severely. "You have already imperilled the whole success of our expedition. Might I beg that you would have the goodness to sit down upon one of those boxes, and not to interfere?"

The solemn Mr. Merryweather perched himself upon a crate, with a very injured expression upon his face, while Holmes fell upon his knees upon the floor, and, with the lantern and a magnifying lens, began to examine minutely the cracks between the stones. A few seconds sufficed to satisfy him, for he sprang to his feet again, and put his glass in his pocket.

"We have at least an hour before us," he remarked, "for they can hardly take any steps until the good pawnbroker is safely in bed. Then they will not lose a minute, for the sooner they do their work the longer time they will have for their escape. We are at present, Doctor—as no doubt you have divined—in the cellar of the City branch of one of the principal London banks. Mr. Merryweather is the chairman of directors, and he will explain to you that there are reasons why the more daring criminals of London should take a considerable interest in this cellar at present."

"It is our French gold," whispered the director. "We have had several warnings that an attempt might be made upon it."

"Your French gold?"

"Yes. We had occasion some months ago to strengthen our resources, and borrowed, for that purpose, thirty thousand napoleons from the Bank of France. It has become known that we have never had occasion to unpack the money, and that it is still lying in our cellar. The crate upon which I sit contains two thousand napoleons packed between layers of lead foil. Our reserve of bullion is much larger at present than is usually kept in a single branch office, and the directors have had misgivings upon the subject."

"Which were very well justified," observed Holmes. "And now it is time that we arranged our little plans. I expect that within an hour matters will come to a head. In the meantime, Mr. Merryweather, we must put the screen over that dark lantern."

"And sit in the dark?"

"I am afraid so. I had brought a pack of cards in my pocket, and I thought that, as we were a *partie carrée*,[2] you might have your rubber after all. But I see that the enemy's preparations have gone so far that we cannot risk the presence of a light. And, first of all, we must choose our positions. These are daring men, and, though we shall take them at a disadvantage they may do us some harm, unless we are careful. I shall stand behind this crate, and do you conceal yourself behind those. Then, when I flash a light upon them, close in swiftly. If they fire, Watson, have no compunction about shooting them down."

I placed my revolver, cocked, upon the top of the wooden case behind which I crouched. Holmes shot the slide across the front of his lantern, and left us in pitch darkness—such an absolute darkness as I have never before experienced. The smell of hot metal remained to assure us that the light was still there, ready to flash out at a moment's notice. To me, with my nerve worked up to a pitch of expectancy, there was something depressing and sub-duing in the sudden gloom, and in the cold, dank air of the vault.

"They have but one retreat," whispered Holmes. "That is back through the house into Saxe-Coburg Square. I hope that you have done what I asked you, Jones?"

"I have an inspector and two officers waiting at the front door."

"Then we have stopped all the holes. And now we must be silent and wait."

What a time it seemed! From comparing notes afterwards it was but an hour and a quarter, yet it appeared to me that the night must have almost gone, and the dawn be breaking above us. My limbs were weary and stiff, for I feared to change my position, yet my nerves were worked up to the highest pitch of tension, and my hearing was so acute that I could not only hear the gentle breathing of my companions, but I could distinguish the deeper, heavier inbreath of the bulky Jones from the thin sighing note of the bank director. From my position I could look over the case in the direction of the floor. Suddenly my eyes caught the glint of a light.

At first it was but a lurid spark upon the stone pavement. Then it lengthened out until it became a yellow line, and then, without any warning or sound, a gash seemed to open and a hand appeared, a white, almost womanly hand, which felt about in the

[2] *partie carrée:* party of four, necessary to play certain card games

centre of the little area of light. For a minute or more the hand, with its writhing fingers, protruded out of the floor. Then it was withdrawn as suddenly as it appeared, and all was dark again save the single lurid spark, which marked a chink between the stones.

Its disappearance, however, was but momentary. With a rending, tearing sound, one of the broad, white stones turned over upon its side, and left a square, gaping hole, through which streamed the light of a lantern. Over the edge there peeped a clean-cut boyish face, which looked keenly about it, and then, with a hand on either side of the aperture, drew itself shoulder high and waist high, until one knee rested upon the edge. In another instant he stood at the side of the hole, and was hauling after him a companion, lithe and small like himself, with a pale face and a shock of very red hair.

"It's all clear," he whispered. "Have you the chisel, and the bags? Great Scott! Jump, Archie, jump, and I'll swing for it!"

Sherlock Holmes had sprung out and seized the intruder by the collar. The other dived down the hole, and I heard the sound of rending cloth as Jones clutched at his skirts. The light flashed upon the barrel of a revolver, but Holmes's hunting-crop came down on the man's wrist, and the pistol clinked upon the stone floor.

"It's no use, John Clay," said Holmes blandly. "You have no chance at all."

"So I see," the other answered with the utmost coolness. "I fancy that my pal is all right, though I see you have got his coat-tails."

"There are three men waiting for him at the door," said Holmes.

"Oh, indeed. You seem to have done the thing very completely. I must compliment you."

"And I you," Holmes answered. "Your red-headed idea was very new and effective."

"You'll see your pal again presently," said Jones. "He's quicker at climbing down holes than I am. Just hold out while I fix the derbies."

"I beg that you will not touch me with your filthy hands," remarked our prisoner, as the handcuffs clattered upon his wrists.

"You may not be aware that I have royal blood in my veins. Have the goodness also when you address me always to say 'sir' and 'please.'"

"All right," said Jones, with a stare and a snigger. "Well, would you please, sir, march upstairs, where we can get a cab to carry your highness to the police station."

"That is better," said John Clay serenely. He made a sweeping bow to the three of us, and walked quietly off in the custody of the detective.

"Really, Mr. Holmes," said Mr. Merryweather, as we followed them from the cellar, "I do not know how the bank can thank you or repay you. There is no doubt that you have detected and defeated in the most complete manner one of the most determined attempts at bank robbery that has ever come within my experience."

"I have had one or two little scores of my own to settle with Mr. John Clay," said Holmes. "I have been at some small expense over this matter, which I shall expect the bank to refund, but beyond that I am amply repaid by having had an experience which is in many ways unique, and by hearing the very remarkable narrative of the Red-Headed League."

"You see, Watson," he explained in the early hours of the morning, as we sat over a glass of whisky-and-soda in Baker Street, "it was perfectly obvious from the first that the only possible object of this rather fantastic business of the advertisement of the League, and the copying of the *Encyclopedia*, must be to get this not overbright pawnbroker out of the way for a number of hours every day. It was a curious way of managing it, but really it would be difficult to suggest a better. The method was no doubt suggested to Clay's ingenious mind by the colour of his accomplice's hair. The four pounds a week was a lure which must draw him, and what was it to them, who were playing for thousands? They put in the advertisement; one rogue has the temporary office, the other rogue incites the man to apply for it, and together they manage to secure his absence every morning in the week. From the time that I heard of the assistant having come for half-wages, it was obvious to me that he had some strong motive for securing the situation."

"But how could you guess what the motive was?"

"Had there been women in the house, I should have suspected a mere vulgar intrigue. That, however, was out of the question. The man's business was a small one, and there was nothing in his house which could account for such elaborate preparations and such an expenditure as they were at. It must then be something out of the house. What could it be? I thought of the assistant's fondness for photography, and his trick of vanishing into the cellar. The cellar! There was the end of this tangled clew. Then I made inquiries as to this mysterious assistant, and found that I had to deal with one of the coolest and most daring criminals in London. He was doing something in the cellar—something which took many hours a day for months on end. What could it be, once more? I could think of nothing save that he was running a tunnel to some other building.

"So far I had got when we went to visit the scene of action. I surprised you by beating upon the pavement with my stick. I was ascertaining whether the cellar stretched out in front or behind. It was not in front. Then I rang the bell, and, as I hoped, the assistant answered it. We have had some skirmishes, but we had never set eyes on each other before. I hardly looked at his face. His knees were what I wished to see. You must yourself have remarked how worn, wrinkled and stained they were. They spoke of those hours of burrowing. The only remaining point was what they were burrowing for. I walked round the corner, saw that the City and Suburban Bank abutted on our friend's premises, and felt that I had solved my problem. When you drove home after the concert I called upon Scotland Yard, and upon the chairman of the bank directors, with the result that you have seen."

"And how could you tell that they would make their attempt tonight?" I asked.

"Well, when they closed their League offices that was a sign that they cared no longer about Mr. Jabez Wilson's presence; in other words, that they had completed their tunnel. But it was essential that they should use it soon, as it might be discovered, or the bullion might be removed. Saturday would suit them better than any other day, as it would give them two days for their escape. For all these reasons I expected them to come tonight."

"You reasoned it out beautifully," I exclaimed in unfeigned admiration. "It is so long a chain, and yet every link rings true."

"It saved me from ennui," he answered, yawning. "Alas, I already feel it closing in upon me! My life is spent in one long effort to escape from the commonplaces of existence. These little problems help me to do so."

"And you are a benefactor of the race," said I.

He shrugged his shoulders. "Well, perhaps, after all, it is of some little use," he remarked. " '*L'homme c'est rien—l'œuvre c'est tout,*' [3] as Gustave Flaubert wrote to George Sand."

[3] "*L'homme c'est rien—l'oeuvre c'est tout*": Man is nothing—work is all. (French)

Questions for discussion

1. Like all the adventures of Sherlock Holmes, this story is told by his friend, Dr. Watson. What did you learn from him about the characteristics and abilities of Holmes that made him such an able and famous sleuth? What did you learn about Holmes from Pete Jones, the Scotland Yard detective?
2. How, in the first pages of the story, did Holmes show his sharp intelligence and brilliant powers of mind? If you were a detective listening to Mr. Wilson's story, which facts would have aroused your suspicion? Why do you think Wilson was "taken in" by the Red-Headed League?
3. Two actions of Sherlock Holmes on his visit to the pawnshop puzzled Dr. Watson. What was Holmes's real purpose for each action?
4. The climax of a story is the point of highest interest or greatest intensity. Usually it marks the turning point in the action which will determine success or failure for the hero. Which scene is the climax of this story? What did the author do to make the climax exciting?
5. Describe the kind of person Holmes's opponent was in this battle of wits. Was it a fair match? What did this contribute to the suspense of the story?
6. Go through the story and list the clues the author gave you. Explain the connection between each clue and the final solution.

Vocabulary growth

WORDS ARE INTERESTING. At the end of the story, Sherlock Holmes says that doing detective work saves him from *ennui*. This is a French word that is used frequently by English-speaking people. It is related to the word *annoy*, but it has a different meaning. To be annoyed is to be displeased or irritated by something unpleasant. But *ennui* is a condition in which we feel that life has nothing to interest us any more. What synonym would you use in its place? Check the meaning in a dictionary and find out how it is pronounced.

Several times, Dr. Watson described Mr. Wilson's story as *bizarre*. This word was originally adopted by the French from the Spanish word *bizarro*. A *bizarro* was a brave and dashing soldier who had fantastic adventures. Gradually, the word came to have its present meaning in English—"odd," "strange," or "fantastic." Why do you think *bizarre* is or is not an appropriate word to describe Mr. Wilson's story?

For composition

1. In a short composition, describe a detective you have admired either in your reading or in motion pictures, TV, or radio. Describe his character and the methods he uses in solving a crime.
2. In a few careful paragraphs, compare the methods Sherlock Holmes used in his investigation and those used by a present-day fictional detective. Give reasons why you think this modern-day sleuth could or could not have learned anything from Holmes.

Phil Fuller had two loves,
which together earned him the name of . . .

The Milk Pitcher

HOWARD BRUBAKER

The Fullers named their son "Philip" after his maternal grand-father. That was an error in judgment because the time came when the name Phil Fuller aroused chuckles and snickers among the pleasure-loving faces of the countryside. At the age of one Phil had practically settled upon red as the best color for hair. Some time in his third year the truth was established that he was left-handed. When given something he did not want, he threw it away with violence.

This act seemed to set up pleasurable emotions in his young soul. His simple face widened into a grin, and before long he was heaving things around for the sheer love of heaving.

At four, Phil sprouted a genuine freckle on his nose, the fore-runner of a bumper crop, and even his prejudiced mother had to admit that his ears were large for their age.

The youth spent his fourth summer in the society of a Jersey calf named Lily, who was tethered in the orchard. Phil had nothing to do except to throw green apples at a tree with his left hand, and Lily's time was also her own. The child learned not to wince when she licked his pink nose with her rough tongue, and the calf put up with some pretty rowdy conduct too. Both infants cried when sepa-rated for the night. The tender attachment between Phil and Lil was the subject of neighborhood gossip as far away as the Doug Morton place at the bend of Squaw Creek.

When Phil was six, he threw a carriage bolt from the wagon shed into the water trough, and he laughed so boisterously over this feat that Mr. Harrington heard the noise while passing in a light spring wagon.

Phil had a misguided sense of humor. It seemed to him that

throwing things was the world's funniest joke. As he picked up a stone and let it fly, the freckles on his face arranged themselves into a pleasure pattern, his features widened, and he grinned expansively, showing vacant spots where he was changing teeth.

By this time his love for the cow stable had become a grand passion. Horses, dogs, cats, and pigs meant rather less in his young life than they do to most farm boys, but cows meant more. Phil attended all the milkings with his father, dealt out bran, and threw down hay. He wandered in and out among bovine legs without fear; hoofs, horns, and teeth had no terrors for him. He was soon old enough to drive the cattle to pasture and bring them back.

At the age of eight he was probably the ablest red-headed cow-boy and left-handed stone-thrower in Clinton Township. At this date in history he had drunk enough milk to float a battleship and thrown enough stones, sticks, bones, horseshoes, apples, corncobs, and base-balls to sink one. He was now the owner in fee simple of Lily's knock-kneed daughter, Dolly. This white-faced blond flapper followed Phil around with adoration and bleated at the barnyard gate until her playmate came home from school.

That fount of knowledge was Clinton Township, District No. 5, known locally as Tamarack School. There he absorbed a reasonable quantity of booklore and learned to pitch a straight ball with speed and control. He is still remembered in educational circles as the southpaw who hurled the Tamarackers to glorious victory over the Squaw Creek outfit, while unveiling the broadest grin ever seen on the lot and issuing many unnecessary noises. Although he had a lot of influence over a baseball, he could not make his face behave.

Baseball was the great joy of Phil's school years. Every spring when the frost came out of the ground his flaming head sprang up on the soggy field like a tulip. He had never learned to bat well, but he was a thrower of great ability and a laugher and yeller of great audibility. In school when asked to give the boundaries of Baluchistan he could scarcely make the teacher hear, but on the diamond his disorderly conduct was noted and deplored as far away as Grandma Longenecker's cottage.

The game uncorked his inhibitions and released his ego. His habitual shyness vanished and gave place to vociferous glee. He did frolicsome things with his feet, his arms went round like a windmill wheel, sometimes he burst into what he wrongly believed to be song.

Miss Willkans, the teacher, testified that Phil had easily the worst singing voice that had attended District No. 5 in her time—which would be nineteen years if she lived through this term, as seemed highly unlikely.

Inevitably there came an afternoon in late May when Phil's career as a Tamaracker had run its course. He twisted a button almost off his new coat, whispered a graduating piece about Daniel Webster, took his books and his well-worn right-hand glove and went back to the cows.

At five o'clock the following morning the fourteen-year-old Phil became the vice president and general manager of the dairy department of the Fuller farm. His father was overworked, help was scarce and expensive, and the graduate of Tamarack was judged strong enough to handle the job. He milked all the cows that summer, cleaned the stalls, helped to get in the hay and fill the silo. He ran the separator, he churned, he carried skim milk to the pigs. The end of the summer found him a stocky lad of rather less than normal height but with a rank growth of feet, arms, and ears. He had the complexion of a boiled beet and hair exactly the shade of a two-cent stamp. His hands were large and fully equipped with freckles, calluses, bumps, cracks, warts, knuckles, and rough red wrists.

Phil could lift with one hand Dolly's new calf, Molly; he could throw a ten-pound sledge-hammer over the hay barn; he could sing like a creaky pump, and he shattered all known speed records from the stable to the dining room. He was an able performer with the table fork as well as with the pitchfork.

In September he took all these assets and liabilities and his first long pants and went to Branford to live with Aunt Mary and Uncle Phineas and attend high school. As he was winding up his affairs preparatory to his great adventure, it was clear that he had something on his mind. It came out one night at supper in the hiatus between the fifth and sixth ears of Golden Bantam.

"It's too bad they don't keep a cow," he said, apropos of nothing.

"Oh, sakes alive, child!" Mother exclaimed in surprise. "They wouldn't want to be bothered with a cow."

Phil's ears went red. He polished off his corncob and returned to the attack. "They wouldn't need to be bothered much. They have no horse any more, and there's room in the barn. I could feed her and milk her and everything. I bet Aunt Mary would be glad to have lots of nice milk and cream. We could tie her behind the buggy and take her in with us."

"Tie who—Aunt Mary?" asked Father with ill-timed facetiousness.

"Dolly," said Phil.

A dozen objections were raised and disposed of. Aunt Mary and Uncle Phineas were consulted by telephone, and after the first shock they agreed to the outrageous plan. And thus it came about that Phil Fuller was the first case in recorded history of a boy who went to Branford High School accompanied by a private and personal cow.

During those first months of strangeness and homesickness, Dolly was his comfort and his joy, his link with the familiar. He brushed and polished that blond cow until her upholstery was threadbare, pampered her with choice viands and clean bedding, scrubbed and whitewashed the interior of the old barn, put in window sashes to give Dolly more sunlight and a better view. Often when the day was fair he led her around the block to take air and see a little city life.

At six o'clock of a dark, bitter morning the neighbors could hear distressing noises issuing from Phineas Rucker's lantern-lit barn, and they knew from sad experiences of the past that another day was about to dawn and the red-headed Fuller boy was singing to his heart's true love.

Dolly was now in the full flush of her splendid young cowhood and home was never like this. Phil plied her with experimental mixtures—beet pulp, ground oats, cottonseed meal—and carefully noted the results. The contented cow responded gratefully to this treatment. Before long she exceeded the needs of the Rucker family and Phil was doing a pleasant little milk business with the neighbors. His immaculate barn, his new white overalls, his vocal excesses, and his free street parades all helped trade. The milk inspector passed Dolly with high honors, and doctors recommended her for ailing babies. Presently she was one of Branford's leading citizens, a self-supporting twenty-quart cow, commanding a premium of three cents over the market price. Phil had discovered his life work.

His second great discovery did not come until spring. On a blustery March day he was out on the diamond behind the high-school building, warming up his left wing and chuckling over his favorite joke, when Mr. Huckley, chemistry teacher and baseball coach, came along.

"Southpaw, eh!" he demanded. "Let's see what you've got, Fuller."

Phil gave a brief exhibition of his wares with Dinky Doolittle holding the catcher's glove.

"Plenty of steam and good control," the teacher said, "and your footwork is terrible. Now show us your curve."

"I haven't got any," Phil answered. "Nobody ever showed me how to pitch a curve."

"Somebody will now," Mr. Huckley said. "Whether you can do it or not is another question."

That was the beginning of a beautiful friendship and a new era in the life of Philip Fuller.

Mr. Huckley had pitched on the team of Athens University, of which he was a graduate. He liked Phil, admired his able hands, his abnormally developed forearms, his keen joy in the game. The coach saw great possibilities in this piece of raw material, and he spent a patient hour teaching Phil some of the rudiments of curve pitching and in time they achieved a perceptible out-curve. At the height of his exultation, the boy pulled out a nickel-plated watch and said:

"I ask you to excuse me now. It's time to milk my cow."

After a week of such instruction, Mr. Huckley handed down this decision: "You have the makings of a good pitcher, Phil, if you're willing to learn. You have a couple of fine qualities and not over twenty-five or thirty serious faults."

Phil's ears flushed with pleasure and embarrassment.

"Well, maybe I can get shut of some of them—I mean those— faults. I've got four years to do it in."

"Right-o. You have good control of your fast one, you have a nice little out, and you have the worst style of windup these eyes have ever seen."

Four years of study, dairying, and baseball, with summers of hard work on the farm, made Phil a different boy—different and yet curiously the same. His shoulders were broader, his arms stronger, but he did not add many inches to his stature. He knew more mathematics, science, and history, but Latin was still Greek to him. Although he took on some of the manners and customs of his town contemporaries, he still had the gait of one walking over a plowed field. In time he learned to talk with girls without being distressed, but as a social light he was a flickering flame in a smoky chimney. He was a conspicuous success on the barn floor but a brilliant failure on the dance floor. His voice changed, but not for the better. His matin song to Dolly now sounded like a bullfrog with a bad attack of static. He wrote a creditable little rural farce for the senior dramatic class and further distinguished himself as the worst actor on the American stage.

Though much ridiculed, he was universally liked and genuinely respected. On the ball field he was a source of low comedy to friend and foe because of the eccentric behavior of his face and feet, but in his succeeding seasons on the mound he pitched the Branford High School out of the cellar position into respectable company, into select society, and finally, in his senior year, into the state championship of the small-town division.

At the joyfest in the assembly hall in celebration of this final triumph, Phil was forced to make a speech. He fixed his eyes upon his third vest button and informed it in confidence that it was Mr. Huckley who had made him what he was today—which wasn't so very much.

When his turn came, the chemist and coach arose and told the world a great secret about this Phil Fuller, who had now pitched his last game for dear old B. H. S. Phil, he said, owed his success as a pitcher to his having been brought up in a cow barn. Constant milking had developed his forearm muscles to surprising strength, and the knots and knobs on his good left hand had enabled him to get a spin on the ball that produced his deadliest curves.

"I therefore propose," he said, "that Phil's girl friend, Dolly, be elected an honorary member of the team."

This motion was seconded with a will and carried with a whoop, and Dolly became, as far as anyone could learn, the only cow that ever belonged to a ball club.

"Phil has told you," Mr. Huckley went on, "that he got some help from my coaching. If so, he has chosen a rotten way to pay his debt. Instead of going to a high-class and fancy culture factory like Athens, he has decided to enter Sparta Agricultural College. Athens and Sparta are deadly enemies in athletics, and some day Phil may use what I have taught him against my own alma mater. There is no use trying to keep Phil from running after the cows; but this is a sad blow to me. I didn't raise my boy to be a Spartan."

It was the county agricultural agent who had first put Sparta into Phil's head. The boy had naturally assumed that his education would cease with high school, but this Mr. Runkleman came into Dolly's palatial quarters one day and spoke an eloquent piece in favor of his own Sparta.

"A boy who intends to be an expert dairy farmer," he said in part, "ought to learn all there is to know on the subject. You have a natural gift for taking care of cows, but what you don't know about scientific dairying would fill a ten-foot shelf."

"That's so," Phil answered, "but I haven't got much money."

"You don't need much money. Lots of the boys are working their way through. I'll guarantee that you get a job in the college dairy barn. The work will pay your board, teach you the practical side, and you'll meet the nicest cows in the world."

This was a weighty inducement, and one crisp day in late September found Phil knocking at the door of the higher education. He was a youth of five feet five with fiery hair and complexion, with ears that stuck out like red semaphores; a homely, awkward, likable boy, full of hope, inexperience, diffidence and whole raw milk. His only regret was that he could not take Dolly with him to college.

Because of Mr. Runkleman's hearty recommendation, he got his job in the dairy barn, and he took a room in a house near by. His days sped by in a new kind of eternal triangle—boardinghouse, dairy and classroom—and he was happy in all three places.

Every morning at the ghastly hour of four he trudged through windy blackness to the big concrete barn. Now followed several hours of milking, feeding, currying, and stable cleaning in company with half a dozen other cow students, then home to breakfast and to class. In the late afternoon there was a repetition of these chores, followed by dinner, some study, and an early bed. Such was the wild college life of this flaming youth.

Football, the great autumn obsession, meant little to him. Basketball was more fun, but a habitual early riser makes a poor customer of night life. In fact, Phil made up his mind that, for the first year, he would waste no time on athletics.

Sibyl Barnett Samboy, the wife of Kenneth Samboy, director of Sparta athletics, said after Phil had been introduced to her at the freshman reception: "That's the first time I ever shook hands with a Stillson wrench."

Although he honestly intended to keep out of baseball, the first warm afternoon in March brought on an attack of the old spring fever. There was no harm, he thought, in getting out a ball and glove and tossing a few to Spider Coppery behind the barn while waiting for milking time. Before long it was a regular practice among the "cowboys" to beguile their idle moments with playing catch and knocking up flies, and presently there was talk of forming a team to play a game with the students of the horticultural department, otherwise the "greenhouse gang."

An insulting challenge was given and taken, and the game took place on a pleasant Saturday.

This contest was held upon the old ball grounds. The new stadium was built upon a better site, and the former athletic grounds with their little grandstand were given over to the general use of the students. Samboy was a firm believer in athletics for everybody. He loved to stir up little wars between classes, dormitories, fraternities, and departments. Often these little home-brew contests developed and uncovered talent for the college teams.

Along about the fifth inning of this ragged ball game, an uninvited guest appeared among the handful of spectators in the grandstand. Phil was on the mound at the time.

So Mr. Samboy's eyes were gladdened by the sight of a stocky, freckled, red-headed southpaw who burned them over with power, who laughed from head to foot and uttered unfortunate noises.

Samboy talked with him after the game, poked his nose into his past and urged him to try for the college team.

Phil protested that he was too busy with his classes and his cows. It was a long argument, but Samboy won.

"Report to Donnigan on Monday," said the director, "and tell him I suggested that he look you over. Every coach has a free hand with his own team, you know, but if he turns you down let me know and I'll give you a tryout on the freshman team. I'll speak to Professor Wetherby, if you like, and ask him to let you shift hours at the dairy while you're trying your luck on the diamond."

"You don't suppose"—Phil was visibly embarrassed—"there wouldn't be any danger of me losing that job—or anything? I wouldn't do that for all the baseball there is."

"Not a chance, Fuller. We don't give fellows positions here because they are good athletes, but we don't fire 'em either."

H. B. Donnigan—"Hard-boiled Donnigan"—had learned his trade under the great Tim Crowley, of the Eagles. Donnigan's big-league days were over and he was making a living coaching college teams. He used the Crowley method and the Crowley philosophy. All ball players were worms and should be treated as such.

He had spent his boyhood among the tin cans and bottles of a vacant lot in New York's gas-house district, and he never really believed that ball players could be grown in the country.

One trouble with his policy was that it did not work at all. It was rumored that when his contract expired at the end of the season, Samboy would let him go. A sense of his failure did not improve the coach's technique—or his temper. It was to this man-eating tiger that Samboy had cheerfully thrown the red-headed rookie from the cow barn.

"And now who let you in?" was Hard-boiled Donnigan's address of welcome.

"Mr. Samboy said would you please look me over."

The phrase was perhaps an unfortunate one. The coach did exactly that.

"All right. Tell him I've done it, and if you're Lillian Gish, I'm Queen Marie."

"I'm a pitcher—southpaw." Phil's hard-earned grammar fled in this crisis. "I done good in high school."

"Oh, all right, stick around," said the testy coach. "When I get time, I'll see if you've got anything."

He seemed to forget all about Phil—who had not the slightest objection. The boy had a bad case of stage fright, partly from Donnigan's ill-nature, but more from the immensity of the empty stadium. He had almost made up his mind to sneak back to his beloved cows when he realized that he was being addressed.

"Hey, you—carrots—come out to the box and pitch to the batters." Donnigan took his place behind the plate. "Murder this guy," he muttered to Risler, a senior and captain of the team.

Risler murdered, instead, the bright April sunshine in three brutal blows. The old miracle had happened again. The moment Phil took hold of the ball and faced the batter he forgot his fears, he remembered only that throwing a baseball was the greatest fun in the world.

"Hey, wipe that grin off your map," yelled the coach. "What do you think this is, a comic opery?"

Phil controlled his features with an effort while two more batters showed their futility. Donnigan handed his catcher's glove to Swede Olson.

"Gimme that stick," he growled. "You birds belong in a home for the blind!"

There were two serious mistakes that Phil could make in this crisis and he made them both without delay. He struck out Hard-boiled Donnigan and he laughed. Of course he knew better than to ridicule the coach, but there was something irresistible about the way Donnigan lunged for that last slow floater.

"All right, now you've done your stuff, get out!" yelled the offended professional. "And stay out. I can't monkey with a guy who won't take his work seriously. Laugh that off."

A few snickers were thrown after the defeated candidate, but the players knew that Donnigan had committed a manager's unpardonable sin of turning down a promising recruit on a personal grudge—and he knew that they knew.

As for Phil, he left the stadium with genuine relief. The more he saw of Donnigan, the better he liked cows. He had kept his promise to Samboy; now he would just sink out of sight and stick to business.

In reply to an inquiry, Samboy got a letter from Mr. Huckley stating that, in the opinion of an old Athens pitcher, Phil Fuller was the best that Branford High School had ever produced. The director showed this tribute to Donnigan.

"Oh, that's the sorrel top. He hasn't got anything but a giggle."

"Are you sure, Hank? We could use a good southpaw."

"I know, but he ain't the answer. This Athens bird is trying to frame us."

"I'll wish him on the freshmen then."

"Sure—give the kid a chanst, Ken," said Donnigan with affected good will. "He might show something if he ever gets over the idea it's all a big wheeze."

Phil was heartily welcomed into the freshman squad. In the presence of Samboy he performed ably in a practice game. His fast ball, well-controlled curve, and change of pace made the inexperienced batters helpless, and his strange conduct landed him in the public eye with a bang.

The college comic paper, *The Cut-up*, had a fine time over Phil. It discovered that the eccentric left-hander was a cow-barner, and it almost died of laughter at this joke. "Phil Fuller the Milk Pitcher" was the title of the piece. He was one of the wide-open faces from the wide-open spaces, the wit said, and sure winner of the standing broad grin. Also, he proved the truth of the old saying, "Little pitchers have big ears."

But the result of the publicity was that the crowd at the freshman-sophomore game was the largest of the season. Among those present were old President Whitman, Professor Wetherby, and Mr. and Mrs. Kenneth Samboy.

The assembled underclassmen laughed until they ached at the grinning, gesticulating, noisy southpaw with the red-thatched roof. They greeted his queer, awkward windup with a yell invented by the sophomore cheer leader, a long, rhythmic "so—o—o, boss." But when he had won the game handily for the freshmen, the jeers turned to cheers.

Sibyl Samboy looked at her husband.

"And why," she asked, "is this infant phenomenon not on the varsity?"

"Hank can't see him somehow, and if I butt in, it upsets my whole system of government. Personally I'd pitch him in a game or two to season him and then try him on Athens. But it isn't worth a rumpus, Sib. After all, Fuller will be with us a long time yet and Donnigan won't."

"Poor old Hank! I wonder what he's got against the boy."

"It's incompatibility of temperament, I guess. Hank thinks baseball is cosmic, and Phil thinks it's comic."

"And you," said Sibyl, "think you're a wisecracker on *The Cut-up*."

In the next issue of that little weekly there was a marked difference in tone. The frosh cowboy, it said, was showing ability as well as risibility. It was time Donnigan tried him out on the team.

There was something inevitable about the Phil Fuller movement. Donnigan did not want him on the team, Samboy was committed to keep his hands off, and Phil himself had no craving to appear in that big stadium. But the team was limping through a disastrous season and there were signs of disaffection among the players. The crowds dwindled, finances were suffering, and the all-important Athens game, the schedule's climax, was approaching like the day of doom.

Donnigan resisted as long as he could, but, schooled as he was in the professional game, he recognized one power greater than players, managers, or owners—the customer. And when white-haired Doctor

Whitman called him into the president's office and intimated ever so gently that it might be just as well to give the public what it wanted, he gave in.

He did not surrender, but he retreated inch by inch. He gave Phil a uniform and let him practice with the team and learn the signals, then put him in at the end of a game that was already hopelessly lost. On the eve of the Athens contest he announced that he would pitch Hagenlaucher with Graybar and Fuller in reserve.

Any contest with the traditional foe always brought out the largest crowd of the season, but this year there was a novelty in the situation. The freshmen were out in full force prepared to make an organized nuisance of themselves on behalf of their favorite character. When he appeared on the field for practice, they gave him a tremendous ovation.

Just before the game started, Phil realized that somebody was calling to him from the edge of the stand. To his great delight, this proved to be Mr. Huckley, who had traveled all the way from Branford to see the game.

"Phil," he said, "if you get a chance today, I want you to do your darnedest."

"I'd kinda hate to play against Athens after all you did for me."

"I know. That's why I spoke. Forget all that, Phil. If they put you in, pitch as you did last year against Milltown, Three Falls, Oderno, and Jefferson. Good luck!"

"Thank you, Mr. Huckley. I'll meet you right here after it's over. I've got something to tell you."

As he took his seat on the bench his smile faded and he lapsed into gloom. "He's scared stiff," thought Donnigan. "I won't dare to stick him in if Haggy blows."

But Hagenlaucher was not blowing up; he was pitching his best game of the season. The Athens moundsman was doing well, too, and there was promise of a tight pitchers' battle. But in time the game grew looser, the pitchers faltered. Haggy was getting wabbly.

The score stood 6 to 5 in favor of the visitors in the fifth when the umpire made the momentous announcement, "Greenwich batting for Hagenlaucher." At the same moment Graybar and Fuller left for the bull pen to warm up. The next inning would see a new face in the box.

Whose face? That was what all Sparta wanted to know; that was what Samboy wanted to know as he stepped out of the stand and walked up to Donnigan.

"Graybar," said the coach. "Fuller is scared to death. I guess he's got a yellow streak."

Samboy hesitated. The teams were changing sides now and the embattled freshmen were booming in unison, like a bass drum: "Phil! Phil! Phil!"

"All right, you're the doctor, Hank. But I'll go and talk to the boy."

The new pitcher did his best, but he was a broken reed. A base on balls, a single, and a hit batter filled the bags, with nobody out, and the air was full of disaster. Captain Risler stepped to the box as if to steady the wabbly pitcher; Swede Olson, the catcher, joined this conference, which was further enriched by the presence of the lanky first baseman, Keeler.

Now Graybar handed the ball to Risler, who made a sign toward the bench. There was an instant of suspense, and then out of the dugout appeared the gaudy head of Phil Fuller.

An avalanche of sound slid down upon the field. From the freshman bloc came the long, rhythmic yell, "So—o—o, boss." In the general confusion, Hard-boiled Donnigan was scarcely seen emerging from the dugout. He seemed to shrink before the wave of noise, then he disappeared through an opening out of the field, and out of the athletics department of Sparta.

Scarcely anyone in the audience knew that Donnigan had not ordered the change of pitchers, nor had Samboy. It was Risler, backed by Olson, Keeler, and the whole team. It was mutiny, it was rebellion.

But this was not the familiar Phil Fuller who had laughed and danced his way into the hearts of the fans. This was a serious Phil, a gloomy Phil. Life was now real, life was earnest. He took his long, queer windup and he threw the ball high, far too high. Olson made a jump for the ball, missed it, and landed in a heap. Before he could recover the ball, two runs had come over and Athens rocked with laughter.

But so, to the amazement of the universe, did Phil Fuller. It suddenly seemed to the misguided youth that it was the funniest thing in the world that he should have thrown away the ball and let in two runs. The infield laughed in imitation. Philip was himself again.

Now the tension under which the team had been working suddenly relaxed as if a tight band had snapped and brought relief. The nervous, eager, do-or-die spirit suddenly disappeared, leaving the natural instinct of youth to have a good time. With the utmost ease the pitcher and the infield disposed of the next three batters and in their half of the inning they began their climb toward victory.

It was a strange, exciting, hilarious game. Phil had never played in such fast company before or faced such a murderous array of bats. He was in hot water half a dozen times, but he never lost the healing gift of laughter.

And the team played as if baseball came under the head of pleasure.

Samboy said to Risler, who sat beside him on the bench in the eighth:

"Whether we win or lose, this is the answer. We're going to build a new idea and a new style of play around that southpaw. You watch our smoke for the next three years, Rissy."

"Just my luck, Ken. In about fifteen minutes I'm through with college baseball forever."

"Well, don't you ever regret what you did today. I can't officially approve it, but—there goes Phil fanning again."

Samboy now addressed the departing warriors.

"All right, boys—last frame and two to the good. All you have to do is hold 'em."

Now it appeared that Phil had been saving the finest joke of all for the end. The season was over and he could take liberties with his arm. He dug his warts and bumps and calluses into the horsehide and proceeded to retire the side with three straight strike-outs, nine rowdy laughs, two informal dances, and an incredible noise that was a hideous parody on song.

But it was an altered and sobered Phil who found his old coach after the game and received his fervent congratulations.

"Were you worried, Phil?" Mr. Huckley asked.

"Yes, but I was glad they let me play. I had so much fun I forgot my trouble."

"What trouble, Phil?"

"Well, I got a letter from Father this morning and my Dolly is terribly sick. Seems she got hold of an old paint can some place. Cows like to lick paint, you know, and it's deadly poison. They don't think Dolly will live. Maybe I left a can of paint somewhere myself. That's what bothers me."

"Listen, Phil. I was supposed to tell you but you got away too quick. Your father telephoned me this morning. Dolly's out of danger. She's doing fine."

"Oh, boy!" cried Phil and his eyes shone with tears.

Down in the field the Sparta students, led by the band, were circling the stadium in that parade of victory that must follow every triumph over Athens.

"There'll be plenty more ball games," said Phil, "but there'll never be another cow like Dolly."

Questions for discussion

1. From the very first paragraph of the story we learn that this is going to be a character story. That is, your attention was centered on a personality who made things happen. You can see him quite clearly and you feel that you know him really very well. You even know how he feels and why. What does Phil look like? How does his name suit him: both his real name and his nickname? How would you describe his character? How would you describe his personality?
2. How did people react to Phil? How did they treat him? What was it about him that enabled him to take criticism so well?
3. Why did he develop into an outstanding baseball pitcher? In what way was he an unusual one?
4. Did you note the sentence on page 114, "Phil had discovered his life work"? When did he discover it? Why was he sure to be a success at it? Why was he a success at his avocation too?
5. What was your impression of Donnigan? What made him like that? Have you ever known anyone like him?

Vocabulary growth

WORD PARTS. The suffix *-ness* is often added to adjectives to make nouns of them. In the story you met, for example *shy-ness* and *strange-ness*. The suffix *-hood* is also used to make nouns either from adjectives or other nouns. In the story you met *neighbor-hood*. The suffix *-ment* is also used to make nouns from verbs and adjectives.

1. Which suffix, *-ment, -hood,* or *-ness* would you add to each of the following words to make it a noun?

likely	retire	knight
govern	man	great
cleanly	manly	arrange

There are several ways of saying *no* in English. One way is by use of prefixes: *non-, un-, in-* as in these words:

nonresident = not a resident
unlikely   = not likely
incomplete   = not complete

2. Which of the negative prefixes would you add to each of the following words to give it a negative meaning?

competent	decent	dependent
consistent	commissioned	natural
combatant	sense	fortunate

WORDS ARE INTERESTING. When Phil Fuller gave Dolly her *viands*, what did he give her? The word *viands* comes from a Latin word *vivere*, meaning "to live." *Viands* are something that help creatures stay alive; namely, *food*. You will find the same Latin root *viv* in *vivacity*, *viable*, *vivid*. If you do not know these words look them up in the dictionary. While you are about it, look for other words built on this root.

From your ability to get context clues you can figure out the meaning of *hiatus* from the sentence, "It came out one night at supper in the hiatus between the fifth and sixth ears of Golden Bantam." The word *hiatus* comes from a Latin word meaning "gap." Can you think of a good synonym for *hiatus*?

For composition

What is your idea of success? Write a paper on "Success," telling what it means to you, what qualities of personality and character are necessary to achieve it, and how it is achieved. Give an example of someone who has achieved the kind of success you are writing about and tell how he went about attaining it.

Everyone knew that it was
Pecos Tommy who carried . . .

Gold-Mounted Guns

F. R. BUCKLEY

EVENING had fallen on Longhorn City, and already, to the
south, an eager star was twinkling in the velvet sky, when a spare,
hard-faced man slouched down the main street and selected a pony
from the dozen hitched beside Tim Geogehan's general store. The
town, which in the daytime suffered from an excess of eye-searing
light in its open spaces, confined its efforts at artificial lighting to the
one store, the one saloon, and its neighbor, the Temple of Chance;
so it was from a dusky void that the hard-faced man heard himself
called by name.

"Tommy!" a subdued voice accosted him.

The hard-faced man made, it seemed, a very slight movement—a
mere flick of the hand at his low-slung belt; but it was a movement
perfectly appraised by the man in the shadows.

"Wait a minute!" the voice pleaded.

A moment later, his hands upraised, his pony's bridle-reins caught
in the crook of one arm, a young man moved into the zone of light
that shone bravely out through Tim Geogehan's back window.

"Don't shoot," he said, trying to control his nervousness before the
weapon unwaveringly trained upon him. "I'm—a friend."

For perhaps fifteen seconds the newcomer and the hard-faced man
examined each other with the unwinking scrutiny of those who take
chances of life and death. The younger, with that lightning draw
fresh in his mind, noted the sinister droop of a gray moustache over
a hidden mouth, and shivered a little as his gaze met that of a pair
of steel-blue eyes. The man with the gun saw before him a rather
handsome face, marred, even in this moment of submission, by a
certain desperation.

"What do you want?" he asked, tersely.

"Can I put my hands down?" countered the other.

The lean man considered.

"All things bein' equal," he said, "I think I'd rather you'd first tell me how you got round to callin' me Tommy. Been askin' people in the street?"

"No," said the boy. "I only got into town this afternoon, an' I ain't a fool anyway. I seen you ride in this afternoon, and the way folks backed away from you made me wonder who you was. Then I seen them gold-mounted guns of yourn, an' of course I knew. Nobody ever had guns like them but Pecos Tommy. I could ha' shot you while you was gettin' your horse, if I'd been that way inclined."

The lean man bit his moustache.

"Put 'em down. What do you want?"

"I want to join you."

"You want to *what?*"

"Yeah, I know it sounds foolish to you, mebbe," said the young man. "But, listen—your side-kicker's in jail down in Rosewell. I figured I could take his place—anyway, till he got out. I know I ain't got any record, but I can ride, an' I can shoot the pips out of a ten-spot at ten paces, an'—I got a little job to bring into the firm, to start with."

The lean man's gaze narrowed.

"Have, eh?" he asked, softly.

"It ain't anythin' like you go in for as a rule," said the boy, apologetically, "but it's a roll of cash an'—I guess it'll show you I'm straight. I only got on to it this afternoon. Kind of providential I should meet you right now."

The lean man chewed his moustache. His eyes did not shift.

"Yeah," he said, slowly. "What you quittin' punchin' for?"

"Sick of it."

"Figurin' robbin' trains is easier money?"

"No," said the young man, "I ain't. But I like a little spice in life. They ain't none in punchin'."

"Got a girl?" asked the lean man.

The boy shook his head. The hard-faced man nodded reflectively.

"Well, what's the job?" he asked.

The light from Geogehan's window was cut off by the body of a man who, cupping his hands about his eyes, stared out into the night, as if to locate the buzz of voices at the back of the store.

"If you're goin' to take me on," said the young man, "I can tell you while we're ridin' toward it. If you ain't—why, there's no need to go no further."

The elder slipped back into its holster the gold-mounted gun he had drawn, glanced once at the obscured window and again, piercingly, at the boy whose face now showed white in the light of the rising moon. Then he turned his pony and mounted.

"Come on," he commanded.

Five minutes later the two had passed the limits of the town, heading for the low range of hills which encircled it to the south—and Will Arblaster had given the details of his job to the unemotional man at his side.

"How do you know the old guy's got the money?" came a level question.

"I saw him come out of the bank this afternoon, grinnin' all over his face an' stuffin' it into his pants-pocket," said the boy. "An' when he was gone, I kind of inquired who he was. His name's Sanderson, an' he lives in this yer cabin right ahead a mile. Looked kind of a soft old geezer—kind that'd give up without any trouble. Must ha' been quite some cash there, judgin' by the size of the roll. But I guess when *you* ask him for it, he won't mind lettin' it go."

"I ain't goin' to ask him," said the lean man. "This is your job."

The boy hesitated.

"Well, if I do it right," he asked, with a trace of tremor in his voice, "will you take me along with you sure?"

"Yeah—I'll take you along."

The two ponies rounded a shoulder of the hill: before the riders there loomed, in the moonlight, the dark shape of a cabin, its windows unlighted. The lean man chuckled.

"He's out."

Will Arblaster swung off his horse.

"Maybe," he said, "but likely the money ain't. He started off home, an' if he's had to go out again, likely he's hid the money some place. Folks know *you're* about. I'm goin' to see."

Stealthily he crept toward the house. The moon went behind a cloud-bank, and the darkness swallowed him. The lean man, sitting his horse, motionless, heard the rap of knuckles on the door—then a pause, and the rattle of the latch. A moment later came the heavy thud of a shoulder against wood—a cracking sound, and a crash as the door went down. The lean man's lips tightened. From within the cabin came the noise of one stumbling over furniture, then the fitful fire of a match illumined the windows. In the quiet, out there in the night, the man on the horse, twenty yards away, could hear the clumping of the other's boots on the rough board floor, and every rustle of the papers that he fumbled in his search. Another match scratched and sputtered, and then, with a hoarse cry of triumph, was flung down. Running feet padded across the short grass and Will Arblaster drew up, panting.

"Got it!" he gasped. "The old fool! Put it in a tea-canister right on the mantelshelf. Enough to choke a horse! Feel it!"

The lean man, unemotional as ever, reached down and took the roll of money.

"Got another match?" he asked.

Willie struck one, and, panting, watched while companion, moistening a thumb, ruffled through the bills.

"Fifty tens," said the lean man. "Five hundred dollars. Guess I'll carry it."

His cold blue eyes turned downward, and focused again with piercing attention on the younger man's upturned face. The bills were stowed in a pocket of the belt right next to one of those gold-mounted guns which, earlier in the evening, had covered Willie Arblaster's heart. For a moment, the lean man's hand seemed to hesitate over its butt; then, as Willie smiled and nodded, it moved away. The match burned out.

"Let's get out of here," the younger urged; whereupon the hand which had hovered over the gun-butt grasped Will Arblaster's shoulder.

"No, not yet," he said quietly, "not just yet. Get on your hawss, an' set still awhile."

The young man mounted. "What's the idea?"

"Why!" said the level voice at his right. "This is a kind of novelty to me. Robbin' trains, you ain't got any chance to see results, like: this here's different. Figure this old guy'll be back pretty soon. I'd like to see what he does when he finds his wad's gone. Ought to be amusin'!"

Arblaster chuckled uncertainly.

"Ain't he liable to—"

"He can't see us," said the lean man with a certain new cheerfulness in his tone. "An' besides, he'll think we'd naturally be miles away; an' besides that, we're mounted, all ready."

"What's that?" whispered the young man, laying a hand on his companion's arm.

The other listened.

"Probably him," he said. "Now stay still."

There were two riders—by their voices, a man and a girl: they were laughing as they approached the rear of the house, where, roughly made of old boards, stood Pa Sanderson's substitute for a stable. They put up the horses; then their words came clearer to the ears of the listeners, as they turned the corner of the building, walking toward the front door.

"I feel mean about it, anyhow," said the girl's voice. "You going on living here, Daddy, while—"

"Tut-tut-tut!" said the old man. "What's five hundred to me? I ain't never had that much in a lump, an' shouldn't know what to do with it if I had. 'Sides, your Aunt Elviry didn't give it you for nothin'. 'If she wants to go to college,' says she, 'let her prove it by workin'. I'll pay half, but she's got to pay t'other half.' Well, you worked, an' —Where on earth did I put that key?"

There was a silence, broken by the grunts of the old man as he contorted himself in the search of his pockets: and then the girl spoke: the tone of her voice was the more terrible for the restraint she was putting on it.

"Daddy—the—the—did you leave the money in the house?"

"Yes. What is it?" cried the old man.

"Daddy—the door's broken down, and—"

There was a hoarse cry: boot-heels stumbled across the boards, and again a match flared. Its pale light showed a girl standing in the doorway of the cabin, her hands clasped on her bosom—while beyond the wreckage of the door a bent figure with silver hair tottered away from the mantelshelf. In one hand Pa Sanderson held the flickering match, in the other a tin box.

"Gone!" he cried in his cracked voice. "Gone!"

Willie Arblaster drew a breath through his teeth and moved uneasily in his saddle. Instantly a lean, strong hand, with a grip like steel, fell on his wrist and grasped it. The man behind the hand chuckled.

"Listen!" he said.

"Daddy—Daddy—don't take on so—please don't," came the girl's voice, itself trembling with repressed tears. There was a scrape of chair-legs on the floor as she forced the old man into his seat by the fireplace. He hunched there, his face in his hands, while she struck a match and laid the flame to the wick of the lamp on the table. As it burned up she went back to her father, knelt by him, and threw her arms about his neck.

"Now, now, now!" she pleaded. "Now, Daddy, it's all right. Don't take on so. It's all right."

But he would not be comforted.

"I can't replace it!" cried Pa Sanderson, dropping trembling hands from his face. "It's gone! Two years you've been away from me; two years you've slaved in a store; and now I've—"

"Hush, hush!" the girl begged. "Now, Daddy—it's all right. I can go on working, and—"

With a convulsive effort, the old man got to his feet. "Two years more slavery, while some skunk drinks your money, gambles it— throws it away!" he cried. "Curse him! Whoever it is, curse him! Where's God's justice? What's a man goin' to believe when years of scrapin' like your aunt done, an' years of slavin' like yours in Laredo there, an' all our happiness today can be wiped out by a thief in a minute?"

The girl put her little hand over her father's mouth.

"Don't, Daddy," she choked. "It only makes it worse. Come and lie down on your bed, and I'll make you some coffee. Don't cry, Daddy darling. Please."

Gently, like a mother with a little child, she led the heartbroken old man out of the watchers' line of vision, out of the circle of lamplight. More faintly, but still with heartrending distinctness, the listeners could hear the sounds of weeping.

The lean man sniffed, chuckled, and pulled his bridle.

"Some circus!" he said appreciatively. "C'mon, boy."

His horse moved a few paces, but Will Arblaster's did not. The lean man turned in his saddle.

"Ain't you comin'?" he asked.

For ten seconds, perhaps, the boy made no answer. Then he urged his pony forward until it stood side by side with his companion's.

"No," he said. "An'—an' I ain't goin' to take that money, neither."

"Huh?"

The voice was slow and meditative.

"Don't know as ever I figured what this game meant," he said. "Always seemed to me that all the hardships was on the stick-up man's side—gettin' shot at an' chased and so on. Kind of fun, at that. Never thought 'bout—old men cryin'.'"

"That ain't my fault," said the lean man.

"No," said Will Arblaster, still very slowly. "But I'm goin' to take that money back. You didn't have no trouble gettin' it, so you don't lose nothin'.'"

"Suppose I say I won't let go of it?" suggested the lean man with a sneer.

"Then," snarled Arblaster, "I'll blow your damned head off an' take it! Don't you move, you! I've got you covered. I'll take the money out myself."

His revolver muzzle under his companion's nose, he snapped open the pocket of the belt and extracted the roll of bills. Then, regardless of a possible shot in the back, he swung off his horse and shambled, with the mincing gait of the born horseman, into the lighted doorway of the cabin. The lean man, unemotional as ever, sat perfectly still, looking alternately at the cloud-dappled sky and at the cabin, from which now came a murmur of voices harmonizing with a strange effect of joy, to the half-heard bass of the night-wind.

It was a full ten minutes before Will Arblaster reappeared in the doorway alone, and made, while silhouetted against the light, a quick movement of his hand across his eyes, then stumbled forward through the darkness toward his horse. Still the lean man did not move.

"I'm sorry," said the boy as he mounted. "But—"

"I ain't," said the lean man quietly. "What do you think I made you stay an' watch for, you young fool?"

The boy made no reply. Suddenly the hair prickled on the back of his neck and his jaw fell.

"Say," he demanded hoarsely at last. "Ain't you Pecos Tommy?"

The lean man's answer was a short laugh.

"But you got his guns, an' the people in Longhorn all kind of fell back!" the boy cried. "If you ain't him, who are you?"

The moon had drifted from behind a cloud and flung a ray of light across the face of the lean man as he turned it, narrow-eyed, toward Arblaster. The pallid light picked out with terrible distinctness the grim lines of that face—emphasized the cluster of sun-wrinkles about the corners of the piercing eyes and marked as if with underscoring black lines the long sweep of the fighting jaw.

"Why," said the lean man dryly, "I'm the sheriff that killed him yesterday. Let's be ridin' back."

Questions for discussion

1. What reason does Willie give for wanting to join the outlaw, Pecos Tommy?
2. What proposal did Willie make to the man he thinks is Tommy, and just how much thought had he given to the consequences of such an act? What does this tell you about Willie?
3. Why does the carrier of the gold-mounted guns go along with the suggestion which Willie makes? He said that he wanted to wait to see how those who were robbed took it. What was his real reason for urging that he and Willie wait for the old man to return?
4. When Willie saw the effects of his criminal act, he experienced a sudden realization or understanding. How does he express what he feels and thinks at that moment?
5. What does the carrier of the gold-mounted guns call Willie at the end of the story? Do you agree with him? Do you think Willie agreed with him?
6. Now that you know who the carrier of the gold-mounted guns really is, do you remember any clues that should have alerted you?
7. What do you think the author is trying to show about people who do the kind of thing Willie did?

Vocabulary growth

CONTEXT. Turn back to page 17 and read again the study of context clues. Then try the following exercises.

1. Using the whole story as context, explain the phrase *gold-mounted*. What are gold-mounted guns?
2. The phrase *dusky void* appears at the end of the first paragraph. Using the entire paragraph as context, figure out what the phrase means.
3. Figure out the meaning of the italicized words in the following sentences:
   a) "The hard-faced man made, it seemed, a very slight movement— a mere flick of the hand at his low-slung belt; but it was a movement perfectly *appraised* by the man in the shadows."

b) "For perhaps fifteen seconds the newcomer and the hard-faced man examined each other with the *unwinking scrutiny* of those who take chances of life and death."

For composition

1. How do you think this experience seemed to Will? Imagine that you are Will, thinking it all over later. How did you happen to make the mistake? How did you feel when you found the money? When you discovered what the money meant to the old man? Write a brief account of the affair from Will's point of view. You might begin, "I couldn't see well in the dark, but I could see the guns and they were Pecos Tommy's guns all right. I must admit that I felt proud when he let me join up with him and when he agreed to go out on the job I had staked out . . ."
2. Have you ever made a mistake about someone's identity? The results can sometimes be very amusing *or* very embarrassing. Write a brief account of such an experience. If you are imaginative, perhaps you can work out a story of what might have happened if . . .

A cattle rustler talks and talks
at his own . . .

Necktie Party

HENRY   GREGOR   FELSEN

DOWN here in Texas we've got a book that is supposed to show
every world's record held by Texas, only it don't. There is one Texas
record that ain't in the book and is unknown about even to Texas.
As the last living survivor of the posse that helped set that record, I
feel it's my duty to claim it for Texas—even if Texas won't want it.

The record I claim is for the longest informal hanging of a cattle
rustler. It was set on a August night in 1886 near Spanish Fort,
Texas, when we strung up the notorious rustler Shawnee Sam.

The funny part of it is, we didn't know until later it was him. At
the time we thought he was just a rustler who needed hanging. He
had a fast horse and a head start, and we never would have caught
him except that his horse fell and throwed him.

There didn't seem to be anything special about the feller at the
time. He dusted himself off and looked around at us and nodded,
and said he sure was glad to see us, and it certainly was funny what
had happened to him. What had happened, he said, was that he had
been riding at night to escape the heat of the day, and he'd fallen
asleep in the saddle until our shooting had woke him up.

To his great surprise, he said, he discovered that his horse had
fallen in behind a herd of stray cattle, and was following them at a
dead run toward the Oklahoma border. Then his horse stepped in a
gopher hole and throwed him, and the fall had somehow pushed his
bandanna up over his face.

When the stranger had said his piece, the sheriff said, "All right,
boys. The trial is over."

A couple of us rode to a nearby cottonwood tree and throwed a
rope over a limb. We got the stranger mounted, tied his hands
behind his back, and positioned him under the limb where the noose

136

was. The sheriff slipped the noose over the feller's head. Then he said to me, "Hank, you stand by. When I lift my hat, you lay a quirt to his horse."

"Sheriff," the stranger said in a mild voice, "I think you're forgetting some of my rights and privileges in this hanging. I'd hate for it to get around how slipshod the hangings are in East Texas."

"If you're so stuck on getting hung West Texas style," the sheriff said, "why didn't you stay to home and rustle West Texas cattle?"

"To tell you the truth, Sheriff," the stranger said, "there ain't better stealing beef in the whole world than in East Texas. But we ain't arguing cattle, we're arguing hangings, and when we have a hanging in West Texas, we extend the condemned man the common courtesies of the occasion."

Well, the sheriff just sat there for a minute scratching his chin and thinking. A quick hanging would have been like admitting that East Texas was satisfied with hangings that didn't come up to West Texas standards. On the other hand, it wouldn't look good if it got out that a West Texas outlaw had to instruct an East Texas sheriff on how to hang.

"Stranger," the sheriff said, "you made a kind remark about our East Texas cattle. I guess we can return the kindness. We'll be happy to hang you West Texas style." He thought a moment. "Who might we be having the pleasure to hang here?" he said grandly.

"The name is Tex," the stranger said. "Tex Tyler."

"Tex Tyler," the sheriff said in a loud official voice, "do you have any last words to say before you swing?"

The outlaw bowed his head. "I would like at this time," he said in a soft voice, "to say a few words about Texas." He cleared his throat, and all of us in the posse uncovered.

"Friends and captors," the outlaw said, lifting his face to the sky, "let us consider together how Texas was born. Two billion years ago a wandering star passed too near the sun and tore off a giant chunk of flaming gas. Once it was off by itself in the sky, the gas cooled and got solid, and that bright fragment of the sun became Texas. . . ."

The stranger spoke on, and we sat on our horses and listened. It got late and cold, but the man was talking about Texas, and we listened.

He told how Texas got all covered over with water a thousand feet deep, and how there was fish swimming over Texas that was a hundred times bigger than the biggest whale. And he told how the water drained off Texas to make the oceans that we have now. He went on to tell how grass began to grow in Texas, and animals to appear—critters with tails as long as trees. If he hadn't been talking about Texas, we wouldn't have believed a word he said.

He talked about them things all night, and the sun was coming up before he took a deep breath and was quiet for a minute. The sheriff came awake with a start, but before he could order the hanging, the stranger said: "So much for the birth of Texas. I would now like to say a few words about Texas history." And he started in with the story of mankind in Texas, beginning about fifteen minutes this side of the ape.

Along about seven o'clock in the morning the horses was getting restless, and it was pretty hard for us to think of Texas instead of coffee.

"Tex," the sheriff said, "the boys and myself appreciate your feelings about Texas, but we've got business elsewhere. I know you don't want your hanging to stand in the way of Texas progress."

"Sheriff," Tex answered, "if this was an ordinary hanging, I'd be glad to oblige your request to speed things up. But this is a momentous occasion. How long have I been talking?"

"Nearly six hours, Tex," the sheriff told him.

The prisoner sighed. "Well, Sheriff, I'll never make it. I'm already getting hoarse."

"You'll never make what?" the sheriff asked.

"That was my little secret," Tex said. "I happen to know that the world's record for long hangings is held by Arizona. It was set about eight years ago. The feller talked for nine hours." Tex shook his head in a sad, tired way. "I ain't going to make it. I don't mind for myself so much, but I hate to see Texas in second place. Just tell the world I done my best. I'm ready, Sheriff."

He was, but we wasn't. The sheriff called us all aside. "It ain't that we're after any glory for ourselves," he said, "but we've got to think about Texas. I think our duty is clear."

Naturally we agreed with the sheriff, and we went back to the prisoner. "Tex," the sheriff said, "me and the boys has decided to help you try for that record. It's only three more hours. You've gotta try!"

And the stranger did. He talked for another hour, but we could tell his voice was getting weaker and weaker. Another half hour and he was barely able to whisper. And in two hours, an hour shy of the record, his voice was quite gone.

"There must be some kind of a noise he can make," Ted Brock said, and then he whispered something into the prisoner's ear. The prisoner straightened up with a look of new confidence, and two seconds later he was whistling "Yellow Rose of Texas." We couldn't help but cheer.

He whistled for twenty minutes, and we began to hope. But at thirty minutes his whistle sounded thin, and at forty minutes we had to stand real close to hear.

At fifty minutes two of us was holding him up in the saddle. At fifty-nine minutes he fell back against me, but I put my ear to his lips and I could still hear that Texas song.

Then a gun went off. The sheriff stood before us with his watch in one hand and his pistol in the other. "Nine hours," he said. "We've tied the Arizona record!"

At those words the rustler pulled himself up straight. He took a big breath and found the strength to *sing* the Texas song and break the record!

Well, you never heard such whooping and hollering in your life. We took the rustler down from his horse and gave him water and shook his hand. It was Ted Brock who brung us back to reality.

"Now that we've got the record," Ted said, "we can finish the hanging and go home."

"Finish the hanging!" one of the boys shouted. "After what this feller done for Texas!"

"We have to," said Ted. "Otherwise it won't be no record. You can't claim a record for the longest hanging unless you hang somebody, can you?"

That sobered us up in a hurry. It was a problem, all right, and it took the sheriff to solve it.

"Men," the sheriff said, "we have to hang this man. But no court of law has passed sentence that he be hung by the neck until dead. This is an informal hanging, and as sheriff, I order that this man be hung until we *think* he's dead."

So we dropped the noose down under the rustler's arms. Then we eased his horse forward until the rustler was hanging from the tree.

"All right, boys," the sheriff called. "I think this man has been hung until dead. Cut him down."

We helped the rustler down and let him go, and Texas held the record.

We rode back to town at top speed and trooped into the saloon to celebrate—all except the sheriff, who had to ride over to the jail first and make his report.

There was the biggest noise and jollity you ever heard in that saloon, until the sheriff come back. He laid a paper on the bar. "Look at this," he said in a shaking voice. "It just came to me by mail."

I looked with the others and saw a WANTED poster with a picture of Tex Tyler, our recent prisoner, on it. But according to this poster it wasn't Tex Tyler at all. It was Shawnee Sam!

"Men," the sheriff said when we had quieted down, "we can't report this record. We can't ever mention it to anybody. What if the world found out that a Texas posse sat around with its hat off while the world's record for talking Texas at a hanging was set by a Oklahoma boy?"

The bitter part of it was that Shawnee Sam was probably the only man in the history of Texas who deserved hanging more *after* he was hung than before.

Questions for discussion

1. To enjoy this story you "play along," and pretend that you really believe this "yarn" but you do realize from the very beginning that you are not to take any of it seriously. You get the feeling that it is being told to you by some "old timer" who is having a good time "pulling your leg," or "stringing you along." What is it about this story that gives it this "yarn" flavor?

2. The "tall tale," was very popular in America during frontier days. Spinning these yarns was a form of entertainment created by a people who had to provide their own diversion. The "Wild West" was an especially good setting for such tales since it wasn't much of a trick to stretch a situation which was somewhat "wild" into one which was really "wild." Did you expect this story to end as it did? Was it an effective ending?

3. There is another story of this type in this book, "The Death of Red Peril," which has its setting on the Erie Canal. Almost every region of America has its tall tales. Does your region have any?

Vocabulary growth

CONTEXT. From the context of the story as a whole, can you figure out the meaning of the words *posse* and *rustler?*

The word *posse* comes from a Latin word meaning "to be able." Long ago in England the word came to mean "able-bodied citizens over the age of 15, except for clergymen." Just what is a *posse* in America?

The word *rustler* once meant "one who bustles about with a great expenditure of energy." As used in this story and in the West of frontier days, it had a special meaning. Just what is a rustler?

Okonkwo and Ekwefi are
concerned about their daughter . . .

Ezinma

CHINUA ACHEBE

OKONKWO stretched himself and scratched his thigh where a
mosquito had bitten him as he slept. Another one was wailing near
his right ear. He slapped the ear and hoped he had killed it. Why
do they always go for one's ears? When he was a child his mother
had told him a story about it. But it was as silly as all women's
stories. Mosquito, she had said, had asked Ear to marry him, whereupon Ear fell on the floor in uncontrollable laughter. "How much
longer do you think you will live?" she asked. "You are already a
skeleton." Mosquito went away humiliated, and any time he
passed her way he told Ear that he was still alive.

Okonkwo turned on his side and went back to sleep. He was
roused in the morning by someone banging on his door.

"Who is that?" he growled. He knew it must be Ekwefi. Of his
three wives Ekwefi was the only one would would have the audacity
to bang on his door.

"Ezinma is dying," came her voice, and all the tragedy and
sorrow of her life were packed in those words.

Okonkwo sprang from his bed, pushed back the bolt on his
door and ran into Ekwefi's hut.

Ezinma lay shivering on a mat beside a huge fire that her
mother had kept burning all night.

"It is *iba*[1]," said Okonkwo as he took his machete and went
into the bush to collect the leaves and grasses and barks of trees
that went into making the medicine for *iba*.

[1] *iba*: fever.

Ekwefi knelt beside the sick child, occasionally feeling with her palm the wet, burning forehead.

Ezinma was an only child and the center of her mother's world. Very often it was Ezinma who decided what food her mother should prepare. Ekwefi even gave her such delicacies as eggs, which children were rarely allowed to eat because such food tempted them to steal. One day as Ezinma was eating an egg Okonkwo had come in unexpectedly from his hut. He was greatly shocked and swore to beat Ekwefi if she dared to give the child eggs again. But it was impossible to refuse Ezinma anything. After her father's rebuke she developed an even keener appetite for eggs. And she enjoyed above all the secrecy in which she now ate them. Her mother always took her into their bedroom and shut the door.

Ezinma did not call her mother *Nne* like all children. She called her by her name, Ekwefi, as her father and other grown-up people did. The relationship between them was not only that of mother and child. There was something in it like the companionship of equals, which was strengthened by such little conspiracies as eating eggs in the bedroom.

Ekwefi had suffered a good deal in her life. She had borne ten children and nine of them had died in infancy, usually before the age of three. As she buried one child after another her sorrow gave way to despair and then to grim resignation. The birth of her children, which should be a woman's crowning glory, became for Ekwefi mere physical agony devoid of promise. The naming ceremony after seven market weeks became an empty ritual. Her deepening despair found expression in the names she gave her children. One of them was a pathetic cry, Onwumbiko—"Death, I implore you." But Death took no notice; Onwumbiko died in his fifteenth month. The next child was a girl, Ozoemena—"May it not happen again." She died in her eleventh month, and two others after her. Ekwefi then became defiant and called her next child Onwuma—"Death may please himself." And he did.

After the death of Ekwefi's second child, Okonkwo had gone to a medicine man, who was also a diviner of the Afa Oracle, to inquire what was amiss. This man told him that the child was an *ogbanje*[2], one of those wicked children who, when they died, entered their mothers' wombs to be born again.

By the time Onwumbiko died Ekwefi had become a very bitter woman. Her husband's first wife had already had three sons, all strong and healthy. When she had borne her third son in succession, Okonkwo had gathered a goat for her, as was the custom. Ekwefi had nothing but good wishes for her. But she had grown so bitter about her own *chi*[3] that she could not rejoice with others over their good fortune. And so, on the day that Nwoye's mother celebrated the birth of her three sons with feasting and music, Ekwefi was the only person in the happy company who went about with a cloud on her brow. Her husband's wife took this for malevolence, as husbands' wives were wont to. How could she know that Ekwefi's bitterness did not flow outwards to others but inwards into her own soul; that she did not blame others for their good fortune but her own evil *chi* who denied her any?

At last Ezinma was born, and although ailing she seemed determined to live. At first Ekwefi accepted her, as she had accepted others—with listless resignation. But when she lived on to her fourth, fifth and sixth years, love returned once more to her mother, and, with love, anxiety. She determined to nurse her child to health, and she put all her being into it. She was rewarded by occasional spells of health during which Ezinma bubbled with energy like fresh palm-wine. At such times she seemed beyond danger. But all of a sudden she would go down again. Everybody knew she was an *ogbanje*. These sudden bouts of sickness and health were typical of her kind. But she had lived so long that perhaps she had decided to stay. Some of them did become tired of their evil rounds of birth and death, or took pity on their mothers, and stayed. Ekwefi believed deep inside her that Ezinma had come to stay. She believed because it was that faith alone that gave her own life any kind of meaning. And this faith had been strengthened when a year or so ago a medicine man had dug up Ezinma's

---

[2] *ogbanje*: a changeling; a child who repeatedly dies and returns to its mother to be reborn. It is almost impossible to bring up an *ogbanje* child without it dying, unless its *iyi-uwa* is destroyed.

[3] *chi*: personal god.

iyi-uwa[4]. Everyone knew then that she would live because her bond with the world of *ogbanje* had been broken. Ekwefi was reassured. But such was her anxiety for her daughter that she could not rid herself completely of her fear. And although she believed that the *iyi-uwa* which had been dug up was genuine, she could not ignore the fact that some really evil children sometimes misled people into digging up a specious one.

But Ezinma's *iyi-uwa* had looked real enough. It was a smooth pebble wrapped in a dirty rag. The man who dug it up was the same Okagbue who was famous in all the clan for his knowledge in these matters. Ezinma had not wanted to cooperate with him at first. But that was only to be expected. No *ogbanje* would yield her secrets easily, and most of them never did because they died too young—before they could be asked questions.

"Where did you bury your *iyi-uwa*?" Okagbue had asked Ezinma. She was nine then and was just recovering from a serious illness.

"What is *iyi-uwa*?" she asked in return.

"You know what it is. You buried it in the ground somewhere so that you can die and return again to torment your mother."

Ezinma looked at her mother, whose eyes, sad and pleading, were fixed on her.

"Answer the question at once," roared Okonkwo, who stood beside her. All the family were there and some of the neighbors too.

"Leave her to me," the medicine man told Okonkwo in a cool, confident voice. He turned again to Ezinma. "Where did you bury your *iyi-uwa*?"

"Where they bury children," she replied, and the quiet spectators murmured to themselves.

"Come along then and show me the spot," said the medicine man.

The crowd set out with Ezinma leading the way and Okagbue following closely behind her. Okonkwo came next and Ekwefi

[4] *iyi-uwa*: a special kind of stone which forms the link between an *ogbanje* and the spirit world. Only if the *iyi-uwa* were discovered and destroyed could the child live.

followed him. When she came to the main road, Ezinma turned left as if she was going to the stream.

"But you said it was where they bury children?" asked the medicine man.

"No," said Ezinma, whose feeling of importance was manifest in her sprightly walk. She sometimes broke into a run and stopped again suddenly. The crowd followed her silently. Women and children returning from the stream with pots of water on their heads wondered what was happening until they saw Okagbue and guessed that it must be something to do with *ogbanje*. And they all knew Ekwefi and her daughter very well.

When she got to the big udala tree Ezinma turned left into the bush, and the crowd followed her. Because of her size she made her way through trees and creepers more quickly than her followers. The bush was alive with the tread of feet on dry leaves and sticks and the moving aside of tree branches. Ezinma went deeper and deeper and the crowd went with her. Then she suddenly turned round and began to walk back to the road. Everybody stood to let her pass and then filed after her.

"If you bring us all this way for nothing I shall beat sense into you," Okonkwo threatened.

"I have told you to let her alone. I know how to deal with them," said Okagbue.

Ezinma led the way back to the road, looked left and right and turned right. And so they arrived home again.

"Where did you bury your *iyi-uwa*?" asked Okagbue when Ezinma finally stopped outside her father's *obi*[5]. Okagbue's voice was unchanged. It was quiet and confident.

"It is near that orange tree," Ezinma said.

"And why did you not say so, you wicked daughter of Akalogoli?" Okonkwo swore furiously. The medicine man ignored him.

"Come and show me the exact spot," he said quietly to Ezinma.

"It is here," she said when they got to the tree.

"Point at the spot with your finger," said Okagbue.

"It is here," said Ezinma touching the ground with her finger. Okonkwo stood by, rumbling like thunder in the rainy season.

[5] *obi*: hut.

"Bring me a hoe," said Okagbue.

When Ekwefi brought the hoe, he had already put aside his goatskin bag and his big cloth and was in his underwear, a long and thin strip of cloth wound round the waist like a belt and then passed between the legs to be fastened to the belt behind. He immediately set to work digging a pit where Ezinma had indicated. The neighbors sat around watching the pit becoming deeper and deeper. The dark top soil soon gave way to the bright red earth with which women scrubbed the floors and walls of huts. Okagbue worked tirelessly and in silence, his back shining with perspiration. Okonkwo stood by the pit. He asked Okagbue to come up and rest while he took a hand. But Okagbue said he was not tired yet.

Ekwefi went into her hut to cook yams. Her husband had brought out more yams than usual because the medicine man had to be fed. Ezinma went with her and helped in preparing the vegetables.

"There is too much green vegetable," she said.

"Don't you see the pot is full of yams?" Ekwefi asked. "And you know how leaves become smaller after cooking."

"Yes," said Ezinma, "that was why the snake-lizard killed his mother."

"Very true," said Ekwefi.

"He gave his mother seven baskets of vegetables to cook and in the end there were only three. And so he killed her," said Ezinma.

"That is not the end of the story."

"Oho," said Ezinma. "I remember now. He brought another seven baskets and cooked them himself. And there were again only three. So he killed himself too."

Outside the *obi* Okagbue and Okonkwo were digging the pit to find where Ezinma had buried her *iyi-uwa*. Neighbors sat around, watching. The pit was now so deep that they no longer saw the digger. They only saw the red earth he threw up mounting higher and higher. Okonkwo's son, Nwoye, stood near the edge of the pit because he wanted to take in all that happened.

Okagbue had again taken over the digging from Okonkwo. He worked, as usual, in silence. The neighbors and Okonkwo's wives were now talking. The children had lost interest and were playing.

Suddenly Okagbue sprang to the surface with the agility of a leopard.

"It is very near now," he said. "I have felt it."

There was immediate excitement and those who were sitting jumped to their feet.

"Call your wife and child," he said to Okonkwo. But Ekwefi and Ezinma had heard the noise and run out to see what it was.

Okagbue went back into the pit, which was now surrounded by spectators. After a few more hoe-fuls of earth he struck the *iyi-uwa*. He raised it carefully with the hoe and threw it to the surface. Some women ran away in fear when it was thrown. But they soon returned and everyone was gazing at the rag from a reasonable distance. Okagbue emerged and without saying a word or even looking at the spectators he went to his goatskin bag, took out two leaves and began to chew them. When he had swallowed them, he took up the rag with left hand and began to untie it. And then the smooth, shiny pebble fell out. He picked it up.

"Is this yours?" he asked Ezinma.

"Yes," she replied. All the women shouted with joy because Ekwefi's troubles were at last ended.

All this had happened more than a year ago and Ezinma had not been ill since. And then suddenly she had begun to shiver in the night. Ekwefi brought her to the fireplace, spread her mat on the floor and built a fire. But she had got worse and worse. As she knelt by her, feeling with her palm the wet, burning forehead, she prayed a thousand times. Although her husband's wives were saying that it was nothing more than *iba*, she did not hear them.

Okonkwo returned from the bush carrying on his left shoulder a large bundle of grasses and leaves, roots and barks of medicinal trees and shrubs. He went into Ekwefi's hut, put down his load and sat down.

"Get me a pot," he said, "and leave the child alone."

Ekwefi went to bring the pot and Okonkwo selected the best from his bundle, in their due proportions, and cut them up. He put them in the pot and Ekwefi poured in some water.

"Is that enough?" she asked when she had poured in about half of the water in the bowl.

"A little more . . . I said *a little*. Are you deaf?" Okonkwo roared at her.

She set the pot on the fire and Okonkwo took up his machete to return to his *obi*.

"You must watch the pot carefully," he said as he went, "and don't allow it to boil over. If it does its power will be gone." He went away to his hut and Ekwefi began to tend the medicine pot almost as if it was itself a sick child. Her eyes went constantly from Ezinma to the boiling pot and back to Ezinma.

Okonkwo returned when he felt the medicine had cooked long enough. He looked it over and said it was done.

"Bring me a low stool for Ezinma," he said, "and a thick mat."

He took down the pot from the fire and placed it in front of the stool. He then roused Ezinma and placed her on the stool, astride the steaming pot. The thick mat was thrown over both. Ezinma struggled to escape from the choking and overpowering steam, but she was held down. She started to cry.

When the mat was at last removed she was drenched in perspiration. Ekwefi mopped her with a piece of cloth and she lay down on a dry mat and was soon asleep.

*   *   *

The night was impenetrably dark. The moon had been rising later and later every night until now it was seen only at dawn. And whenever the moon forsook evening and rose at cock-crow the nights were as black as charcoal.

Ezinma and her mother sat on a mat on the floor after their supper of yam foo-foo and bitter-leaf soup. A palm-oil lamp gave out yellowish light. Without it, it would have been impossible to eat; one could not have known where one's mouth was in the darkness of that night. There was an oil lamp in all the four huts on Okonkwo's compound, and each hut seen from the others looked like a soft eye of yellow half-light set in the solid massiveness of night.

The world was silent except for the shrill cry of insects, which was part of the night, and the sound of wooden mortar and pestle as Nwayieke pounded her foo-foo. Nwayieke lived four compounds away, and she was notorious for her late cooking. Every woman in the neighborhood knew the sound of Nwayieke's mortar and pestle. It was also part of the night.

Okonkwo had eaten from his wives' dishes and was now reclining with his back against the wall. He searched his bag and brought out his snuff-bottle. He turned it on to his left palm, but nothing came out. He hit the bottle against his knee to shake up the tobacco. That was always the trouble with Okeke's snuff. It very quickly went damp, and there was too much saltpeter in it. Okonkwo had not bought snuff from him for a long time. Idigo was the man who knew how to grind good snuff. But he had recently fallen ill.

Low voices, broken now and again by singing, reached Okonkwo from his wives' huts as each woman and her children told folk stories. Ekwefi and her daughter, Ezinma, sat on a mat on the floor. It was Ezinma's turn to tell a story.

"Once upon a time," Ezinma began, "Tortoise and Cat went to wrestle against Yams—no, that is not the beginning. Once upon a time there was a great famine in the land of animals. Everybody was lean except Cat, who was fat and whose body shone as if oil was rubbed on it . . ."

She broke off because at that very moment a loud and high-pitched voice broke the outer silence of the night. It was Chielo, the priestess of Agbala, prophesying. There was nothing new in that. Once in a while Chielo was possessed by the spirit of her god and she began to prophesy. But tonight she was addressing her prophecy and greetings to Okonkwo, and so everyone in his family listened. The folk stories stopped.

"Agbala do-o-o-o! Agbala ekeneo-o-o-o-o," came the voice like a sharp knife cutting through the night. "Okonkwo! Agbala ekene gio-o-o-o! Agbala cholu ifu ada ya Ezinmao-o-o-o!"

At the mention of Ezinma's name Ekwefi jerked her head sharply like an animal that had sniffed death in the air. Her heart jumped painfully within her.

The priestess had now reached Okonkwo's compound and was talking with him outside his hut. She was saying again and again that Agbala wanted to see his daughter, Ezinma. Okonkwo pleaded with her to come back in the morning because Ezinma was now asleep. But Chielo ignored what he was trying to say and went on shouting that Agbala wanted to see his daughter. Her voice was as clear as metal, and Okonkwo's women and children heard from their huts all that she said. Okonkwo was still pleading that the girl had been ill of late and was asleep. Ekwefi quickly took her to their bedroom and placed her on their high bamboo bed.

The priestess screamed. "Beware, Okonkwo!" she warned. "Beware of exchanging words with Agbala. Does a man speak when a god speaks? Beware!"

She walked through Okonkwo's hut into the circular compound and went straight toward Ekwefi's hut. Okonkwo came after her.

"Ekwefi," she called, "Agbala greets you. Where is my daughter, Ezinma? Agbala wants to see her."

Ekwefi came out from her hut carrying her oil lamp in her left hand. There was a light wind blowing, so she cupped her right hand to shelter the flame. Nwoye's mother, also carrying an oil lamp, emerged from her hut. The children stood in the darkness outside their hut watching the strange event. Okonkwo's youngest wife also came out and joined the others.

"Where does Agbala want to see her?" Ekwefi asked.

"Where else but in his house in the hills and the caves?" replied the priestess.

"I will come with you, too," Ekwefi said firmly.

"*Tufia-a!*" the priestess cursed, her voice cracking like the angry bark of thunder in the dry season. "How dare you, woman, to go before the mighty Agbala of your own accord? Beware, woman, lest he strike you in his anger. Bring me my daughter."

Ekwefi went into her hut and came out again with Ezinma.

"Come, my daughter," said the priestess. "I shall carry you on my back. A baby on its mother's back does not know that the way is long."

Ezinma began to cry. She was used to Chielo calling her "my daughter." But it was a different Chielo she now saw in the yellow half-light.

"Don't cry, my daughter," said the priestess, "lest Agbala be angry with you."

"Don't cry," said Ekwefi, "she will bring you back very soon. I shall give you some fish to eat." She went into the hut again and brought down the smoke-black basket in which she kept her dried fish and other ingredients for cooking soup. She broke a piece in two and gave it to Ezinma, who clung to her.

"Don't be afraid," said Ekwefi, stroking her head, which was shaved in places, leaving a regular pattern of hair. They went outside again. The priestess bent down on one knee and Ezinma climbed on her back, her left palm closed on her fish and her eyes gleaming with tears.

"*Agbala do-o-o-o! Agbala ekeneo-o-o-o!* . . ." Chielo began once again to chant greetings to her god. She turned round sharply and walked through Okonkwo's hut, bending very low at the eaves. Ezinma was crying loudly now, calling on her mother. The two voices disappeared into the thick darkness.

A strange and sudden weakness descended on Ekwefi as she stood gazing in the direction of the voices like a hen whose only chick has been carried away by a kite. Ezinma's voice soon faded away and only Chielo was heard moving farther and farther into the distance.

"Why do you stand there as though she had been kidnapped?" asked Okonkwo as he went back to his hut.

"She will bring her back soon," Nwoye's mother said.

But Ekwefi did not hear these consolations. She stood for a while, and then, all of a sudden, made up her mind. She hurried through Okonkwo's hut and went outside. "Where are you going?" he asked.

"I am following Chielo," she replied and disappeared in the darkness. Okonkwo cleared his throat, and brought out his snuffbottle from the goatskin bag by his side.

The priestess' voice was already growing faint in the distance. Ekwefi hurried to the main footpath and turned left in the direction of the voice. Her eyes were useless to her in the darkness. But she picked her way easily on the sandy footpath hedged on either side by branches and damp leaves. She began to run, holding her breasts with her hands to stop them flapping noisily against her body. She hit her left foot against an outcropped root, and terror seized her. It was an ill omen. She ran faster. But Chielo's voice was still a long way away. Had she been running too? How could she go so fast with Ezinma on her back? Although the night was cool, Ekwefi was beginning to feel hot from her running. She continually ran into the luxuriant weeds and creepers that walled in the path. Once she tripped up and fell. Only then did she realize, with a start, that Chielo had stopped her chanting. Her heart beat violently and she stood still. Then Chielo's renewed outburst came from only a few paces ahead. But Ekwefi could not see her. She shut her eyes for a while and opened them again in an effort to see. But it was useless. She could not see beyond her nose.

There were no stars in the sky because there was a rain-cloud. Fireflies went about with their tiny green lamps, which only made the darkness more profound. Between Chielo's outbursts the night was alive with the shrill tremor of forest insects woven into the darkness.

"*Agbala do-o-o-o! . . . Agbala ekeneo-o-o-o! . . .*" Ekwefi trudged behind, neither getting too near nor keeping too far back. She thought they must be going towards the sacred cave. Now that she walked slowly she had time to think. What would she do when they got to the cave? She would not dare to enter. She would wait at the mouth, all alone in that fearful place. She thought of all the terrors of the night. She remembered that night, long ago, when she had seen *Ogbu-agali-odu,* one of those evil essences loosed upon the world by the potent "medicines" which the tribe had made in the distant past against its enemies but had now forgotten how to control. Ekwefi had been returning from the stream with her mother on a dark night like this when they saw its glow as it flew in their direction. They had thrown down their water-pots and lain by the roadside expecting the sinister light to descend on them and kill them. That was the only time Ekwefi ever saw *Ogbu-agali-odu.* But although it had happened so long ago, her blood still ran cold whenever she remembered that night.

The priestess' voice came at longer intervals now, but its vigor was undiminished. The air was cool and damp with dew. Ezinma sneezed. Ekwefi muttered, "Life to you." At the same time the priestess also said, "Life to you, my daughter." Ezinma's voice from the darkness warmed her mother's heart. She trudged slowly along.

And then the priestess screamed. "Somebody is walking behind me!" she said. "Whether you are spirit or man, may Agbala shave your head with a blunt razor! May he twist your neck until you see your heels!"

Ekwefi stood rooted to the spot. One mind said to her: "Woman, go home before Agbala does you harm." But she could not. She stood until Chielo had increased the distance between them and she began to follow again. She had already walked so long that she began to feel a slight numbness in the limbs and in the head. Then it occurred to her that they could not have been heading for the cave. They must have by-passed it long ago; they must be going towards Umuachi, the farthest village in the clan. Chielo's voice now came after long intervals.

It seemed to Ekwefi that the night had become a little lighter. The cloud had lifted and a few stars were out. The moon must be preparing to rise, its sullenness over. When the moon rose late in the night, people said it was refusing food, as a sullen husband refuses his wife's food when they have quarrelled.

"*Agbala do-o-o-o! Umuachi! Agbala ekene unuo-o-o!*" It was just as Ekwefi had thought. The priestess was now saluting the village of Umuachi. It was unbelievable, the distance they had covered. As they emerged into the open village from the narrow forest track the darkness was softened and it became possible to see the vague shape of trees. Ekwefi screwed her eyes up in an effort to see her daughter and the priestess, but whenever she thought she saw their shape it immediately dissolved like a melting lump of darkness. She walked numbly along.

Chielo's voice was now rising continuously, as when she first set out. Ekwefi had a feeling of spacious openness, and she guessed they must be on the village *ilo*, or playground. And she realized too with something like a jerk that Chielo was no longer moving forward. She was, in fact, returning. Ekwefi quickly moved away from her line of retreat. Chielo passed by, and they began to go back the way they had come.

It was a long and weary journey and Ekwefi felt like a sleepwalker most of the way. The moon was definitely rising, and although it had not yet appeared on the sky its light had already melted down the darkness. Ekwefi could now discern the figure of the priestess and her burden. She slowed down her pace so as to increase the distance between them. She was afraid of what might happen if Chielo suddenly turned round and saw her.

She had prayed for the moon to rise. But now she found the half-light of the incipient moon more terrifying than darkness. The world was now peopled with vague, fantastic figures that dissolved under her steady gaze and then formed again in new shapes. At one stage Ekwefi was so afraid that she nearly called out to Chielo for companionship and human sympathy. What she had seen was the shape of a man climbing a palm tree, his head pointing to the earth and his legs skywards. But at that very moment Chielo's voice rose again in her possessed chanting, and Ekwefi recoiled, because there was no humanity there. It was not the same Chielo who sat with her in the market and sometimes bought beancakes for Ezinma, whom she called her daughter. It was a different woman—the priestess of Agbala, the Oracle of the Hills and Caves. Ekwefi trudged along between two fears. The sound of her benumbed steps seemed to come from some other person walking behind her. Her arms were folded across her bare breasts. Dew fell heavily and the air was cold. She could no longer think, not even about the terrors of night. She just jogged along in a half-sleep, only waking to full life when Chielo sang.

At last they took a turning and began to head for the caves. From then on, Chielo never ceased in her chanting. She greeted her god in a multitude of names—the owner of the future, the messenger of earth, the god who cut a man down when his life was sweetest to him. Ekwefi was also awakened and her benumbed fears revived.

The moon was now up and she could see Chielo and Ezinma clearly. How a woman could carry a child of that size so easily and for so long was a miracle. But Ekwefi was not thinking about that. Chielo was not a woman that night.

"*Agbala do-o-o-o! Agbala ekeneo-o-o! Chi negbu madu ubosi ndu ya nato ya uto daluo-o-o!* . . ."

Ekwefi could already see the hills looming in the moonlight. They formed a circular ring with a break at one point through which the foot-track led to the center of the circle.

As soon as the priestess stepped into this ring of hills her voice was not only doubled in strength but was thrown back on all sides. It was indeed the shrine of a great god. Ekwefi picked her way carefully and quietly. She was already beginning to doubt the wisdom of her coming. Nothing would happen to Ezinma, she thought. And if anything happened to her could she stop it? She would not dare to enter the underground caves. Her coming was quite useless, she thought.

As these things went through her mind she did not realize how close they were to the cave mouth. And so when the priestess with Ezinma on her back disappeared through a hole hardly big enough to pass a hen, Ekwefi broke into a run as though to stop them. As she stood gazing at the circular darkness which had swallowed them, tears gushed from her eyes, and she swore within her that if she heard Ezinma cry she would rush into the cave to defend her against all the gods in the world. She would die with her.

Having sworn that oath, she sat down on a stony ledge and waited. Her fear had vanished. She could hear the priestess' voice, all its metal taken out of it by the vast emptiness of the cave. She buried her face in her lap and waited.

She did not know how long she waited. It must have been a very long time. Her back was turned on the footpath that led out of the hills. She must have heard a noise behind her and turned round sharply. A man stood there with a machete in his hand. Ekwefi uttered a scream and sprang to her feet.

"Don't be foolish," said Okonkwo's voice. "I thought you were going into the shrine with Chielo," he mocked.

Ekwefi did not answer. Tears of gratitude filled her eyes. She knew her daughter was safe.

Questions for discussion

1. This story takes place at the turn of the century in an Ibo village in what is now Biafra. "Ezinma" is taken from *Things Fall Apart*, a novel by a modern African writer who recreates Ibo village life at the time of its first contact with colonialism and Christianity. He shows how the coming of the white man led to a breakup of traditional ways. In this selection from the novel, what is the author's attitude toward the traditional ways?

2. According to Ekwefi, why have nine of her children died? Why do you think they died? Is it mere coincidence or the result of the *obanje*? Do many Ibo babies die? What evidence do you have?

3. Do you think Ezinma buried the *iyi-uwa*? Why did she lead the village on a "wild goose chase" before showing them the stone?

4. Why does Ekwefi allow Chielo to carry off Ezinma? How do we know that Chielo is interested in the child's welfare? How does Chielo appear by day? by night? Why does Ekwefi say that she is not the same person (page 155)?

5. Why does Ekwefi become even more frightened when the moon rises? What does she see in the moonlight? If you were in the jungle at night, what sort of things would frighten you? Would they be real or imagined? Would they be the same sort of things that frightened Ekwefi? What are her "two fears" (page 155)?

6. How does the author use Chielo's chanting to make the journey to the cave more suspenseful?

7. Why are we surprised when Okonkwo appears at the cave? What sort of person is Okonkwo? How does he treat Ekwefi?

8. Why aren't we surprised that Ekwefi follows the priestess?

9. What would *family* mean to an Ibo? How would it differ from your idea of *family*? Who would be included in an Ibo family? What evidence do you have that this is a very close-knit society?

Vocabulary growth

WORDS ARE INTERESTING.

1. In her despair, Ekwefi gives her children very expressive names like "Death I implore you" and "May it not happen again." Most of our names have meanings, although we are not always aware of them. What do the names of the members of your family mean?

2. Why does the author use African words in some cases instead of translating them into English? What effect does this create?

For composition

Ezinma is asked by the adults of the tribe to produce her *iyi-uwa*. To avoid their anger, she plays along and seems to enjoy the attention. Have you ever been asked by your relatives or friends to do something you thought was ridiculous? What did you do?

The Frill

PEARL BUCK

"**M**Y dear, the only way to manage these native tailors is to be firm!"

Mrs. Lowe, the postmaster's wife, settled herself with some difficulty into the wicker rocking chair upon the wide veranda of her house. She was a large woman, red-faced from more food than necessary and little exercise over the ten-odd years she had spent in a port town on the China coast. Now as she looked at her caller and thus spoke, her square hard-fleshed face grew a little redder. Beside her stood a Chinese manservant who had just announced in a mild voice:

"Tailor have come, missy."

Little Mrs. Newman looked at her hostess with vague admiration.

"I'm sure I wish I had your way with them, Adeline," she murmured, fanning herself slowly with a palm-leaf fan. She went on in a plaintive complaining way: "Sometimes I think it is scarcely worth while to bother with new clothes, although they are so cheap here, especially if you buy the native silks. But it is so much trouble to have them made, and these tailors say—my dear, my tailor promises me faithfully he will make a dress in three days and then he doesn't come for a week or two!" Her weak voice dwindled and ended in a sigh and she fanned herself a trifle more quickly.

"Watch me now," said Mrs. Lowe commandingly. She had a deep firm voice and round hard gray eyes set a little near together beneath closely waved dead brown hair. She turned these eyes upon the Chinese manservant as he stood looking decorously down to the floor, his head drooping slightly, and said, "Boy, talkee tailor come this side."

"Yes, missy," murmured the servant and disappeared.

Almost instantly there was the sound of soft steady footsteps through the open doors, and from the back of the house through the hall following the manservant there came the tailor. He was a tall man, taller than the servant, middle-aged, his face quiet with a sort of closed tranquillity. He wore a long robe of faded blue grasscloth, patched neatly at the elbows and very clean. Under his arm he carried a bundle wrapped in a white cloth. He bowed to the two white women and then squatting down put this bundle upon the floor of the veranda and untied its knots. Inside was a worn and frayed fashion book from some American company and a half-finished dress of a spotted blue and white silk. This dress he shook out carefully and held up for Mrs. Lowe to see. From its generous proportions it could be seen that it was made for her. She surveyed it coldly and with hostility, searching its details.

Suddenly she spoke in a loud voice: "No wantchee that collar, tailor! I have talkee you wantchee frill—see, so fashion!" She turned the pages of the book rapidly to a section devoted to garments for ample women. "See, all same fashion this lady. What for you makee flat collar? No wantchee—no wantchee—take it away!"

Upon the tailor's calm patient face a perspiration broke forth. "Yes, missy," he said faintly. And then he pressed his lips together slightly and took a breath and began: "Missy, you first talkee frill, then you say no frill. Other day, you say wantchee flat collar, frill too fat."

He looked imploringly at the white woman. But Mrs. Lowe waved him away with a fat ringed hand.

"No, you talkee lie, tailor," she cried sternly. "I know how I talkee. I never say I wantchee flat collar—never! No lady have flat collar now. What for you talkee so fashion?"

"Yes, missy," said the tailor. Then, brightening somewhat, he suggested, "Have more cloth, missy. Suppose I makee frill, never mind."

But Mrs. Lowe was not to be thus easily appeased. "Yes, never mind you, but you have spoil so much my cloth. What do you think, I buy this cloth no money? Plenty money you make me lose." She turned to her guest. "I have been counting on that dress, Minnie, and now look at it! I wanted to wear it to the garden party at the consulate day after tomorrow. I told him a frill—just look at that silly collar!"

"Yes, I know. It's just what I was saying," said Mrs. Newman in her tired, peevish voice. "What I want to know is how will you manage it?"

"Oh, I'll manage it," replied Mrs. Lowe grimly.

She ignored the tailor for a while and stared out over her trim garden. In the hot sunshine a blue-coated coolie squatted over a border of zinnias, glittering in the September noon. A narrow sanded path ran about a square of green lawn. She said nothing, and the tailor stood acutely uncomfortable, the dress still held delicately by the shoulders. A small trickle of perspiration ran down each side of his face. He wet his lips and began in a trembling voice:

"Missy wantchee try?"

"No, I do not," snapped Mrs. Lowe. "What for wantchee try? All wrong—collar all wrong—what for try?" She continued to stare out into the shining garden.

"Can makee all same frill," said the tailor eagerly, persuasively. "Yes, yes, missy, I makee all same you say. What time you want?"

"I want it tomorrow," replied the white woman. "You bring tomorrow twelve o'clock. Suppose you no bring, then I no pay—savee? All time you talkee what time you bring and you never bring."

"Can do, missy," said the tailor quietly. He squatted gracefully, folded the dress into the cloth again and tied it tenderly, careful to crush nothing. Then he rose and stood waiting, upon his face some agony of supplication. His whole soul rose in this silent supplication, so that it was written upon his quiet high-cheeked face, upon his close-set lips. Sweat broke out upon him afresh. Even Mrs. Lowe could feel dimly that imploring soul. She paused in her rocking, and looked up.

"What is it?" she asked sharply. "What more thing?"

The tailor wet his lips again and spoke in a faint voice. "Missy, can you give me litty money—one dollar, two dollar—" Before her outraged look his voice dropped yet lower. "My brother's son he die today, I think—he have three piecee baby, one woman—no money buy coffin—no nothing—he very ill today——"

Mrs. Lowe looked at her caller. "Well, of all the nerve!" she breathed, genuinely aghast. Mrs. Newman answered her look.

"It's just what I said," she replied. "They are more trouble than they are worth—and the way they *cut*—and then they think about nothing but money!"

Mrs. Lowe turned her rolling gray eyes upon the tailor. He did not look up, but he wiped his lip furtively with his sleeve. She stared at him an instant, and then her voice came forth filled with righteous anger.

"No," she said. "No. You finish dress all proper with frill, I pay you. No finish dress, no pay. Never. You savee, tailor?"

"Yes, missy," sighed the tailor. All vestige of hope had now disappeared from his face. The atmosphere of supplication died away. A look of cold despair came over his face like a curtain. "I finish tomorrow twelve o'clock, missy," he said and turned away.

"See that you do," shouted Mrs. Lowe triumphantly after him, and she watched his figure with contempt as it disappeared into the hall. Then she turned to her caller. "If I say tomorrow," she explained, "perhaps it will be ready by the day after." She thought of something and reaching forward in her chair pressed a bell firmly. The servant appeared.

"Boy," she said, "look see tailor—see he no takee something."

Her loud voice penetrated into the house, and the tailor's body, still visible at the end of the hall, straightened itself somewhat and then passed out of sight.

"You never can tell," said Mrs. Lowe. "You can't tell whether they are making up these stories or not. If they need money—but they always do need money. I never saw such people. They must make a lot, though, sewing for all these foreigners here in the port. But this tailor is worse than most. He is forever wanting money before his work is done. Three separate times he has come and said a child was dying or something. I don't believe a word of it. Probably smokes opium or gambles. They all gamble—you can't believe a word they say!"

"Oh, I know—" sighed Mrs. Newman, rising to depart. Mrs. Lowe rose also.

"After all, one simply has to be firm," she said again.

Outside the big white foreign house the tailor went silently and swiftly through the hot street. Well, he had asked her, and she would not give him anything. After all his dread and fear of her refusal, all his summoning of courage, she would not give him anything. The dress was more than half done, except for the frill, too. She had given him the silk two days ago, and he had been glad because it would bring him in a few dollars for this nephew of his who was like his own son now that the gods had taken away his own little children, three of them.

He had therefore clung the more to this only son of his dead younger brother, a young man apprenticed to an ironsmith, and he had three little children now, too. Such a strong young man—who could have thought he would have been seized for death like this? Two months ago it was the long piece of red-hot iron he was beating into the shape of a plowshare had slipped somehow from his pincers and had fallen upon his leg and foot and seared the flesh away almost to the bone. It had fallen on his naked flesh, for it was summer and the little shop was hot and he had only his thin cotton trousers on rolled to his thighs.

Well, and they had tried every sort of ointment, but what ointment will grow sound flesh again, and what balm is there for such a wound? The whole leg had swollen, and now on this hot day in the ninth moon the young man lay dying. There were black plasters on his leg from hip to foot, but they were of no avail.

Yes, the tailor had seen that for himself this morning when he went to see his nephew—he had seen death there plainly. The young wife sat weeping in the doorway of the one room that was their home, and the two elder children stared at her gravely, too stricken for play. The third was but a babe she held in her bosom.

The tailor turned down an alleyway and into a door in a wall. He passed through a court filled with naked children screaming and quarreling and shouting at play.

Above his head were stretched bamboo poles upon which were hung ragged garments washed in too scanty water and without any soap. Here about these courts a family lived in every room and poured its waste into the court so that even though it was a dry day —and the days had been dry for a moon or more—yet the court was slimy and running with waste water.

But he did not notice this. He passed through three more courts like the first and turned to an open door at the right and went into the dark windowless room. There was a different odor here. It was the odor of dying rotten flesh. The sound of a woman's wailing rose from beside the curtained bed, and thither the tailor went, his face not changed from the look it had borne away from the white woman's house. The young wife did not look up at his coming. She sat crouched on the ground beside the bed, and her face was wet with tears. Her long black hair had come uncoiled and stretched over her shoulder and hung to the earth. Over and over she moaned: "Oh my husband—oh, my man—I am left alone—oh, my husband—"

The babe lay on the ground beside her, crying feebly now and again. The two elder children sat close to their mother, each of them holding fast to a corner of her coat. They had been weeping, too, but now they were silent, their streaked faces upturned to look at their uncle.

But the tailor paid no heed to them now. He looked into the hempen curtains of the bed and said gently:

"Are you still living, my son?"

The dying man turned his eyes with difficulty. He was horribly swollen, his hands, his naked upper body, his neck, his face. But these were nothing to the immense loglike swelling of his burned leg. It lay there so huge it seemed he was attached to it, rather than it to him. His glazed eyes fixed themselves upon his uncle. He opened his puffed lips and after a long time and a mighty effort of concentration his voice came forth in a hoarse whisper:

"These children—"

The tailor's face was suddenly convulsed with suffering. He sat down upon the edge of the bed and began to speak earnestly:

"You need not grieve for your children, my son. Die peacefully. Your wife and your children shall come to my house. They shall take the place of my own three. Your wife shall be daughter to me and to my wife, and your children shall be our grandchildren. Are you not my own brother's son? And he dead, too, and only I left now."

He began to weep quietly, and it could be seen that the lines upon his face were set there by other hours of this repressed silent weeping, for as he wept his face hardly changed at all, only the tears rolled down his cheeks.

After a long time the dying man's voice came again with the same rending effort, as though he tore himself out of some heavy stupor to say what must be said:

"You—are poor—too—"

But the uncle answered quickly, bending toward the dying man, for the swollen eyes were now closed and he could not be sure he was heard: "You're not to worry. Rest your heart. I have work—these white women are always wanting new dresses. I have a silk dress now nearly finished for the postmaster's wife—nearly done, except for a frill, and then she will give me money for it and perhaps more sewing. We shall do very well—"

But the young man made no further reply. He had gone into that stupor forever, and he could rouse himself no more.

Nevertheless he still breathed slightly throughout that long hot day. The tailor rose once to place his bundle in a corner and to remove his robe, and then he took his place again beside the dying man and remained immovable through the hours. The woman wailed on and on, but at last she was exhausted and sat leaning against the end of the bed, her eyes closed, sobbing now and again softly. But the children grew used to it. They grew used even to their father's dying, and they ran out into the court to play. Once or twice a kindly neighbor woman came and put her head into the door, and the last time she picked up the babe and carried him away, holding him to her own full breast to comfort him. Outside, her voice could be heard shouting in cheerful pity:

"Well, his hour is come, and he is foul already as though he had been dead a month!"

So the hot day drew on at last to its end and when twilight came the young man ceased breathing and was dead.

Only then did the tailor rise. He rose and put on his gown and took his bundle, and he said to the crouching woman, "He is dead. Have you any money at all?"

Then the young woman rose also and looked at him anxiously, smoothing the hair back from her face. It could now be seen that she was still very young—not more than twenty years of age—a young common creature such as may be seen anywhere on any street in any day, neither pretty nor ugly, slight, and somewhat slovenly even on ordinary occasions, and now unwashed for many days. Her grimy face was round, the mouth full and projecting, the eyes a little stupid. It was clear that she had lived from day to day, never foreseeing the catastrophe that had now befallen her. She looked at the tailor humbly and anxiously.

"We have nothing left," she said. "I pawned his clothes and my winter clothes and the table and stools, and we have only that bed on which he lies."

The look of despair deepened on the man's face. "Is there anyone of whom you might borrow?" he asked.

She shook her head. "I do not know anyone except these people in the court. And what have they?" Then as the full terror of her position came upon her she cried out shrilly, "Uncle, we have no one but you in the world!"

"I know," he said simply. He looked once more at the bed. "Cover him," he said in a low voice. "Cover him against the flies."

He passed through the courts quickly then, and the neighbor woman, who was still holding the babe, bawled at him as he went, "Is he dead yet?"

"He is dead," said the tailor and went through the gate into the street and turned to the west where his own home was.

It seemed to him that this was the most hot day of that whole summer. So is the ninth moon hot sometimes, and so does summer often pass burning fiercely into autumn. The evening had brought no coolness, and thunderous clouds towered over the city. The streets were filled with half-naked men and with women in thinnest garb, sitting upon little low bamboo couches they had moved out of their houses. Some lay flat upon the street on mats of reed or strips of woven matting. Children wailed everywhere, and mothers fanned their babes wearily, dreading the night.

Through this crowd the tailor passed swiftly, his head bent down. He was now very weary but still not hungry, although he had fasted the whole day. He could not eat—no, not even when he reached the one room in a court which was his home, and he could not eat even when his poor stupid old wife, who could not keep her babies alive, came shuffling and panting out of the street and placed a bowl of cold rice gruel on the table for him to eat. There was that smell about his clothes—it filled his nostrils still. He thought suddenly of the silk dress. Suppose the white woman noticed the odor there! He rose suddenly and opened the bundle and shook out the dress, and turning it carefully inside out he hung it to air upon a decrepit dressmaker's form that stood by the bed.

But it could not hang there long. He must finish it and have the money. He took off his robe and his undershirt and his shoes and stockings and sat in his trousers. He must be careful in this heat that his sweat did not stain the dress. He found a gray towel and wrapped it about his head to catch the drops of sweat and put a rag upon the table on which to wipe his hands from time to time.

While he sewed swiftly, not daring to hasten beyond what he

was able to do well lest she be not pleased, he pondered on what he could do. He had had one apprentice last year, but the times were so evil he had had to let the lad go, and so had now but his own ten fingers to use. But that was not altogether ill because the lad had made so many mistakes and the white woman said insistently, "You must makee yourself, tailor—no give small boy, makee spoil." Yes, but with just these ten fingers of his could he hope to make another dress in three days—suppose she had another silk dress—that would be ten dollars for the two. He could buy a coffin for ten dollars down and the promise of more later.

But supposing she had no more work to give him now—then what could he do? What indeed, but go to a usurer? And yet that he did not dare to do. A man was lost if he went to a usurer for the interest ran faster than a tiger upon him—in a few months double and triple what he had borrowed. Then when the coffin was buried he must bring the young wife and the three babies here. There was only this one room for them all, too. His heart warmed somewhat at the thought of the babies and then stopped in terror at the thought that he must feed them.

Midnight drew on, and he was not finished. There was the worst of all yet to be made—the frill. He fetched his fashion book and pored over it beneath the flickering light of the small tin kerosene lamp. So the frill went, here it turned, a long wide frill, closely pleated. He folded the small pleats, his hands trembling with fatigue. His wife lay snoring in the bed now. Nothing would wake her, not even the rackety noisy sewing machine with which he set fast the carefully basted frill. At dawn there remained but the edge to whip by hand and the irons to heat on the charcoal brazier. Well, he would sleep a little and rest his aching eyes and then get up to finish it. He hung the dress upon the form, and then he lay down beside his wife and fell instantly into deep sleep.

But not for long could he sleep. At seven he rose and went to his work again and worked until nearly noon, stopping only for a mouthful of the food he could not eat the night before. Then he was finished. It had taken him longer than he hoped it would. He squinted up at the sun. Yes, he could just get to the house by noon. He must hasten. He must not make her angry so that she would perhaps refuse him the other dress. No, somehow he must have the other dress. Then if he sewed this afternoon and tonight he could finish it in another day. He smelled the finished dress anxiously. A little odor, perhaps—would she notice it?

But fortunately she did not notice it. She was sitting in that strange moving chair she had on the veranda, and she looked at the dress critically.

"All finish?" she asked in her loud sudden way.

"Yes, missy," he answered humbly.

"All right, I go try."

She had gone into her room then, and he held his breath, waiting. Perhaps there was some odor to it yet? But she came back wearing the dress, a satisfied look upon her face; but not too satisfied.

"How much?" she said abruptly.

He hesitated. "Five dollar, missy, please." Then seeing her angry eyes he added hastily, "Silk dress, five dollar, please, missy. Any tailor five dollar."

"Too much—too much," she declared. "You spoil my cloth, too!" But she paid the money to him grudgingly, and he took it from her, delicately careful not to touch her hand.

"Thank you, missy," he said gently.

He dropped to his heels and began to tie up his bundle, his fingers trembling. He must ask her now. But how could he? What would he do if she refused? He gathered his courage together desperately.

"Missy," he said, looking up humbly but avoiding her eyes. "You have more dress I can do?"

He waited, hanging on her answer, staring into the shining garden. But she had already turned to go into the house again to take off the dress. She called back at him carelessly.

"No—no more! You makee too muchee trouble. You spoil my cloth—plenty more tailor more cheap and not so muchee trouble!"

The next day at the garden party she met little Mrs. Newman, sitting languidly in a wicker chair, watching white figures move about the lawn intent upon a game of croquet. Mrs. Newman's faded blue eyes brightened somewhat at the sight of the new dress.

"You really did get your dress after all," she said with faint interest. "I didn't think you really would. He did that frill nicely, didn't he?"

Mrs. Lowe looked down upon her large bosom. There the frill

lay, beautifully pleated, perfectly ironed. She said with satisfaction, "Yes, it is nice, isn't it? I am glad I decided to have the frill, after all. And so cheap! My dear, with all this frill the dress cost only five dollars to be made—that's less than two dollars at home! What's that? Oh, yes, he brought it punctually at twelve, as I told him he must. It's as I said—you simply have to be firm with these native tailors!"

Questions for discussion

1. This story is obviously that of a personal conflict between two people. Who are the two people? What is the conflict? What causes it?
2. Why does Mrs. Lowe act as she does? What was your reaction to her? What was your reaction to the tailor?
3. What emotions did you experience as you read the story?
4. Could you stand by and watch such a scene, as Mrs. Newman does, and not try to do something about it? What would you do?
5. You'll remember that in "The Most Dangerous Game" the observation is made that the people of the world are divided into two classes, the hunters and the hunted. In this story the people of the world are also divided into two classes but the classification is made on a different basis. What would you say the two classes are here? What is your reaction to this arrangement?
6. What comments about people and their conduct toward or treatment of each other could one make as a result of having read this story?
7. This story is set in a foreign country. Have you ever seen or heard of something comparable to this as having happened in this country?
8. What is the significance of the title, "The Frill," beyond naming an object which plays a central part in the story?

Vocabulary growth

WORDS ARE INTERESTING. 1. You know by now that a great many English words come from Latin. You may not know how far apart the modern English meanings and the old Latin meanings are. This is because English is a living, growing language in which we are constantly giving new meanings to old words.

In this story, you read on page 158, "She . . . in a *plaintive complaining* way. . . ." Both *plaintive* and *complaining* come from the same Latin word *plangere*, meaning "to beat the breast; to lament." One meaning of *plaintive* is fairly close to this: "melancholy, sorrowful." However, the most common meaning of *complain* is "to find fault." When someone finds fault, he is not usually speaking sorrowfully, but angrily.

You can see that the author knew what she was doing in putting the words *plaintive* and *complaining* together. They do not mean the same thing. Can you now substitute your own meanings for those words in the sentence quoted above?

2. When we are amused at the angry remarks and actions of someone, we may say that he was "in high *dudgeon*." The word *dudgeon* is interesting. It comes from a word meaning "the wood from which the handles of daggers were made." Apparently, when a man was in anger, his hand flew to his dagger.

Curiously enough, no one is ever in low dudgeon. It is *high* dudgeon or occasionally deep dudgeon, but there is no rule to prevent your speaking of "low dudgeon" if you have a mind to.

For composition

1. Write a character sketch of Mrs. Lowe as she would look to herself, to Mrs. Newman, to the Chinese tailor, to the Chinese servants in her house, and finally to you, the reader of this story.
2. Write a sketch of an American in a foreign country (a real person or a fictitious character), showing how he looks to the people of that country.

They say that caterpillar racing was
good sport all along the Big Ditch until the . . .

Death of Red Peril

WALTER D. EDMONDS

1

JOHN brought his off eye to bear on me:—

What do them old coots down to the store do? Why, one of
'em will think up a horse that's been dead forty year and then
they'll set around remembering this and that about that horse until
they've made a resurrection of him. You'd think he was a regular Grattan Bars, the way they talk, telling one thing and another,
when a man knows if that horse hadn't 've had a breeching to keep
his tail end off the ground he could hardly have walked from here
to Boonville.

A horse race is a handsome thing to watch if a man has his money
on a sure proposition. My pa was always a great hand at a horse
race. But when he took to a boat and my mother he didn't have
no more time for it. So he got interested in another sport.

Did you ever hear of racing caterpillars? No? Well, it used to
be a great thing on the canawl. My pa used to have a lot of them
insects on hand every fall, and the way he could get them to run
would make a man have his eyes examined.

The way we raced caterpillars was to set them in a napkin ring
on a table, one facing one way and one the other. Outside the
napkin ring was drawed a circle in chalk three feet acrost. Then
a man lifted the ring and the handlers was allowed one jab with a
darning needle to get their caterpillars started. The one that got
outside the chalk circle the first was the one that won the race.

I remember my pa tried out a lot of breeds, and he got hold of
some pretty fast steppers. But there wasn't one of them could
equal Red Peril. To see him you wouldn't believe he could run.
He was all red and kind of stubby, and he had a sort of wart be-

hind that you'd think would get in his way. There wasn't anything fancy in his looks. He'd just set still studying the ground
and make you think he was dreaming about last year's oats; but
when you set him in the starting ring he'd hitch himself up behind
like a man lifting on his galluses, and then he'd light out for glory.

Pa come acrost Red Peril down in Westernville. Ma's relatives
resided there, and it being Sunday we'd all gone in to church. We
was riding back in a hired rig with a dandy trotter, and Pa was
pushing her right along and Ma was talking sermon and clothes,
and me and my sister was setting on the back seat playing poke
your nose, when all of a sudden Pa hollers, "Whoa!" and set the
horse right down on the breeching. Ma let out a holler and come
to rest on the dashboard with her head under the horse. "My
gracious land!" she says. "What's happened?" Pa was out on the
other side of the road right down in the mud in his Sunday pants,
a-wropping up something in his yeller handkerchief. Ma begun to
get riled. "What you doing, Pa?" she says. "What you got there?"
Pa was putting his handkerchief back into his inside pocket. Then
he come back over the wheel and got him a chew. "Leeza," he says,
"I got the fastest caterpillar in seven counties. It's an act of Providence I seen him, the way he jumped the ruts." "It's an act of God
I ain't laying dead under the back end of that horse," says Ma. "I've
gone and spoilt my Sunday hat." "Never mind," says Pa; "Red Peril
will earn you a new one." Just like that he named him. He was the
fastest caterpillar in seven counties.

When we got back onto the boat, while Ma was turning up the
supper, Pa set him down to the table under the lamp and pulled
out the handkerchief. "You two devils stand there and there," he
says to me and my sister, "and if you let him get by I'll leather the
soap out of you."

So we stood there and he undid the handkerchief, and out walked
one of them red, long-haired caterpillars. He walked right to the
middle of the table, and then he took a short turn and put his nose
in his tail and went to sleep.

"Who'd think that insect could make such a break for freedom
as I seen him make?" says Pa, and he got out a empty Brandreth
box and filled it up with some towel and put the caterpillar inside.
"He needs a rest," says Pa. "He needs to get used to his stall. When
he limbers up I'll commence training him. Now then," he says,

putting the box on the shelf back of the stove, "don't none of you say a word about him."

He got out a pipe and set there smoking and figuring, and we could see he was studying out just how he'd make a world-beater out of that bug. "What you going to feed him?" asks Ma. "If I wasn't afraid of constipating him," Pa says, "I'd try him out with milkweed."

Next day we hauled up the Lansing Kill Gorge. Ned Kilbourne, Pa's driver, come aboard in the morning, and he took a look at that caterpillar. He took him out of the box and felt his legs and laid him down on the table and went clean over him. "Well," he says, "he don't look like a great lot, but I've knowed some of that red variety could chug along pretty smart." Then he touched him with a pin. It was a sudden sight.

It looked like the rear end of that caterpillar was racing the front end, but it couldn't never quite get by. Afore either Ned or Pa could get a move Red Peril had made a turn around the sugar bowl and run solid aground in the butter dish.

Pa let out a loud swear. "Look out he don't pull a tendon," he says. "Butter's a bad thing. A man has to be careful. Jeepers," he says, picking him up and taking him over to the stove to dry, "I'll handle him myself. I don't want no rum-soaked bezabors dishing my beans."

"I didn't mean harm, Will," says Ned. "I was just curious."

There was something extraordinary about that caterpillar. He was intelligent. It seemed he just couldn't abide the feel of sharp iron. It got so that if Pa reached for the lapel of his coat Red Peril would light out. It must have been he was tender. I said he had a sort of wart behind, and I guess he liked to find it a place of safety.

We was all terrible proud of that bird. Pa took to timing him on the track. He beat all known time holler. He got to know that as soon as he crossed the chalk he would get back safe in his quarters. Only when we tried sprinting him across the supper table, if he saw a piece of butter he'd pull up short and bolt back where he come from. He had a mortal fear of butter.

Well, Pa trained him three nights. It was a sight to see him there at the table, a big man with a needle in his hand, moving the lamp around and studying out the identical spot that caterpillar wanted most to get out of the needle's way. Pretty soon he found it, and then he says to Ned, "I'll race him agin all comers at all odds." "Well, Will," says Ned, "I guess it's a safe proposition."

2

We hauled up the feeder to Forestport and got us a load of potatoes. We raced him there against Charley Mack, the bank-walker's, Leopard Pillar, one of them tufted breeds with a row of black buttons down the back. The Leopard was well liked and had won several races that season, and there was quite a few boaters around that fancied him. Pa argued for favorable odds, saying he was racing a maiden caterpillar; and there was a lot of money laid out, and Pa and Ned managed to cover the most of it. As for the race, there wasn't anything to it. While we was putting him in the ring—one of them birchbark and sweet grass ones Indians make—Red Peril didn't act very good. I guess the smell and the crowd kind of upset him. He was nervous and kept fidgeting with his front feet; but they hadn't more'n lifted the ring than he lit out under the edge as tight as he could make it, and Pa touched him with the needle just as he lepped the line. Me and my sister was supposed to be in bed, but Ma had gone visiting in Forestport and we'd snuck in and was under the table, which had a red cloth onto it, and I can tell you there was some shouting. There was some couldn't believe that insect had been inside the ring at all; and there was some said he must be a cross with a dragon fly or a side-hill gouger; but old Charley Mack, that'd worked in the camps, said he guessed Red Peril must be descended from the caterpillars Paul Bunyan used to race. He said you could tell by the bump on his tail, which Paul used to put on all his caterpillars, seeing as how the smallest pointed object he could hold in his hand was a peavy.

Well, Pa raced him a couple of more times and he won just as easy, and Pa cleared up close to a hundred dollars in three races. That caterpillar was a mammoth wonder, and word of him got going and people commenced talking him up everywhere, so it was hard to race him around these parts.

But about that time the dock-keeper of Number One on the feeder come across a pretty swift article that the people round Rome thought high of. And as our boat was headed down the gorge, word got ahead about Red Peril, and people began to look out for the race.

We come into Number One about four o'clock, and Pa tied up right there and went on shore with his box in his pocket and Red Peril inside the box. There must have been ten men crowded into the shanty, and as many more again outside looking in the windows and door. The lock-tender was a skinny bezabor from Stittville, who thought he knew a lot about racing caterpillars; and, come to think of it, maybe he did. His name was Henry Buscerck, and he had a bad tooth in front he used to suck at a lot.

Well, him and Pa set their caterpillars on the table for the crowd to see, and I must say Buscerck's caterpillar was as handsome a brute as you could wish to look at, bright bay with black points and a short fine coat. He had a way of looking right and left, too, that made him handsome. But Pa didn't bother to look at him. Red Peril was a natural marvel, and he knew it.

Buscerck was a sly, twerpish man, and he must've heard about Red Peril—right from the beginning, as it turned out; for he laid out the course in yeller chalk. They used Pa's ring, a big silver one he'd bought secondhand just for Red Peril. They laid out a lot of money, and Dennison Smith lifted the ring. The way Red Peril histed himself out from under would raise a man's blood pressure twenty notches. I swear you could see the hair lay down on his back. Why, that black-pointed bay was left nowhere! It didn't seem like he moved. But Red Peril was just gathering himself for a fast finish over the line when he seen it was yeller. He reared right up; he must've thought it was butter, by Jeepers, the way he whirled on his hind legs and went the way he'd come. Pa begun to get scared, and he shook his needle behind Red Peril, but that caterpillar was more scared of butter than he ever was of cold steel. He passed the other insect afore he'd got halfway to the line. By Cripus, you'd ought to've heard the cheering from the Forestport crews. The Rome men was green. But when he got to the line, danged if that caterpillar didn't shy again and run around the circle twicet, and then it seemed like his heart had gone in on him, and he crept right back to the middle of the circle and lay there hiding his head. It was the pitifulest sight a man ever looked at. You could almost hear him moaning, and he shook all over.

I've never seen a man so riled as Pa was. The water was running right out of his eyes. He picked up Red Peril and he says, "This here's no race." He picked up his money and he says, "The course was illegal, with that yeller chalk." Then he squashed the other caterpillar, which was just getting ready to cross the line, and he looks at Buscerck and says, "What're you going to do about that?"

Buscerck says, "I'm going to collect my money. My caterpillar would have beat."

"If you want to call that a finish you can," says Pa, pointing to the squashed bay one, "but a baby could see he's still got to reach the line. Red Peril got to wire and come back and got to it again afore your hayseed worm got half his feet on the ground. If it was any other man owned him," Pa says, "I'd feel sorry I squashed him."

He stepped out of the house, but Buscerck laid a-hold of his pants and says, "You got to pay, Hemstreet. A man can't get away with no such excuses in the city of Rome."

Pa didn't say nothing. He just hauled off and sunk his fist, and Buscerck come to inside the lock, which was at low level right then. He waded out the lower end and he says, "I'll have you arrested for this." Pa says, "All right; but if I ever catch you around this lock again I'll let you have a feel with your other eye."

Nobody else wanted to collect money from Pa, on account of his build, mostly, so we went back to the boat. Pa put Red Peril to bed for two days. It took him all of that to get over his fright at the yeller circle. Pa even made us go without butter for a spell, thinking Red Peril might know the smell of it. He was such an intelligent, thinking animal, a man couldn't tell nothing about him.

3

But next morning the sheriff comes aboard and arrests Pa with a warrant and takes him afore a justice of the peace. That was old Oscar Snipe. He'd heard all about the race, and I think he was feeling pleasant with Pa, because right off they commenced talking breeds. It would have gone off good only Pa'd been having a round with the sheriff. They come in arm in arm, singing a Hallelujah meeting song; but Pa was polite, and when Oscar says, "What's this?" he only says, "Well, well."

"I hear you've got a good caterpillar," says the judge.

"Well, well," says Pa. It was all he could think of to say.

"What breed is he?" says Oscar, taking a chew.

"Well," says Pa, "well, well."

Ned Kilbourne says he was a red one.

"That's a good breed," says Oscar, folding his hands on his stummick and spitting over his thumbs and between his knees and into the sandbox all in one spit. "I kind of fancy the yeller ones myself. You're a connesewer," he says to Pa, "and so'm I, and between connesewers I'd like to show you one. He's as neat a stepper as there is in this county."

"Well, well," says Pa, kind of cold around the eyes and looking at the lithograph of Mrs. Snipe done in a hair frame over the sink.

Oscar slews around and fetches a box out of his back pocket and shows us a sweet little yeller one.

"There she is," he says, and waits for praise.

"She was a good woman," Pa said after a while, looking at the picture, "if any woman that's four times a widow can be called such."

"Not her," says Oscar. "It's this yeller caterpillar."

Pa slung his eyes on the insect which Oscar was holding, and it seemed like he'd just got an idee.

"Fast?" he says, deep down. "That thing run! Why, a snail with the stringhalt could spit in his eye."

Old Oscar come to a boil quick.

"Evidence. Bring me the evidence."

He spit, and he was that mad he let his whole chew get away from him without noticing. Buscerck says, "Here," and takes his hand off'n his right eye.

Pa never took no notice of nothing after that but the eye. It was the shiniest black onion I ever see on a man. Oscar says, "Forty dollars!" And Pa pays and says, "It's worth it."

But it don't never pay to make an enemy in horse racing or caterpillars, as you will see, after I've got around to telling you.

Well, we raced Red Peril nine times after that, all along the Big Ditch, and you can hear to this day—yes, sir—that there never was a caterpillar alive could run like Red Peril. Pa got rich onto him. He allowed to buy a new team in the spring. If he could only've started a breed from that bug, his fortune would've been made and Henry Ford would've looked like a bent nickel alongside me today. But caterpillars aren't built like Ford cars. We beat all the great caterpillars of the year, and it being a time for a late winter, there was some fast running. We raced the Buffalo Big Blue and Fenwick's Night Mail and Wilson's Joe of Barneveld.

There wasn't one could touch Red Peril. It was close into October when a crowd got together and brought up the Black Arrer of Ava to race us, but Red Peril beat him by an inch. And after that there wasn't a caterpillar in the state would race Pa's.

He was mighty chesty them days and had come to be quite a figger down the canawl. People come aboard to talk with him and admire Red Peril; and Pa got the idea of charging five cents a sight, and that made for more money even if there wasn't no more running for the animile. He commenced to get fat.

And then come the time that comes to all caterpillars. And it goes to show that a man ought to be as careful of his enemies as he is lending money to friends.

4

We was hauling down the Lansing Kill again and we'd just crossed the aqueduct over Stringer Brook when the lock-keeper, that minded it and the lock just below, come out and says there was quite a lot of money being put up on a caterpillar they'd collected down in Rome.

Well, Pa went in and he got out Red Peril and tried him out. He was fat and his stifles acted kind of stiff, but you could see with half an eye he was still fast. His start was a mite slower, but he made great speed once he got going.

"He's not in the best shape in the world," Pa says, "and if it was any other bug I wouldn't want to run him. But I'll trust the old brute," and he commenced brushing him up with a toothbrush he'd bought a-purpose.

"Yeanh," says Ned. "It may not be right, but we've got to consider the public."

By what happened after, we might have known that we'd meet up with that caterpillar at Number One Lock; but there wasn't no sign of Buscerck, and Pa was so excited at racing Red Peril again that I doubt if he noticed where he was at all. He was all rigged out for the occasion. He had on a black hat and a new red boating waistcoat, and when he busted loose with his horn for the lock you'd have thought he wanted to wake up all the deef-and-dumbers in seven counties. We tied by the upper gates and left the team to graze; and there was quite a crowd on hand. About nine morning boats was tied along the towpath, and all the afternoon boats waited. People was hanging around, and when they heard Pa whanging his horn they let out a great cheer. He took off his hat to some of the ladies, and then he took Red Peril out of his pocket and everybody cheered some more.

"Who owns this-here caterpillar I've been hearing about?" Pa asks. "Where is he? Why don't he bring out his pore contraption?"

A feller says he's in the shanty.

"What's his name?" says Pa.

"Martin Henry's running him. He's called the Horned Demon of Rome."

"Dinged if I ever thought to see him at my time of life," says Pa. And he goes in. Inside there was a lot of men talking and smoking and drinking and laying money faster than Leghorns can lay eggs, and when Pa comes in they let out a great howdy, and when Pa put down the Brandreth box on the table they crowded round; and you'd ought to've heard the mammoth shout they give when Red Peril climbed out of his box. And well they might. Yes, sir!

You can tell that caterpillar's a thoroughbred. He's shining right down to the root of each hair. He's round, but he ain't too fat. He don't look as supple as he used to, but the folks can't tell that. He's got the winner's look, and he prances into the center of the ring with a kind of delicate canter that was as near single-footing as I ever see a caterpillar get to. By Jeepers Cripus! I felt proud to be in the same family as him, and I wasn't only a little lad.

Pa waits for the admiration to die down, and he lays out his money, and he says to Martin Henry, "Let's see your ring-boned swivel-hocked imitation of a bug."

Martin answers, "Well, he ain't much to look at, maybe, but you'll be surprised to see how he can push along."

And he lays down the dangedest lump of worm you ever set your eyes on. It's the kind of insect a man might expect to see in France or one of them furrin lands. It's about two and a half inches long and stands only half a thumbnail at the shoulder. It's green and as hairless as a newborn egg, and it crouches down squinting around at Red Peril like a man with sweat in his eye. It ain't natural or refined to look at such a bug, let alone race it.

When Pa seen it, he let out a shout and laughed. He couldn't talk from laughing.

But the crowd didn't say a lot, having more money on the race than ever was before or since on a similar occasion. It was so much that even Pa commenced to be serious. Well, they put 'em in the ring together and Red Peril kept over on his side with a sort of intelligent dislike. He was the brainiest article in the caterpillar line I ever knowed. The other one just hunkered down with a mean look in his eye.

Millard Thompson held the ring. He counted, "One—two—three—and off." Some folks said it was the highest he knew how to count, but he always got that far anyhow, even if it took quite a while for him to remember what figger to commence with.

The ring come off and Pa and Martin Henry sunk their needles —at least they almost sunk them, for just then them standing close to the course seen that Horned Demon sink his horns into the back end of Red Peril. He was always a sensitive animal, Red Peril was, and if a needle made him start you can think for yourself what them two horns did for him. He cleared twelve inches in one jump— but then he sot right down on his belly, trembling.

"Foul!" bellers Pa. "My 'pillar's fouled."

"It ain't in the rule book," Millard says.

"It's a foul!" yells Pa; and all the Forestport men yell, "Foul! Foul!"

But it wasn't allowed. The Horned Demon commenced walking to the circle—he couldn't move much faster than a barrel can roll uphill, but he was getting there. We all seen two things, then. Red Peril was dying, and we was losing the race. Pa stood there kind of foamy in his beard, and the water running right out of both eyes. It's an awful thing to see a big man cry in public. But Ned saved us. He seen Red Peril was dying, the way he wiggled, and he figgered, with the money he had on him, he'd make him win if he could.

He leans over and puts his nose into Red Peril's ear, and he shouts, "My Cripus, you've gone and dropped the butter!"

Something got into that caterpillar's brain, dying as he was, and he let out the smallest squeak of a hollering fright I ever listened to a caterpillar make. There was a convulsion got into him. He looked like a three-dollar mule with the wind colic, and then he gave a bound. My holy! How that caterpillar did rise up. When he come down again, he was stone dead, but he lay with his chin across the line. He'd won the race. The Horned Demon was blowing bad and only halfway to the line. . . .

Well, we won. But I think Pa's heart was busted by the squeal he heard Red Peril make when he died. He couldn't abide Ned's face after that, though he knowed Ned had saved the day for him. But he put Red Peril's carcase in his pocket with the money and walks out.

And there he seen Buscerck standing at the sluices. Pa stood looking at him. The sheriff was alongside Buscerck and Oscar Snipe on the other side, and Buscerck guessed he had the law behind him.

"Who owns that Horned Demon?" said Pa.

"Me," says Buscerck with a sneer. "He may have lost, but he done a good job doing it."

Pa walks right up to him.

"I've got another forty dollars in my pocket," he says, and he connected sizably.

Buscerck's boots showed a minute. Pretty soon they let down the water and pulled him out. They had to roll a couple of gallons out of him afore they got a grunt. It served him right. He'd played foul. But the sheriff was worried, and he says to Oscar, "Had I ought to arrest Will?" (Meaning Pa.)

Oscar was a sporting man. He couldn't abide low dealing. He looks at Buscerck there, shaping his belly over the barrel, and he says, "Water never hurt a man. It keeps his hide from cracking." So they let Pa alone. I guess they didn't think it was safe to have a man in jail that would cry about a caterpillar. But then they hadn't lived alongside of Red Peril like us.

Questions for discussion

1. In the very first line you sense that this story is being *told* to you by and old "canawler," perhaps as you are sitting around a cracker barrel or a pot-bellied stove in the general store of a small community along the Erie Canal or the "Big Ditch," as it was called. Why is the story written in "canawl" dialect?
2. What indications are there that, like "Necktie Party," this is a tall tale? Have you ever read Mark Twain's "The Celebrated Jumping Frog of Calaveras County"? What similarities can you see?
3. From this story you can learn a great deal about life along the Erie Canal. At about what date would you set the time of this story? Why is it important that you have some notion of the time when the events of this story occurred? What are some of the things you learned about the canalers?

4. Did you observe the frequent references, direct and indirect, to horses and horse racing? Did you observe the names given the various racing caterpillars? What do the names remind you of? How do you account for all this?
5. Does the author give you a clue that Buscerck would show up in the story again? Or that the climax of the story would occur at Lock Number One? Did you anticipate either of these?
6. What was your emotional reaction to this story as a whole? How do you think the author felt while he was writing it? What was his purpose in writing it?

Vocabulary growth

WORDS ARE INTERESTING. A real, genuine *coot* is a water bird that long ago in England acquired a reputation for being silly. In part, no doubt, this was because of the bird's unfortunate appearance. Its broad white bill extended back into its forehead so that it had the appearance of being bald. It was quite natural, then, to speak of a man as being "bald as a coot" or "silly as a coot." Gradually, the comparison was dropped and the *coot* came to mean "a foolish person" as it does today in informal speech and writing.

For composition

1. What kind of man was Pa? How did he look? How did he act? What kind of person would cry over the death of a caterpillar and while still crying punch a man in the eye? Write a character sketch of Pa.
2. Have you listened to radio broadcasts of sports events? Imagine that you are a radio reporter. Write your account of Red Peril's last fight. You might begin, "Here he comes now, folks. Here comes Will Hemstreet with the famous Brandreth box under his arm . . ."

Two desperate men become kidnappers
and figure out a scheme to collect . . .

The Ransom of Red Chief

O. HENRY

IT looked like a good thing: but wait till I tell you. We were
down South, in Alabama—Bill Driscoll and myself—when this kidnapping idea struck us. It was, as Bill afterward expressed it, "during
a moment of temporary mental apparition"; but we didn't find that
out till later.

There was a town down there, as flat as a flannel-cake, and
called Summit, of course. It contained inhabitants of as undeleterious and self-satisfied a class of peasantry as ever clustered around
a Maypole.

Bill and me had a joint capital of about six hundred dollars,
and we needed just two thousand dollars more to pull off a fraudu-
lent town-lot scheme in Western Illinois with. We talked it over
on the front steps of the hotel. Philoprogenitiveness, says we, is
strong in semi-rural communities; therefore, and for other reasons,
a kidnapping project ought to do better there than in the radius of
newspapers that send reporters out in plain clothes to stir up talk
about such things. We knew that Summit couldn't get after us with
anything stronger than constables and, maybe, some lackadaisical
bloodhounds and a diatribe or two in the *Weekly Farmers' Budget*.
So, it looked good.

We selected for our victim the only child of a prominent citizen
named Ebenezer Dorset. The father was respectable and tight, a
mortgage fancier and a stern, upright collection-plate passer and
forecloser. The kid was a boy of ten, with bas-relief freckles, and
hair the color of the cover of the magazine you buy at the news-
stand when you want to catch a train. Bill and me figured that
Ebenezer would melt down for a ransom of two thousand dollars
to a cent. But wait till I tell you.

About two miles from Summit was a little mountain, covered with a dense cedar brake. On the rear elevation of this mountain was a cave. There we stored provisions.

One evening after sundown, we drove in a buggy past old Dorset's house. The kid was in the street, throwing rocks at a kitten on the opposite fence.

"Hey, little boy!" says Bill, "would you like to have a bag of candy and a nice ride?"

The boy catches Bill neatly in the eye with a piece of brick.

"That will cost the old man an extra five hundred dollars," says Bill, climbing over the wheel.

That boy put up a fight like a welterweight cinnamon bear; but, at last, we got him down in the bottom of the buggy and drove away. We took him up to the cave, and I hitched the horse in the cedar brake. After dark I drove the buggy to the little village, three miles away, where we had hired it, and walked back to the mountain.

Bill was pasting court-plaster over the scratches and bruises on his features. There was a fire burning behind the big rock at the entrance of the cave, and the boy was watching a pot of boiling coffee, with two buzzard tail-feathers stuck in his red hair. He points a stick at me when I come up, and says:

"Ha! cursed paleface, do you dare to enter the camp of Red Chief, the terror of the plains?"

"He's all right now," says Bill, rolling up his trousers and examining some bruises on his shins. "We're playing Indian. We're making Buffalo Bill's show look like magic-lantern views of Palestine in the town hall. I'm Old Hank, the Trapper, Red Chief's captive, and I'm to be scalped at daybreak. By Geronimo! that kid can kick hard."

Yes, sir, that boy seemed to be having the time of his life. The fun of camping out in a cave had made him forget that he was a captive himself. He immediately christened me Snake-eye, the Spy, and announced that, when his braves returned from the warpath, I was to be broiled at the stake at the rising of the sun.

Then we had supper; and he filled his mouth full of bacon and bread and gravy, and began to talk. He made a during-dinner speech something like this:

"I like this fine. I never camped out before; but I had a pet 'possum once, and I was nine last birthday. I hate to go to school. Rats ate up sixteen of Jimmy Talbot's aunt's speckled hen's eggs.

Are there any real Indians in these woods? I want some more gravy.
Does the trees moving make the wind blow? We had five puppies.
What makes your nose so red, Hank? My father has lots of money.
Are the stars hot? I whipped Ed Walker twice, Saturday. I don't like
girls. You dassent catch toads unless with a string. Do oxen make any
noise? Why are oranges round? Have you got beds to sleep on in this
cave? Amos Murray has got six toes. A parrot can talk, but a monkey
or a fish can't. How many does it take to make twelve?"

Every few minutes he would remember that he was a pesky red-
skin, and pick up his stick rifle and tiptoe to the mouth of the cave
to rubber for the scouts of the hated paleface. Now and then he
would let out a war-whoop that made Old Hank the Trapper shiver.
That boy had Bill terrorized from the start.

"Red Chief," says I to the kid, "would you like to go home?"

"Aw, what for?" says he. "I don't have any fun at home. I hate
to go to school. I like to camp out. You won't take me back home
again, Snake-eye, will you?"

"Not right away," says I. "We'll stay here in the cave a while."

"All right!" says he. "That'll be fine. I never had such fun in all
my life."

We went to bed about eleven o'clock. We spread down some
wide blankets and quilts and put Red Chief between us. We weren't
afraid he'd run away. He kept us awake for three hours, jumping up
and reaching for his rifle and screeching: "Hist! pard," in mine and
Bill's ears, as the fancied crackle of a twig or the rustle of a leaf revealed to his young imagination the stealthy approach of the outlaw
band. At last, I fell into a troubled sleep, and dreamed that I had
been kidnapped and chained to a tree by a ferocious pirate with red
hair.

Just at daybreak, I was awakened by a series of awful screams
from Bill. They weren't yells, or howls, or shouts, or whoops, or
yawps, such as you'd expect from a manly set of vocal organs—they
were simply indecent, terrifying, humiliating screams, such as women
emit when they see ghosts or caterpillars. It's an awful thing to hear
a strong, desperate, fat man scream incontinently in a cave at daybreak.

I jumped up to see what the matter was. Red Chief was sitting
on Bill's chest, with one hand twined in Bill's hair. In the other he
had the sharp case-knife we used for slicing bacon; and he was indus-

triously and realistically trying to take Bill's scalp, according to the sentence that had been pronounced upon him the evening before.

I got the knife away from the kid and made him lie down again. But, from that moment, Bill's spirit was broken. He laid down on his side of the bed, but he never closed an eye again in sleep as long as that boy was with us. I dozed off for a while, but along toward sun-up I remembered that Red Chief had said I was to be burned at the stake at the rising of the sun. I wasn't nervous or afraid; but I sat up and lit my pipe and leaned against a rock.

"What you getting up so soon for, Sam?" asked Bill.

"Me?" says I. "Oh, I got a kind of a pain in my shoulder. I thought sitting up would rest it."

"You're a liar!" says Bill. "You're afraid. You was to be burned at sunrise, and you was afraid he'd do it. And he would, too, if he could find a match. Ain't it awful, Sam? Do you think anybody will pay out money to get a little imp like that back home?"

"Sure," said I. "A rowdy kid like that is just the kind that parents dote on. Now, you and the Chief get up and cook breakfast, while I go up on the top of this mountain and reconnoiter."

I went up on the peak of the little mountain and ran my eye over the contiguous vicinity. Over toward Summit I expected to see the sturdy yeomanry of the village armed with scythes and pitchforks beating the countryside for the dastardly kidnappers. But what I saw was a peaceful landscape dotted with one man ploughing with a dun mule. Nobody was dragging the creek; no couriers dashed hither and yon, bringing tidings of no news to the distracted parents. There was a sylvan attitude of somnolent sleepiness pervading that section of the external outward surface of Alabama that lay exposed to my view. "Perhaps," says I to myself, "it has not yet been discovered that the wolves have borne away the tender lambkin from the fold. Heaven help the wolves!" says I, and I went down the mountain to breakfast.

When I got to the cave I found Bill backed up against the side of it, breathing hard, and the boy threatening to smash him with a rock half as big as a cocoanut.

"He put a red-hot boiled potato down my back," explained Bill, "and then mashed it with his foot; and I boxed his ears. Have you got a gun about you, Sam?"

I took the rock away from the boy and kind of patched up the argument. "I'll fix you," says the kid to Bill. "No man ever yet struck the Red Chief but what he got paid for it. You better beware!"

After breakfast the kid takes a piece of leather with strings wrapped around it out of his pocket and goes outside the cave unwinding it.

"What's he up to now?" says Bill, anxiously. "You don't think he'll run away, do you, Sam?"

"No fear of it," says I. "He don't seem to be much of a home body. But we've got to fix up some plan about the ransom. There don't seem to be much excitement around Summit on account of his disappearance; but maybe they haven't realized yet that he's gone. His folks may think he's spending the night with Aunt Jane or one of the neighbors. Anyhow, he'll be missed today. Tonight we must get a message to his father demanding the two thousand dollars for his return."

Just then we heard a kind of war-whoop, such as David might have emitted when he knocked out the champion Goliath. It was a sling that Red Chief had pulled out of his pocket, and he was whirling it around his head.

I dodged, and heard a heavy thud and a kind of a sigh from Bill, like a horse gives out when you take his saddle off. A niggerhead rock the size of an egg had caught Bill just behind his left ear. He loosened himself all over and fell in the fire across the frying pan of hot water for washing the dishes. I dragged him out and poured cold water on his head for half an hour.

By and by, Bill sits up and feels behind his ear and says: "Sam, do you know who my favorite Biblical character is?"

"Take it easy," says I. "You'll come to your senses presently."

"King Herod," says he. "You won't go away and leave me here alone, will you, Sam?"

I went out and caught that boy and shook him until his freckles rattled.

"If you don't behave," says I, "I'll take you straight home. Now, are you going to be good, or not?"

"I was only funning," says he sullenly. "I didn't mean to hurt Old Hank. But what did he hit me for? I'll behave, Snake-eye, if you won't send me home, and if you'll let me play the Black Scout today."

"I don't know the game," says I. "That's for you and Mr. Bill to decide. He's your playmate for the day. I'm going away for a while, on business. Now, you come in and make friends with him and say you are sorry for hurting him, or home you go, at once."

I made him and Bill shake hands, and then I took Bill aside and told him I was going to Poplar Cove, a little village three miles from the cave, and find out what I could about how the kidnapping had been regarded in Summit. Also, I thought it best to send a peremptory letter to old man Dorset that day, demanding the ransom and dictating how it should be paid.

"You know, Sam," says Bill, "I've stood by you without batting an eye in earthquakes, fire and flood—in poker games, dynamite outrages, police raids, train robberies and cyclones. I never lost my nerve yet till we kidnapped that two-legged skyrocket of a kid. He's got me going. You won't leave me long with him, will you, Sam?"

"I'll be back some time this afternoon," says I. "You must keep the boy amused and quiet till I return. And now we'll write the letter to old Dorset."

Bill and I got paper and pencil and worked on the letter while Red Chief, with a blanket wrapped around him, strutted up and down, guarding the mouth of the cave. Bill begged me tearfully to make the ransom fifteen hundred dollars instead of two thousand. "I ain't attempting," says he, "to decry the celebrated moral aspect of parental affection, but we're dealing with humans, and it ain't human for anybody to give up two thousand dollars for that forty-pound chunk of freckled wildcat. I'm willing to take a chance at fifteen hundred dollars. You can charge the difference up to me."

So, to relieve Bill, I acceded, and we collaborated a letter that ran this way:

Ebenezer Dorset, Esq.:
We have your boy concealed in a place far from Summit. It is useless for you or the most skilful detectives to attempt to find him. Absolutely, the only terms on which you can have him restored to you are these: We demand fifteen hundred dollars in large bills for his return; the money to be left at midnight tonight at the same spot and in the same box as your reply—as hereinafter described. If you agree to these terms, send your answer in writing by a solitary messenger tonight at half-past eight o'clock. After crossing Owl Creek, on the road to Poplar Cove, there are three large trees about a hundred yards apart, close to the fence of the

wheat field on the right-hand side. At the bottom of the fence-post, opposite the third tree, will be found a small pasteboard box.

The messenger will place the answer in this box and return immediately to Summit.

If you attempt any treachery or fail to comply with our demand as stated, you will never see your boy again.

If you pay the money as demanded, he will be returned to you safe and well within three hours. These terms are final, and if you do not accede to them no further communication will be attempted.

Two Desperate Men.

I addressed this letter to Dorset, and put it in my pocket. As I was about to start, the kid comes up to me and says:

"Aw, Snake-eye, you said I could play the Black Scout while you was gone."

"Play it, of course," says I. "Mr. Bill will play with you. What kind of a game is it?"

"I'm the Black Scout," says Red Chief, "and I have to ride to the stockade to warn the settlers that the Indians are coming. I'm tired of playing Indian myself. I want to be the Black Scout."

"All right," says I. "It sounds harmless to me. I guess Mr. Bill will help you foil the pesky savages."

"What am I to do?" asks Bill, looking at the kid suspiciously.

"You are the hoss," says Black Scout. "Get down on your hands and knees. How can I ride to the stockade without a hoss?"

"You'd better keep him interested," said I, "till we get the scheme going. Loosen up."

Bill gets down on his all fours, and a look comes in his eye like a rabbit's when you catch it in a trap.

"How far is it to the stockade, kid?" he asks, in a husky manner of voice.

"Ninety miles," says the Black Scout. "And you have to hump yourself to get there on time. Whoa, now!"

The Black Scout jumps on Bill's back and digs his heels in his side.

"For Heaven's sake," says Bill, "hurry back, Sam, as soon as you can. I wish we hadn't made the ransom more than a thousand. Say, you quit kicking me or I'll get up and warm you good."

I walked over to Poplar Cove and sat around the postoffice and store, talking with the chawbacons that came in to trade. One whiskerando says that he hears Summit is all upset on account of Elder Ebenezer Dorset's boy having been lost or stolen. That was all I wanted to know. I bought some smoking tobacco, referred casually to the price of black-eyed peas, posted my letter surreptitiously and came away. The postmaster said the mail-carrier would come by in an hour to take the mail on to Summit.

When I got back to the cave Bill and the boy were not to be found. I explored the vicinity of the cave, and risked a yodel or two, but there was no response.

So I lighted my pipe and sat down on a mossy bank to await developments.

In about half an hour I heard the bushes rustle, and Bill wabbled out into the little glade in front of the cave. Behind him was the kid, stepping softly like a scout, with a broad grin on his face. Bill stopped, took off his hat and wiped his face with a red handkerchief. The kid stopped about eight feet behind him.

"Sam," says Bill, "I suppose you'll think I'm a renegade, but I couldn't help it. I'm a grown person with masculine proclivities and habits of self-defense, but there is a time when all systems of egotism and predominance fail. The boy is gone. I have sent him home. All is off. There was martyrs in old times," goes on Bill, "that suffered death rather than give up the particular graft they enjoyed. None of 'em ever was subjugated to such supernatural tortures as I have been. I tried to be faithful to our articles of depredation; but there came a limit."

"What's the trouble, Bill?" I asks him.

"I was rode," says Bill, "the ninety miles to the stockade, not barring an inch. Then, when the settlers was rescued, I was given oats. Sand ain't a palatable substitute. And then, for an hour I had to try to explain to him why there was nothin' in holes, how a road can run both ways and what makes the grass green. I tell you, Sam, a human can only stand so much. I takes him by the neck of his clothes and drags him down the mountain. On the way he kicks my legs black-and-blue from the knees down; and I've got to have two or three bites on my thumb and hand cauterized.

"But he's gone"—continues Bill—"gone home. I showed him the road to Summit and kicked him about eight feet nearer there at one kick. I'm sorry we lose the ransom; but it was either that or Bill Driscoll to the madhouse."

Bill is puffing and blowing, but there is a look of ineffable peace and growing content on his rose-pink features.

"Bill," says I, "there isn't any heart disease in your family, is there?"

"No," says Bill, "nothing chronic except malaria and accidents. Why?"

"Then you might turn around," says I, "and have a look behind you."

Bill turns and sees the boy, and loses his complexion and sits down plump on the ground and begins to pluck aimlessly at grass and little sticks. For an hour I was afraid of his mind. And then I told him that my scheme was to put the whole job through immediately and that we would get the ransom and be off with it by midnight if old Dorset fell in with our proposition. So Bill braced up enough to give the kid a weak sort of a smile and a promise to play the Russian in a Japanese war with him as soon as he felt a little better.

I had a scheme for collecting that ransom without danger of being caught by counterplots that ought to commend itself to professional kidnappers. The tree under which the answer was to be left —and the money later on—was close to the road fence with big, bare fields on all sides. If a gang of constables should be watching for any one to come for the note they could see him a long way off crossing the fields or in the road. But no, sirree! At half-past eight I was up in that tree as well hidden as a tree toad, waiting for the messenger to arrive.

Exactly on time, a half-grown boy rides up the road on a bicycle, locates the pasteboard box at the foot of the fence-post, slips a folded piece of paper into it and pedals away again back toward Summit.

I waited an hour and then concluded the thing was square. I slid down the tree, got the note, slipped along the fence till I struck the woods, and was back at the cave in another half an hour. I opened the note, got near the lantern and read it to Bill. It was written with a pen in a crabbed hand, and the sum and substance of it was this:

Two Desperate Men.

Gentlemen: I received your letter today by post, in regard to the ransom you ask for the return of my son. I think you are a little high in your demands, and I hereby make you a counter-proposition, which I am inclined to believe you will accept. You bring Johnny home and pay me two hundred and fifty dollars in cash, and I agree to take him off your hands. You had better come at night, for the neighbors believe he is lost, and I couldn't be responsible for what they would do to anybody they saw bringing him back. Very respectfully,

·EBENEZER DORSET.

"Great pirates of Penzance!" says I; "of all the impudent——"

But I glanced at Bill, and hesitated. He had the most appealing look in his eyes I ever saw on the face of a dumb or a talking brute.

"Sam," says he, "what's two hundred and fifty dollars, after all? We've got the money. One more night of this kid will send me to a bed in Bedlam. Besides being a thorough gentleman, I think Mr. Dorset is a spendthrift for making us such a liberal offer. You ain't going to let the chance go, are you?"

"Tell you the truth, Bill," says I, "this little he ewe lamb has somewhat got on my nerves too. We'll take him home, pay the ransom and make our get-away."

We took him home that night. We got him to go by telling him that his father had bought a silver-mounted rifle and a pair of moccasins for him, and we were going to hunt bears the next day.

It was just twelve o'clock when we knocked at Ebenezer's front door. Just at the moment when I should have been abstracting the fifteen hundred dollars from the box under the tree, according to the original proposition, Bill was counting out two hundred and fifty dollars into Dorset's hand.

When the kid found out we were going to leave him at home he started up a howl like a calliope and fastened himself as tight as a leech to Bill's leg. His father peeled him away gradually, like a porous plaster.

"How long can you hold him?" asks Bill.

"I'm not as strong as I used to be," says old Dorset, "but I think I can promise you ten minutes."

"Enough," says Bill. "In ten minutes I shall cross the Central, Southern and Middle Western States, and be legging it trippingly for the Canadian border."

And, as dark as it was, and as fat as Bill was, and as good a runner as I am, he was a good mile and a half out of Summit before I could catch up with him.

Questions for discussion

1. To whom is this a funny situation? To Bill? To Sam? To Red Chief? To Red Chief's father? To the author of the story? To you? Why?
2. What situation in the story struck you as being especially funny? Why?
3. Why does Red Chief react the way he does? Why isn't he afraid?
4. When did you get the first hint as to the kind of boy he is?
5. When did the "two desperate men" regret what they had done?
6. Did you sympathize with any of the characters in this story?
7. What was your reaction to their signing the ransom note as "Two Desperate Men"?
8. Do you think that Ebenezer Dorset had any idea of what was going on where his son was?
9. Did the story develop as you thought it would? Did it end as you thought it would? Very early in the story the author gives you a hint as to how things would turn out. Do you see it now? How did you react to the end of the story?
10. In what respect is this story and "The Death of Red Peril" similar?

Vocabulary growth

WORDS ARE INTERESTING. In this story O. Henry had fun with words by deliberately misusing some, and choosing long, fancy words when shorter words would have been better. For example, Bill speaks of a "temporary mental apparition." Do you know what he should have said instead of *apparition*?

In the next sentence, O. Henry speaks of the residents of Summit as *undeleterious*. You probably won't find this word in a dictionary. O. Henry made it up from the prefix *un-*, which means "not" or "the opposite of" plus the word *deleterious*, which means "harmful, injurious." O. Henry was taking a long way around to say that the people of Summit were harmless.

Later on, he says "There was a sylvan attitude of somnolent sleepiness pervading that section of the external outward surface of Alabama . . ." Look up the words that you do not know. Rewrite the sentence in the fewest words that will convey its meaning.

CONTEXT. You can often get the meaning of a word from the context, that is, from the other words with which it is used. Figure out a meaning for each of the italicized words in the following sentences. Check your meanings with a dictionary.

1. "We knew that Summit couldn't get after us with anything

stronger than constables and, maybe, some lackadaisical blood-hounds and a *diatribe* or two in the *Weekly Farmers' Budget*."

2. "About two miles from Summit was a little mountain, covered with a dense cedar *brake*."
3. "Now, you and the Chief get up and cook breakfast, while I go up on the top of this mountain and *reconnoiter*."
4. "Also, I thought it best to send a *peremptory* letter to old man Dorset that day, demanding the ransom and dictating how it should be paid."

For composition

1. Have you or your family ever had something they wanted to get rid of but couldn't figure out how to do it? A car, perhaps? A bike? Some useless and troublesome gift? Write a short account of the thing and why it was so troublesome.
2. You are one of Mr. Dorset's neighbors. You are writing a letter to the editor of the town paper under the heading "Twenty-four Hours of Peace." You suggest that a search be made for the kidnappers so they can be rewarded, and perhaps even persuaded to take Red Chief far away. Of course, you will have to tell some of the things that Red Chief did day after day, to make the neighbors glad he was gone.

Mme. Loisel could not possibly anticipate
what would happen because of . . .

The Necklace

GUY DE MAUPASSANT

SHE was one of those pretty and charming girls who are sometimes, as if by a mistake of destiny, born in a family of clerks. She
had no dowry, no expectations, no means of being known, understood, loved, wedded, by any rich and distinguished man; and she
let herself be married to a little clerk at the Ministry of Public
Instruction.

She dressed plainly because she could not dress well, but she
was as unhappy as though she had really fallen from her proper
station; since with women there is neither caste nor ranks; and
beauty, grace, and charm act instead of family and birth. Natural
fineness, instinct for what is elegant, suppleness of wit, are the
sole hierarchy, and make from women of the people the equals of
the very greatest ladies.

She suffered ceaselessly, feeling herself born for all the delicacies
and all the luxuries. She suffered from the poverty of her dwelling,
from the wretched look of the walls, from the worn-out chairs,
from the ugliness of the curtains. All those things, of which another woman of her rank would never even have been conscious,
tortured her and made her angry. The sight of the little Breton
peasant who did her humble housework aroused in her regrets
which were despairing, and distracted dreams. She thought of the
silent ante-chambers hung with Oriental tapestry, lit by tall bronze
candelabra, and of the two great footmen in knee-breeches who
sleep in the big armchairs, made drowsy by the heavy warmth of
the hot-air stove. She thought of the long *salons* fitted up with
ancient silk, of the delicate furniture carrying priceless curiosities,
and of the coquettish perfumed boudoirs made for talks at five
o'clock with intimate friends, with men famous and sought after,
whom all women envy and whose attention they all desire.

When she sat down to dinner, before the round table covered

with a table-cloth three days old, opposite her husband, who uncovered the soup tureen and declared with an enchanted air, "Ah,
the good *pot-au-feu!* I don't know anything better than that," she
thought of dainty dinners, of shining silverware, of tapestry which
peopled the walls with ancient personages and with strange birds
flying in the midst of a fairy forest; and she thought of delicious
dishes served on marvelous plates, and of the whispered gallantries
which you listen to with a sphinx-like smile, while you are eating
the pink flesh of a trout or the wings of a quail.

She had no dresses, no jewels, nothing. And she loved nothing
but that; she felt made for that. She would so have liked to please,
to be envied, to be charming, to be sought after.

She had a friend, a former schoolmate at the convent, who was
rich, and whom she did not like to go and see any more, because
she suffered so much when she came back.

But, one evening, her husband returned home with a trium-
phant air, and holding a large envelope in his hand.

"There," said he, "here is something for you."

She tore the paper sharply, and drew out a printed card which
bore these words:

"The Minister of Public Instruction and Mme. Georges Ram-
ponneau request the honor of M. and Mme. Loisel's company at
the palace of the Ministry on Monday evening, January 18th."

Instead of being delighted, as her husband hoped, she threw
the invitation on the table with disdain, murmuring:

"What do you want me to do with that?"

"But, my dear, I thought you would be glad. You never go out,
and this is such a fine opportunity. I had awful trouble to get it.
Every one wants to go; it is very select, and they are not giving many
invitations to clerks. The whole official world will be there."

She looked at him with an irritated eye, and she said, impa-
tiently:

"And what do you want me to put on my back?"

He had not thought of that; he stammered:

"Why, the dress you go to the theater in. It looks very well, to
me."

He stopped, distracted, seeing that his wife was crying. Two
great tears descended slowly from the corners of her eyes towards
the corners of her mouth. He stuttered:

"What's the matter? What's the matter?"

But, by a violent effort, she had conquered her grief, and she replied, with a calm voice, while she wiped her wet cheeks:

"Nothing. Only I have no dress, and therefore I can't go to this ball. Give your card to some colleague whose wife is better equipped than I."

He was in despair. He resumed:

"Come, let us see, Mathilde. How much would it cost, a suitable dress, which you could use on other occasions, something very simple?"

She reflected several seconds, making her calculations and wondering also what sum she could ask without drawing on herself an immediate refusal and a frightened exclamation from the economical clerk.

Finally, she replied, hesitatingly:

"I don't know exactly, but I think I could manage it with four hundred francs."

He had grown a little pale, because he was laying aside just that amount to buy a gun and treat himself to a little shooting next summer on the plain of Nanterre, with several friends who went to shoot larks down there, of a Sunday.

But he said:

"All right. I will give you four hundred francs. And try to have a pretty dress."

The day of the ball drew near, and Mme. Loisel seemed sad, uneasy, anxious. Her dress was ready, however. Her husband said to her one evening:

"What is the matter? Come, you've been so queer these last three days."

And she answered:

"It annoys me not to have a single jewel, not a single stone, nothing to put on. I shall look like distress. I should almost rather not go at all."

He resumed:

"You might wear natural flowers. It's very stylish at this time of the year. For ten francs you can get two or three magnificent roses."

She was not convinced.

"No; there's nothing more humiliating than to look poor among other women who are rich."

But her husband cried:

"How stupid you are! Go look up your friend Mme. Forestier, and ask her to lend you some jewels. You're quite thick enough with her to do that."

She uttered a cry of joy:

"It's true. I never thought of it."

The next day she went to her friend and told of her distress.

Mme. Forestier went to a wardrobe with a glass door, took out a large jewel-box, brought it back, opened it, and said to Mme. Loisel:

"Choose, my dear."

She saw first of all some bracelets, then a pearl necklace, then a Venetian cross, gold, and precious stones of admirable workmanship. She tried on the ornaments before the glass, hesitated, could not make up her mind to part with them, to give them back. She kept asking:

"Haven't you any more?"

"Why, yes. Look. I don't know what you like."

All of a sudden she discovered, in a black satin box, a superb necklace of diamonds; and her heart began to beat with an immoderate desire. Her hands trembled as she took it. She fastened it around her throat, outside her high-necked dress, and remained lost in ecstasy at the sight of herself.

Then she asked, hesitatingly, filled with anguish:

"Can you lend me that, only that?"

"Why, yes, certainly."

She sprang upon the neck of her friend, kissed her passionately, then fled with her treasure.

The day of the ball arrived. Mme. Loisel made a great success. She was prettier than them all, elegant, gracious, smiling, and crazy with joy. All the men looked at her, asked her name, endeavored to be introduced. All the attachés of the Cabinet wanted to waltz with her. She was remarked by the minister himself.

She danced with intoxication, with passion, made drunk by pleasure, forgetting all, in the triumph of her beauty, in the glory of her success, in a sort of cloud of happiness composed of all this homage, of all this admiration, of all these awakened desires, and of that sense of complete victory which is so sweet to woman's heart.

She went away about four o'clock in the morning. Her husband had been sleeping since midnight, in a little deserted anteroom, with three other gentlemen whose wives were having a good time.

He threw over her shoulders the wraps which he had brought, modest wraps of common life, whose poverty contrasted with the elegance of the ball dress. She felt this and wanted to escape so as not to be remarked by the other women, who were enveloping themselves in costly furs.

Loisel held her back.

"Wait a bit. You will catch cold outside. I will go and call a cab."

But she did not listen to him, and rapidly descended the stairs. When they were in the street they did not find a carriage; and they began to look for one, shouting after the cabmen whom they saw passing by at a distance.

They went down towards the Seine, in despair, shivering with cold. At last they found on the quay one of those ancient noctambulant coupés which, exactly as if they were ashamed to show their misery during the day, are never seen around Paris until after nightfall.

It took them to their door in the Rue des Martyrs, and once more, sadly, they climbed up homeward. All was ended for her. And as to him, he reflected that he must be at the Ministry at ten o'clock.

She removed the wraps, which covered her shoulders, before the glass, so as once more to see herself in all her glory. But suddenly she uttered a cry. She had no longer the necklace around her neck!

Her husband already half-undressed, demanded:

"What is the matter with you?"

She turned madly towards him:

"I have—I have—I've lost Mme. Forestier's necklace."

He stood up, distracted.

"What!—how?—Impossible!"

And they looked in the folds of her dress, in the folds of her cloak, in her pockets, everywhere. They did not find it.

He asked:

"You're sure you had it on when you left the ball?"

"Yes, I felt it in the vestibule of the palace."

"But if you had lost it in the street we should have heard it fall. It must be in the cab."

"Yes. Probably. Did you take his number?"

"No. And you, didn't you notice it?"

"No."

They looked, thunderstruck, at one another. At last Loisel put on his clothes.

"I shall go back on foot," said he, "over the whole route which we have taken, to see if I can't find it."

And he went out. She sat waiting on a chair in her ball dress, without strength to go to bed, overwhelmed, without fire, without a thought.

Her husband came back about seven o'clock. He had found nothing.

He went to Police Headquarters, to the newspaper offices, to offer a reward; he went to the cab companies—everywhere, in fact, whither he was urged by the least suspicion of hope.

She waited all day, in the same condition of mad fear before this terrible calamity.

Loisel returned at night with a hollow, pale face; he had discovered nothing.

"You must write to your friend," said he, "that you have broken the clasp of her necklace and that you are having it mended. That will give us time to turn round."

She wrote at his dictation.

At the end of the week they had lost all hope.

And Loisel, who had aged five years, declared:

"We must consider how to replace that ornament."

The next day they took the box which had contained it, and they went to the jeweler whose name was found within. He consulted his books.

"It was not I, madame, who sold that necklace; I must simply have furnished the case."

Then they went from jeweler to jeweler, searching for a necklace like the other, consulting their memories, sick both of them with chagrin and with anguish.

They found, in a shop at the Palais Royal, a string of diamonds which seemed to them exactly like the one they looked for. It was worth forty thousand francs. They could have it for thirty-six.

So they begged the jeweler not to sell it for three days yet. And they made a bargain that he should buy it back for thirty-four thousand francs, in case they found the other one before the end of February.

Loisel possessed eighteen thousand francs which his father had left him. He would borrow the rest.

He did borrow, asking a thousand francs of one, five hundred of another, five louis here, three louis there. He gave notes, took up ruinous obligations, dealt with usurers, and all the race of lenders. He compromised all the rest of his life, risked his signature without even knowing if he could meet it; and, frightened by the pains yet to come, by the black misery which was about to fall upon him, by the prospect of all the physical privations and of all the mortal tortures which he was to suffer, he went to get the new necklace, putting down upon the merchant's counter thirty-six thousand francs.

When Mme. Loisel took back the necklace Mme. Forestier said to her, with a chilly manner:

"You should have returned it sooner, I might have needed it."

She did not open the case, as her friend had so much feared. If she had detected the substitution, what would she have thought, what would she have said? Would she not have taken Mme. Loisel for a thief?

Mme. Loisel now knew the horrible existence of the needy. She took her part, moreover, all on a sudden, with heroism. That dreadful debt must be paid. She would pay it. They dismissed their servant; they changed their lodgings; they rented a garret under the roof.

She came to know what heavy housework meant and the odious cares of the kitchen. She washed the dishes, using her rosy nails on the pots and pans. She washed the dirty linen, the shirts, and the dish-cloths, which she dried upon a line; she carried the slops down to the street every morning, and carried up the water, stopping for breath at every landing. And, dressed like a woman of the people, she went to the fruiterer, the grocer, the butcher, her basket on her arm, bargaining, insulted, defending her miserable money sou by sou.

Each month they had to meet some notes, renew others, obtain more time.

Her husband worked in the evening making a fair copy of some tradesman's accounts, and late at night he often copied manuscript for five sous a page.

And this life lasted ten years.

At the end of ten years they had paid everything, everything with the rates of usury, and the accumulations of the compound interest.

Mme. Loisel looked old now. She had become the woman of impoverished households—strong and hard and rough. With frowsy hair, skirts askew, and red hands, she talked loud while washing the floor with great swishes of water. But sometimes, when her husband was at the office, she sat down near the window, and she thought of that gay evening of long ago, of that ball where she had been so beautiful and so fêted.

What would have happened if she had not lost that necklace? Who knows? Who knows? How life is strange and how changeful! How little a thing is needed for us to be lost or to be saved!

But, one Sunday, having gone to take a walk in the Champs Elysées to refresh herself from the labors of the week, she suddenly perceived a woman who was leading a child. It was Mme. Forestier, still young, still beautiful, still charming.

Mme. Loisel felt moved. Was she going to speak to her? Yes, certainly. And now that she had paid, she was going to tell her all about it. Why not?

She went up.

"Good-day, Jeanne."

The other, astonished to be familiarly addressed by this plain good-wife, did not recognize her at all, and stammered:

"But—madame!—I do not know—You must be mistaken."

"No. I am Mathilde Loisel."

Her friend uttered a cry.

"Oh, my poor Mathilde! How you are changed!"

"Yes, I have had days hard enough, since I have seen you, days wretched enough—and that because of you!"

"Of me! How so?"

"Do you remember that diamond necklace which you lent me to wear at the ministerial ball?"

"Yes. Well?"

"Well, I lost it."

"What do you mean? You brought it back."

"I brought you back another just like it. And for this we have been ten years paying. You can understand that it was not easy for us, us who had nothing. At last it is ended, and I am very glad."

Mme. Forestier had stopped.

"You say that you bought a necklace of diamonds to replace mine?"

"Yes. You never noticed it, then! They were very like."

And she smiled with a joy which was proud and naïve at once. Mme. Forestier, strongly moved, took her two hands.

"Oh, my poor Mathilde! Why, my necklace was paste.[1] It was worth at most five hundred francs!"

[1] paste: a hard, brilliant glass used to make artificial gems

Questions for discussion

"The Necklace" is one of the world's most widely read short stories. You have just read an English translation of the original, which was written in French.

1. The first six paragraphs of the story present the main character, Madame Loisel. The author wants you to understand something about her character and personality before he tells you what happens to her. What kind of person is Mme. Loisel? Do you feel sympathetic or critical of her? Why?

2. Why do you think Mme. Loisel selected the necklace rather than any of the other pieces of jewelry? What do you think it symbolized to her?

3. Do you think Mme. Loisel and her husband were right or wrong in not telling Mme. Forestier about the necklace? Why?

4. To what extent did Mme. Loisel contribute to her own misfortune? To what extent was she a victim of fate?

5. Describe the change that took place in Mme. Loisel during the ten years following her great misfortune. Although she suffered during this period, do you think she gained anything from this experience?

6. De Maupassant's use of *irony* (see Glossary, page 299) in this story makes for power and suggestiveness.
   a) At the close of the story, it is clear that Mme. Forestier owes the Loisels many thousands of francs. Supposing that the money was repaid, what irony would there be in the fact that Mme. Loisel could then afford pretty dresses and other extravagances?
   b) Do you see anything ironical in the fact that Monsieur Loisel worked so hard to get a ticket to the ball and was so pleased at his success?
   c) Point out the irony of the final sentence in the story. What point do you think the author is making?

Vocabulary Growth

WORD BUILDING. On page 196 is the sentence, "For ten francs you can get two or three magnificent roses." The word *magnificent* belongs to an interesting word family. Give the common root and meaning of each of the following words:

magnify   magnate

magnitude   magnanimous

CONTEXT. By examining their contexts, what meaning do you get from the following italicized words:

a. He *compromised* all the rest of his life. (page 200)

b. ". . . cloud of happiness *composed* of all this *homage*, of all this admiration . . ." (page 197)

For composition

1. Do you think there are people like Mme. Loisel today? Write a composition in which you describe such a person. Include the things and achievements this person feels are important to his happiness. Also, what object or objects symbolize success and importance for him? State to what extent you think these attitudes are justified and profitable.

2. Some people clearly contribute to a misfortune because of the kind of person they are. Describe an actual or imaginary incident where a person caused an accident because of his personality. Tell what happened to him or to others because of this one unfortunate incident.

At last Mr. Baumer gets what he has been
waiting for—and at a . . .

Bargain

A . B . GUTHRIE , JR .

MR. Baumer and I had closed the Moon Dance Mercantile
Company and were walking to the post office, and he had a bunch
of bills in his hand ready to mail. There wasn't anyone or anything
much on the street because it was suppertime. A buckboard and a
saddle horse were tied at Hirsch's rack, and a rancher in a wagon
rattled for home ahead of us, the sound of his going fading out as
he prodded his team. Freighter Slade stood alone in front of the
Moon Dance Saloon, maybe wondering whether to have one more
before going to supper. People said he could hold a lot without
showing it except in being ornerier even than usual.

Mr. Baumer didn't see him until he was almost on him, and
then he stopped and fingered through the bills until he found the
right one. He stepped up to Slade and held it out.

Slade said, "What's this, Dutchie?"

Mr. Baumer had to tilt his head up to talk to him. "You know
vat it is."

Slade just said, "Yeah?" You never could tell from his face
what went on inside his skull. He had dark skin and shallow cheeks
and a thick-growing mustache that fell over the corners of his
mouth.

"It is a bill," Mr. Baumer said. "I tell you before it is a bill.
For twenty-vun dollars and fifty cents."

"You know what I do with bills, don't you, Dutchie?" Slade
asked.

Mr. Baumer didn't answer the question. He said, "For mer-
chandise."

Slade took the envelope from Mr. Baumer's hand and squeezed
it up in his fist and let it drop on the plank sidewalk. Not saying
anything, he reached down and took Mr. Baumer's nose between

the knuckles of his fingers and twisted it up into his eyes. That was all. That was all at the time. Slade half turned and slouched to the door of the bar and let himself in. Some men were laughing in there.

Mr. Baumer stooped and picked up the bill and put it on top of the rest and smoothed it out for mailing. When he straightened up I could see tears in his eyes from having his nose screwed around.

He didn't say anything to me, and I didn't say anything to him, being so much younger and feeling embarrassed for him. He went into the post office and slipped the bills in the slot, and we walked on home together. At the last, at the crossing where I had to leave him, he remembered to say, "Better study, Al. Is good to know to read and write and figure." I guess he felt he had to push me a little, my father being dead.

I said, "Sure. See you after school tomorrow"—which he knew I would anyway. I had been working in the store for him during the summer and after classes ever since pneumonia took my dad off.

Three of us worked there regularly, Mr. Baumer, of course, and me and Colly Coleman, who knew enough to drive the delivery wagon but wasn't much help around the store except for carrying orders out to the rigs at the hitchpost and handling heavy things like the whisky barrel at the back of the store which Mr. Baumer sold quarts and gallons out of.

The store carried quite a bit of stuff—sugar and flour and dried fruits and canned goods and such on one side and yard goods and coats and caps and aprons and the like of that on the other, besides kerosene and bran and buckets and linoleum and pitchforks in the storehouse at the rear—but it wasn't a big store like Hirsch Brothers up the street. Never would be, people guessed, going on to say, with a sort of slow respect, that it would have gone under long ago if Mr. Baumer hadn't been half mule and half beaver. He had started the store just two years before and, the way things were, worked himself close to death.

He was at the high desk at the end of the grocery counter when I came in the next afternoon. He had an eyeshade on and black sateen protectors on his forearms, and his pencil was in his hand instead of behind his ear and his glasses were roosted on the nose that Slade had twisted. He didn't hear me open and close the door or hear my feet as I walked back to him, and I saw he wasn't doing anything with the pencil but holding it over paper. I stood and studied him for a minute, seeing a small, stooped man with a little paunch bulging through his unbuttoned vest. He was a man you wouldn't remember from meeting once. There was nothing in his looks to set itself in your mind unless maybe it was his chin, which was a small, pink hill in the gentle plain of his face.

While I watched him, he lifted his hand and felt carefully of his nose. Then he saw me. His eyes had that kind of mistiness that seems to go with age or illness, though he wasn't really old or sick, either. He brought his hand down quickly and picked up the pencil, but he saw I still was looking at the nose, and finally he sighed and said, "That Slade."

Just the sound of the name brought Slade to my eye. I saw him slouched in front of the bar, and I saw him and his string coming down the grade from the buttes, the wheel horses held snug and the rest lined out pretty, and then the string leveling off and Slade's whip lifting hair from a horse that wasn't up in the collar. I had heard it said that Slade could make a horse scream with that whip. Slade's name wasn't Freighter, of course. Our town had nicknamed him that because that was what he was.

"I don't think it's any good to send him a bill, Mr. Baumer," I said. "He can't even read."

"He could pay yet."

"He don't pay anybody," I said.

"I think he hate me," Mr. Baumer went on. "That is the thing. He hate me for coming not from this country. I come here, sixteen years old, and learn to read and write, and I make a business, and so I think he hate me."

"He hates everybody."

Mr. Baumer shook his head. "But not to pinch the nose. Not to call Dutchie."

The side door squeaked open, but it was only Colly Coleman coming in from a trip so I said, "Excuse me, Mr. Baumer, but you shouldn't have trusted him in the first place."

"I know," he answered, looking at me with his misty eyes. "A man make mistakes. I think some do not trust him, so he will pay me because I do. And I do not know him well then. He only came back to town three-four months ago, from being away since before I go into business."

"People who knew him before could have told you," I said.

"A man make mistakes," he explained again.

"It's not my business, Mr. Baumer, but I would forget the bill."

His eyes rested on my face for a long minute, as if they didn't see me but the problem itself. He said, "It is not twenty-vun dollars and fifty cents now, Al. It is not that any more."

"What is it?"

He took a little time to answer. Then he brought his two hands up as if to help him shape the words. "It is the thing. You see, it is the thing."

I wasn't quite sure what he meant.

He took his pencil from behind the ear where he had put it and studied the point of it. "That Slade. He steal whisky and call it evaporation. He sneak things from his load. A thief, he is. And too big for me."

I said, "I got no time for him, Mr. Baumer, but I guess there never was a freighter didn't steal whisky. That's what I hear."

It was true, too. From the railroad to Moon Dance was fifty miles and a little better—a two-day haul in good weather, heck knew how long in bad. Any freight string bound home with a load had to lie out at least one night. When a freighter had his stock tended to and maybe a little fire going against the dark, he'd tackle a barrel of whisky or of grain alcohol if he had one aboard, consigned to Hirsch Brothers or Mr. Baumer's or the Moon Dance Saloon or the Gold Leaf Bar. He'd drive a hoop out of place, bore a little hole with a nail or bit and draw off what he wanted. Then he'd plug the hole with a whittled peg and pound the hoop back. That was evaporation. Nobody complained much. With freighters you generally took what they gave you, within reason.

"Moore steals it, too," I told Mr. Baumer. Moore was Mr. Baumer's freighter.

"Yah," he said, and that was all, but I stood there for a minute, thinking there might be something more. I could see thought swimming in his eyes, above that little hill of chin. Then a customer came in, and I had to go wait on him.

Nothing happened for a month, nothing between Mr. Baumer and Slade, that is, but fall drew on toward winter and the first flight of ducks headed south and Mr. Baumer hired Miss Lizzie Webb to help with the just-beginning Christmas trade, and here it was, the first week in October, and he and I walked up the street again with the monthly bills. He always sent them out. I guess he had to. A bigger store, like Hirsch's, would wait on the ranchers until their beef or wool went to market.

Up to a point things looked and happened almost the same as they had before, so much the same that I had the crazy feeling I was going through that time again. There was a wagon and a rig tied up at Hirsch's rack and a saddle horse standing hipshot in front of the harness shop. A few more people were on the street now, not many, and lamps had been lit against the shortened day.

It was dark enough that I didn't make out Slade right away. He was just a figure that came out of the yellow wash of light from the Moon Dance Saloon and stood on the board walk and with his head made the little motion of spitting. Then I recognized the lean, raw shape of him and the muscles flowing down into the sloped shoulders, and in the settling darkness I filled the picture in—the dark skin and the flat cheeks and the peevish eyes and the mustache growing rank.

There was Slade and here was Mr. Baumer with his bills and here I was, just as before, just like in the second go-round of a bad dream. I felt like turning back, being embarrassed and half scared by trouble even when it wasn't mine. Please, I said to myself, don't stop, Mr. Baumer! Don't bite off anything! Please, shortsighted the way you are, don't catch sight of him at all! I held up and stepped around behind Mr. Baumer and came up on the outside so as to be between him and Slade where maybe I'd cut off his view.

But it wasn't any use. All along I think I knew it was no use, not the praying or the walking between or anything. The act had to play itself out.

Mr. Baumer looked across the front of me and saw Slade and hesitated in his step and came to a stop. Then in his slow, business way, his chin held firm against his mouth, he began fingering through the bills, squinting to make out the names. Slade had turned and was watching him, munching on a cud of tobacco like a bull waiting.

"You look, Al," Mr. Baumer said without lifting his face from the bills. "I cannot see so good."

So I looked, and while I was looking Slade must have moved. The next I knew Mr. Baumer was staggering ahead, the envelopes spilling out of his hands. There had been a thump, the clap of a heavy hand swung hard on his back.

Slade said, "Haryu, Dutchie?"

Mr. Baumer caught his balance and turned around, the bills he had trampled shining white between them and, at Slade's feet, the hat that Mr. Baumer had stumbled out from under.

Slade picked up the hat and scuffed through the bills and held it out. "Cold to be goin' without a sky-piece," he said.

Mr. Baumer hadn't spoken a word. The lampshine from inside the bar caught his eyes, and in them it seemed to me a light came and went as anger and the uselessness of it took turns in his head.

Two men had come up on us and stood watching. One of them was Angus McDonald, who owned the Ranchers' Bank, and the other was Dr. King. He had his bag in his hand.

Two others were drifting up, but I didn't have time to tell who. The light came in Mr. Baumer's eyes, and he took a step ahead and swung. I could have hit harder myself. The fist landed on Slade's cheek without hardly so much as jogging his head, but it let hell loose in the man. I didn't know he could move so fast. He slid in like a practiced fighter and let Mr. Baumer have it full in the face.

Mr. Baumer slammed over on his back, but he wasn't out. He started lifting himself. Slade leaped ahead and brought a boot heel down on the hand he was lifting himself by. I heard meat and bone under that heel and saw Mr. Baumer fall back and try to roll away.

Things had happened so fast that not until then did anyone have a chance to get between them. Now Mr. McDonald pushed at Slade's chest, saying, "That's enough, Freighter. That's enough now," and Dr. King lined up, too, and another man I didn't know, and I took a place, and we formed a kind of screen between them. Dr. King turned and bent to look at Mr. Baumer.

"Damn fool hit me first," Slade said.

"That's enough," Mr. McDonald told him again while Slade looked at all of us as if he'd spit on us for a nickel. Mr. McDonald went on, using a half-friendly tone, and I knew it was because he didn't want to take Slade on any more than the rest of us did. "You go on home and sleep it off, Freighter. That's the ticket."

Slade just snorted.

From behind us Dr. King said, "I think you've broken this man's hand."

"Lucky for him I didn't kill him," Slade answered. "Damn Dutch penny-pincher!" He fingered the chew out of his mouth. "Maybe he'll know enough to leave me alone now."

Dr. King had Mr. Baumer on his feet. "I'll take him to the office," he said.

Blood was draining from Mr. Baumer's nose and rounding the curve of his lip and dripping from the sides of his chin. He held his hurt right hand in the other. But a thing was that he didn't look beaten even then, not the way a man who has given up looks beaten. Maybe that was why Slade said, with a show of that fierce anger, "You stay away from me! Hear? Stay clear away, or you'll get more of the same!"

Dr. King led Mr. Baumer away, Slade went back into the bar, and the other men walked off, talking about the fight. I got down and picked up the bills, because I knew Mr. Baumer would want me to, and mailed them at the post office, dirty as they were. It made me sorer, someway, that Slade's bill was one of the few that wasn't marked up. The cleanness of it seemed to say that there was no getting the best of him.

Mr. Baumer had his hand in a sling the next day and wasn't much good at waiting on the trade. I had to hustle all afternoon and so didn't have a chance to talk to him even if he had wanted to talk. Mostly he stood at his desk, and once, passing it, I saw he was practicing writing with his left hand. His nose and the edges of the cheeks around it were swollen some.

At closing time I said, "Look, Mr. Baumer, I can lay out of school a few days until you kind of get straightened out here."

"No," he answered as if to wave the subject away. "I get somebody else. You go to school. Is good to learn."

I had a half notion to say that learning hadn't helped him with Slade. Instead, I blurted out that I would have the law on Slade.

"The law?" he asked.

"The sheriff or somebody."

"No, Al," he said. "You would not."

I asked why.

"The law, it is not for plain fights," he said. "Shooting? Robbing? Yes, the law come quick. The plain fights, they are too many. They not count enough."

He was right. I said, "Well, I'd do something anyhow."

"Yes," he answered with a slow nod of his head. "Something you vould do, Al." He didn't tell me what.

Within a couple of days he got another man to clerk for him —it was Ed Hempel, who was always finding and losing jobs— and we made out. Mr. Baumer took his hand from the sling in a couple or three weeks, but with the tape on it it still wasn't any use to him. From what you could see of the fingers below the tape it looked as if it never would be.

He spent most of his time at the high desk, sending me or Ed out on the errands he used to run, like posting and getting the mail. Sometimes I wondered if that was because he was afraid of meeting Slade. He could just as well have gone himself. He wasted a lot of hours just looking at nothing, though I will have to say he worked hard at learning to write left-handed.

Then, a month and a half before Christmas, he hired Slade to haul his freight for him.

Ed Hempel told me about the deal when I showed up for work. "Yessir," he said, resting his foot on a crate in the storeroom where we were supposed to be working. "I tell you he's throwed in with Slade. Told me this morning to go out and locate him if I could and bring him in. Slade was at the saloon, o' course, and says to hell with Dutchie, but I told him this was honest-to-God business, like Baumer had told me to, and there was a quart of whisky right there in the store for him if he'd come and get it. He was out of money, I reckon, because the quart fetched him."

"What'd they say?" I asked him.

"Search me. There was two or three people in the store and Baumer told me to wait on 'em, and he and Slade palavered back by the desk."

"How do you know they made a deal?"

Ed spread his hands out. " 'Bout noon, Moore came in with his string, and I heard Baumer say he was makin' a change. Moore didn't like it too good, either."

It was a hard thing to believe, but there one day was Slade with a pile of stuff for the Moon Dance Mercantile Company, and that was proof enough with something left for boot.

Mr. Baumer never opened the subject up with me, though I gave him plenty of chances. And I didn't feel like asking. He didn't talk much these days but went around absent-minded, feeling now and then of the fingers that curled yellow and stiff out of the bandage like the toes on the leg of a dead chicken. Even on our walks home he kept his thoughts to himself.

I felt different about him now, and was sore inside. Not that I blamed him exactly. A hundred and thirty-five pounds wasn't much to throw against two hundred. And who could tell what Slade would do on a bellyful of whisky? He had promised Mr. Baumer more of the same, hadn't he? But I didn't feel good. I couldn't look up to Mr. Baumer like I used to and still wanted to. I didn't have the beginning of an answer when men cracked jokes or shook their heads in sympathy with Mr. Baumer, saying Slade had made him come to time.

Slade hauled in a load for the store, and another, and Christmas time was drawing on and trade heavy, and the winter that had started early and then pulled back came on again. There was a blizzard and then a still cold and another blizzard and afterwards a sunshine that was ice-shine on the drifted snow. I was glad to be busy, selling overshoes and sheep-lined coats and mitts and socks as thick as saddle blankets and Christmas candy out of buckets and hickory nuts and the fresh oranges that the people in our town never saw except when Santa Claus was coming.

One afternoon when I lit out from class the thermometer on the school porch read 42° below. But you didn't have to look at it to know how cold the weather was. Your nose and fingers and toes and ears and the bones inside you told you. The snow cried when you stepped on it.

I got to the store and took my things off and scuffed my hands at the stove for a minute so's to get life enough in them to tie a parcel. Mr. Baumer—he was always polite to me—said, "Hello, Al. Not so much to do today. Too cold for customers." He shuddered a little, as if he hadn't got the chill off even yet, and rubbed his broken hand with the good one. "Ve need Christmas goods," he said, looking out the window to the furrows that wheels had made in the snow-banked street, and I knew he was thinking of Slade's string, inbound from the railroad, and the time it might take even Slade to travel those hard miles.

Slade never made it at all.

Less than an hour later our old freighter, Moore, came in, his beard white and stiff with frost. He didn't speak at first but looked around and clumped to the stove and took off his heavy mitts, holding his news inside him.

Then he said, not pleasantly, "Your new man's dead, Baumer."

"My new man?" Mr. Baumer said.

"Who the hell do you think? Slade. He's dead."

All Mr. Baumer could say was, "Dead!"

"Froze to death, I figger," Moore told him while Colly Coleman and Ed Hempel and Miss Lizzie and I and a couple of customers stepped closer.

"Not Slade," Mr. Baumer said. "He know too much to freeze."

"Maybe so, but he sure's God's froze now. I got him in the wagon."

We stood looking at one another and at Moore. Moore was enjoying his news, enjoying feeding it out bit by bit so's to hold the stage. "Heart might've give out for all I know."

The side door swung open, letting in a cloud of cold and three men who stood, like us, waiting on Moore. I moved a little and looked through the window and saw Slade's freight outfit tied outside with more men around it. Two of them were on a wheel of one of the wagons, looking inside.

"Had a extra man, so I brought your stuff in," Moore went on. "Figgered you'd be glad to pay for it."

"Not Slade," Mr. Baumer said again.

"You can take a look at him."

Mr. Baumer answered no.

"Someone's takin' word to Connor to bring his hearse. Anyhow I told 'em to. I carted old Slade this far. Connor can have him now."

Moore pulled on his mitts. "Found him there by the Deep Creek crossin', doubled up in the snow an' his fire out." He moved toward the door. "I'll see to the horses, but your stuff'll have to set there. I got more'n enough work to do at Hirsch's."

Mr. Baumer just nodded.

I put on my coat and went out and waited my turn and climbed on a wagon wheel and looked inside, and there was Slade piled on some bags of bran. Maybe because of being frozen, his face was whiter than I ever saw it, whiter and deader, too, though it never had been lively. Only the mustache seemed still alive, sprouting thick like greasewood from alkali. Slade was doubled up all right, as if he had died and stiffened leaning forward in a chair.

I got down from the wheel, and Colly and then Ed climbed up. Moore was unhitching, tossing off his pieces of information while he did so. Pretty soon Mr. Connor came up with his old hearse, and he and Moore tumbled Slade into it, and the team that was as old as the hearse made off, the tires squeaking in the snow. The people trailed on away with it, their breaths leaving little ribbons of mist in the air. It was beginning to get dark.

Mr. Baumer came out of the side door of the store, bundled up, and called to Colly and Ed and me. "We unload," he said. "Already is late. Al, better you get a couple lanterns now."

We did a fast job, setting the stuff out of the wagons on to the platform and then carrying it or rolling it on the one truck that the store owned and stowing it inside according to where Mr. Baumer's good hand pointed.

A barrel was one of the last things to go in. I edged it up and Colly nosed the truck under it, and then I let it fall back. "Mr. Baumer," I said, "we'll never sell all this, will we?"

"Yah," he answered. "Sure we sell it. I get it cheap. A bargain, Al, so I buy it."

I looked at the barrel head again. There in big letters I saw WOOD ALCOHOL—DEADLY POISON.

"Hurry now," Mr. Baumer said. "Is late." For a flash and no longer I saw through the mist in his eyes, saw, you might say, that hilly chin repeated there. "Then ve go home, Al. Is good to know to read."

Questions for discussion

1. "Bargain" is the story of a conflict between two men: Mr. Baumer and Freighter Slade. They are seen through the eyes of Al, the boy who works in Mr. Baumer's store, who tells the story. How does Al describe (a) Mr. Baumer; (b) Freighter Slade? What does Al's opinion of each seem to be? What would you say is the dominant character trait of Mr. Baumer? Of Slade?
2. Describe Slade's attitude toward Mr. Baumer. Give evidence to support your answer. Why did Slade hate Mr. Baumer?
3. Mr. Baumer says that he doesn't care about the money Slade owes him. "It is the thing," he says (page 207). What do you think Mr. Baumer meant by "the thing"?
4. Why didn't the law in the community—the sheriff, for instance— come to Mr. Baumer's aid?
5. You should know that grain alcohol is an intoxicating liquor; wood alcohol is a deadly poison and is always carefully labeled as such. Why is this fact important to an understanding of what happens at the end of the story? Point out information or clues along the way that make what occurs convincing.

6. Some people would say that Mr. Baumer obtained justice for himself—a justice which the law could not give him. Others would say that what he obtained was not justice but revenge. What is your opinion on this matter? Give reasons to defend your opinion. You may want to look up the words *justice* and *revenge*.
7. Part of the credibility of the story is in the setting, which you should try to picture clearly. What kind of community is Moon Dance? In what part of America is it located? When, approximately, does the story take place? How does the weather contribute to the events in the story?

Vocabulary growth

CONTEXT. To help create atmosphere in this story, A. B. Guthrie, Jr. uses many words and phrases that have a peculiarly western flavor. You may already be familiar with some of these expressions. From the contexts of the following sentences, try to discover the meaning of the italicized words. Then check the meaning in a dictionary.

a. "A *buckboard* and a saddle horse were tied at Hirsch's rack . . ." (page 204).
b. "People said he could hold a lot without showing it except in being *ornerier* even than usual." (page 204)
c. ". . . I saw him and his string coming down the *grade* from the *buttes* . . ." (page 206)
d. ". . . he and Slade *palavered* back by the desk." (page 211)
e. "*scuffed* my hands at the stove for a minute so's to get life enough in them to tie a parcel." (page 212)
f. "He didn't speak at first but looked around and *clumped* to the stove . . ." (page 212)

For composition

1. What do you think was going on in Al's mind when he looked at the label on the barrel of wood alcohol? This might be called the story's "moment of truth," the moment when Al suddenly understands. Imagine you are Al. Write a short composition in which you describe what you were thinking and what you felt at that time.
2. Write an account of a particularly frustrating conflict in which you (or a group of which you were a member) were the underdog. Explain the situation, describe your adversary, and tell how you felt. You may need to look up the meaning of the word *frustrating* first.

When Laurie came home from school
he kept talking about . . .

Charles

SHIRLEY JACKSON

THE day my son Laurie started kindergarten he renounced corduroy overalls with bibs and began wearing blue jeans with a belt; I watched him go off the first morning with the older girl next door, seeing clearly that an era of my life was ended, my sweet-voiced nursery-school tot replaced by a long-trousered, swaggering character who forgot to stop at the corner and wave good-bye to me.

He came home the same way, the front door slamming open, his cap on the floor, and the voice suddenly become raucous shouting, "Isn't anybody *here?*"

At lunch he spoke insolently to his father, spilled his baby sister's milk, and remarked that his teacher said we were not to take the name of the Lord in vain.

"How *was* school today?" I asked, elaborately casual.

"All right," he said.

"Did you learn anything?" his father asked.

Laurie regarded his father coldly. "I didn't learn nothing," he said.

"Anything," I said. "Didn't learn anything."

"The teacher spanked a boy, though," Laurie said, addressing his bread and butter. "For being fresh," he added, with his mouth full.

"What did he do?" I asked. "Who was it?"

Laurie thought. "It was Charles," he said. "He was fresh. The teacher spanked him and made him stand in a corner. He was awfully fresh."

"What did he do?" I asked again, but Laurie slid off his chair, took a cookie, and left, while his father was still saying, "See here, young man."

The next day Laurie remarked at lunch, as soon as he sat down,

216

"Well, Charles was bad again today." He grinned enormously and said, "Today Charles hit the teacher."

"Good heavens," I said, mindful of the Lord's name, "I suppose he got spanked again?"

"He sure did," Laurie said. "Look up," he said to his father.

"What?" his father said, looking up.

"Look down," Laurie said. "Look at my thumb. Gee, you're dumb." He began to laugh insanely.

"Why did Charles hit the teacher?" I asked quickly.

"Because she tried to make him color with red crayons," Laurie said. "Charles wanted to color with green crayons so he hit the teacher and she spanked him and said nobody play with Charles but everybody did."

The third day—it was Wednesday of the first week—Charles bounced a see-saw on to the head of a little girl and made her bleed, and the teacher made him stay inside all during recess. Thursday Charles had to stand in a corner during story-time because he kept pounding his feet on the floor. Friday Charles was deprived of blackboard privileges because he threw chalk.

On Saturday I remarked to my husband, "Do you think kindergarten is too unsettling for Laurie? All this toughness, and bad grammar, and this Charles boy sounds like such a bad influence."

"It'll be all right," my husband said reassuringly. "Bound to be people like Charles in the world. Might as well meet them now as later."

On Monday Laurie came home late, full of news. "Charles," he shouted as he came up the hill; I was waiting anxiously on the front steps. "Charles," Laurie yelled all the way up the hill, "Charles was bad again."

"Come right in," I said, as soon as he came close enough. "Lunch is waiting."

"You know what Charles did?" he demanded, following me through the door. "Charles yelled so in school they sent a boy in from first grade to tell the teacher she had to make Charles keep quiet, and so Charles had to stay after school. And so all the children stayed to watch him."

"What did he do?" I asked.

"He just sat there," Laurie said, climbing into his chair at the table. "Hi, Pop, y'old dust mop."

"Charles had to stay after school today," I told my husband. "Everyone stayed with him."

"What does this Charles look like?" my husband asked Laurie. "What's his other name?"

"He's bigger than me," Laurie said. "And he doesn't have any rubbers and he doesn't ever wear a jacket."

Monday night was the first Parent-Teachers meeting, and only the fact that the baby had a cold kept me from going; I wanted passionately to meet Charles's mother. On Tuesday Laurie remarked suddenly, "Our teacher had a friend come to see her in school today."

"Charles's mother?" my husband and I asked simultaneously.

"Naaah," Laurie said scornfully. "It was a man who came and made us do exercises, we had to touch our toes. Look." He climbed down from his chair and squatted down and touched his toes. "Like this," he said. He got solemnly back into his chair and said, picking up his fork, "Charles didn't even *do* exercises."

"That's fine," I said heartily. "Didn't Charles want to do exercises?"

"Naaah," Laurie said. "Charles was so fresh to the teacher's friend he wasn't *let* do exercises."

"Fresh again?" I said.

"He kicked the teacher's friend," Laurie said. "The teacher's friend told Charles to touch his toes like I just did and Charles kicked him."

"What are they going to do about Charles, do you suppose?" Laurie's father asked him.

Laurie shrugged elaborately. "Throw him out of school, I guess," he said.

Wednesday and Thursday were routine; Charles yelled during story hour and hit a boy in the stomach and made him cry. On Friday Charles stayed after school again and so did all the other children.

With the third week of kindergarten Charles was an institution in our family; the baby was being a Charles when she cried all afternoon; Laurie did a Charles when he filled his wagon full of mud and pulled it through the kitchen; even my husband, when he caught his elbow in the telephone cord and pulled telephone, ashtray, and a bowl of flowers off the table, said, after the first minute, "Looks like Charles."

During the third and fourth weeks it looked like a reformation in Charles; Laurie reported grimly at lunch on Thursday of the third week, "Charles was so good today the teacher gave him an apple."

"What?" I said, and my husband added warily, "You mean Charles?"

"Charles," Laurie said. "He gave the crayons around and he picked up the books afterward and the teacher said he was her helper."

"What happened?" I asked incredulously.

"He was her helper, that's all," Laurie said, and shrugged.

"Can this be true, about Charles?" I asked my husband that night. "Can something like this happen?"

"Wait and see," my husband said cynically. "When you've got a Charles to deal with, this may mean he's only plotting."

He seemed to be wrong. For over a week Charles was the teacher's helper; each day he handed things out and he picked things up; no one had to stay after school.

"The P.T.A. meeting's next week again," I told my husband one evening. "I'm going to find Charles's mother there."

"Ask her what happened to Charles," my husband said. "I'd like to know."

"I'd like to know myself," I said.

On Friday of that week things were back to normal. "You know what Charles did today?" Laurie demanded at the lunch table, in a voice slightly awed. "He told a little girl to say a word and she said it and the teacher washed her mouth out with soap and Charles laughed."

"What word?" his father asked unwisely, and Laurie said, "I'll have to whisper it to you, it's so bad." He got down off his chair and went around to his father. His father bent his head down and Laurie whispered joyfully. His father's eyes widened.

"Did Charles tell the little girl to say *that*?" he asked respectfully.

"She said it *twice*," Laurie said. "Charles told her to say it *twice*."

"What happened to Charles?" my husband asked.

"Nothing," Laurie said. "He was passing out the crayons."

Monday morning Charles abandoned the little girl and said the evil word himself three or four times, getting his mouth washed out with soap each time. He also threw chalk.

My husband came to the door with me that evening as I set out for the P.T.A. meeting. "Invite her over for a cup of tea after the meeting," he said. "I want to get a look at her."

"If only she's there," I said prayerfully.

"She'll be there," my husband said. "I don't see how they could hold a P.T.A. meeting without Charles's mother."

At the meeting I sat restlessly, scanning each comfortable matronly face, trying to determine which one hid the secret of Charles. None of them looked to me haggard enough. No one stood up in the meeting and apologized for the way her son had been acting. No one mentioned Charles.

After the meeting I identified and sought out Laurie's kindergarten teacher. She had a plate with a cup of tea and a piece of chocolate cake; I had a plate with a cup of tea and a piece of marshmallow cake. We maneuvered up to one another cautiously, and smiled.

"I've been so anxious to meet you," I said. "I'm Laurie's mother."

"We're all so interested in Laurie," she said.

"Well, he certainly likes kindergarten," I said. "He talks about it all the time."

"We had a little trouble adjusting, the first week or so," she said primly, "but now he's a fine little helper. With occasional lapses, of course."

"Laurie usually adjusts very quickly," I said. "I suppose this time it's Charles's influence."

"Charles?"

"Yes," I said, laughing, "you must have your hands full in that kindergarten, with Charles."

"Charles?" she said. "We don't have any Charles in the kindergarten."

Questions for discussion

1. Why did Laurie behave as he did at school? Why did he say that it was Charles who was guilty of all this unacceptable behavior? Have you ever seen this sort of thing happen to people, not only little people like Laurie or Charles but people of high school age? What is the cure for this sort of behavior?
2. Did you suspect the outcome of the story? Look back for the clue given you very early in the story (page 216). It is very subtle but it is there.
3. Notice that Laurie describes Charles (page 218) as being bigger than he, as wearing no rubbers or jacket. What does this tell you about Laurie?

4. Did you like the way the story ended or would you rather have had the whole thing spelled out for you?
5. What do you think was going on in the kindergarten teacher's mind as she was talking to Laurie's mother? What do you think was going on in the mind of Laurie's mother as she spoke with the teacher?

Vocabulary growth

WORD PARTS. Most prefixes have more than one meaning. You may have to try more than one of these meanings in order to work out the meaning of the word in which it appears. The prefix *in-* means "not, in, or within." It is also used to heighten or intensify meaning. For example, in *intensify* the prefix is used to heighten or strengthen the meaning. You might translate its meaning as "very."

Similarly, the prefix *un-* means "not," as in *unable* or "the opposite of," as in *untie.*

Work out the meaning of the prefix in each of the following words. Then check your work with a dictionary. You may find some help in the etymology, that is, the part of the entry that tells the word's origin.

insolent	unwise	income
unsettling	indefinite	inflammable
incredulous	unwind	unravel
insane	uneventful	inculcate

WORDS ARE INTERESTING. "He was *fresh*." Just exactly what does *fresh* mean used in this way? Is it slang in this usage? Try the dictionary. You may be in for a surprise.

" 'How was school today?' I asked, elaborately *casual*." Exactly what does *casual* mean in this usage? How could anyone be *elaborately* casual? What other meanings does the word have? Is it acceptable to speak of *casual clothes*, or is this a slang usage? Try your dictionary.

For composition

1. How do you get along with your conscience? What do you find the best thing to do when you have done something wrong? Is it hard for you to say, "I was wrong"? Why? Write a paper on the general subject "My Conscience and I."
2. Laurie's parents were quite eager to meet Charles's mother. Part of the fun of the story lies in their surprise at the end. Write a narrative account of a great surprise that you or someone you know has had.

An Ornery Kind of Kid

WILLIAM SAROYAN

MAYO Maloney at eleven was a little shrimp of a fellow who was not rude so much as he was rudeness itself, for he couldn't even step inside a church, for instance, without giving everybody who happened to see him an uncomfortable feeling that he, Mayo, despised the place and its purpose.

It was much the same everywhere else that Mayo went: school, library, theater, home. Only his mother felt that Mayo was not a rude boy, but his father frequently asked him to get down off his high horse and act like everybody else. By this, Michael Maloney meant that Mayo ought to take things easy and stop finding so much fault with everything.

Mayo was the most self-confident boy in the world, and he found fault with everything, or so at least it seemed. He found fault with his mother's church activities. He found fault with his father's interest in Shakespeare and Mozart. He found fault with the public-school system, the Government, the United Nations, the entire population of the world. And he did all this fault-finding without so much as going into detail about anything. He did it by being alive, by being on hand at all. He did it by being nervous, irritable, swift, wise and bored. In short, he was a perfectly normal boy. He had contempt for everything and everybody, and he couldn't help it. His contempt was unspoken but unmistakable. He was slight of body, dark of face and hair, and he went at everything in a hurry because everything was slow and stupid and weak.

The only thing that didn't bore him was the idea of hunting, but his father wouldn't buy him a gun, not even a .22-caliber single-shot rifle. Michael Maloney told Mayo that as soon as he was sure that Mayo had calmed down a little, he would think about buying him a gun. Mayo tried to calm down a little, so he could have his gun, but he gave it up after a day and a half.

222

"O.K.," his father said, "if you don't want your gun, you don't have to try to earn it."

"I did try to earn it," Mayo said.

"When?"

"Yesterday and today."

"I had in mind," his father said, "a trial covering a period of at least a month."

"A month?" Mayo said. "How do you expect a fellow to stay calm all through October with pheasant to shoot in the country?"

"I don't know how," Mike Maloney said, "but if you want a gun, you've got to calm down enough so I can believe you won't shoot the neighbors with it. Do you think my father so much as let me sit down to my dinner if I hadn't done something to earn it? He didn't invite me to earn any gun to shoot pheasant with. He told me to earn my food, and he didn't wait until I was eleven, either. I started earning it when I was no more than eight. The whole trouble with you is you're too pent-up from not doing any kind of work at all for your food or shelter or clothing to be decently tired and ordinary like everybody else. You're not human, almost. Nobody's human who doesn't know how hard it is to earn his food and the other basic things. It's the fault of your mother and father that you're such a sarcastic and fault-finding man instead of a calm, handsome one. Everybody in this whole town is talking about how your mother and father have turned you into an arrogant ignoramus of a man by not making you earn your right to judge things."

Mr. Maloney spoke as much to the boy's mother as to the boy himself, and he spoke as well to the boy's younger brother and younger sister, for he had left his office at half past four, as he did once a week, to sit down with the whole family for early supper, and it was his intention to make these mid-week gatherings at the table memorable to everyone, including himself.

"Now, Mike," Mrs. Maloney said. "Mayo's not as bad as all that. He just wants a gun to hunt pheasant with."

Mike Maloney laid down his fork that was loaded with macaroni baked with tomatoes and cheese, and he stared at his wife a long time, rejecting one by one two dozen different angry remarks he knew would do no one present any good at all to hear, and only serve to make the gathering unpleasantly memorable.

At last he said, "I suppose you think I ought to get him a gun, just like that?"

"Mayo isn't really rude," the boy's mother said. "It's just that he's restless, the way every human being's got to be once in his lifetime for a while."

Mayo didn't receive this defense of himself with anything like gratitude. If anything, it appeared as if he were sick and tired of having so much made of a simple little matter like furnishing him with an inexpensive .22-caliber single-shot rifle.

"Now don't you go to work and try to speak up for him," Mike Maloney said to his wife, "because, as you can see for yourself, he doesn't like it. He doesn't enjoy being spoken up for, not even by his mother, poor woman, and you can see how much he thinks of what his father's saying this minute."

"What did I say?" Mayo asked.

"You didn't say anything," his father said. "You didn't need to." He turned to Mrs. Maloney. "Is it a gun I must buy for him now?" he said.

Mrs. Maloney didn't quite know how to say that it was. She remained silent and tried not to look at either her husband or her son.

"O.K.," Mike Maloney said to both his wife and his son. "I have to go back to the office a minute, so if you'll come along with me I'll drop into Archie Cannon's and buy you a gun."

He got up from the table and turned to Mrs. Maloney.

"Provided, of course," he said, "that that meets with your approval."

"Aren't you going to finish your food?" Mrs. Maloney said.

"No, I'm not," Mike Maloney said. "And I'll tell you why, too. I don't want him to be denied anything he wants or anything his mother wants him to have, without earning it, for one unnecessary moment, and as you can see, his cap's on his head, he's at the door, and every moment I stand here explaining is unnecessary."

"Couldn't you both finish your food first?" Mrs. Maloney said.

"Who wants to waste time eating," Mike Maloney said, "when it's time to buy a gun?"

"Well," Mrs. Maloney said, "perhaps you'll have something after you buy the gun."

"We should have been poor," Mike Maloney said. "Being poor would have helped us in this problem."

Mike Maloney went to the door where his nervous son was standing waiting for him to shut up and get going.

He turned to his wife and said, "I won't be able to account for him after I turn the gun over to him, but I'll be gone no more than an hour. If we'd been poor and couldn't afford it, he'd know the sinfulness of provoking me into this sort of bitter kindness."

When he stepped out of the house onto the front porch, he saw that his son was at the corner, trying his best not to run. He moved quickly and caught up with him, and then he moved along as swiftly as his son did.

At last he said, "Now, I'm willing to walk the half mile to Archie Cannon's, but I'm not going to run, so if you've got to run, go ahead, and I'll meet you outside the place as soon as I get there."

He saw the boy break loose and disappear far down the street. When he got to Archie Cannon's, the boy was waiting for him. They went in and Mike Maloney asked Archie to show him the guns.

"What kind of a gun do you want, Mike?" Archie said. "I didn't know you were interested in hunting."

"It's not for myself," Mike Maloney said. "It's for Mayo here, and it ought to be suitable for pheasant shooting."

"That would be a shotgun," Archie said.

"Would that be what it would be?" Mike Maloney asked his son, and although the boy hadn't expected anything so precisely suitable for pheasant shooting, he said that a shotgun would be what it would be.

"O.K., Archie," Mike said. "A shotgun."

"Well, Mike," Archie said, "I wouldn't like to think a shotgun would be the proper gun to turn over to a boy."

"Careful," Mike Maloney said. "He's right here with us, you know. Let's not take any unnecessary liberties. I believe he indicated the gun ought to be a shotgun."

"Well, anyway," Archie said, "it's going to have a powerful kick."

"A powerful kick," Mike Maloney repeated, addressing the three words to his son, who received them with disdain.

"That is no matter to him," Mike Maloney said to Archie Cannon.

"Well, then," Archie Cannon said, "this here's a fine double-barrel twelve-gauge shotgun and it's just about the best bargain in the store."

"You shouldn't have said that, Archie," Mike Maloney said. "This man's not interested in bargains. What he wants is the best shotgun you've got that's suitable for pheasant shooting."

"That would be this twelve-gauge repeater," Archie Cannon said, "that sells for ninety-eight fifty, plus tax, of course. It's the best gun of its kind."

"Anybody can see it's a better gun," Mike Maloney said. "No need to waste time with inferior firearms."

He handed the gun to Mayo Maloney, who held it barrel down, resting over his right arm, precisely as a gun, loaded or not, ought to be held.

"Anything else?" Mike Maloney said to his son, who said nothing, but with such irritation that Mike quickly said to Archie Cannon, "Shells, of course. What good is a shotgun without shells?"

Archie Cannon jumped to get three boxes of his best shotgun shells, and as he turned them over to Mike Maloney, who turned them over to Mayo, Archie said, "A hunting coat in which to carry the shells? A red hunting cap?"

Mayo Maloney was gone, however.

"He didn't want those things," Mike Maloney said.

"Some hunters go to a lot of trouble about costume," Archie Cannon said.

"He doesn't," Mike Maloney said. "What do I owe you?"

"One hundred and five dollars and sixty-nine cents, including tax," Archie said. "Has he got a license?"

"To hunt?" Mike Maloney said. "He hasn't got a license to eat, but damned if I don't halfway admire him sometimes. He must know something to be so sure of himself and so contemptuous of everybody else."

"To tell you the truth," Archie Cannon said, "I thought you were kidding, Mike. I thought you were kidding the way you sometimes do in court when you're helping a small man fight a big company. I didn't expect you to actually buy a gun and turn it over to an eleven-year-old boy. Are you sure it's all right?"

"Of course it's all right," Mike Maloney said. "You saw for yourself the way he held the gun." He began to write a check. "Now, what did you say it came to?"

"A hundred and five sixty-nine," Archie Cannon said. "I hope you know there's no pheasant to speak of anywhere near here. The Sacramento Valley is where the pheasant shooting is."

"Where you going to be around ten o'clock tonight?" Mike Maloney said.

"Home, most likely," Archie Cannon said. "Why?"

"Would you like to drop over to my house for a couple of bottles of beer around ten?" Mike said.

"I'd like that very much," Archie said. "Why?"

"Well," Mike said, "the way I figure is this: It's a quarter after five now. It'll take him about three minutes to hitch a ride with somebody going out to Riverdale, which is about twenty-five miles from here. That would take an average driver forty or forty-five minutes to make, but he'll get the driver, whoever he is, or she is, for that matter, to make it in about half an hour or a little under. He'll do it by being excited, not by saying anything. He'll get the driver to go out of his or her way to let him off where the hunting is, too, so he'll start hunting right away, or a little before six. He'll hunt until after dark, walking a lot in the meantime. He won't get lost or anything like that, but he'll have to walk back to a road with a little traffic. He'll hitch a ride back, and he'll be home a little before or a little after ten."

"How do you know?" Archie said. "How do you even know he's going hunting at all tonight? He just got the gun, and he may not even know how to work it."

"You saw him take off, didn't you?" Mike Maloney said. "He took off to go hunting. And you can be sure he either knows how to work the gun or will find out by himself in a few minutes."

"Well," Archie said, "I certainly would like to drop by for some beer, Mike, if you're serious."

"Of course I'm serious," Mike said.

"I suppose you want to have somebody to share your amusement with when he gets back with nothing shot and his body all sore from the powerful kick of the gun," Archie said.

"Yes," Mike said. "I want to have somebody to share my amusement with but not for those reasons. He may be a little sore from the powerful kick of the gun, but I think he'll come back with something."

"I've never heard of anybody shooting any pheasant around Riverdale," Archie said. "There's a little duck shooting out there in season, and jack rabbits, of course."

"He said pheasants," Mike Maloney said. . . . . "Here's my check. Better make it a little before ten, just in case."

"I thought you were only kidding about the gun," Archie said. "Are you sure you did the right thing? I mean, considering he's only eleven years old, hasn't got a hunting license and the pheasant-shooting season doesn't open for almost a month?"

"That's one of the reasons why I want you to come by for some beer," Mike said.

"I don't get it," Archie said.

"You're game warden of this area, aren't you?"

"I am."

"Okay," Mike said. "If it turns out that he's broken the law, I want you to know it."

"Well," Archie said, "I wouldn't want to bother about a small boy shooting a few days out of season without a license."

"I'll see you a little before ten, then," Mike Maloney said.

He spent a half hour at his office, then walked home slowly, to find the house quiet and peaceful, the kids in bed and his wife doing the dishes. He took the dish cloth and began to dry dishes.

"I bought him the best shotgun Archie Cannon had for pheasant shooting," he said.

"I hope he didn't make you too angry," Mrs. Maloney said.

"He did for a while," Mike said, "but all of a sudden he didn't, if you know what I mean."

"I don't know what you mean," Mrs. Maloney said.

"I mean," Mike said, "it's all right not being poor."

"What's being poor got to do with it?" Mrs. Maloney said.

"I mean it's all right, that's all," Mike said.

"Well, that's fine," Mrs. Maloney said. "But where is he?"

"Hunting, of course," Mike said. "You don't think he wanted a gun to look at."

"I don't know what I think now," Mrs. Maloney said. "You've had so much trouble with him all along, and now all of a sudden you buy him an expensive gun and believe it's perfectly all right for him to go off hunting in the middle of the night on the third day of October. Why?"

"Well," Mike Maloney said, "it's because while I was preaching to him at the table this afternoon, something began to happen. It was as if my own father were preaching to me thirty years ago when I was Mayo's age. Oh, I did earn my food, as I said, and I wanted a gun, just as he's been wanting one. Well, my father preached to me, and I didn't get the gun. I mean, I didn't get it until almost five years later, when it didn't mean very much to me any more. Well, while I was preaching to him this afternoon I remembered that when my father preached to me I was sure he was mistaken to belittle me so, and I even believed that somehow—somehow or other, perhaps because we were so poor, if that makes sense—he would suddenly stop preaching and take me along without any fuss of any kind and buy me a gun. But of course he didn't. And I remembered that he didn't, and I decided that I'd do for my son what my father had not done for me."

"Do you mean you and Mayo are alike?" Mrs. Maloney said.

"I do," Mike said, "I do indeed."

"Very much alike?"

"Almost precisely," Mike said. "Oh, he'll not be the great man he is now for long, but I don't want to be the one to cheat him out of a single moment of his greatness."

"You must be joking," Mrs. Maloney said.

"I couldn't be more serious," Mike said. "Archie Cannon thought I was joking, too, but why would I be joking? I bought him the gun and shells, and off he went to hunt, didn't he?"

"Well, I hope he doesn't hurt himself," Mrs. Maloney said.

"We'll never know if he does," Mike said. "I've asked Archie to come by around ten for some beer because I figure he'll be back by then."

"Is Mrs. Cannon coming with Archie?"

"I don't think so," Mike said. "Her name wasn't mentioned."

"Then I suppose you don't want me to sit up with you," Mrs. Maloney said.

"I don't know why not, if you want to," Mike said.

But Mrs. Maloney knew it wouldn't do to sit up, so she said, "No, I'll be getting to bed long before ten."

Mike Maloney went out on the front porch with his wife, and they sat and talked about their son Mayo and their other kids until a little after nine, and then Mrs. Maloney went inside to see if the beer was in the icebox and to put some stuff out on the kitchen table, to go with the beer. Then she went to bed.

Around a quarter to ten Archie Cannon came walking up the street and sat down in the rocker on the front porch.

"I've been thinking about what you did," he said, "and I still don't know if you did right."

"I did right, all right," Mike Maloney said. "Let's go inside and have some beer. He'll be along pretty soon."

They went inside and sat down at the kitchen table. Mike lifted the caps off two bottles of cold beer, filled two tall glasses, and they began to drink. There was a plate loaded with cold roast beef, ham, Bologna and sliced store cheese, and another plate with rye bread on it, already buttered.

When it was almost twelve and Mayo Maloney hadn't come home, Archie Cannon wondered if he shouldn't offer to get up and go home or maybe even offer to get his car and go looking for the boy, but he decided he'd better not. Mike Maloney seemed excited and angry at himself for having done such a foolish thing, and he might not like Archie to rub it in.

A little before one in the morning, after they had finished a half dozen bottles of beer apiece and all the food Mrs. Maloney had set out for them, and talked about everything in the world excepting Mayo Maloney, they heard footsteps on the back stairs, and then on the porch, and after a moment he came into the kitchen.

He was a tired man. His face was dirty and flushed, and his clothes were dusty and covered with prickly burs of all kinds. His hands were scratched and almost black with dirt. His gun was slung over his right arm, though, and nested in his left arm were two beautiful pheasants.

He set the birds on the kitchen table, then broke his gun up for cleaning. He wrapped a dry dish towel around the pieces and put the bundle in the drawer in which he kept his junk. He then brought six unused shells out of his pockets and placed them in the drawer, too, locked the drawer with his key and put the key back into his pocket. Then he went to the kitchen sink and rolled up his sleeves and washed his hands and arms and face and neck, and after he'd dried himself, he looked into the refrigerator and brought out some Bologna wrapped in butcher paper and began to eat it without bread while he fetched bread and butter and a chair. He sat down and began to put three thick slices of Bologna between two slices of buttered bread. Mike Maloney had never before seen him eat so heartily.

He didn't look restless and mean any more, either.

Mike Maloney got up with Archie Cannon, and they left the house by the back door in order not to disturb Mrs. Maloney and the sleeping kids.

When they were in the back yard, Archie Cannon said, "Well, aren't you going to ask him where he got them?"

"He's not ready to talk about it just yet," Mike said. "What's the fine? I'll pay it, of course."

"Well," Archie said, "there won't be any fine because there's not supposed to be any pheasants in the whole area of which I'm game warden. I didn't believe he'd get anything, let alone pheasants. Damned if I don't admire him a little myself."

"I'll walk you home," Mike said.

In the kitchen, the boy finished his sandwich, drank a glass of milk and rubbed his shoulder.

The whole evening and night had been unbelievable. Suddenly at the table, when his father had been preaching to him, he'd begun to understand his father a little better, and himself, too, but he'd known he couldn't immediately stop being the way he had been for so long, the way that was making everybody so uncomfortable. He'd known he'd have to go on for a while longer and see the thing through. He'd have to go along with his father. He'd known all this very clearly, because his father had suddenly stopped being a certain way—the way everybody believed a father ought to be—and Mayo had known it was going to be necessary for him to stop being a certain way, too —the way he had believed he had to be.

In the kitchen, almost asleep from weariness, he decided he'd tell his father exactly what he'd done, but he'd wait awhile first, maybe ten years.

He'd had a devil of a time finding out how the gun worked, and he hadn't been able to hitch a ride at all, so he'd walked and run six miles to the countryside around Clovis, and there he'd loaded the gun and aimed it at a blackbird in a tree leaning over Clovis Creek and pressed the trigger.

The kick had knocked him down, and he had missed the bird by a mile. He'd had to walk a long way through tall dry grass and shrubs for something else to shoot at, but all it was was another blackbird, and again the kick had knocked him down, and he'd missed it by a mile.

It was getting dark fast by then, and there didn't seem to be anything alive around at all, so he began to shoot the gun just to get used to it. Pretty soon he could shoot it and not get knocked down. He kept shooting and walking, and finally it was dark and it seemed he was lost. He stumbled over a hidden rock and fell and shot the gun by accident and got a lot of dirt in his eyes. He got up and almost cried, but he managed not to, and then he found a road, but he had no idea where it went to or which direction to take. He was scratched and sore all over and not very happy about the way he'd shot the gun by accident. He was scared, too, and he said a prayer a minute and meant every word of what he said. And he understood for the first time in his life why people liked to go to church.

"Please don't let me make a fool of myself," he prayed. "Please let me start walking in the right direction on this road."

He started walking down the road, hoping he was getting nearer home, or at least to a house with a light in it, or a store or something that would be open. He felt a lot of alive things in the dark now that he knew must be imaginary, and he said, "Please don't let me get so scared." And pretty soon he felt so tired and small and lost and hopeless and foolish that he could barely keep from crying, and he said, "Please don't let me cry."

He walked a long time, and then far down the road he saw a small light, and he began to walk faster. It was a country store with a gasoline pump out front and a new pickup truck beside the pump. Inside the store was the driver of the truck and the storekeeper, and he saw that it was twenty minutes to twelve. The storekeeper was an old man who was sitting on a box talking to the driver of the truck, who was about as old as the boy's father.

He saw the younger man wink at the older one, and he thanked God for both of them, and for the wink, too, because he didn't think people who could wink could be unfriendly.

He told them exactly what he had done, and why, and the men looked at him and at each other until he was all through talking. They both examined the brand-new gun too. Then the storekeeper handed the gun back to the boy and said to the younger man, "I'll be much obliged to you, Ed, if you'll get this man home in our truck."

They were a father and a son, too, apparently, and good friends, besides. Mayo Maloney admired them very much, and on account of them, he began to like people in general too.

"Not at all," the younger man said.

"And I'd like to think we might rustle up a couple of pheasant for him to take home too."

"That might not be easy to do this hour of the night," the younger man said, "but we could try."

"Isn't there an all-night Chinese restaurant in town that serves pheasant in and out of season?" the old man said. "Commercial pheasant, that is?"

"I don't know," the younger man said, "but we could phone and find out."

"No," the older man said. "No use phoning. They wouldn't be

apt to understand what we were talking about. Better just drive up to it and go on in and find out. It's on Kern Street between F and G, but I forget the name. Anyhow, it's open all night, and I've heard you can get pheasant there any time you like."

"It certainly is worth looking into," the younger man said.

The younger man got up, and Mayo Maloney, speechless with amazement, got up too. He tried to say something courteous to the older man, but nothing seemed to want to come out of his dry mouth. He picked up his gun and went out to the truck and got in beside the younger man, and they went off. He saw the older man standing in the doorway of the store, watching.

The younger man drove all the way to town in silence, and when the boy saw familiar places, he thought in prayer again, saying, *I certainly don't deserve this, and I'm never going to forget it.*

The truck crossed the Southern Pacific tracks to Chinatown, and the driver parked in front of Willie Fong's, which was in fact open, although nobody was inside eating. The driver stepped out of the truck and went into the restaurant, and the boy saw him talk to a waiter. The waiter disappeared and soon came back with a man in a business suit. This man and the driver of the truck talked a moment, and then they both disappeared into the back of the restaurant. After a few minutes the driver of the truck came back, and he was holding something that was wrapped in newspaper. He came out of the restaurant and got back into the truck, and they drove off again.

"How's your father?" the man said suddenly.

"He's fine," Mayo managed to say.

"I mean," the man said, "you are Mike Maloney's boy, aren't you?"

"Yes, I am," Mayo Maloney said.

"I thought you were," the man said. "You look alike and have a lot in common. You don't have to tell me where you live. I know where it is. And I know you want to know who I am, but don't you think it would be better if I didn't tell you? I've had dealings with your father, and he lent me some money once when I needed it badly and we both weren't sure I'd ever be able to pay him back. So it's all right. I mean, nobody's going to know anything about this from me."

"Did they have any pheasants?" the boy said.

"Oh, yes," the man said. "I'm sorry I forgot to tell you. They're in that newspaper. Just throw the paper out the window."

The boy removed the paper from around the birds and looked at them. They were just about the most wonderful-looking things in the whole world.

"Do they have any shot in them?" he asked. "Because they ought to."

"No, I'm afraid they don't," the driver said, "but we'll drive out here a little where it's quiet and we won't disturb too many sleeping farmers, and between the two of us we'll get some shot into them. You can do the shooting, if you like."

"I might spoil them," the boy said.

"I'll be glad to attend to it, then," the driver said.

They drove along in silence a few minutes, and then the truck turned into a lonely road and stopped. The driver got out and placed the two birds on some grass by the side of the road in the light of the truck's lights about twenty yards off. Then he took the gun, examined it, aimed, fired once, unloaded the gun, fetched the birds, got back into the truck and they drove off again.

"They're just right now," he said.

"Thanks," the boy said.

When the truck got into his neighborhood Mayo said, "Could I get off a couple of blocks from my house, so nobody will see this truck accidentally?"

"Yes, that's a good idea," the driver said.

The truck stopped. The boy carefully nested the two birds in his left arm, then got out, and the driver helped him get the gun slung over his right arm.

"I never expected anything like this to happen," the boy said.

"No, I suppose not," the man said. "I never expected to find a man like your father when I needed him, either, but I guess things like that happen just the same. Well, good night."

"Good night," the boy said.

The man got into the truck and drove off, and the boy hurried home and into the house.

When Mike Maloney got back from walking Archie Cannon home, he was surprised to find the boy asleep on his folded arms on the kitchen table. He shook the boy gently, and Mayo Maloney sat up with a start, his eyes bloodshot and his ears red.

"You better get to bed," Mike said.

"I didn't want to go," the boy said, "until you got back, so I could thank you for the gun."

"That wasn't necessary," the man said. "That wasn't necessary at all."

The boy got up and barely managed to drag himself out of the room without falling.

Alone in the kitchen, the father picked up the birds and examined them, smiling because he knew whatever was behind their presence in the house, it was certainly something as handsome as the birds themselves.

Questions for discussion

1. What kind of boy was Mayo? What made him like this? How did his father feel about him? In what way was his father right about Mayo and in what way was he wrong? Did you notice that when his father talked to him he called him a *man?* What does this tell you about Mr. Maloney?
2. Was Mayo the same inside as outside? When do we really find out what he is like inside? Think back to other stories in this book. Which characters were so presented that we could see what they were really like inside? How did the authors manage this trick of revealing a character?
3. Was Mayo's orneriness the same kind as Laurie's? Were they ornery for the same reason?
4. This story is built in two parts. From whose point of view is Mayo presented in the first part? From whose in the second? Why does the author build the story in this way?
5. What happened to Mayo's attitude during the story? (Remember what happened to Willie Arblaster's attitude?) What brought about the change? At what point were you sure that Mayo was a changed boy? Did you approve of the change?
6. Did Mayo think or do anything which you understood particularly well because you have thought or done something like it?
7. What does the story say about men and boys? About fathers and sons?
8. What does the last sentence of the story mean to you?

Vocabulary growth

WORD PARTS. Suffixes are used to make adjectives out of nouns and verbs. Thus, we can greatly expand the number of words in the language, stretching and adapting basic ideas to whatever our need may be. For example, we take the verb *confide* and by adding *-ent,* we make the adjective *confident*. Or we take the noun *comfort* and by adding *-able*, we make the adjective *comfortable*. Here are some of the most useful and frequent adjective suffixes:

-ous	-ent (ant)
-al	-ive
-ic	-ful

Find the base word to which the adjective suffix has been added in each of the following. Keep in mind that in adding a suffix, the spelling of the base word is sometimes slightly changed.

irritable	memorable	officious
normal	pleasant	populous
unmistakable	expensive	imitative
dreadful	suitable	original
arrogant	decisive	alergic
dramatic	cautious	frightful

For composition

Why is it, do you think, that young people and their parents sometimes have conflicts of one kind or another? Write an article giving your answer to this question. You might expand your answer to include a discussion of the reasons why young people as a group and adults as a group do not always understand and like each other. Do you know of a way in which mutual understanding and respect between these two groups can be achieved?

On the planet Venus it was . . .

All Summer in a Day

RAY BRADBURY

"Ready?"
"Ready."
"Now?"
"Soon."
"Do the scientists really know? Will it happen today, will it?"
"Look, look; see for yourself!"

The children pressed to each other like so many roses, so many weeds, intermixed, peering out for a look at the hidden sun.

It rained.

It had been raining for seven years; thousands upon thousands of days compounded and filled from one end to the other with rain, with the drum and gush of water, with the sweet crystal fall of showers and the concussion of storms so heavy they were tidal waves come over the islands. A thousand forests had been crushed under the rain and grown up a thousand times to be crushed again. And this was the way life was forever on the planet Venus, and this was the schoolroom of the children of the rocket men and women who had come to a raining world to set up civilization and live out their lives.

"It's stopping, it's stopping!"
"Yes, yes!"

Margot stood apart from them, from these children who could never remember a time when there wasn't rain and rain and rain. They were all nine years old, and if there had been a day, seven years ago, when the sun came out for an hour and showed its face to the stunned world, they could not recall. Sometimes, at night, she heard them stir, in remembrance, and she knew they were dreaming and remembering gold or a yellow crayon or a coin large enough to buy the world with. She knew they thought they remembered a warmness, like a blushing in the face, in the body, in the arms and legs and trembling hands. But then they always awoke to the tatting drum, the endless shaking down of clear bead necklaces upon the roof, the walk, the gardens, the forests, and their dreams were gone.

All day yesterday they had read in class about the sun. About how like a lemon it was, and how hot. And they had written small stories or essays or poems about it:

> *I think the sun is a flower,*
> *That blooms for just one hour.*

That was Margot's poem, read in a quiet voice in the still classroom while the rain was falling outside.

"Aw, you didn't write that!" protested one of the boys.

"I did," said Margot. "I *did*."

"William!" said the teacher.

But that was yesterday. Now the rain was slackening, and the children were crushed in the great thick windows.

"Where's teacher?"

"She'll be back."

"She'd better hurry, we'll miss it!"

They turned on themselves, like a feverish wheel, all tumbling spokes.

Margot stood alone. She was a very frail girl who looked as if she had been lost in the rain for years and the rain had washed out the blue from her eyes and the red from her mouth and the yellow from her hair. She was an old photograph dusted from an album, whitened away, and if she spoke at all her voice would be a ghost. Now she stood, separate, staring at the rain and the loud wet world beyond the huge glass.

"What're *you* looking at?" said William.

Margot said nothing.

"Speak when you're spoken to." He gave her a shove. But she did not move; rather she let herself be moved only by him and nothing else.

They edged away from her, they would not look at her. She felt them go away. And this was because she would play no games with them in the echoing tunnels of the underground city. If they tagged her and ran, she stood blinking after them and did not follow. When the class sang songs about happiness and life and games her lips barely moved. Only when they sang about the sun and the summer did her lips move as she watched the drenched windows.

And then, of course, the biggest crime of all was that she had come here only five years ago from Earth, and she remembered the sun and the way the sun was and the sky was when she was four in Ohio. And they, they had been on Venus all their lives, and they had been only two years old when last the sun came out and had long since forgotten the color and heat of it and the way it really was. But Margot remembered.

"It's like a penny," she said once, eyes closed.

"No it's not!" the children cried.

"It's like a fire," she said, "in the stove."

"You're lying, you don't remember!" cried the children.

But she remembered and stood quietly apart from all of them and watched the patterning windows. And once, a month ago, she had refused to shower in the school shower rooms, had clutched her hands to her ears and over her head, screaming the water mustn't touch her head. So after that, dimly, dimly, she sensed it, she was different and they knew her difference and kept away.

There was talk that her father and mother were taking her back to Earth next year; it seemed vital to her that they do so, though it would mean the loss of thousands of dollars to her family. And so, the children hated her for all these reasons of big and little consequence. They hated her pale snow face, her waiting silence, her thinness, and her possible future.

"Get away!" The boy gave her another push. "What're you waiting for?"

Then, for the first time, she turned and looked at him. And what she was waiting for was in her eyes.

"Well, don't wait around here!" cried the boy savagely. "You won't see nothing!"

Her lips moved.

"Nothing!" he cried. "It was all a joke, wasn't it?" He turned to the other children. "Nothing's happening today. *Is* it?"

They all blinked at him and then, understanding, laughed and shook their heads. "Nothing, nothing!"

"Oh, but," Margot whispered, her eyes helpless. "But this is the day, the scientists predict, they say, they *know*, the sun . . ."

"All a joke!" said the boy, and seized her roughly. "Hey, everyone, let's put her in a closet before teacher comes!"

"No," said Margot, falling back.

They surged about her, caught her up and bore her, protesting, and then pleading, and then crying, back into a tunnel, a room, a closet, where they slammed and locked the door. They stood looking at the door and saw it tremble from her beating and throwing herself against it. They heard her muffled cries. Then, smiling, they turned and went out and back down the tunnel, just as the teacher arrived.

"Ready, children?" She glanced at her watch.

"Yes!" said everyone.

"Are we all here?"

"Yes!"

The rain slackened still more.

They crowded to the huge door.

The rain stopped.

It was as if, in the midst of a film concerning an avalanche, a tornado, a hurricane, a volcanic eruption, something had, first, gone wrong with the sound apparatus, thus muffling and finally cutting off all noise, all of the blasts and repercussions and thunders, and then, second, ripped the film from the projector and inserted in its place a peaceful tropical slide which did not move or tremor. The world ground to a standstill. The silence was so immense and unbelievable that you felt your ears had been stuffed or you had lost your hearing altogether. The children put their hands to their ears. They stood apart. The door slid back and the smell of the silent, waiting world came in to them.

The sun came out.

It was the color of flaming bronze and it was very large. And the sky around it was a blazing blue tile color. And the jungle burned with sunlight as the children, released from their spell, rushed out, yelling, into the springtime.

"Now, don't go too far," called the teacher after them. "You've only two hours, you know. You wouldn't want to get caught out!"

But they were running and turning their faces up to the sky and feeling the sun on their cheeks like a warm iron; they were taking off their jackets and letting the sun burn their arms.

"Oh, it's better than the sun lamps, isn't it?"

"Much, much better!"

They stopped running and stood in the great jungle that covered Venus, that grew and never stopped growing, tumultuously, even as you watched it. It was a nest of octopi, clustering up great arms of fleshlike weed, wavering, flowering in this brief spring. It was the

· color of rubber and ash, this jungle, from the many years without sun. It was the color of stones and white cheeses and ink, and it was the color of the moon.

The children lay out, laughing, on the jungle mattress, and heard it sigh and squeak under them, resilient and alive. They ran among the trees, they slipped and fell, they pushed each other, they played hide-and-seek and tag, but most of all they squinted at the sun until tears ran down their faces, they put their hands up to that yellowness and that amazing blueness and they breathed of the fresh, fresh air and listened and listened to the silence which suspended them in a blessed sea of no sound and no motion. They looked at everything and savored everything. Then, wildly, like animals escaped from their caves, they ran and ran in shouting circles. They ran for an hour and did not stop running.

And then—

In the midst of their running one of the girls wailed.

Everyone stopped.

The girl, standing in the open, held out her hand.

"Oh, look, look," she said, trembling.

They came slowly to look at her opened palm.

In the center of it, cupped and huge, was a single raindrop.

She began to cry, looking at it.

They glanced quietly at the sky.

"Oh. Oh."

A few cold drops fell on their noses and their cheeks and their mouths. The sun faded behind a stir of mist. A wind blew cool around them. They turned and started to walk back toward the underground house, their hands at their sides, their smiles vanishing away.

A boom of thunder startled them and like leaves before a new hurricane, they tumbled upon each other and ran. Lightning struck ten miles away, five miles away, a mile, a half mile. The sky darkened into midnight in a flash.

They stood in the doorway of the underground for a moment until it was raining hard. Then they closed the door and heard the gigantic sound of the rain falling in tons and avalanches, everywhere and forever.

"Will it be seven more years?"

"Yes. Seven."

Then one of them gave a little cry.

"Margot!"

"What?"

"She's still in the closet where we locked her."

"Margot."

They stood as if someone had driven them, like so many stakes, into the floor. They looked at each other and then looked away. They glanced out at the world that was raining now and raining and raining steadily. They could not meet each other's glances. Their faces were solemn and pale. They looked at their hands and feet, their faces down.

"Margot."

One of the girls said, "Well . . . ?"

No one moved.

"Go on," whispered the girl.

They walked slowly down the hall in the sound of cold rain. They turned through the doorway to the room in the sound of the storm and thunder, lightning on their faces, blue and terrible. They walked over to the closet door slowly and stood by it.

Behind the closet door was only silence.

They unlocked the door, even more slowly, and let Margot out.

Questions for discussion

1. This kind of story might be called a fantasy. It is a story in which the author lets his imagination take him out into space and ahead into the future. We know perfectly well that conditions on the planet Venus are not as he describes them and that the incident which he shows us could not possibly happen. But this does not bother us a bit because the setting and the incident are not really what the story is about. What is really important here is that the author is making a profound observation about the behavior of people. What is the author trying to tell you about people—perhaps about yourself?

2. Could you visualize the setting and feel its atmosphere? Which of your senses came into play while you were reading the story? Which was the most active? Why?

3. Did you notice that the setting of this story is a combination of a very strange planet and a very familiar classroom? What is accomplished by this strange combination?

4. Between whom is the conflict in this story? What was your reaction to this lining up of the two sides? Is this a realistic situation? Do things like this really happen? Have you observed it?

5. How do the Venus children feel about Margot? The author says:

"They edged away from her . . ." What does *edged away from* mean to you? What was her crime? Was it really a crime? Why does the author use that word?

6. What was your reaction to the way they treated her? What was their "crime"? Is this crime common among people?

7. How did the children feel when they remembered about Margot? Which lines in the story tell you how they felt?

8. How did you react to the way the story ended? Have you any idea why the author ended the story in this way?

9. Now let's go back to the very first question asked above: What is the author saying about the behavior of people? Is this true only of children? Can you think of a reason why he chose Venus as his setting rather than Earth?

Vocabulary growth

WORD PARTS. Many English words are made by adding syllables before (prefixes) and after (suffixes) a base word. One frequently used prefix is *re-* which has two basic meanings. It means "back" as in *repay*, "to pay back." It also means "again" as in *reprint*, "to print again."

Suffixes are very useful in English, since they help us multiply the uses of a basic meaning. Thus, with suffixes such as *-ness*, *-ation* (*-tion*, *-ion*), *-ment*, *-ence*, we can make nouns out of adjectives and verbs. A word like *govern*, for example, names an action; it is a verb. When we want to speak of the various acts of governing together, we do not say "the govern of our state." In this phrase, we need a noun, since only nouns are preceded by *the*. Hence, we add a *noun suffix* and produce the word *government*. We can speak of "the *government* of our state."

1. Which meaning of the prefix *re-* occurs in each of the following words?

recall	replace
remembrance	report
repercussion	retouch
result	review

2. We add *-ment* or *-ence* to some words, and *-ness* or *-ation* to others. We do not add them indiscriminately, and usually we do not add more than one suffix to the same base. Which ending do we add to each of the following words to make nouns of them?

blue	state	estimate
movie	argument	confer
happy	derive	excel
differ	sweet	graduate

For composition

Unfortunately, people do not always conduct themselves in an admirable way. It is likely that you have observed or heard of some person or some group of people who do or say things which you feel are not respectable or commendable. It is not always easy (or diplomatic) to tell people directly that they are acting badly. It is surprisingly easy, however, for most people to see that others are misbehaving. For this reason, it is sometimes an effective device to tell a story about "some other people" who misbehave in a certain way, disguising the situation by changing the time and place where it happened or is happening. It is possible, then, that those who read or listen to this "parable" or "fantasy" will come to see it as a mirror and see in it that they, too, are acting or have acted in this way. This is what "All Summer in a Day" does.

Select some instance of human misconduct (cheating, for instance) committed by an individual, or a group of people, or a country. Then set the story out in space somewhere so that the people whom you are going to portray will not recognize themselves immediately. Tell the story in such a way that, without your even hinting that you intend this to be a sort of "look into the mirror" experience, the readers will be led to make an observation about human behavior, perhaps even their own.

The boys could not believe that their dog was "no
'count" and resented his being called . . .

The Biscuit Eater

JAMES STREET

LONNIE poked out his lower lip and blew as hard as he could,
trying to blow back the tousled brown hair that flopped over his
forehead and got in his eyes. He couldn't use his hands to brush back
his hair, for his hands were full of puppies. He held the puppies up,
careful to protect their eyes from the sun, and examined them.

Then he cocked his head as his father often did and said solemnly,
as though he were an expert on such matters, "Yes siree bobtail. Fine
litter of puppies. Pure D scutters, sure as my name is Lonnie McNeil."

"Think so, Son?" Harve McNeil glanced up at his only son. He
wanted to laugh at Lonnie's solemn expression, but he wouldn't.
Never treat a child as a child, treat him as an equal. That's what
Harve McNeil believed. The boy was serious, so the father must be
serious, too. "Mighty glad you think so. You're an A No. 1 bird-dog
man and I have a heap of respect for your judgment."

Lonnie's heart swelled until it filled his chest and lapped over
into his throat. He stuck out his chest and swaggered a bit. Then he
put the puppies back into the big box where he and his father were
working.

They were Bonnie Blue's pups, seven squirming, yelping little
fellows that tumbled over themselves in greedy attempts to reach
their mother, lying in a corner of the box and watching her litter
proudly. They were nine days old and their eyes were open.

The boy sat on his feet next to his father in the crowded box and
helped him doctor the puppies. Now that their eyes were open they
must be prepared to face a blinding sun. Soon they must have shots
to ward off diseases, but first their eyes and ears must be cleaned.
A bird dog with defective sight and hearing is no 'count.

This was the first time Lonnie had ever been allowed to help his father with a new litter. Harve held a puppy in his big hand, wiped each eye with a clean piece of cotton, then bathed the pup's ears.

"Hand me another, Son," he said. "But handle him gently. Ol' Bonnie's got her eye on you, and if you hurt one of them she'll jump you like a jay jumps a June bug."

Lonnie picked up a puppy and cuddled it. "Hi, puppy dog. How you doing, ol' puppy dog? Know me now that you got your eyes open?" The pup flicked out his tongue and ran it across Lonnie's face. Then he caught Lonnie's ear and began sucking it. The boy laughed and handed the puppy to his father.

Harve looked the dog over carefully. "He's a beaut all right." He ran his finger over a small knot on the pup's head. "Ummhh. Little knot there. But it'll go away. Then he'll be perfect. Ought to be. Good blood line in this litter. Hey, Bonnie Blue, ol' girl. I'm bragging on your pups."

Bonnie Blue perked up her ears and rubbed her nose against Harve. She was a champion. She was almost as good a dog as Silver Belle, the pride of the place. Bonnie had won more than her share of field trials, and once she had run in the Grand National up at Grand Junction, Tennessee, the world series for bird dogs. But the puppies had a doubtful strain in them, inherited from their father, a fair to middlin' bird dog until he killed one of Farmer Eben's sheep, and was shot, according to the code of the piney woods. Farmer Eben lived across the hollow from the McNeils.

Mr. Eben warned Harve that any puppies that had the sheep killer's blood in them were bound to be no 'count by the law of heritage. Bonnie's litter was on the way when the father was killed, and Harve believed he could cure the pups of any bad habits. The father had had a lot of courage, a strong heart, and a good nose. Maybe the pups would be all right.

Harve scratched the pup on the belly, then passed him back to a huge grinning Negro, black as a swamp at midnight. The Negro was First-and-Second-Thessalonians, the handyman around the place. Everybody called him Thes.

"Yas, suh, Mistah Harve," Thes said as he put the pup into another box. "Me and you and Mistah Lon and ol' Bonnie Blue got us a good litter this go-round. And ol' Mistah Lon handles 'em just like he was born with a pup in each hand. Just like a natchel bird-dawg man."

It was too much for Lonnie. He was so happy he wanted to cry. Everybody bragging on him. His father beamed and resumed his work. It was good working there in the shade, with his son at his side and good dogs to work with. Harve McNeil was very proud of his boy and his dogs and his job. He trained dogs for Mr. Ames, the Philadelphia sportsman, and Ames' dogs, handled by McNeil, were known at every important field trial from Virginia to Texas. The Ames plantation, almost hidden in the piney woods of South Mississippi, was Lonnie's home. There were many bird dogs in the kennel, pointers and setters, and some were as valuable as race horses. Mr. Ames could have named his own price for Bonnie Blue and Silver Belle, but money couldn't buy them.

Cicadas sang in the water oaks as Harve worked. Hummingbirds darted around the red cannas and the mellow Cape jasmine. June bugs buzzed around the fig trees. Jay birds scolded in a pecan tree and mockingbirds warbled. In a field near by, a bobwhite whistled, and Bonnie Blue lifted her ears. Yes, Harve McNeil thought, it was good, working there with his boy in such a beautiful, peaceful land. So he began humming:

> Went to the river and couldn't get across,
> Singing polly-wolly-doodle all day—

Lonnie took up the melody:

> Paid five dollars for an old gray hoss,
> Singing polly-wolly-doodle all day—

Thes doubled up with laughter. "Listen to ol' Mistah Lon sing that gray-hoss song. Just like a natchel man. Know this 'un, Mistah Lon?"

The big Negro tilted his head, shuffled his feet, and chanted:

> Peckerwood a-sittin' on a swingin' limb,
> Bluejay a-struttin' in the garden—

Lonnie joined in:

> Ol' gray goose a-settin' in the lane,
> She'll hatch on the other side of Jordan.

Thes slapped his thigh. "Hot ziggity-dog. How 'bout this 'un: 'Thought I heard somebody say—.'"

"Soda pop, soda pop, take it away." Lonnie sang so loudly that the pups quit yelping and looked up at him.

They doctored six pups, and as Harve finished the last one he told his son, "Run in the house and tell Mamma we'll be in for dinner in a minute."

Lonnie jumped up and started away. Then he stopped suddenly. "But we got another puppy, Papa. We only done six. There's seven in the litter."

Harve looked over at Thes and the big Negro turned his head. The father reached down and lifted the seventh pup. "We won't fix him, Son."

"How come?" asked Lonnie. He stared at the pup, a scrawny little fellow with spots that looked like freckles, a stringy tail, and watery brown eyes. He was the most forlorn looking pup Lonnie had ever seen.

"He's no 'count, Son," Harve said sadly. "He's the runt of the litter. Thes will get rid of him."

"You mean kill him?" Lonnie said.

"Now don't look at me that way," Harve said. "He'll go easy. You're a bird-dog man, Son. You know there's a bad 'un in 'most every litter. All these dogs got one strike on them 'cause their papa was a sheep killer. But this one has got two strikes on him."

All the blood drained from Lonnie's face and his heart went to the pit of his stomach. "I was a runt," he said. "And I got freckles. Why didn't you drown me?"

"Don't talk that away, Mistah Lon," Thes said. "Its hard 'nuff to kill him without you carryin' on so."

Harve McNeil looked at his boy a long time, then at the runt. Slowly he began cleaning the puppy's ears. "We'll keep him, Thes," he said. "If my boy wants to keep this dog, we'll keep him."

Lonnie's heart climbed from his stomach back to his chest and he choked up again. "Is he mine, Papa?"

"He's yours." Harve got up and put his hand on his boy's shoulder. "He's your dog, Son. But don't feel bad if he's no good. I'll help you train him, but he looks like a biscuit eater."

"He sho' do," said Thes.

"He don't neither," said Lon. It was his dog now and nobody could defame him. "He ain't no biscuit eater. Are you, puppy dog?"

He held the dog close to him and began running toward the branch, beyond which lived his friend, Text. Text was Thes's little brother and was just as black.

Harve and Thes watched the boy out of sight. "How come Mistah Lon want that li'l ol' pup, you reckon?" Thes scratched his head.

"Nobody, Thes," Harve said, "has ever understood the way of a boy with a dog. I reckon the boy wanted him because nobody else did."

"Reckon he's a biscuit eater?" Thes asked.

"It sticks out all over him," Harve said. "He ain't worth a shuck. But he's Lonnie's dog, and Heaven help the boy who calls him a biscuit eater."

A biscuit eater is an ornery dog. He won't hunt anything except his own biscuits. And he'll suck eggs and steal chickens and run coons and jump rabbits. To a bird-dog man, a biscuit eater is the lowest form of animal life. Strangers in Mississippi often are puzzled by the expression until natives, who usually eat biscuits instead of light bread, explain that a biscuit eater is a no 'count hound that isn't good for anything except to hunt his meat and biscuits.

Lonnie found Text down at the branch, fishing for shiners, long silver minnows that thrived near the bank. Text was the youngest of Aunt Charity's brood. A shouting, sanctified, foot-washing Baptist, Aunt Charity lived close to God and had given her children names that should be fitting in the eyes of the Lord. She had heard her preacher take text from this and text from that, so she reckoned Text was a superfine name.

The white boy held the puppy in his arms so Text couldn't see him and said, "Guess what I got."

"A gopher," Text suggested.

Lonnie sat on the ground and opened his arms. The puppy tumbled out, and Text's eyes popped open. "A puppy dawg. Be John dogged, Lon. And he's ours!"

"Mine," said Lonnie.

Text took the dog in his arms and ignored Lonnie's claim of complete possession. "We finally got us a dawg. Heah, pup."

The pup's tail drooped, but his big eyes watched Text. He was awkward, scrawny, and wobbly-legged. "Ain't he a beaut, Lon?" Text said. "Boy, we got us a dog."

There was no denying Text a claim to the pup, so Lonnie said, "You tell 'um. We got us a dog."

The pup whimpered and licked Lonnie's hand. "Knows me already. Better get him back to his mamma."

Text went with him, but before they put the pup in the kennel, the little Negro turned him over, placed his hand over the pup's heart, and muttered:

> Possum up a sweetgum stump, raccoon in the holler,
> Wake, snake! June bug done stole yo' half-a-dollar.

Lonnie said, "What's that for?"

"Luck," said Text. "I put the ol' charm on him. I got better charms than that, but I'm savin' 'em."

The boys hung around Bonnie Blue's kennel all day, watching their dog. They called him Pup for lack of a better name, and in the weeks that followed they worked hard at his training. The dog developed fast. The freckles grew into big spots. His chest filled out and the muscles rippled in his legs. The boys saw only love and loyalty in his eyes, but Harve and Thes saw meanness there, and stubbornness. He was slow to learn, but the boys were patient.

A bird dog must know many things. How to carry an egg in his mouth without breaking it. How to get bird scents from the air and how to stand motionless for an hour if necessary, pointing birds, showing the master where the covey is. A bird dog knows instinctively that quail live in flocks, or coveys, usually a brood. They feed on the ground and fly in coveys until scattered. A bird dog must know all the habits of quail and never try to round them up, or crawl and putter around them. Only a biscuit eater who can't catch air scents rounds up birds in an effort to sight-point them. A quail's only protection is his color, and when a dog sight-points him the bird knows he's been seen and will take off. Good dogs must know how to keep their heads up and hold birds on the ground until the master is ready to flush the covey by frightening the quail. Then, when the birds take wing fast as feathered lightning, bird dogs must stand still until the hunter shoots the birds and orders his dog to fetch the kill.

He must know how to cover every likely looking spot, passing up bare ground where quail can't hide. He should have a merry tail that whips back and forth. And he must cast with wisdom and range wide.

He must know how to honor the other dog's point by backing him up and standing still while the other dog holds the birds. A good dog knows that if he moves while another dog is on a point he might flush the birds. Such behavior is instinct with good dogs and not really a sense of honor.

Harve tried to help the boys train the pup, but was not able to get close to his affections. There was no feeling between him and the pup, no understanding. The pup cowered at Lonnie's feet when Harve ordered him into the fields to hunt. And then one night Harve caught him in the henhouse, sucking eggs.

An egg-sucking dog simply is not tolerated. It hurt Harve to get rid of the dog, but there was nothing else to do. He walked with Lonnie out to the barn and they sat down. Harve told his son, "You're a bird-dog man, Son. A hunter. It's in your blood."

Lonnie sensed what was coming and asked, "What's my dog done now?"

"Sucked eggs. I caught him last night."

"No, Papa. Not that. He ain't no suck-egger."

"Yes, he is, Son, and remember his father was a sheep killer. The bad streak's coming out. He's a biscuit eater, and there's no cure for a biscuit eater. We've got to get rid of him. He'll teach my good dogs bad habits. He's got to go."

Lonnie didn't say anything. He compressed his lips, knowing that if he opened them he would cry. He walked out of the barn and down to the branch where he could think over his problem. Text could keep the dog. That was the solution. They could keep him away from Harve's fine dogs. Lonnie ran to tell Text the plan, but while he was away Harve took the dog across the ridge and gave him to a Negro. He didn't have the heart to kill him or let Thes kill him.

Harve shoved the dog toward the Negro and said, "He's yours, if you want him. He'll run rabbits. But I warn you, he's no good. He's a suck-egg biscuit eater."

The Negro accepted the dog because he knew he could swap him. That very night, however, the dog stole eggs from the Negro's henhouse, and the Negro tied a block and rope around his neck and beat him and called him a low-life biscuit eater. The dog immediately associated the block and rope and the beating with the term biscuit eater and he was sorely afraid and hurt. He was hurt because the man was displeased with him and he didn't know why. So when the Negro called him biscuit eater, he ran under the cabin and sulked.

When Lonnie learned what his father had done with the outcast, he went to Text, and together they went over the ridge to bargain for the dog. On the way, Text paused, crossed his fingers and muttered:

> Green corn, sweet corn,
> Mister, fetch a demijohn,
> Fat meat, fat meat,
> That's what the Injuns eat.

Lonnie said, "Puttin' on a good-luck spell?"

"Uh huh. That's one of my best charms. We going to need luck to make this swap."

The Negro man was wily. He sensed a good bargain and was trader enough to know that if he low-rated the dog, the boys would want him more than ever. The dog had a cotton rope around his neck, and the rope was fastened to a block, and when the dog walked, his head pulled sideways as he tugged the block. The dog walked to Lonnie and rubbed against his legs. The boy ignored him. He mustn't let the Negro man know how badly he wanted the dog. The man grabbed the rope and jerked the dog away.

"He's a biscuit eater!" The Negro nudged the dog with his foot. The animal looked sideways at his master and slunk away. "He ain't worth much."

"He's a suck-egg biscuit eater, ain't he?" Lonnie asked. The dog watched him, and when the boy said "biscuit eater," the dog ran under the cabin, pulling the block behind him. "He's scared," Lonnie said. "You been beating him. And ever' time you jump him, you call him 'biscuit eater.' That's how come he's scared. Whatcha take for him?"

The man said, "Whatcha gimme?"

"I'll give you my frog-sticker." Lonnie showed his knife. "And I got a pretty good automobile tire. Ain't but one patch on it. It'd make a prime superfine swing for your young 'uns."

The Negro asked Text, "What'll you chip in to boot?"

Text said, "You done cussed out the dawg so much I don't want no share of him. You done low-rated him too much. If he sucks eggs at my house, my Maw'll bust me in two halves. Whatcha want to boot?"

"Whatcha got?"

"Nothin'," said Text "cep'n two big hands what can tote a heap of wood. Tote your shed full of light'r knots for boot."

"What else?"

Text thought for a minute, weighing the deal. "Lon wants that dawg. I know where there's a pas'l of May haws and a honeybee tree."

The Negro man said, "It's a deal, boys, if'n you pick me a lard bucket full of May haws and show me the bee tree."

Lonnie took the block from the dog and led him across the field. Then Text led him awhile. Out of sight of the Negro's shack, the boys stopped and examined their possession.

Text ran his hand over the dog, smoothing the fur. "He's a good dawg, ain't he, Lon? Look at them big ol' eyes, and them big ol' feet, and that big ol' short tail. Bet he can point birds from here to yonder. Betcha if he tries, he can point partridge on light bread." He looked down at the big, brooding dog. "We got to give him a name. We can't keep on calling him Pup. He's a big dawg and if'n you call a big dawg Pup it's like calling a growed-up man young 'un. What we going to name him, Lon?"

Lonnie said, "Dunno, Text. But listen, don't ever call him—" He looked at the dog, then at Text. "You know." He held his fingers in the shape of a biscuit and pantomimed as though he were eating. The dog didn't understand. Neither did Text. So Lonnie whispered, "You know, 'biscuit eater.' Don't ever call him that. That's what's the matter with him. He expects a beating when he hears it."

"It's a go," Text whispered. "Let's name him Moreover. It's in the Bible."

"Where 'bouts?"

"I heard the preacher say so. He said, 'Moreover, the dog,' and he was reading from the Bible."

Lonnie held the dog's chin with one hand and stroked his chest with the other. "If Moreover is good enough for the Bible, then it's good enough for us. He's Moreover then. He's a good dog, Text. And he's ours. You keep him and I'll furnish the rations. I can snitch 'em from Papa. Will Aunt Charity raise Cain if you keep him?"

"Naw," said Text. "I 'member the time that big ol' brother of mine, ol' First-and-Second-Thessalonians, fetched a goat home, and Maw didn't low-rate him. She just said she had so many young 'uns she didn't mind a goat. I 'spects she feels the same way 'bout a dawg, if'n he's got a Bible name."

"I reckon so, too," said Lonnie and ran home and told his father about the deal.

Harve told his son, "It's all right for you and Text to keep the dog, but keep him away from over here. I don't want him running around my good dogs. You know why."

Lonnie said, "He's a good dog, Papa. He just ain't had no chance."

Harve looked at his son. The boy was growing, and the man was proud.

He noticed his son collecting table scraps the next morning, but didn't mention it. "I'm going to work Silver Belle today. Want to come along?"

Lonnie shook his head. Harve knew then how much the boy loved Moreover for, ordinarily, Lonnie would have surrendered any pleasure to accompany his father when he worked Silver Belle. She was the finest pointer in the Ames kennels and Harve had trained her since puppyhood. Already, she had won the Grand National twice. A third win would give his employer permanent possession of the Grand National trophy, and Harve wanted to win the prize for Mr. Ames more than he wanted anything in the world. He pampered Silver Belle. She was a magnificent pointer, trim and beautiful. There were no characteristics of a biscuit eater in Silver Belle. She was everything that Moreover was not, and when hunting she ranged so far and so fast that she had to wear a bell so the hunters could keep track of her. She had seen Moreover only once and that was from a distance. The aristocrat had sniffed and Moreover had turned his big head and stared at her, awe and admiration in his eyes. And then he had tucked his head and run away. He knew his place.

Lonnie set the greasy bag of table scraps on a hummock of wire grass and leaned over the branch, burying his face in the cool water.

A lone ant poked its head from around a clover leaf, surveyed the scene, and scurried boldly to the scraps. The adventurer scrambled about the sack and then turned away. Soon the ant reappeared with a string of fellow workers and they circled the bag, seeking an opening. But the boy didn't notice the ants. He lifted his head out of the water, took a deep breath, and plunged it in again.

A beetle lumbered from behind a clod and stumbled toward the scraps. One of the working ants spied it and signaled the others, and the little army retreated into the grass to get reinforcements. The beetle went to the scraps and was preparing for a feast when the ants attacked.

Lonnie paid no mind to the drama of life. He wiped his mouth with the back of his hand. Hundreds of black, frisky water bugs, aroused at his invasion of their playground, scooted to the middle of the stream, swerved as though playing follow-the-leader, and scooted back to the bank.

The boy laughed at their capers. Slowly, he stooped over the water. His hand darted as a cottonmouth strikes, and he snatched one of the bugs and smelled it. There was a sharp, sugary odor on the bug.

"A sweet stinker, sure as I'm born," the boy muttered. If you caught a sweet stinker among water bugs, it meant good luck, maybe. Lonnie mumbled slowly:

> Eerie, oarie, eekerie, Nan,
> Fillison, follison, Nicholas, Buck,
> Queavy, quavy, English navy,
> Sticklum, stacklum, come good luck.

That should help the charm. Everybody knew that. Lonnie held the mellow bug behind him, closed his eyes, tilted his head, and whispered to the pine trees, the branch, the wire grass and anything else in the silence that wanted to hear him and would never tell his wish: "I hope Moreover is always a good dog."

Then Lonnie put the bug back in the branch. It darted in circles for a second and skedaddled across the creek, making a beeline for the other bugs. There were tiny ripples in its wake. The boy grinned. He was in for some good luck. If the sweet stinker had changed its course, it would have broken the charm.

He picked up his bag of scraps and brushed off the beetle and ants, crushing some of the ants. The beetle landed on its back, and a blue jay swooped down and snatched it. Lonnie watched the bird fly away. Then he studied the earth near the stream. No telling what a fellow would find if he looked around. Maybe he would find a doodlebug hole and catch one on a straw. That was good luck, too; better luck than finding a ladybug and telling her, "Ladybug, ladybug, fly away home; your house is on fire and your children are alone." He found no doodlebug hole, but there was a crawdad castle, a house of mud that a crawfish had built. There was no luck in a crawdad, but Lonnie marked the place. Crawdads are good fish bait. He crossed the branch on a log and moseyed to the edge of the woods where the cleared land began. The land was choked with grass and stumps. Lonnie pursed his lower lip, and whistled the call of the catbird, watching the cabin in the field where Text lived.

Lonnie saw Text run to the rickety front gallery of the cabin and listen. He whistled again. Text answered and ran around the house, and a minute later he was racing across the field with Moreover at his heels. The white boy opened his arms and the dog ran to him and tried to lick his face. The dog almost bowled the boy over. Lonnie jerked off his cap and his long, brown uncombed hair fell over his face. He put his face very close to the dog's right ear and muttered to him the things that boys always mutter to dogs. The dog's tail wagged and his big eyes looked quizzically at the boy. He rubbed against the boy's legs and Lonnie scratched him.

Text waited until Lonnie and the dog had greeted each other properly and then he said, "Hydee, Lon. Ol' Moreover is glad to see you. Me and him bof'."

Lonnie said, "Hi, Text. He looks slick as el-lem sap, don't he? Been working him?"

"A heap and whole lot," said Text. "Turned him loose in the wire grass yestiddy and he pointed two coveys 'fore I could say, 'Lawd 'a' mercy.' He's a prime superfine bird dawg, Lon. He ain't no no 'count biscuit eater."

Lonnie put his arm around his friend. "You mighty come a'right he ain't no biscuit eater."

The dog had wiped away all class and race barriers between Lonnie and Text, and they were friends in a way that grownups never understand. They didn't brag about their friendship or impose upon it, but each knew he could count upon the other.

They worked hard and patiently trying to train the dog, and sometimes the task seemed hopeless. Once he pointed a flock of chickens, a disgraceful performance. Again he ran a rabbit and once he left a point to dash across a field and bark at Mr. Eben, who was plowing a mule. Mr. Eben threw a clod at him.

The boys couldn't teach the dog to carry an egg in his mouth, for he always broke the egg and ate it. Once when he sucked an egg, Lon put his arms around the dog and cried, not in anger but in anguish.

Cotton hung loosely in the bolls and dog days passed. Indian summer came and the forest smelled woodsy and smoky. Sumac turned to yellow and gold, and the haze of autumn hugged the earth.

Moreover improved slowly, but the boys still were not satisfied. "Let's work him across the ridge today," Lon said. "Papa's got Silver Belle in the south forty and he won't want us and Moreover around."

Text said, "It's a go, Lon. I'll snitch ol' Thes's shotgun and meet you 'cross the ridge. But that there lan' over there is pow'ful close to Mister Eben's place. I don't want no truck with that man."

"I ain't afraid of Mr. Eben," said Lonnie.

"Well, I am. And so are you! And so is your Paw!"

Lonnie's face flushed and he clenched his fists. It was the first time he had ever clenched his fist at Text, but nobody could talk about his papa. "Papa's not afraid of anything and I'll bust you in two halves if you say so." He jerked off his cap and hurled it to the ground.

Text rolled his eyes until the whites showed. He had never seen Lon angry before, but he wasn't afraid. "Then how come your Paw didn't whup Mister Eben when Mister Eben kicked his dawg about two years ago?"

Negroes heard everything and forgot nothing. Everybody in the county had wondered why Harve McNeil hadn't thrashed Eben when the farmer kicked one of McNeil's dogs without cause. The code of the county was, "Love me, love my dog." And one of the favorite sayings was, "It makes no difference if he is a hound, don't you kick my dog around."

But Harve had done nothing when Eben kicked his dog. Harve didn't believe in settling disputes with his fists. As a young man he had fought often for many reasons, but now that he was a father he tried to set a good example for his son. So he had taken the Eben insult although it was hard to do.

Lonnie often had wondered why his father didn't beat up Mr. Eben. His mother tried to explain and had said, "Gentlemen don't go around fighting. Your father is a gentleman and he wants you to be one."

Lonnie was ashamed and embarrassed because some of the other boys had said Harve was afraid of Eben. And now Text said the same thing. "Papa didn't whip Mr. Eben 'cause Mother asked him not to, that's why," Lonnie said defiantly.

Text realized that his friend was hurt and he 'lowed that Mr. McNeil was the best bird-dog man in the county. The flattery might help to offset the charge of cowardice that the little Negro had made against his friend's father. Text couldn't stand to see Lonnie hurt. He jammed his hands in his overall pockets and grinned at Lonnie. "Lady folks sho' are buttinskies," Text said. "All time trying to keep men folks from whupping each other. Lady folks sho' are scutters. All 'cept your maw and my maw, huh, Lon?"

Lonnie said, "Mr. Eben is just a crotchety man. Mother said so. He don't mean no harm."

"That's what you say," Text said. "But he's a scutter from 'way back. Maw says when he kills beeves he drinks the blood, and I'se popeyed scared of him. His lan' say, 'Posted. Keep off. Law.' And I ain't messin' around over there."

They turned Moreover loose near a field of stubble and watched him range. Lonnie often had worked dogs with his father and had seen the best run at field trials. He trained Moreover by inspiring confidence in him. The first time Text shot over him, Moreover cowered, but now he no longer was gun shy, and he worked for the sheer joy of working. Lonnie never upbraided him. When Moreover showed a streak of good traits, the boys patted him; when he erred, they simply ignored him. The dog had a marvelous range and moved through the saw grass at an easy gait, never tiring.

He had a strange point. He cocked his long head in the air, then turned slowly toward Lonnie as he froze to his point. But having caught Lonnie's eye, he always turned his head back and pointed his nose toward the birds, his head high, his tail as stiff as a ramrod. He was not spectacular, but constant. He ran at a sort of awkward lope, twisting his head as though he still were tugging a block. But he certainly covered ground.

"He sho' is a good dawg," Text said.

They were working him near Eben's farm and Moreover, catching wind of a huge covey, raced through the stubble and disappeared in the sage. When the boys found him he was frozen on a point far inside Farmer Eben's posted land. And watching Moreover from a pine thicket was Eben, a shotgun held loosely in the crook of his arm.

Text was terror-stricken and gaped at Eben as though the stubble-faced man were an ogre. Lonnie took one look at his dog, then at the man, and walked to the thicket. Text was in his shadow. "Please don't shoot him, Mr. Eben," Lonnie said.

The farmer said, "Huh?"

"Naw, suh, please don't shoot him." Text found his courage. "He couldn't read yo' posted sign."

Eben scowled. "I don't aim to shoot him. That is, less'n he gets 'round my sheep. I was watching his point. Right pretty, ain't it?"

Lonnie said, "Mighty pretty. He's a good dog, Mr. Eben. If ever you want a mess of birds, I'll give you the loan of him."

"Nothin' shaking," Eben said. "He's that biscuit eater your paw gave that Negro over the ridge."

Moreover still was on the point and when Lon heard the dreaded word he turned quickly to his dog. The dog's eyes blinked, but he didn't break his point. Text protested, "Don't go callin' him that, please, suh. He don't like it."

"He can't read my posted sign, but he can understand English, huh?" Eben laughed. He admired the dog's point again and then flushed the birds by rustling the grass. The quail got up and Eben shot one. Moreover didn't flinch. Eben ordered him to fetch, but the big, brooding dog turned his head toward Lonnie and just stood there. He wouldn't obey Mr. Eben and the farmer was furious. He picked up a stick and started toward the dog, but Lon and Text jumped beside Moreover.

The dog showed his fangs.

"I'll teach that biscuit eater to fetch dead birds," Eben snarled.

"If you touch my dog, I'll tell Papa," Lon said, slowly.

"I'm not afraid of your papa. And get that dog off'n my land or I'll sprinkle him with bird shot." He glared at Moreover, and the dog crouched to spring. "I believe that dog would jump me," Eben said.

"He will if'n you bother me or Lon," said Text. 'He won't 'low nobody to bother us."

Lonnie patted his dog and whistled, and Moreover followed him and Text.

Lonnie was moody at supper and his mother reckoned he needed a tonic or something. He didn't eat but one helping of chicken pie, corn on the cob, string beans, light bread, molasses, butter, and sweet-potato pie. Usually he had two helpings and at least two glasses of buttermilk. His mother was worried about him, but his father knew that something was bothering the boy and kept his peace.

Finally, Lon took a deep breath and asked his father, "How come you didn't whip Mr. Eben that time he kicked your dog?"

Harve looked quickly at his wife and swallowed. "What made you think of that question?"

"Nothin'," said Lon. "I was just wondering. If a man kicked my dog, I'd bust him open."

"Well, I tell you, Son. I've had my share of fighting. It never proves anything. Anything can fight. Dogs, cats, skunks, and such things. But a man is supposed to be different. He's supposed to have some sense. I don't mind a good fight if there's something to fight for. I'd fight for you and your mother and our country, but I won't fight for foolishness." He knew his wife was pleased with his words, but he wasn't pleased with himself. He wished there was some way he could meet Eben without everybody knowing about it. He was a peace-loving man, but not too peace-loving.

Harve knew his son wasn't satisfied with the explanation. He frowned and glanced at his wife. He hadn't punished Eben simply because he didn't think the crime of kicking a dog justified a beating. There had been a time when he thought differently. But he was older now, and respected. He wondered if Lonnie thought he was afraid of Eben, and the thought bothered him.

"I wish we had the papers on Moreover," Lonnie changed the subject. "I want to register him."

Harve said, "I got the papers, Son. You can have 'em. What you gonna do, run your dog against my Belle in the county-seat trials?" He was joshing the boy. Ordinarily, Harve wouldn't enter Silver Belle in such two-bit trials as the county meets. She was a national champion and no dogs in the little meet would be in her class. But Harve wanted to get her in perfect shape for the big meet, and the county trials would help.

Lonnie looked at his father. "That's what I aim to do," he said. "Run my dog against yours."

The father laughed loudly, and his laughter trailed off into a chuckle. Lonnie enjoyed hearing his father laugh that way. "It's a great idea, Son. So you have trained that biscuit eater for the trials! Where are you going to get your entry fee?"

"He ain't no biscuit eater!" Lonnie said defiantly.

His mother was startled at his impudence to his father. But Harve shook his head at his wife and said, " 'Course he ain't, Son. I'm sorry. And just to show that me and Belle ain't scared of you and Moreover, I'll give you and Text the job of painting around the kennels. You can earn your entry fee. Is it a go?"

"Yes siree bob." Lonnie stuffed food in his mouth and hurried through his meal. "I'm going to high-tail it over and tell Text and Moreover."

Harve walked down the front path with his son. It was nice to walk down the path with his son. The father said simply and in man's talk, "Maybe I'm batty to stake you and your dog to your entry fee. You might whip me and Belle, and Mr. Ames might give you my job of training his dogs."

Lonnie didn't reply. But at the gate he paused and faced his father. "Papa, you ain't scared of Mr. Eben, are you?"

The trainer leaned against the gate and lit his pipe. "Son," he said, "I ain't scared of nothing but God. But don't tell your mother." He put his hand on his boy's shoulder. "You're getting to be a big boy, Lonnie. Before long you'll be a man. I'm mighty proud of you."

"I'm proud of you, too, Papa, even if you didn't whip Mr. Eben."

"You and Text have done a mighty fine job with your dog. It takes a good man to handle a dog like yours. He ain't had much chance in life. He really ain't much 'count. But you boys have shown patience and courage with him. So I'll tell you what I'll do. If you fellows make a good showing at the trials, I'll let you bring that dog back to the kennels."

"Is it a deal, Papa? If we do good, can I bring my li'l ol' dog back home?"

"It's a deal," said Harve, and they shook hands.

Lonnie ran down to the branch and whistled for Text and told him the good news.

"Gee m'netty," Text said. "But who's going to handle him, me or you? Can't but one of us work him."

"Count out," said Lonnie. "That'll make it fair and square."

Text began counting out, pointing his finger at Lon, then at himself as he recited slowly:

> William come Trimble-toe,
> He is a good fisherman.
> Catches hens, puts 'em in pens,
> Some lay eggs, some lay none.
> Wire, brier, Limberlock,
> Three geese in a flock,
> One flew east, one flew west,
> One flew over the cuckoo's nest.
> O–U–T spells out and out you go,
> You dirty old dish rag you.

Text was pointing at himself when he said the last word, so he was out. "You're it, Lon," he said. "You work him and I'll help."

Mr. Ames sat on the steps of the gun-club lodge and laughed when he saw his truck coming up the driveway. His cronies, who had come to the county seat for the trials—a sort of minor-league series—laughed, too. Harve was driving. Silver Belle was beside him. Lonnie and Text were on the truck bed with dogs all around them, and behind the truck, tied with cotton rope, loped Moreover. Mr. Ames shook hands with his trainer and met the boys.

"We got competition," Harve said, and nodded toward Moreover.

Ames studied the big dog. "By Joe, Harve! That used to be my dog. Is that the old bis—"

"Sh-h-h!" Harve commanded. "Don't say it. It hurts the dog's feelings. Or so the boys say."

Ames understood. He had a son at home. He walked around Moreover and looked at him. "Mighty fine dog, boys. . . . If he beats Belle, I might hire you, Lonnie, and fire your father." He winked at Harve, but the boys didn't see him.

They took Moreover to the kennels. They didn't have any money to buy rations, so Text ran to the kitchen of the lodge and soon had a job doing chores. Moreover's food was assured, for it was easy for Text to slip liver and bits of good beef for the dog.

Lonnie bedded his dog down carefully and combed him and tried to make him look spruce. But Moreover would not be spruce. There was a quizzical look in his eyes. The other dogs took attention as though they expected it, but Moreover rubbed his head along the ground and scratched his ears against the kennel box and mussed himself up as fast as Lonnie cleaned him. But he seemed to know that Lonnie expected something of him. All the other dogs were yelping and were nervous. But Moreover just flopped on his side and licked Lonnie's hands.

Inside the lodge, Ames asked Harve, "How's Belle?"

"Tiptop," said Harve. "She'll win hands down here, and I'm laying that she'll take the Grand National later. I'm gonna keep my boy with me, Mr. Ames. Text can stay with the help."

"What do those kids expect to do with that biscuit eater?" Ames laughed.

"You know how boys are. I'll bet this is the first time in history a colored boy and a white boy ever had a joint entry in a field trial. They get riled if anybody calls him a biscuit eater."

"Can't blame them, Harve," Ames said. "I get mad if anybody makes fun of my dogs. We are all alike, men and boys."

"You said it. Since the first, I reckon, boys have got mad if a fellow said anything against their mothers or dogs."

"Or fathers?" Ames suggested.

"Depends on the father," said Harve. "Wish Lonnie's dog could make a good showing. Do the boy a heap of good."

They were standing by the fireplace and Ames said, "I hope that big brute is not in a brace with Belle. She's a sensitive dog." Then he laughed. "Be funny, Harve, if that dog whipped us. I'd run you bowlegged."

All the men laughed, but when a waiter told the pantry maid the story, he neglected to say that the threat was a jest. The pantry maid told the barkeeper. The barkeeper told the cook, and by the time the story was circulated around the kitchen, the servants were whispering that rich Mr. Ames had threatened to fire poor Mr. Harve because his son had fetched a biscuit eater to the field trials.

The morning of the first heat, Text met Lonnie at the kennels, and together they fed Moreover. "Let's put some good ol' gunpowder in his vittles," Text said. "Make him hunt better."

"Aw, that's superstition," said Lonnie.

"I don't care what it is, it helps," said Text.

Lonnie didn't believe in tempting luck, so Moreover was fed a sprinkling of gunpowder.

Text said, "I got my lucky buckeye along. We bound to have luck, Lon."

Lonnie was getting too big for such foolishness, but then he remembered. "I caught a sweet stinker not so long ago," he whispered, "and he swum the right way."

"A good ol' sweet-stinking mellow bug?" asked Text eagerly. "Lon, good luck gonna bust us in two halves."

Harve took Silver Belle out in an early brace and the pointer completely outclassed her rival. Her trainer sent her back to her kennel and went into the fields with Ames to watch Moreover in his first race. He was braced with a rangy setter. Even the judges smiled at the two boys and their dog. Text, in keeping with the rules of the sport, gave no orders.

The spectators and judges were mounted, but the handlers were on foot. Lonnie put his dog down on the edge of a clover field and the judges instructed that the dogs be set to work. Moreover's competitor leaped away and began hunting, but Moreover just rolled over, then jumped up and loped around the boy, leaping on him and licking his face. The judges scowled. It was bad behavior for a bird dog. Lonnie and Text walked into the field, and Moreover followed. Lonnie leaned over his dog and whispered in his ear. The big dog jerked up his head, cocked it, and began casting. He ranged to the edge of the field and worked in. He loped past a patch of saw grass, slowed suddenly, wheeled and pointed, his head high, his right leg poised, and his tail stiff as a poker.

Lonnie kept his dog on the point until the judges nodded approval, and then the boy threw a stick among the birds and flushed them. Moreover didn't blink an eye when the birds whirred away and Lonnie shot over him. Then the boy called his dog to the far edge of a field and set him ranging again. He was on a point in a flash.

Ames looked at Harve. "That's a good dog, McNeil. He's trained beautifully. He'll give us a run for our money sure as shooting. If that dog beats Belle, it'll make us look bad."

Harve was beaming with pride. "It proves what I've always preached. A bird dog will work for a man, if the man understands him. I couldn't do anything with that dog, but he'll work his heart out for my boy and Text. But don't worry, Mr. Ames, he can't beat Belle."

To the utter amazement of everybody, except Lonnie and Text, Moreover swept through to the final series, or heat, and was pitted against Silver Belle for the championship. Harve regretted then that he had entered Belle. He wasn't worried about his dog winning. He had confidence in Silver Belle, but the mere fact that a grand champion was running against a biscuit eater was bad. And, too, Harve hated to best his own son in the contest. News that father and son were matched, with the famous Belle against a biscuit eater, brought sportsmen and sportswriters swarming to the county seat. Harve and Lonnie slept and ate together, but the man didn't discuss the contest with his son. He didn't want to make him nervous. He treated Lonnie as he would treat any other trainer.

Neither Harve nor Lonnie had much to say that morning at breakfast. Once the father, his mouth full of batter cakes, looked over at his son and winked. Lonnie winked back. But the boy didn't eat much. He was too excited. The excitement, however, didn't interfere with Text's eating. The other sportsmen kidded Harve and joshed him about the possibility of a biscuit eater beating Silver Belle.

The spectators and judges rode to the edge of a field of stubble, and Harve snapped a bell on his dog's collar. It was the first time he had used the bell during the trials and Lonnie knew what it meant. His father was going to give Silver Belle her head, let her show all that was in her, let her range far and wide. Lonnie's heart sank and Text rolled his eyes. Silver Belle stood there beautifully, but Moreover tucked his head and flopped his ears. The judges gave the signal and Harve said, "Go get 'em, girl."

The champion dashed into the stubble and soon was out of sight. Moreover didn't leap away as he should have, but rubbed against Lonnie's legs and watched Silver Belle for a minute, then began running along her trail. There was no order between Lonnie and his dog, only understanding. Moreover looked like a biscuit eater all right. He didn't race as most bird dogs do, but he sort of trotted away, taking his time. The judges smiled.

The men heard the tinkling of the bell on Silver Belle and knew that the champion was still casting. The dog had ranged far beyond a ridge and Harve did his best to keep her in sight. Suddenly, the bell was silent and Harve ran to his dog. Belle was on a point and was rigid. Her trim body was thrown forward a bit; her nose, perfectly tilted, was aimed toward a clump of sage. She didn't flex a muscle. She might have been made of marble.

"Point!" Harve shouted, and the judges came.

Moreover crept behind Silver Belle and stopped, honoring her point. Harve smiled at his son and Lonnie's heart beat faster. It was a beautiful point. The judges nodded approval, and Harve flushed the birds and shot over his dog, and Belle took it as a champion should.

When the echo of the shot died away, Belle walked to her master and he patted her. Lonnie took Moreover by the collar and the judges gave the signal that the dogs be released again. Belle raced into the stubble, but Moreover swung along at an easy gait. He cast a bit to the right, sniffed, and found the trail that Belle had just made. He never depended on ground scents but on body scents, and kept his nose high enough to catch any smells the wind blew his way.

He got the odor of birds and the muscles of his legs suddenly bunched. He leaped away, easing his nose higher in the air, and raced back up the trail Belle had made. Suddenly, he crouched. Slowly, noiselessly, he took two steps, then three, and froze to a point. His right leg came up slowly, deliberately. He cocked his head in that strange fashion, and the quizzical, comical look came into his eyes. Moreover was a still hunter and never waited for orders. Lonnie clicked the safety off his gun and watched his dog. Text was beside him. The judges and spectators were far away.

"Look at that li'l ol' dawg," said Text. "He's got himself a mess of birds."

Lonnie cupped his hands and shouted to the judges, "Point!"

"Pint!" Text whooped.

Moreover held his point as Lonnie shot over him. Belle honored his point, and as soon as the gun sounded and Moreover got a nod from Lonnie, the big dog dashed to the right and flashed to another point.

The judges whistled softly. "Most beautiful work I ever saw," whispered one. Ames's face took on a worried look. So did Harve's. The big dog had picked up a covey almost under Belle's nose.

Belle settled down to hunt. She seemed everywhere. She dashed to a point on the fringe of a cornfield and got a big covey. She raced over the ridge, her nose picking up scents in almost impossible places. Moreover sort of ambled along, never wasting energy, but every time Belle got a covey he honored her and then cast for a few minutes, pointed, and held. He waited for her to set the pace and it was a killing pace.

Belle held a covey for ten minutes near a rabbit's den. The smell of rabbit was strong in her nose, but she knew birds were there and she handled them.

It was then that Moreover pulled his downwind point. He was running with the wind and didn't get the odor of the covey until he had passed it. But when the hot odor of birds filled his nose, he leaped, reversed himself in mid-air and landed on a point, his front feet braced, his choke-bore nose held high.

It was the most beautiful performance of the morning. Belle tried to match it, but couldn't. She was hunting because she was bred to hunt. Moreover was hunting from habit and because Lonnie expected him to.

It was exasperating. Belle tried every trick of her training, but her skill was no match for his stamina. Her heart was pumping rapidly and she was tired when the crowd passed near the clubhouse and the judges suggested refreshments. Harve and Lon rubbed their dogs while they waited. Belle's tongue was hanging out, but Moreover just sat on his haunches and watched his master. Text ran into the lodge to help fetch food and drink to the crowd. He strutted into the kitchen and told the servants that Moreover was running Silver Belle ragged.

The servants shook their heads, and one told him that Mr. Ames would fire Harve if Moreover beat Belle. Text couldn't swallow his food. He ran out of the lodge and called Lonnie aside. Lonnie's thorat hurt when he heard the story that Moreover's victory would cost his father the job of training Mr. Ames's dogs. He stared at Moreover and then at Text.

"That Mr. Ames sho' is a scutter," said Text. "A frazzlin' scutter. He's worse'n Mr. Eben. What we gonna do, Lon?"

Lonnie said sadly, "He's half your dog, Text. What you say?"

The little Negro put his hand on his friend's arm. "We can't let yo' paw get in no trouble on account of us. He got to have a job. He got to eat, ain't he?"

Lonnie nodded and bit his lip. He noticed that his father's face was drawn as the contest was renewed. Ames was nervous. The two men had worked for years to get Belle to perfection and win the

Grand National for the third time. And here an outcast dog was hunting her heart out at a minor meet. Lonnie thought his father was worried about his job and that Ames was angry.

His mind was made up. He watched Moreover leap across a branch, then race toward a rail fence. He and Text were right behind him.

The big dog held his head high for a split second, then sprang. He balanced himself perfectly on the rail fence, turned his face to Lonnie, and seemed to smile. Then he tilted his nose and pointed a covey just beyond the fence.

Lonnie and Text just stood there for a minute, their mouths wide open. Pointing quail from a rail fence! Lonnie choked up with pride, but he didn't shout "point." He didn't want the judges to know, but the judges saw Moreover.

They stopped their horses and gaped. One judge said in a whisper, "That's the best dog I ever saw."

Harve said, "Pointing from a fence. I'm looking right at him but I can't believe it. No dog's that good. That beats Belle."

A judge told Lonnie to flush the birds and shoot over his dog. The boy didn't move, however. His tongue was frozen to the roof of his mouth. Then he cupped his hands and said, hoarsely, "Hep!" It was an order Moreover had never heard. Lonnie thought the strange order would startle his dog and cause him to break his point, but Moreover stood rigid.

Again Lon called, "Hep!" The dog didn't budge. The judges couldn't understand the action of the boy and Harve was puzzled.

Lonnie tried again, and Moreover turned his head and faced his master, amazement in his eyes.

Ames whispered, "He's breaking. That good-for-nothing streak is cropping out."

Moreover didn't break, however. He settled to the point, and in desperation Lonnie walked close to him and hissed, "Biscuit eater! Low-life, no 'count, egg-sucking biscuit eater."

Text cringed when he heard the words. Moreover faced the boy again and blinked his eyes. Slowly his tail dropped. Then his head. Lonnie repeated it. "Biscuit eater." There were tears in his eyes and his voice quivered.

Moreover tucked his tail between his legs and leaped from the fence, flushing the birds. Then he turned his big, sad eyes toward

Lonnie. He couldn't believe his ears and must see for himself that his master had thrown him down. Lonnie stood there by the fence, his fists clenched and tears rolling down his face. Moreover ran to the lodge and hid under it. He wanted to be alone, away from the sight and smell of men.

Lonnie and Text ran after him. They couldn't face the crowd. The judges didn't know what to make of it and the spectators muttered at the strange performance.

Ames looked at Harve for an explanation, and Harve said, "I don't get it. My son called his dog off. He quit. He threw his dog down."

The judges awarded the trophy to Mr. Ames, but the sportsman wouldn't touch it. "We didn't earn it. Those kids and their dog beat us. I won't have it. You take it, Harve."

Harve shook his head slowly. "It's not mine. I don't want the thing. I can't understand my son. I can't understand why he quit. That dog worked hard for those boys and they double-crossed him. I heard my boy call his dog a biscuit eater. He would fight anybody else who called him a biscuit eater. My boy broke his dog's heart. . . ."

It took Lonnie and Text a long time to coax Moreover from under the lodge. The dog crawled to Lonnie's feet and rolled over. Lonnie patted him, but Moreover didn't lick his face. "He's mad at us," Text said. "He don't like us no more."

"His feelings are hurt," Lonnie said, as Moreover lay down and thumped his tail. . . . "I'm sorry I said it, Moreover. I had to."

Text said, "We sorry, puppy dawg. We didn't mean it. But us had to say it, huh, Lon? Aw, don't cry, Lon. Ol' Moreover knows you didn't mean it. Please don't cry. Don't let ol' Moreover see us bawlin'."

Harve didn't speak to the boys as they loaded the truck. Mr. Ames wanted to tell the boys good-by, but they walked away from him. Harve had his boy sit on the front seat by him. They said good-by to the crowd and rolled away.

Finally, Harve asked Lonnie, "How come you did that, Son?"

Lonnie didn't reply and the father didn't press the point. "Don't ever quit, Son, if you're winning or losing. It ain't fair to the dog."

"My dog is mad at me," Lonnie said.

"We'll give him a beef heart when we get home. His feelings are hurt because you threw him down. But he'll be all right. Dogs are not like folks. They'll forgive a fellow." He knew then that Lonnie had a reason for what he had done, and he knew that if his son wanted him to know the reason, he would tell him.

Back home, Lonnie cooked a beef heart and took the plate to the back gallery where the dog was tied. Moreover slunk into the shadows and Harve said, "Untie him, Son. You can let him run free over here. I made a deal with you and I'll stick to it. You can keep your dog right here. He needn't go back to Text's house."

The boy hugged his father gratefully and untied his dog. Moreover sniffed the food and toyed with it. He never had had such good food before. Lonnie and his father went back into the house.

After supper, Lonnie went to see about his dog. The meat hadn't been eaten and Moreover was gone.

"He's still mad at me," Lon said. "He don't like me no more. He's gone off and I'm going after him."

"I'll go with you," said Harve, and got a lantern.

Text hadn't seen the dog. He joined the search and the three hunted through the woods for an hour or so, Lonnie whistling for Moreover, and Text calling him, "Heah, heah, fellow. Heah."

Harve sat on a stump, put the lantern down, and called the boys to him. He had seen only a few dogs that would refuse to eat beef heart as Moreover had done.

"Text," he said sharply, "did Moreover ever suck eggs at your place?"

Text rolled his eyes and looked at Lonnie. "Yas, suh." He was afraid to lie to Harve. "But I didn't tell Lon. I didn't want to hurt his feelings. Moreover was a suck-egger, good and proper."

Harve said, "Go on, tell us about it."

"Maw put hot pepper in a raw egg, but it didn't break him. My ol' brother, ol' First-and-Second Thessalonians, reckoned he'd kill Moreover less'n he quit suck-egging. So I got to snitching two eggs ever' night and feedin' them to him. He sho' did like eggs."

Lonnie said sharply, "You hadn't ought to have done that, Text."

Harve said, "Did you feed him eggs tonight?"

"Naw, suh," said Text. "I reckoned he had vittles at yo' house. We had done gathered all the eggs, and Maw had counted them by nightfall."

Harve got up. "I'm worried. Let's walk up the branch. . . . Text, you take the left side . . . Lonnie, you take the right side. I'll walk up the bank."

Lonnie found Moreover's body, still warm, only a few feet from the water. He stooped over his dog, put the lantern by his head, and opened his mouth. The dog had been poisoned. Lonnie straightened. He didn't cry. His emotions welled up within him, and having no outlet, hurt him.

He knelt beside his dog and stroked Moreover's head. Then he pulled the dog's body into his lap and whispered, "My li'l ol' dog, my li'l ol' dog. . . ."

He looked up at his father and said simply, "I'm sorry I called him a biscuit eater."

Harve was too choked up to speak, and Text sat down by Lonnie and stroked the dog, too. "He was trying to get to water. I sho' hate to think of him dying, wanting just one swallow of good ol' water."

"Who killed him, Papa?" Lonnie got to his feet and faced his father.

"That's what I'm aiming to find out." The man picked up the lantern and walked away, the boys at his heels. They walked over the ridge to Eben's house, and Harve pounded on the front gallery until the farmer appeared.

"My boy's dog is dead," Harve said. "Reckoned you might know something about it."

Eben said, "If he was poisoned, I do. He's a suck-egg dog. I put poison in some eggs and left them in the field. Seems he must have committed suicide, McNeil."

"Seems you made it powerful easy for him to get those poisoned eggs," Harve said.

"Ain't no room round here for suck-egg dogs. His daddy was a sheep killer, too. It's good riddance. You ain't got no cause to jump me, Harve McNeil."

Harve said, "He's right, boys. A man's got a right to poison eggs on his own land, and if a dog sucks 'em and dies, the dog's to blame."

Eben said, "Reckon you young 'uns want to bury that dog. Buzzards will be thick tomorrow. You can have the loan of my shovel."

Lonnie looked at the man a long time. He bit his lip so he couldn't cry. "Me and Text will dig a hole with a stick," he said, and turned away.

"You boys go bury him," Harve said. "I'll be home in a few minutes."

Lonnie and Text walked silently into the woods. Text said, "He sho' was a good dawg, huh, Lon? You ain't mad at me 'cause I fed him eggs, are you, Lon?"

"No, Text. Ain't no use in being mad at you. Getting mad at you won't bring ol' Moreover back. Let's wait up here and watch Papa. He can't see us."

Back at Eben's gallery, Harve propped against a post and spoke slowly, "I would have paid you for all the eggs the dog took. My boy loved that dog, Eben."

"Looka heah!" Eben said. "I know my rights."

"I know mine," Harve said. "I always pay my debts, Eben. And I always collect them. I ain't got no cause to get riled because that dog stole poisoned eggs. But I ain't got no use for a man who will poison a dog. If a dog is mad, shoot him. It's low-life to plant poisoned eggs where a dog can find them. But you were within your rights. I ain't forgot another little thing, however. Two years ago you kicked one of my dogs . . ."

"He barked at me and scared my team on the road," Eben said.

"A dog has got a right on the road, and he's got a right to bark." Harve straightened slowly. A look of fear came into Eben's eyes and he backed away. Harve said softly, "You're a bully. I don't like bullies. I don't like folks who go around causing trouble, picking on their neighbors and keeping everything upset. I'm a peace-loving man, but even peace-loving folks get fed up sometimes." He reached out and grabbed Eben by the collar.

"I'll law you!" Eben shouted.

Harve didn't reply. He slapped the man with his open palm, and when Eben squared off to fight, Harve knocked him down.

In the shadows of the woods, Lonnie whispered to Text, "What did I tell you? Papa ain't scared of nothing, cep'n God."

They buried their dog near the branch. Text poured water in the grave. "I can't stand to think of him wanting water when there's a heap of water so close. Reckon if he could have got to the ol' branch he could have washed out that poison? Reckon, Lon?"

"Maybe so."

They were walking to Lonnie's house. "My ol' buckeye and your sweet-stinking mellow bug ain't helped us much, eh, Lon? Luck is plum' mad at us, ain't it, Lon?"

Lonnie waited at the gate until his father arrived. "Me and Text saw the fight," he said. "I won't tell Mother. Women are scutters, ain't they, Papa? Always trying to keep men folks from fighting."

Harve smiled and kept his right hand in his pocket. He didn't offer the boys another dog. He could have easily, but he was too wise. Lonnie and Text would have other dogs, but there would never be another dog like their first dog. And Harve knew it would be crude to suggest another dog might replace Moreover.

He peered into the darkness and saw a car parked behind the house, then hurried inside. Mr. Ames was warming himself by the fire and talking with Mrs. McNeil. She went to the kitchen to brew coffee, and left the men alone, after calling for Lonnie and Text to follow her.

Ames said, "I heard why your boy called his dog off. Call him and that little colored boy in here. I can't go back East with those boys thinking what they do of me."

Lonnie and Text stood by the fire, and Ames said, "That story you heard about me isn't true. I wouldn't have fired this man if your dog had won. We were joking about it and the servants got the story all wrong. I just wanted you boys to know that."

Harve said, "Yes. But even if Mr. Ames would have fired me, it wouldn't have made any difference. You did what you thought was right, but you were wrong. Don't ever quit a race once you start it."

Lonnie told Mr. Ames, "My dog is dead. I'm sorry I called him a biscuit eater. He wasn't. I just want you to know that."

Ames lit his pipe and passed his tobacco pouch to Harve. He saw Harve's bloody hand as the trainer accepted the tobacco.

"Ran into some briars," Harve said.

"Lots of them around here." Ames's eyes twinkled. "Just been thinking, Harve. We got some fine pups coming along. You need help down here. Better hire a couple of good men."

"Good men are sort of scarce," Harve said.

"The kind I want are mighty scarce," said Ames. "They've got to be men with a lot of courage who can lose without grumbling and win without crowing."

"Believe I know where I can get hold of a couple to fill the bill." Harve put his hand on Lon's shoulder and smiled at his son and at Text.

"Well, I'll trust your judgment," Ames said. He shook hands all around. "I've got to be going. Good night, men."

Questions for discussion

1. To appreciate this story fully, you have to have some understanding about the community in which it is set, and the environment in which the characters of the story move. You must be aware that it is in the South, that it is a community in which hunting with dogs is a very important sport, and that there is here a very strict code about the conduct of dogs. What kind of behavior on the part of dogs is absolutely not tolerated?
2. What was your reaction to Mr. Eben? Have you ever encountered a person like him? What makes people act the way Mr. Eben acted?
3. Why does Lonnie love Moreover? Can you understand this? What are Moreover's particular characteristics? How did he develop them? Why were the boys so successful in training him?
4. What conflict exists between the two dogs, Silver Belle and Moreover?
5. What was the conflict between Lonnie and his father? What caused it? In what way was it different from the conflict between Mayo Maloney and his father? How was this conflict between father and son finally resolved?
6. Mr. McNeil's advice to the boys was: "Don't ever quit a race once you start it." What do you think of this idea? Have you ever heard it stated in another way?
7. What was Mr. Ames' definition of a good man? What is your opinion of this definition? You noticed that at the end of the story, when Mr. Ames left, he said: "Good night, *men*." Why did he use the word *men*? What effect did this probably have on Lonnie and Text?
8. Why did Lonnie keep saying: "I'm sorry I called him a biscuit eater"?
9. What did the boys learn about adults?

Vocabulary growth

CONTEXT. Figure out a meaning for the italicized words in each of the following sentences. Check your meaning with a dictionary.

 a. "Good dogs must know how to keep their heads up and hold birds on the ground until the master is ready to *flush* the *covey* by frightening the quail." (page 250)

 b. On page 257 you read the sentence, "Once when he sucked an egg, Lon put his arms around the dog and cried, not in anger but in *anguish*."

 c. On page 246 you read, "But the puppies had doubtful *strain* in them, inherited from their father. . . ." You know what *doubtful* means. What does *strain* mean in this context?

WORDS ARE INTERESTING. There is a fascinating group of words in English, used to refer to a group of individuals of a certain species. You have seen *covey* referring to a group of quail. A number of lions together is called a *pride* of lions. Look up the following words and determine what group they are used to describe.

gam	gaggle	bevy	clutch
pod	swarm	farrow	flight

For composition

During this story the boys do some "growing up." That is, they learn certain things about life and people that advance them on the road to becoming adults. Write a paper on what it was that they learned. Or write a paper on what "Growing Up" means to you.

The Test

ANGELICA GIBBS

On the afternoon Marian took her second driver's test, Mrs. Ericson went with her. "It's probably better to have someone a little older with you," Mrs. Ericson said as Marian slipped into the driver's seat beside her. "Perhaps last time your Cousin Bill made you nervous, talking too much on the way."

"Yes, Ma'am," Marian said in her soft unaccented voice. "They probably do like it better if a white person shows up with you."

"Oh, I don't think it's *that*," Mrs. Ericson began, and subsided after a glance at the girl's set profile. Marian drove the car slowly through the shady suburban streets. It was one of the first hot days of June, and when they reached the boulevard they found it crowded with cars headed for the beaches.

"Do you want me to drive?" Mrs. Ericson asked. "I'll be glad to if you're feeling jumpy." Marian shook her head. Mrs. Ericson watched her dark, competent hands and wondered for the thousandth time how the house had ever managed to get along without her, or how she had lived through those earlier years when her household had been presided over by a series of slatternly white girls who had considered housework demeaning and the care of children an added insult. "You drive beautifully, Marian," she said. "Now, don't think of the last time. Anybody would slide on a steep hill on a wet day like that."

"It takes four mistakes to flunk you," Marian said. "I don't remember doing all the things the inspector marked down on my blank."

"People say that they only want you to slip them a little something," Mrs. Ericson said doubtfully.

"No," Marian said. "That would only make it worse, Mrs. Ericson. I know."

The car turned right, at a traffic signal, into a side road and slid up to the curb at the rear of a short line of parked cars. The inspectors had not arrived yet.

"You have the papers?" Mrs. Ericson asked. Marian took them out of her bag: her learner's permit, the car registration, and her birth certificate. They settled down to the dreary business of waiting.

"It will be marvellous to have someone dependable to drive the children to school every day," Mrs. Ericson said.

Marian looked up from the list of driving requirements she had been studying. "It'll make things simpler at the house, won't it?" she said.

"Oh, Marian," Mrs. Ericson exclaimed, "if I could only pay you half of what you're worth!"

"Now, Mrs. Ericson," Marian said firmly. They looked at each other and smiled with affection.

Two cars with official insignia on their doors stopped across the street. The inspectors leaped out, very brisk and military in their neat uniforms. Marian's hands tightened on the wheel. "There's the one who flunked me last time," she whispered, pointing to a stocky, self-important man who had begun to shout directions at the driver at the head of the line. "Oh, Mrs. Ericson."

"Now, Marian," Mrs. Ericson said. They smiled at each other again, rather weakly.

The inspector who finally reached their car was not the stocky one but a genial, middle-aged man who grinned broadly as he thumbed over their papers. Mrs. Ericson started to get out of the car. "Don't you want to come along?" the inspector asked. "Mandy and I don't mind company."

Mrs. Ericson was bewildered for a moment. "No," she said, and stepped to the curb. "I might make Marian self-conscious. She's a fine driver, Inspector."

"Sure thing," the inspector said, winking at Mrs. Ericson. He slid into the seat beside Marian. "Turn right at the corner, Mandy-Lou."

From the curb, Mrs. Ericson watched the car move smoothly up the street.

The inspector made notations in a small black book. "Age?" he inquired presently, as they drove along.

"Twenty-seven."

He looked at Marian out of the corner of his eye. "Old enough to have quite a flock of pickaninnies, eh?"

Marian did not answer.

"Left at this corner," the inspector said, "and park between that truck and the green Buick."

The two cars were very close together, but Marian squeezed in between them without too much maneuvering. "Driven before, Mandy-Lou?" the inspector asked.

"Yes, sir. I had a license for three years in Pennsylvania."

"Why do you want to drive a car?"

"My employer needs me to take her children to and from school."

"Sure you don't really want to sneak out nights to meet some young blood?" the inspector asked. He laughed as Marian shook her head.

"Let's see you take a left at the corner and then turn around in the middle of the next block," the inspector said. He began to whistle "Swanee River." "Make you homesick?" he asked.

Marian put out her hand, swung around neatly in the street, and headed back in the direction from which they had come. "No," she said. "I was born in Scranton, Pennsylvania."

The inspector feigned astonishment. "You-all ain't Southern?" he said. "Well, dog my cats if I didn't think you-all came from down yondah."

"No, sir," Marian said.

"Turn onto Main Street here and let's see how you-all does in heavier traffic."

They followed a line of cars along Main Street for several blocks until they came in sight of a concrete bridge which arched high over the railroad tracks.

"Read that sign at the end of the bridge," the inspector said.

" 'Proceed with caution. Dangerous in slippery weather,' " Marian said.

"You-all sho can read fine," the inspector exclaimed. "Where d'you learn to do that, Mandy?"

"I got my college degree last year," Marian said. Her voice was not quite steady.

As the car crept up the slope of the bridge the inspector burst out laughing. He laughed so hard he could scarcely give his next direction. "Stop here," he said, wiping his eyes, "then start 'er up again. Mandy got her degree, did she? Dog my cats!"

Marian pulled up beside the curb. She put the car in neutral, pulled on the emergency, waited a moment, and then put the car into gear again. Her face was set. As she released the brake her foot slipped off the clutch pedal and the engine stalled.

"Now, Mistress Mandy," the inspector said, "remember your degree."

"*Damn* you!" Marian cried. She started the car with a jerk.

The inspector lost his joviality in an instant. "Return to the starting place, please," he said, and made four very black crosses at random in the squares on Marian's application blank.

Mrs. Ericson was waiting at the curb where they had left her. As Marian stopped the car the inspector jumped out and brushed past her, his face purple. "What happened?" Mrs. Ericson asked, looking after him with alarm.

Marian stared down at the wheel and her lip trembled.

"Oh, Marian, *again?*" Mrs. Ericson said.

Marian nodded. "In a sort of different way," she said, and slid over to the right-hand side of the car.

Questions for discussion

1. In the opening paragraphs of the story, you learned that Marian was about to take a driver's test for the second time. What else did you learn about her?
2. As you understand it, why had Marian failed the test the first time? Was it because she was not yet a good driver?
3. Besides the fact that having a driver's license would make things more convenient for both Marian and her employer, why was it so important for her to pass the second time?
4. From the very beginning, Marian and the inspector have attitudes toward each other that are bound to erupt into open conflict. What was Marian's attitude as she approached the second test? Was it justified? What was the inspector's attitude toward Marian? Where did he get his ideas? Why did he laugh so hard?
5. What is your impression of the inspector? How do you visualize him as to manner, voice, facial expression? What impression did you get as to his probable degree of intelligence and education? How did you react to his treatment of Marian?

6. At what point did Marian's control begin to crack? As you read the story, at what point did you begin to get angry? If you had been in Marian's place, would you have exploded earlier than she? At the same time? Or would you have been able to restrain yourself?

7. Do you think that the inspector was deliberately maneuvering or baiting Marian into an outburst? Or do you think that he was genuinely surprised by it? How do you think he would have explained later what he had done? Would you attribute the inspector's conduct to malice? Insensitivity? Contempt? A combination of several of these?

8. In your opinion, did Marian have any chance of passing that test? If so, what would she have had to do to pass? In your opinion, would it have been worth the price?

9. In what part of the United States does "The Test" take place? What significance does this setting have in the story?

10. What test did the inspector fail? One might say that they were both taking a "test of character." What does this mean?

Vocabulary growth

WORD PARTS. 1. On page 277, you read "The car turned right, at a traffic signal, into a side road . . ." The word *signal* is based on the Latin root word *signum*, meaning "a mark or sign." Give the roots and definitions of the following words based on *signum*. Use a dictionary to check your answers.

signature	designate
resign	signet
signify	design

2. On page 278, you read "The two cars were very close together, but Marian squeezed in between them without too much maneuvering." *Maneuver* is built on two Latin root words, *manus*, "a hand," and *opera*, the plural of *opus*, "a work." Thus *maneuver* indicates "to work by hand." But it has come to have the more general meaning of "any movement or procedure intended as a skillful step toward some objective." In some of the following words, the original meaning of *manus* has been transformed to have more general meanings. Find the roots and definitions of the following words. Explain, in each case, what relation the meaning of *manus* has to the definition.

manipulate	demand
manifest	manual
mandatory	manacle

For composition

1. Write an encouraging letter to Marian in which you give her some helpful suggestions for her third try at passing the driver's test. Be sure you do not make the mistake the inspector did of talking down to her.
2. Write a letter to the inspector in which you hope to set him straight about his stereotyped notion of Negroes.
3 Contempt is an ugly, but common, method we have of making less of other people as a means of building ourselves up in our own eyes. Sometimes contempt is obvious, as in racial discrimination; sometimes it is less obvious and may be taken for granted, as when people get together and gossip about someone or make fun of him behind his back. Write a composition in which you describe one or two everyday situations where you have seen people showing contempt. Give reasons why you think it is bad.

Three boys play a dangerous game
while taking . . .

A Ride on The Short Dog

JAMES STILL

WE flagged the bus on a curve at the mouth of Lairds Creek by
jumping and waving in the road and Dee Buck Engle had to tread
the brake the instant he saw us. He wouldn't have halted unless
compelled. Mal Dowe and I leaped aside finally, but Godey Spurlock
held his ground. The bus stopped a yard from Godey and vexed
faces pressed the windows and we heard Old Liz Hyden cry, "I'd not
haul them jaspers."

Dee Buck opened the door and blared, "You boys trying to get
killed?"

We climbed on grinning and shoved fares to Roscoe into his hand
and for once we didn't sing out, To Knuckle Junction, and Pistol
City, and Two Hoots. We even strode the aisle without raising
elbows to knock off hats, having agreed among ourselves to sort of
behave and make certain of a ride home. Yet Dee Buck was wary.
He warned, "Bother my passengers, you fellers, and I'll fix you. I've
put up with your mischief till I won't."

That set Godey and Mal laughing for Dee Buck was a bluffer.
We took the seat across from Liz Hyden and on wedging into
it my bruised arm started aching. Swapping licks was Godey's
delight.

The bus wheezed and jolted in moving away, yet we spared Dee
Buck our usual advice: Feed her a biscuit and see will she mend,
and, Twist her tail and teach her a few manners. The vehicle was
scarcely half the length of regular buses—"The Short Dog" everybody called it. It traveled from Thacker to Roscoe and back twice a
day. Enos Webb occupied the seat in front and Godey greeted,
"Hey-o, chum. How's your fat?" Enos tucked his head, fearing a
rabbit lick, and he changed his seat. He knew how Godey served

282

exposed necks. Godey could cause you to see forked lightning and hear thunder balls. Though others shunned us, Liz Hyden gazed in our direction. Her eyes were scornful, her lips puckered sour. She was as old as a hill.

Godey and Mal couldn't sit idle. They rubbed the dusty pane with their sleeves and looked abroad and everything they saw they remarked on: hay doodles in Alonzo Tate's pasture, a crazy chimney leaning away from a house, long-johns on clotheslines. They kept a count of the bridges. They pointed toward the mountain ahead, trying to fool, calling, "Gee-o, looky yonder." But they couldn't trick a soul. My arm throbbed and I had no notion to prank, and after a while Godey muttered, "I want to know what's eating you."

"We'd better decide what we can do in town," I grouched. Roscoe folk looked alive at sight of us. And except for our return fares we hadn't a dime. The poolroom had us ousted. We'd have to steer clear of the courthouse where sheriffs were thick. And we dare not rouse the county prisoners again. On our last trip we'd bellowed in front of the jail, "Hey-o, you wife-beaters, how are you standing the times?" We'd jeered and mocked until they had begged the turnkey to fetch us inside, they'd notch our ears, they'd trim us. The turnkey had told them to be patient, we'd get in on our own hook.

Godey said, "We'll break loose in town, no two ways talking."

I gloomed. "The law will pen us for the least thing. We'll be thrown in amongst the meanest fellers that ever breathed."

Godey screwed his eyes narrow. "My opinion, the prisoners scared you plumb. You're ruint for trick-pulling." He knotted a fist and hit me squarely on my bruise.

My arm ached the fiercer. My eyes burned and had I not glanced sideways they'd come to worse. "Now, no," I said; but Godey's charge was true.

"Well, act like it," he said. "And pay me."

I returned the blow.

Old Liz was watching and she blurted, "I swear to my Gracious. A human being can't see a minute's peace."

Godey chuckled, "What's fretting you old woman?"

"Knock and beat and battle is all you think on," she snorted.

"We're not so bad we try to hinder people from riding the bus," he countered. "Aye, we heard you squall back yonder."

Old Liz's lips quivered, her veiny hands trembled. "Did I have strength to reach," she croaked, "I'd pop your jaws. I'd addle you totally."

Godey thrust his head across the aisle and turned a cheek. He didn't mind a slap. "See your satisfaction," he invited.

"Out o' my face," she ordered, lifting her voice to alert Dee Buck. She laced her fingers to stay their shaking.

Dee Buck adjusted the rear-view mirror and inquired, "What's the matter, Aunt Liz?"

"It's these boys tormenting me," she complained. "They'd drive a body to raving."

Dee Buck slowed. "I told you fellers—"

"What've we done now?" Godey asked injuredly.

"Didn't I say not to bother my passengers?"

"I never tipped the old hen."

"One more antic and off you three go."

Godey smirked. "Know what?" he said. "We've been treating you pretty but we've done no good. Suit a grunt-box, you can't."

"You heard me," Dee Buck said.

The twins got on at Lucus. They were about nine years old, as like as two peas, and had not a hair on their heads. Their polls were shaven clean. Godey chirruped, "Gee-o, look who's coming," and he beckoned them to the place quitted by Enos Webb. Dee Buck seated the two up front and Godey vowed, "I'll trap the chubs, just you wait," and he made donkey ears with his hands and brayed. The twins stared, their mouths open.

Mal said, "Why don't we have our noggins peeled?"

"Say we do," laughed Godey, cocking a teasing eye on me. "They can't jail us for that shorely."

I replied, "We're broke as grasshoppers, keep in mind."

It didn't take Godey long to entice the twins. He picked nothings out of the air and chewed them—chewed to match a sheep eating ivy; he feigned to pull teeth, pitch them again into his mouth, to swallow. The twins stole a seat closer, the better to see, and then two more. Directly Godey had them where he wanted. He spoke: "Hey-o, Dirty Ears."

The twins nodded, too shy to answer.

"What's you little men's names?" he asked.

They swallowed timidly, their eyes meeting.

"Ah, tell."

"Woodrow," ventured one; "Jethro," said the other. They were solemn as fire pokers.

"Hustling to a store to spend a couple of nickels, I bet."

"Going to Cowen," said one. "To Grandpaw's," said his image.

"Well, who skinned you alive, I want to know?"

"Pap," they said.

Godey gazed at their skulls, mischief tingling him. He declared, "Us fellers aim to get cut bald in Roscoe. Too hot to wear hair nowadays."

I slipped a hand over my bruise and crabbed, "I reckon you know haircuts cost money in town." Plaguing Godey humored me.

"Witless," Godey said, annoyed, "we'll climb into the chairs, and when the barbers finish we'll say, 'Charge it on your short list.' "

"They'd summons the law in an eye-bat."

"Idjit," he snapped, "people can't be jailed for a debt." Yet he wouldn't pause to argue. He addressed the twins: "You little gents have me uneasy. There are swellings on your noggins and I'm worried on your behalf."

The twins rubbed their crowns. They were smooth as goose eggs.

"Godey's sharp on this head business," said Mal.

"Want me to examine you and find your ailment?" asked Godey. The twins glanced one to the other. "We don't care," said one.

Godey tipped a finger to their polls. He squinted and frowned. And then he drew back and gasped, "Oh-oh." He punched Mal and blabbed, "Do you see what I see? Horns, if ever I saw them."

"The tom truth," Mal swore.

"Sprouting horns like bully-cows," Godey said. "Budding under the hide and ready to pip."

"You're in a bad way," Mal moaned.

"In the fix of a boy on Lotts Creek," Godey said. "He growed horns, and he turned into a brute and went hooking folks. Mean? Upon my word and honor, the bad man wouldn't claim him."

"A feller at Scuddy had the disease," Mal related. "Kept shut in a barn, he was, and they fed him hay and cornstalks, and he never tasted victuals. I saw him myself, I swear to my thumb. I saw him chewing a cud and heard him bawl a big bawl."

Godey sighed. "The only cure is to deaden the nubs before they break the skin."

"And, gee-o, you're lucky," Mal poured on. "Godey Spurlock's a horn-doctor. Cured a hundred, I reckon."

"Oh, I've treated a few," admitted Godey.

"Spare the little masters," pled Mal.

Dee Buck was trying to watch both road and mirror, his head bobbing like a chicken drinking water. Old Liz's eyes glinted darkly. I poked Godey, grumbling, "Didn't we promise to mind ourselves?" But he went on:

"They may enjoy old long hookers, may want to bellow and snort and hoof up dirt."

"We don't neither," a twin denied.

Godey brightened. "Want me to dehorn you?"

The boys nodded.

Though I prodded Godey's ribs, he ignored me. He told the twins, "The quicker the medicine the better the cure," and he made short work of it. Without more ado he clapped a hand on each of their heads, drew them wide apart, and bumped them together. The brakes began to screech and Old Liz to fill the bus with her groans. The twins sat blinking. Dee Buck halted in the middle of the road and commanded: "All right, you scamps, pile off."

We didn't stir.

"You're not deaf. Trot."

"Deef in one ear, and can't hear out of the other'n," Godey jested.

Dee Buck slapped his knee with his cap. "I said Go."

Old Liz was in a fidget. "Shut of them," she rasped, her arms a-jiggle, her fingers dancing. "See that they walk. Make 'em foot it."

"Old Liz," Godey chided, "if you don't check yourself you're liable to fly to pieces."

"Rid the rascals," she shrilled to Dee Buck. "Are ye afraid? Are ye man enough?"

Godey scoffed, "He'll huff and he'll puff—all he ever does. He might as well feed the hound a sup of gas and travel."

Dee Buck blustered, "I've got a bait of you fellers. I'm offering you a chance to leave of your own free will."

"Collar and drag'em off," Old Liz taunted. "A coward, are ye?"

"Anybody spoiling to tussle," Godey challenged, "well, let 'em come humping."

Dee Buck flared, "Listen, you devils, I can put a quietus on you and not have to soil my hands. My opinion, you'll not want to be aboard when I pull into town. I can draw up at the courthouse and fetch the law in two minutes."

"Sick a sheriff on us," Godey said, "and you'll wish to your heart you hadn't. We paid to ride this dog."

"Walk off and I'll return your fares."

"Now, no."

"I won't wait all day."

"Dynamite couldn't budge us."

Dee Buck swept his cap onto his head. He changed gear, readying to leave. "I'm willing to spare you and you won't have it."

"Drive on, Big Buddy."

The bus started and Old Liz flounced angrily in her seat. She turned her back and didn't look round until we got to Roscoe.

We crossed two bridges. We passed Hilton and Chunk Jones's sawmill and Gayheart and Thorne. Beyond Thorne the highway began to rise. We climbed past the bloom of coal veins and tipples of mines hanging the slope; we mounted until we'd gained the saddle of the gap and could see Roscoe four miles distant. Godey and Mal cut up the whole way, no longer trying to behave. They hailed newcomers with, "Take a seat and sit like you were at home, where you ought to be," and sped the departers, "I'll see you later, when I can talk to you straighter." The twins left at Cowen and Godey shouted, "Good-by, Dirty Ears. Recollect I done you a favor." We rolled through the high gap and on down the mountain.

I nursed my hurt and sulked, and eventually Godey growled, "I want to know, did you come along just to pout?"

"You've fixed us," I accused bitterly, and I openly covered my crippled arm.

Godey scoffed, "Dee Buck can't panic me. You watch him turn good-feller by the time we reach town, watch him unload in the square the same as usual. Aye, he knows what suits his hide." He grabbed loose my arm and his fist shot out.

It was too much. My face tore up, my lips quivered and tears smeared my cheeks. Godey stared in wonder. His mouth fell open. Mal took my part, rebuking him, "No use to injure people."

"I don't give knocks I can't take myself," Godey said; and he invited, "Pay me double. Hit me a rabbit lick, I don't care. Make me see lightning." He leaned forward and bared his neck.

I wiped the shameful tears, thinking to join no more in Godey's game.

"Whap him and even up," Mal said. "We're nearly to the bottom of the mountain."

"Level up with me," said Godey, "or you're no crony of mine. You'll not run with my bunch."

I shook my head.

"Hurry," said Mal. "I see town smoking."

I wouldn't.

Mal advised Godey, "Nettle him. Speak a thing he can't let pass. Make him mad."

Godey said, "Know what I'm in the opinion of? Hadn't it been for Mal and me you'd let Dee Buck bounce you off the bus and never lifted a finger. You'd have turned chicken."

"I'd not," I gulped.

"Jolt him," Mal urged. "What I'd do."

"You're a chicken leg," Godey said, "and everybody akin to you is a chicken leg, and if you're yellow enough to take that I'll call you 'Chicken Leg' hereinafter."

I couldn't get around Godey. Smite him I must, and I gripped a fist and struck as hard as I could in close quarters, mauling his chest.

"Is that your best?" he belittled. "Anyhow, didn't I call for a rabbit lick? Throw one and let me feel it; throw one, else you know your name." Again he leaned and exposed his neck.

"He's begging," Mal incited.

I'd satisfy him, I resolved, and I half rose to get elbowroom. I swung mightily, my fist striking the base of his skull. I made his head pitch upward and thump the seat board; I made his teeth grate. "That ought to do," I blurted.

Godey walled his eyes and clenched his jaws. He began to gasp and strain and flounder. His arms lifted, clawing the air. Tight as we were wedged the seat would hardly hold him. Mal was ready to back up a sham and he chortled, "Look, you people, if you want to see a feller perish." But none bothered to glance.

Then Mal and me noticed the odd twist of Godey's neck. We saw his lips tinge, his ears turn tallow. His tongue waggled to speak and could not. And of a sudden we knew and we sat frozen. We sat like posts while he heaved and pitched and his soles rattled the floor and his knees banged the forward seat. He bucked like a spoiled nag. . . . He quieted presently. His arms fell, his hands crumpled. He slumped and his gullet rattled.

We rode on. The mountain fell aside and the curves straightened. The highway ran a beeline. We crossed the last bridge and drew into Roscoe, halting in the square. Dee Buck stood at the door while the passengers alighted and all hastened except Old Liz and us. Old Liz ordered over her shoulder, "Go on ahead. I'll not trust a set o' jaspers coming behind me." We didn't move. She whirled and her eyes lit on Godey. She sputtered, "What's the matter with him?"

Mal opened his mouth numbly. "He's doing no good," he said.

Questions for discussion

1. Imagine yourself in the bus when the three boys flag it down. Watch them and listen to them. How do Dee Buck and Old Liz react to them? What impression do they make as a group? What reputation have they apparently gained for themselves in the community? How do they affect the adults on the bus? The little boys? What is your reaction to what Godey does to the twins?
2. How does the fact that the story is set on this bus, "The Short Dog," affect the events of the story?
3. Why did the author choose to present this story in the first person and why from the point of view of this particular boy? Why not through Godey or Mal? Why not through Dee Buck or Old Liz?
4. Did you notice that the boy who narrates the story is never named? Did this have any effect on you, the reader? Did you feel that you were listening to the boy or that you were following his thinking and his feeling?
5. Does the narrator make a different impression on you when you consider him as an individual than when you saw him as a member of a "gang"? How did you feel about each of the boys as individuals? How did you feel about them as a group? Why did these boys act like that?
6. There are several conflicts going on here at the same time. What are they? Which would be the most obvious to the passengers on the bus? Which did you feel most keenly? What does the story suggest about the relationship between young people as a group and adults as a group? What is the reason for this?
7. At what point did you *know* that something had happened? Had you anticipated it? What emotion did you experience at that point? Do you know why? Why does the story not actually *say* what really happened?
8. Using the events of this story as an illustration, what observation about the behavior of young people could be made?

9. What observation could you make about your understanding of *why* people behave as they do?

Vocabulary growth

CONTEXT. There are a number of interesting words in this story and a number of words used in an interesting way. See what you can do to work out a meaning for each of the italicized words in the following sentences. Remember that you can never get all of a word's meaning from one encounter with it. Try for enough meaning, a synonym perhaps, to give you enough of an idea to make sense out of the sentence. Turn back to the story and read the sentences before and after. They may provide you with clues. Check your meaning with a dictionary.

1. "We'd jeered and mocked until they had begged the *turnkey* to fetch us inside, they'd notch our ears, they'd trim us. . . ." (page 283)
2. "Did I have strength to reach," she croaked, "I'd pop your jaws. I'd *addle* you totally." (pages 283–284)
3. "One more *antic* and off you three go." (page 284)
4. "It didn't take Godey long to *entice* the twins . . . he *feigned* to pull teeth, pitch them again into his mouth, to swallow." (page 284)
5. "Dee Buck blustered, 'I've got a *bait* of you fellers.' " (page 286)

For composition

Pretend that you are one of the characters in this story, or the parent of one of the boys, or someone who lives in their community. You are asked to come to the inquest to testify either about what happened on the bus or about the characters or reputation of one or all of the boys. Write your testimony as a monologue.

When these testimonies, presumably given by the various characters on the bus and from the community, are read aloud, your class will have created quite a courtroom scene!

About the Authors

Chinua Achebe (1930–   ) is a Nigerian writer whose first novel, *Things Fall Apart*—now considered a classic of modern African literature—was published in 1958. Mr. Achebe was educated at Government College, Umuahia and at University College, Ibadan. He was a producer of the Nigerian Broadcasting Corporation, director of *Voice of Nigeria*, and the recipient of Rockefeller and UNESCO Fellowships. Other books by Mr. Achebe include *Arrow of God, Man of the People, No Longer at Ease*, and the most recent, *Girls at War*, published in 1972. Mr. Achebe has won the Nigerian National Trophy, the Margaret Wrong Memorial Prize, and the Jock Campbell *New Statesman* Award.

Joseph N. Bell (1921–   ) gave up regular employment as an advertising and public relations man to devote full time to writing. In recent years, he has enjoyed an increasingly successful career as a free-lance writer of articles and books. His interest in flying, as revealed in "I'm Coming In," probably dates back to World War II days when he served as a Navy pilot and flight instructor in the South Pacific.

Bell is a graduate of the University of Missouri where he studied journalism. His books and articles have dealt chiefly with flight and with space exploration. He hopes to succeed as a writer of musical comedy.

Ray Bradbury (1920–   ) has been surrounded by books for as long as he can remember. A boyhood fascination for the adventures of Buck Rogers sparked his interest in the reading, as well as the writing, of science fiction. While still in high school, he began to write stories and to send them to various magazines. "All Summer in a Day" reveals Bradbury's fascination for the world of eerie fantasy. Though he is known chiefly for his short stories, he has written novels as well.

291

Howard Brubaker (1882–1957) became a magazine editor and then a writer after a brief career as a social worker in New York City. His stories and sketches, mostly humorous, have appeared in many popular magazines. "The Milk Pitcher," with its warm and humorous portrait of an unusual young boy, is characteristic of much of Brubaker's work.

Pearl S. Buck (1892–1973) made American literary history with the record-breaking success of her novel, *The Good Earth*, a story about a Chinese family. Ms. Buck knew China intimately for, as the daughter of American missionaries, she grew up in China and attended boarding school in Shanghai. At seventeen she was taken to Europe, England, and then home to America where she completed her education at Randolph Macon College in Virginia. Later, with her husband, she returned to China to teach English at the University of Nanking. Her story, "The Frill," reflects her keen understanding of the Chinese people and their problems. *The Good Earth*, often called her most distinguished novel, won the Pulitzer Prize and was made into a successful motion picture. In 1938, Pearl Buck became the first American woman to win the Nobel Prize in literature. Ms. Buck was active in child welfare work. Her autobiography is titled *My Several Worlds*.

F. R. Buckley (1896–   ) began his professional life as an artist and later turned to writing. He was born and educated in England but, during the first World War, came to the United States as a junior member of a military mission. He remained in the United States becoming first a newspaperman, then a scenario writer, and finally a fiction writer. His early stories, like "Gold-Mounted Guns," have a western setting. His later stories have a nautical setting and are often based on Buckley's own experiences at sea traveling on cargo boats.

Richard Connell (1893–1949) began his career as a boy reporter for his father's newspaper in Poughkeepsie, New York. He covered local baseball games and other sporting events and was paid at the rate of ten cents for each story. After one year at

Georgetown College, he served as secretary to his father, who had been elected to Congress. Later, he attended Harvard and, following his graduation, was a reporter and advertising copywriter. At the outbreak of the war, he enlisted as a private and served in France. When he returned home, he started in earnest to make a career of writing. In addition to short stories and novels, he has written screen plays for motion pictures, among them *Meet John Doe* and *Brother Orchid.* Connell won the O. Henry Memorial Award in 1924 for his short story, "The Most Dangerous Game."

Sir Arthur Conan Doyle (1859–1930), an English writer and creator of the fictional detective Sherlock Holmes, began his career as a physician, but he seems not to have pursued it with much enthusiasm. He preferred writing stories and he introduced Sherlock Holmes to the public for the first time in "A Study in Scarlet" (1887). The second Holmes story, "The Sign of the Four," appeared in 1890. The following year Doyle began a series for *The Strand* magazine called *The Adventures of Sherlock Holmes.* Handling his hero with deftness and imagination, he aroused the public's enthusiasm beyond all of his fondest hopes. When, in the course of time, he became bored with Holmes, he had the famous detective killed in a dramatic fall from a precipice. The public was outraged and protested so vigorously that Doyle was forced to bring Holmes back to life. In his next story, Doyle explained that Holmes had miraculously escaped death in the fall. From that time on, Doyle continued the adventures of Sherlock Holmes and his friend, Dr. Watson, to the public's never-ending delight.

Walter D. Edmonds (1903–   ) was born on a farm near Utica, New York, and has used his native state and its early history as the setting for many of his short stories and novels. While studying chemical engineering at Harvard, he began to write stories about the Erie Canal and the Mohawk River region. When one of his stories was published in *Scribner's Magazine,* he decided to make writing his life's work. His first successful novel, *Rome Haul,* deals with the early days of the Erie Canal. One of Edmonds' best loved stories, "Death of Red Peril," gives a humorous and affectionate portrait of the canal people along Lake Erie.

Stanley Ellin (1916–   ) has had a varied and colorful career as a promoter for a newspaper distributor, a Hudson Valley farmer, a junior college teacher, and as an ironworker. He began his writing career when, on leaving the Army, he needed something to do. His first story, entitled "The Specialty of the House," won the award of "Best Short Story" in the *Ellery Queen Mystery Magazine* contest for 1948. "Unreasonable Doubt," like many of his first stories, is concerned with the solving of a mystery. His first major novel, *The Winter After This Summer*, was published in 1960.

Henry Gregor Felsen (1916–   ) was born in Brooklyn, New York. Following his graduation from Erasmus Hall High School, he attended the University of Iowa. He was forced to leave in his junior year when he could no longer pay his tuition. On returning to New York, he shipped out as a seaman on a freighter bound for South America.

Felsen started his career as a writer of fact-detective stories—those based on actual police and court records. He wrote his first book, *Jungle Highway*, while working as a staff writer for a large publishing house. Within the next year he sold five more books and many stories. He spent two-and-a-half years in the Marine Corps as a roving editor in the Pacific area for *Leatherneck* magazine. "Necktie Party" is a good example of the tall tale—a story so far-fetched that nobody could possibly believe it.

A. B. Guthrie, Jr. (1901–   ) grew up in a small ranch town in Montana, where he developed a love for the West and its history. After getting his degree from the University of Montana, he became a newspaper reporter. In 1944 he began writing his first novel, *The Big Sky*, which won a favorable reception from the critics. In 1947 he gave up his newspaper work and wrote *The Way West*, for which he won the Pulitizer Prize for fiction. His short stories, like "Bargain," deal with life in small, primitive western towns.

Henry Sydnor Harrison (1880–1930) was born in Sewanee, Tennessee, where his father was Professor of Greek and Latin at the University of the South. While attending Columbia University, Harrison edited student publications and starred in productions of the Columbia Dramatic Society. Like many writers, Harrison began his career as a newspaper reporter. His first novel, *Queed*, published in 1911, was written in six months, and, like its successor, *V. V.'s Eyes*, enjoyed tremendous popular success. Thereafter, Harrison's short stories were much in demand. His reputation as a writer was firmly established. "Miss Hinch" is still a favorite among readers who enjoy an intriguing mystery.

O. Henry (1862–1910) is the pen name of William Sydney Porter, one of America's most popular short story writers. He began writing stories while serving a prison sentence for stealing money from the bank in which he worked. The charges against him were never completely proved, and much doubt remains even today about Porter's actual guilt. This experience did, however, give him a keen insight into the minds and emotions of criminals. Some of his most famous stories are uproarious accounts of shady characters and their skirmishes with the law. Often, underlying the humorous mood, there is a note of pathos. O. Henry is considered the master of the surprise ending.

Shirley Jackson (1919–1965) was born in San Francisco and spent most of her early life in California. Following her marriage, she moved to a quiet Vermont community—an ideal spot for raising a family and writing books. Ms. Jackson was a writer of great versatility. Short stories, novels, and informal essays have all come from her pen. Many of her stories, as is seen in the modern classic, "The Lottery," reveal her concern with fantasy and horror. In stories like "Charles," however, Ms. Jackson reveals a talent for the humorous as well.

Jack London (1876–1916) was born in San Francisco, California, the son of a wandering Irish astrologer. As a youth, he was an avid reader of books of travel, adventure, sea voyages, and discoveries. Formal education was postponed so that he could help support his family by working on ice wagons and in bowling alleys, canneries and jute mills. Working ten hours a day for ten cents an hour, he gained a deep respect and sympathy for working class people. At fifteen he was traveling on the road as a tramp, and at sixteen he became an oyster pirate in and around the bay of San Francisco. He entered the freshman class at Oakland High School when he was nineteen years old. By cramming nineteen hours of study into each day, he was soon able to enter the University of California. However, the needs of his impoverished family again forced him to go back to work—this time as a helper in a laundry. When gold was discovered in the Klondike in 1896, he was among those who crossed the Chilkoot Pass to the gold fields of the Far North. From his experiences in this far, cold land, he created such books as *The Call of the Wild* and *White Fang*, and the short story "To Build a Fire."

H. H. Munro (1870–1916) was born in Burma and educated in England. On completing his education, he returned to Burma to serve with the military police. When ill health forced him to return to England, he tried to earn a living as a writer for various British publications. Later, as a foreign correspondent, he traveled to Poland, Russia, and France. Although he was nearly forty-five when World War I broke out, he enlisted in the army as a private, refusing the commission offered him. He was killed in the attack on Beaumont-Hamel on the thirteenth day of the month.

Munro took the pseudonym of Saki from *The Rubáiyát* of Omar Khayyám. He is still considered one of England's most famous writers of humorous short stories. "The Open Window" reveals his special talent for achieving the bizarre through a perfect blending of humor and horror.

William Saroyan (1908–   ) went directly from junior high school into various odd jobs—telegraph messenger, office worker, farm hand, and newspaper reporter. From the age of thirteen, he wrote constantly. In 1934, a story called "The Daring Young Man on the Flying Trapeze" won him instant recognition. His books of short stories, including *My Name Is Aram*, and his novel, *The Human Comedy*, have placed him in the front rank of American writers. In 1940, he was awarded the Pulitzer Prize for his play, *The Time of Your Life*. Like "An Ornery Kind of Kid," many of his stories are simple, heart-warming tales of young people going through the difficult process of growing up.

James Still (1906–   ) was born in Double Creek, Alabama, the son of a veterinarian. He planned to follow in his father's footsteps and would often stay up all night in stables and barnyards attending sick animals. He received his early education at a mountain school in Tennessee, paying all his expenses out of wages he earned working in a rock quarry. Later, he took degrees at both the University of Illinois and Vanderbilt University. While working as a librarian, he started to write poems and short stories. "A Ride on The Short Dog" is considered one of his finest stories. Among his other works are a novel, *River of Earth*, and a volume of poetry, *Hounds on the Mountain*.

James Street (1903–1954) became a reporter at eighteen, after an eleventh-grade education. When he tired of journalism, he decided to become a minister and enrolled in a Baptist seminary. Following his graduation, he had his own church, but soon gave it up to try several other fields, including law. Eventually, he returned to his first love, writing, and came to New York as a reporter for the New York *World Telegram*. His first short story, "Nothing Sacred," was made into a movie and later formed the basis for the successful musical comedy *Hazel Flagg*. Often, as in "The Biscuit Eater," his stories present a warm and sympathetic picture of Southern life.

Glossary of Literary Terms

action: what takes place during the course of a short story.

falling action: See *denouement.*

rising action: the series of incidents that grow out of the problem to be solved and that build up to the climax.

allusion: a reference to some person, place, or event with literary, historical, or geographical significance.

analogy: a comparison of ideas or objects which are essentially different but which are alike in one significant way; for example, the analogy between the grasshopper and the man who lives only for the moment.

antagonist: the force (usually a person) that opposes the main character (the protagonist) in his attempt to solve a problem and thus to resolve the conflict in which he is involved.

anticlimax: an outcome of a situation or series of events that, by contrast to what was anticipated, is ludicrous or disappointing. The anticlimax can often create a humorous effect.

atmosphere: the general over-all feeling of a story conveyed in large part by the setting and the mood.

character: a person in a work of fiction; sometimes an animal or object.

consistent character: a character whose actions, decisions, attitudes, etc., are in keeping with what the author has led the reader to expect.

dynamic character: a character who changes or develops during the course of a work of fiction.

static character: a character who does *not* change or develop during the course of a work of fiction.

characterization: the portrayal in a story of an imaginary person by what he says or does, by what others say about him or how they react to him, and by what the author reveals directly or through a narrator.

cliché: an expression so often used that it has lost its freshness and effectiveness.

climax: the point of highest interest or dramatic intensity. Usually it marks a turning point in the action, since the reader is no longer in doubt about the outcome.

298

coincidence: the chance occurrence of two events which take place at the same time.

conflict: the struggle between two opposing forces, ideas, or beliefs which form the basis of the plot. The conflict is resolved when one force—usually the protagonist—succeeds or fails in overcoming the opposing force or gives up trying.

external conflict: a struggle between the protagonist and some outside force.

internal conflict: a struggle between conflicting forces within the heart and mind of the protagonist.

connotation: the implied or suggested meaning of a word or expression.

contrast: the bringing together of ideas, images, or characters to show how they differ.

denotation: the precise, literal meaning of a word or expression.

denouement: the unraveling of the plot, following the climax, in which the writer explains how and why everything turned out as it did. See also *resolution*.

episode: a related group of incidents, or a major event, that comprises all or part of the main plot or, in a long work, is related to the main plot.

fantasy: a tale involving such unreal characters and improbable events that the reader is not expected to believe it. Some fantasies are intended merely to entertain; others have a serious purpose as well; namely, to poke fun at outmoded customs or at the stupidity of certain people or groups of people.

flashback: a device by which a writer interrupts the main action of a story to recreate a situation or incident of an earlier time as though it were occurring in the present.

foreshadowing: the dropping of important hints by the author to prepare the reader for what is to come and to help him to anticipate the outcome.

image: a general term for any representation of a particular thing with its attendant and evocative detail. It may be a metaphor, a simile, or a straightforward description. An image may also have a symbolic meaning.

incident: one of the events (usually minor) that make up the total action or plot of a work of fiction.

initial incident: the event in a story that introduces the conflict.

irony: a mode of expression in which the author says one thing and means the opposite. The term also applies to a situation, or to the outcome of an event (or series of events), that is the opposite of what might be expected or considered appropriate.

locale: the particular place in which the action in a work of fiction occurs.

metaphor: a figure of speech in which two things are compared without the use of *like* or *as*; for example, "The fog was a gray veil through which I viewed the city."

mood: the frame of mind or state of feeling created by a piece of writing; for example, the *eerie* mood of a story by Poe.

moral: the lesson taught by a literary work.

narration: an account or story of an event, or series of events, whether true or imaginary.

paradox: a statement which seems on the surface to be contradictory; yet if interpreted figuratively, it involves an element of truth; for example: "The country mobilized for peace."

pathos: that quality in prose that evokes in the reader a feeling of pity and compassion.

plot: the series of events or episodes that make up the action in a work of fiction.

point of view: the method used by the short story writer to tell his story; the position, psychological as well as physical, from which he presents what happens and the characters involved in it.

　first person point of view: the narration of a story by the main character or, possibly, a minor character. As the narrator, he was the pronoun *I* in referring to himself.

　omniscient point of view: the narration of a story as though by an all-knowing observer, who can be in several places at the same time and can see into the hearts and minds of all characters.

　omniscient third person point of view: the narration of a story by an all-knowing observer but limited primarily to what one of the characters (usually the main character) can see, know, hear, or experience.

protagonist: usually the main character, who faces a problem and, in his attempt to solve it, becomes involved in a conflict with an opposing force.

realism: the faithful portrayal of people, scenes, and events as they are, not as the writer would like them to be.

resolution: the events following the climax in a work of fiction; sometimes called the *falling action*.

satire: a piece of writing that criticizes manners, individuals, or political and social institutions by holding them up to ridicule.

sentimentality: a superabundance of emotion in a story.

setting: the time and place in which the events in a work of fiction occur.

simile: a figure of speech in which a comparison is made between two objects essentially unlike but resembling each other in one or more respects. This comparison is always introduced by *like* or *as*; for examle, "The moon shone like a silver dollar."

stereotype: a character in a story who is presented according to certain widely accepted ideas of how such a person should look, think, or act; for example, a "good" student wears glasses and is poor at sports.

style: the distinctive manner in which the writer uses language; his choice and arrangement of words.

suspense: a feeling of excitement, curiosity, or expectation about the outcome of a work of fiction.

symbol: an object that stands for, or represents, an idea, belief, superstition, social or political institution, etc.; for example, a pair of scales is often used as a symbol for justice.

theme: the idea, general truth, or commentary on life or people brought out through a story.

tone: the feeling conveyed by the author's attitude toward his subject and the particular way in which he writes about it.

unity: an arrangement of parts or material that will produce a single, harmonious design or effect in a literary work.